Masculinity in Male-Authored Fiction 1950–2000

Masculinity in Male-Authored Fiction 1950–2000

Keeping it Up

Alice Ferrebe
School of Media, Critical and Creative Arts
Liverpool John Moores University

© Alice Ferrebe 2005

All rights reserved. No reproduction, copy or transmission of this publication may be made without written permission.

No paragraph of this publication may be reproduced, copied or transmitted save with written permission or in accordance with the provisions of the Copyright, Designs and Patents Act 1988, or under the terms of any licence permitting limited copying issued by the Copyright Licensing Agency, 90 Tottenham Court Road, London W1T 4LP.

Any person who does any unauthorized act in relation to this publication may be liable to criminal prosecution and civil claims for damages.

The author has asserted her right to be identified as the author of this work in accordance with the Copyright, Designs and Patents Act 1988.

First published in 2005 by
PALGRAVE MACMILLAN
Houndmills, Basingstoke, Hampshire RG21 6XS and
175 Fifth Avenue, New York, N.Y. 10010
Companies and representatives throughout the world.

PALGRAVE MACMILLAN is the global academic imprint of the Palgrave Macmillan division of St. Martin's Press, LLC and of Palgrave Macmillan Ltd. Macmillan® is a registered trademark in the United States, United Kingdom and other countries. Palgrave is a registered trademark in the European Union and other countries.

ISBN-13: 978–1–4039–4550–1 hardback
ISBN-10: 1–4039–4550–0 hardback

This book is printed on paper suitable for recycling and made from fully managed and sustained forest sources.

A catalogue record for this book is available from the British Library.

Library of Congress Cataloging-in-Publication Data

Ferrebe, Alice, 1970–
    Masculinity in male-authored fiction 1950–2000 : keeping it up / Alice Ferrebe.
        p. cm.
    Includes bibliographical references (p.) and index.
    ISBN 1–4039–4550–0
        1. English fiction – 20th century – History and criticism.
    2. English fiction – Male authors – History and criticism. 3. Masculinity in literature. 4. Sex role in literature. 5. Men in literature. I. Title.

PR888.M45F47 2005
823'.91409353—dc22   2005048764

10 9 8 7 6 5 4 3 2 1
14 13 12 11 10 09 08 07 06 05

Transferred to digital printing in 2007.

For Mum and Dad

Contents

Acknowledgements

I would like to thank Professors Cairns Craig and Berthold Schoene for their careful reading, comments and suggestions. Randall Stevenson was hugely generous with his time, and his encouragement and insights informed and improved this book throughout: may the pigeons always nest on your *left* window-sill. Most of all, thanks to Jonathan, for always listening, and always knowing what's important.

1
Introduction

> Tolson's hand fell to that part of his body which seemed to torment and mesmerize Leonard the most. 'Well? What theory are you going to make up about that?'
>
> David Storey, *Radcliffe* (1963)

To begin with exclusions; this study does not consider the fictional output in the post-Second World War period of women, non-whites, or the non-English. It takes as its focus the white, middle-class, English, heterosexual, male, fiction-making majority, or rather, and crucially, a group of authors who strove to portray themselves as such. In it, I will consider the functions and significance of the category of the masculine in selected novels, arguing that masculinity has profound implications for the fictional narratives, textual styles and definitions of selfhood that emerged from the social and economic energies following the war and its aftermath in Britain. As Kaja Silverman writes in the introduction to *Male Subjectivity at the Margins*, of her focus upon the United States during and after the Second World War:

> This book will isolate a historical moment at which the equation of the male sexual organ with the phallus could no longer be sustained, and it will show the disjuncture of those two terms to have led to a collective loss of belief in the whole of the dominant fiction. In doing so, it will foreground masculinity as a crucial site for renegotiating our *vraisemblance*. (2)

The decades following the Second World War are here upheld as a similar, if lengthy, 'historical moment', one in which masculinity, even when defined and displayed in a traditional manner, was conceived to

1

be failing to pay the traditional dividends. Belief in the 'dominant fiction' of male superiority has been systematically eroded, and, as this term suggests, fictional narrative, as a key space for self-definition and ideological exertion, provides a promising object of investigation, both for conclusions over the historical, cultural and masculine specifics of the era and for wider insights into the construction of gender itself.

This book conducts a series of contextualised case studies of individual novels selected because they seem to focus on key issues, rather than a systematic analysis of the presiding themes and trajectories of canonical authors. As such, it is by no means a history or developmental narrative of English post-war fiction. Rather, it presents the male-authored fiction of the 1950s and 1960s, most frequently understood as an apathetic and uncoordinatedly rebellious decade respectively, as the basis of under- standing the dominant mode of male self-representation in English fiction in the early years of the twenty-first century. At the heart of the study, then, is an interrogation of the male response in fiction to femi- nism's Second and Third Waves, through a comparison of recent con- temporary novels with those produced before the concerted ideological and political promptings of the Women's Liberation Movement (WLM).

My intention is not to detract from the Copernican revolution of soci- ety and culture that feminism achieved in Britain. Nor is it to suggest that the WLM was the fount of female emancipation, for as Deborah Philips and Ian Haywood discuss in *Brave New Causes: Women in British Postwar Fictions*, its members colluded to some extent in suppressing the contribution of their mothers' generation in order to glorify the group's emergence.[1] It does, however, uphold Juliet Mitchell's claim for British feminism that, in 1971, on the publication of her book *Woman's Estate*, there was no indication that 'the organized movement can claim more than nuisance value' (13). Feminism, which after the Second World War progressed first into political influence, then onwards to a hugely authoritative intellectual framework, may properly be conceived in the 1950s and 1960s as minor disruption rather than targeted impetus. Doris Lessing's 1962 novel *The Golden Notebook*, for example, can best be understood as symptomatic of a time in which patriarchal power and masculine identity are under threat, but in which there is no articulate political critique of the power structures at stake as yet (even as, in its reworking of Saul's story by Anna in the aspirationally androgynous golden notebook, it does explicitly acknowledge the gendered nature of contemporaneous narrative). A vital date in the calendar of this study is the 1971 British publication of Kate Millett's *Sexual Politics*, the book which exploded the traditional literary connection of the male with the universal and initiated a consideration of the exclusionary tactics of the male fiction-making community. Writing and reading *as a man* was, in the vast majority of the novels considered here, still conflated with writing and reading in general, but, as we shall see, this identification is not without its anxiety. Of course, by the rise of Ladlit in the 1990s, a genre which forms the focus of Chapter 5, the representation of masculinity necessitates a negotiation of the gender theories that have arisen from feminism, and from wider contemporary renegotiations of identity.

In choosing to concentrate upon male authors, I am aware that I may be interpreted as promoting a separatist scholarship. There is some sense in which this is true. Just as I would baulk at the concept of a comprehensive study of masculinity in some way 'completing' the feminist literary project, so I believe that maleness needs to, and is, finding its own revolution, and masculinity its own means of deconstruction, without a reliance upon the female/feminine as example or opposition. In her 1986 article 'Gender: A Useful Category of Historical Analysis', Joan W. Scott claims that 'we need a refusal of the fixed and permanent quality of the binary opposition, a genuine historicization and deconstruction of the terms of sexual difference' (1065). This book aims to achieve the former by means of the latter, and will assess the extent of such a revolution within post-war English male writing. I examine exemplary masculinity as defined by male authors during the period, where the term 'exemplary' combines a sense of the ideal with the notion of the admonitory; masculinity as great white hope (the designated colour is appropriate), and as cautionary tale.

Reading: resisting resistance

In the introduction to her 1978 book *The Resisting Reader*, Judith Fetterley claims of American literature:

> Though one of the most persistent of literary stereotypes is the castrating bitch, the cultural reality is not the emasculation of men by women but the *immasculation* of women by men. As readers and teachers and scholars, women are taught to think as men, to identify with a male point of view, and to accept as normal and legitimate a male system of values, one of whose central principles is misogyny. (xx)

Fetterley's prescribed female response to this compromise is clear-cut: 'The first act of the feminist critic must be to become a resisting rather than an assenting reader and, by this refusal to assent, to begin the process of exorcizing the male mind that has been implanted in us' (xxii). This book does not, of course, seek to deny the necessary immasculation of women by a great majority of English (or American) literature; necessary in that, in order to identify with these literary works, a female reader must for the most part identify against her own gender in act after act of psychic transvestism. Nor does it seek to deny the extraordinary privilege entailed in the act of being born a man throughout Western social and cultural history. It does, however, reject a purely resistant reading as a productive or pleasurable response to the male textual viewpoint. Just as Second Wave feminism's early stumbling block was its attempt to define womanhood as universal and in total opposition to a totalised manhood, so the assumption that the only valid female response to a text demonstrating misogynist tendencies is a proud, self-imposed exile seems both profitless and miserable.[2] In the essay 'Reading as a Woman', Jonathan Culler critiques feminist appeals in reader-response theory to the experience of 'Woman', whilst maintaining emphasis upon the importance of *hypothesising* a female reader so as to deconstruct the situation in which a male reader/critic is assumed to be sexually neutral. He sums up the way in which a female reader, through determinedly resistant reading, repeatedly reproduces a limiting binary:

> In literary criticism, a powerful strategy is to produce readings that identify and situate male misreadings. Though it is difficult to work out in positive, independent terms what it might mean to read as a woman, one may confidently propose a purely differential definition: to read as a woman is to avoid reading as a man, to identify the specific defences and distortions of male readings and provide correctives. (516)

Once again in this strategy, female identity becomes a matter of what it is not: 'positive, independent terms' are avoided in favour of being different from, and by implication, eternally deferential to, the mighty male. Identity, and identification during the reading process, is presented to be possible only with reference to the gender of the reading self, so perpetuating the dichotomy. Masculine reading is figured as active, and feminine reading as responsive and retaliatory; there is no liberation here, and no feminist strategy of any rigour or promise. As Judith Butler notes in *Gender Trouble*: 'Feminist critique ought to explore the totalizing claims of a masculinist signifying economy, but also remain self-critical with respect to the totalizing gestures of feminism. The effort to identify the enemy as singular in form is a reverse-discourse that uncritically mimics the strategy of the oppressor instead of offering a different set of terms' (13). For the female example to act as 'corrective' to masculine tyranny is nothing but another distortion, one that will be encountered in a number of the texts considered in the following chapters, in particular those of John Berger and John Fowles. Lynda Broughton's stance in her essay 'Portrait of the Subject as a Young Man: The Construction of Masculinity Ironized in "Male" Fiction' seems similarly unproductive:

> Rereading 'male' fictions also enables the feminist reader to apply the same playful analysis to the subject of masculinity, since this is frequently the 'hidden' subject of 'male' writing. Masculinity's sense of itself, recent commentary on the question has suggested, is a construct so frail that it must be constantly reinforced, constantly rewritten; the woman reader of the 'male' text frequently finds herself, to use Simone de Beauvoir's phrase [...], in the position of one listening to a little boy telling himself stories, rebuilding himself as subject through the hierarchical structures of sexual difference. (137)

Identification with this constantly alienated and superior attitude – reading male-authored texts as listening to little boys bolstering their egos – is as problematic for a contemporary reader as would be empathy with Geoffrey H. Hartman's creepy simile for the reading process: 'Reading is a modest word, and to defend reading may give the impression of venturing on the minimal. Much reading is indeed, like girl-watching, a simple expense of spirit' (248).

Listening to boys or watching girls – infantilising the enemy must surely now be rejected for a concerted and united attempt at understanding, intellectual profit and enjoyment. My own experience of many of the texts considered here has involved a level of pleasure in their reading that I wish to interrogate beyond the assumption of that outdated feminist term of dismissal, 'false consciousness'. In 'Reading Ourselves: toward a feminist theory of reading', Patrocinio P. Schweickart, in her consideration of the lingering appeal of some texts after a feminist reading has rendered them objectionably sexist, asserts:

> Fredric Jameson advances a study that seems to me to be a good starting point for the feminist reconsideration of male texts: 'The effectively ideological is also at the same time necessarily utopian.'

> This study implies that the male text draws its power over the female reader from authentic desires, which it rouses and then harnesses to the process of immasculation. (534)

The selection process for the fictional texts considered in this study will be justified more explicitly in the succeeding chapters, but in general the novels under consideration demonstrate the way in which texts can both be gendered themselves and function to engender a particular type of reader. Schweickart's point, in brief, will form one of the main tenets of belief in this study: that identification with a text, rather than a betrayal of feminist principles, is precisely a product of 'authentic desires', desires that deserve closer consideration in order fully to understand the reading process for a reader of either gender.

The problematisation of my own response to the strategies of reader 'immasculation' in these selected male-authored texts leads to a further crucial assumption. This study will conduct its examination of post-Second World War fiction with the conviction that the process of, in Fetterley's term, 'immasculation', uncomfortable and compromising for a female reader, is no simplistic process if the reader is male. As Ben Knights has noted in *Writing Masculinities*, 'the comfortable normality of reading as a man is an ideologically induced illusion' (23), and this ideology functions precisely to ensure that the category of the 'masculine' (and, by implication, the feminine) is conceived and enforced in order to normalise a specifically distorted experience of both life and text. Gender, in other words, will here be understood as an influential, complex, contradictory and debilitating illusion. Readings of the selected novels will interrogate the ways in which textual immasculation may be considered to be both a fraught and a profitable process for all readers, be they women or men. In other words, the purpose here is not to be accusatory, but rather diagnostic. Any analysis of textual pleasure or desire will avoid subjective assertion in favour of the consideration of a more bilateral reader-response, and ultimately one that posits the dissolution of the gender dichotomy altogether.

Following in many cases the taxonomies of the work of Dorrit Cohn, narrative voice is here apprehended as an interpersonal phenomenon, an interaction between narrator, character, reader and author (as those persona are variously conceived), rather than the purely structural arrangement of traditional poetics. Work in film studies has long made use of the concept of 'suture' (as, for example, in Stephen Heath's 'Notes on Suture') in a theorising of the process whereby the reader becomes part of a filmic text's structure through the inferential work s/he is drawn into performing. By making sense of the text, by interpreting it, the reader becomes enmeshed in its structures of power and judgement. Succumbing to these imposed codes can involve conscious surrender as well as conscious sacrifice. Belonging is a powerful and alluring emotion, and identifying with the narratives of these novels, as we shall see, frequently puts the reader in a position of superior vision, situating them at the seat of sense-making. It seems counter-productive to be puritanical about the immorality of this pleasure of kinship or clubbiness, to reject the process of suture as disempowering to the individual. The homosocial community, for all its repulsive tactics, and in spite of the illusory nature of its bonds, remains a symbol of solidarity seductive in its enduring power. It is also untruthful to assert that identification with an immasculatory text does not pay out dividends for both male and female readers. In addition to a close analysis of the textual tactics that might achieve both the enmeshment and immasculation of the reader, this book also ultimately examines the possibility of a textual belonging to male-authored novels, and thence to fiction in general, that does not involve the exclusion or compromise of readers with reference to their gender or any other solitary characteristic, assessing how far this has become a reality in the fiction of the turn of the millennium.

This is not to suggest, of course, that there is one, 'masculine', reading available for each text considered. As Sara Mills points out in *Gendering the Reader*, such an assumption would make reading product- rather than process-orientated. Rather, the individual reader is here envisaged as neither wholly free to interpret at whim, nor wholly constrained in the interpretation available to them. Readers have choices. In coining the term 'masculine text', however, I assume that more dominant readings *do* exist, and although the reader is ultimately able to resist, or adopt, a masculine reading at will, a masculine text retains an ultimate political aim – to channel desires for traditional narrative pleasure and privilege into the acceptance of a range of masculine definitions and principles. In *Feminism and the Politics of Reading*, Lynne Pearce notes how feminist writing frequently marks its addressees as allies using an intimate coded language. She continues: 'The reason that such signs of intimacy are absent in much male-authored work is precisely because men have traditionally assumed a universal male readership: all the world, as it were, is "his" ally' (39). The male-authored novels considered here will be used to demonstrate that these 'signs of intimacy' are, to the contrary, rife, and that their purpose is as political as those of feminist discourse.

Although a single reading or meaning is impossible, the masculine text can be characterised as striving towards that impossibility, and towards a passive, immasculated reader. It seeks to prevent illegitimate interpretations. In the same way, a patriarchal system strives for the universal recognition of a unitary principle of social organisation – congenital male superiority. Analysis of the attempts at formal and philosophical manipulation in selected novels will thus engage with the intellectual confrontation of two of the reader-response field's most influential theorists, and negotiate between their positions. For Wolfgang Iser, the text is primary, and the reader engages in a cognitive activity of selecting and prioritising from the multiplicity of structures and strategies that constitute it. A masculine text works precisely towards the reduction of this multiplicity to one particular set of standards and judgements. For Stanley Fish, the influence of the particular interpretive community in which the reader is situated is primary in the selection of a reading. For a male community anxious over its waning influence, this sense of solidarity within an interpretive community is crucial, and many texts of this era shall be shown to function precisely to create an illusion of cohesive community, rather than relying on its pre-existence to prompt the 'right' reading. Such ideal solidarity is conceived to be impossible amidst specific contemporary conditions. Immasculation, then, is a social and cultural project, implemented by textual means.

Defining masculinity(/-ies?)

This study does not uphold a concept of masculinity as a psychological state of impoverished emotional development with its roots in childhood separation from a once-available mother and an always-absent father.[3] The literalism of object-relations theory tends to limit gender to a product of home and family, rather than making it a pervasive and dynamic facet of experience. Masculinity will instead be read here as an effect of the way in which the power relationships of signification, and especially narrative, are organised.

'Being a man', in other words, is read as a particular *style* of being. My focus may be upon male-authored works, but my argument is for universal involvement in (and thus some level of culpability with) the fostering of the continuing illusion of masculinity. While excluding (for the most part) female authors, there need be no logical progression to excluding or excusing female readers and critics. As Eve Kosofsky Sedgwick asserts in her essay ' "Gosh, Boy George, You Must Be Awfully Secure in Your Masculinity" ', 'As a woman, I am a consumer of masculinities but I am not more so than men are; and, like men, I as a woman am also a producer of masculinities, and a performer of them' (13).

She rehearses this point in *Between Men: English Literature and Male Homosocial Desire*: ' "Patriarchy" is not a monolithic mechanism for subordinating "the female" to "the male"; it is a web of valences and significations that, while deeply tendentious, can historically through its articulations and divisions offer both material and ideological affordances to women as well as to men' (141). Yet despite the fact that women both consume and produce masculinity, and occupy a central place in its systems of symbolism, they are without influence in its ultimate evaluation. As Michael S. Kimmel points out in 'Masculinity as Homophobia: Fear, Shame and Silence in the Construction of Gender Identity', masculinity is 'a homosocial enactment' (128), because, as men, 'we are under the constant careful scrutiny of other men. Other men watch us, rank us, grant our acceptance into the realm of manhood. Manhood is demonstrated for other men's approval. It is other men who evaluate the performance' (128). Though continually couched as rational, independent and isolated, masculinity as a project in fact involves an intense level both of emotional investment and of public performance and validation. Following the introduction in the previous section of the possibility of a text functioning to *immasculate* its readers, I wish to extend this notion of the 'homosocial', to allow its feasible application to a readership of both men and women, provided they accept, for whatever reason, the masculine standards of self and behaviour established by a text. These novels will be approached as public enactments of masculinity that function through their dominant readings and modes of indirect address to inculcate homosocial investment and approval, achieved through a determined immasculation of the reader, whatever their sex.

As already stated, this study takes a still further exclusionary focus beyond the gender of its chosen authors: it rejects a consideration of multiple definitions of masculinity beyond a hegemonic, white, heterosexual, English 'ideal'. Such is the influence of this paradigm, it may be noted how counter-discourses to hegemonic masculinity, throughout the period following the Second World War, delineate themselves with reference to characteristics *other than* masculinity – sexuality, for example, or race. David Rosen's *The Changing Fictions of Masculinity* takes as its focus the inherent instability of this concept of hegemonic masculinity, and he notes in his introduction how:

When men experience abrasion between the masculine ideal and the surrounding world, between a shifting sense of self and world and a restrictive or dysfunctional sense of role, they often try to create a new definition of masculinity. In each epoch groups of men try to pass on a stable 'masculinity' that can encompass traditional roles, accommodate new experiences, ensure a meaningful contribution to society, and insulate from the shock of change. But in each new creation, the concept of 'masculinity' multiplies and one concept contests another. Moreover, within this contestation, accommodations take place, so that older masculine ideals inhabit spaces in new ones, although they are transmuted by their new residence. In every age, men experience an abrasion between the concepts of privileged manhood that they inherit and try to satisfy and other experiences to which they try to fit their masculine ideals. (xiii)

Rosen's book is exemplary, though not unusual in studies of its type, in its repeated reference to a 'definition of masculinity' alongside a determined refusal to define the said definition. The book as a whole tacitly assumes, however, as in the extract above, that 'masculinity' *does* exist as a conceptual entity, and that although social change prompts the need for new definitions, some residual core of meaning remains and is recognisable to all who encounter the term. In the ideas of Eve Kosofsky Sedgwick we have already witnessed another common response to the need for masculine definition. Sedgwick pluralises 'masculinity', then avoids providing definitions for any of the word's supposedly heterogeneous brood. This failure to pin down the meaning of masculinity, hegemonic or otherwise, is crucially instructive. Definitions of 'masculinity' are routinely avoided precisely because the concept is impossible to define.

In *The End of Masculinity*, John MacInnes traces the importance of the idea of gender (though not the term itself) to the work of a number of seventeenth-century theorists of the social contract, for whom it functioned to conceal a troubling contradiction between the patriarchal hierarchy and the universalising tendencies of modernisation:

The concept of gender thus implied being able to hold two diametrically opposed beliefs at once: that masculinity (and its counterpart femininity) was socially constructed (and thus in theory constructable by members of either sex) and that it was naturally determined (so that there was a special connection between masculinity and being male). Without both sides of this paradox the concept of masculinity does not work. Without the first masculinity collapses back into maleness, without the second it loses all connection to sex at all. (25)

The contemporary concept of gender, MacInnes argues, perpetuates this contradictory 'doublethink'. We are content to pluralise masculinity and grant equal opportunities to exercise and consume masculinities, as gender is a social construction, and thus mobile and mutable. This definition of gender allows a decisive rejection of the biological determinism implied in patriarchal social organisation. However, we are also loath to abandon the link between masculinity and maleness, as this link allows us, depending upon our inclination, both a means of punishing men for their legacy of oppression and a potential mode of liberation for a sex debilitated by this legacy in specific psychological ways. Masculinity requires both a material and a social explanation, leaving us dangling, or in MacInnes's memorable phrase, 'swinging from penis to phallus' (78). Here is the root of the failure to define either masculinity or masculinities: the concept, fissured with contradiction, cannot sustain a definite meaning. Attempts to define it as cultural construction still perpetuate a tacit essentialism, and attempts to link it to congenital difference must always acknowledge its public, performative qualities. 'Masculinity' is a fallacy, or rather, a phallusy – a signifier for a concept that does not exist. Yet, as Joan W. Scott notes: ' "Man" and "woman" are at once empty and overflowing categories. Empty because they have no ultimate, transcendent meaning. Overflowing because even when they appear to be fixed, they still contain within them alternative, denied, or suppressed definitions' (1074). The mere non-existence of masculinity does nothing to exclude it from a powerful political and cultural role.

Masculinity, then, is an illusion. Instability is further built into the epistemological structure of that illusion itself, dependent as it is upon hierarchical binary oppositions as a means of definition. Joining the literary fraternity depends upon a knowledge of binaries, and of the correct side to which privilege should be attributed. When definition depends upon the establishment of the Other, though, the Other is unavoidably positioned in a site of power, and *its* Other simultaneously undermined and antagonised by that power. Attempts to establish masculinity as a coherent concept, doomed as these may be, depend upon a constant process of othering all Others, discrediting them on as many scales of judgement as possible. (The phenomenon of textual 'subaltern-bashing' is examined in detail in Chapter 2.) This process of discreditation puts the masculine subject, or text, in a position to which it can never admit – a position of response rather than initiation, reaction rather than assertion. The most potent Other in the novels selected here, both as an instrument of masculine triumph and masculine challenge, is the feminine. This is manifested in the fictional figure of the woman, and also in that of the homosexual male, as hegemonic masculinity relies so heavily upon the pre-emption and repudiation of homosexual desire. Of the category 'homosexual', Sedgwick notes a 'potential for giving whoever wields it a structuring definitional leverage over the whole range of male bonds that shape the social constitution' (1985, 86). Gay-subaltern-bashing (the first two terms forming a tautology in all the fictional texts examined here) is a process offering a uniquely powerful method of masculine self-definition.

The masculine self

Masculinity may be characterised as being founded upon an ontology of binary oppositions. Yet as Judith Butler notes in *Gender Trouble*, 'Ontology is [...] not a foundation, but a normative injunction that operates insidiously by installing itself into political discourse as its necessary ground' (148). A patriarchal political discourse will involve the installation of a masculine ontology in order to naturalise its particular power structure and conceal its essential contradictions. This ontology should be traceable in all arenas properly designated as political. Fiction, as a ludic and liminal cultural space in which the political both dictates theories of identity and is influenced by innovatory new ones, represents such an arena. This book makes and explores the assumption that the self, as initially apprehended in post-war England, is based upon traditional masculine principles, or rather, that the means used to apprehend subjectivity are compulsively based upon tenets that are properly designated as masculine. As Luce Irigaray asserts in *Speculum of the Other Woman*, her analysis of the function of feminine references in the major texts of Western philosophy, 'we can assume that any theory of the subject has always been appropriated by the "masculine" ' (133). Masculinity thus becomes a crucial site of negotiating the identity of self and subject, and for understanding the tenets of identity of the post-war period as a whole. The masculine self is characterised with reference to its isolation, independence and rigorous exclusion of what it is not. The definition of the feminine self, by contrast, is precisely that it cannot be defined. Reinforcing the age-old gender stereotypes, the feminine self is fluid and indefinable, and the masculine, rigid and rational.

An examination of the 'masculine self' will predictably prove to be rife with the contradiction implied by the epithet 'masculine'; that of a simultaneous belief of gender as socially defined and naturally provided. Two opposing paradigms of selfhood are in evidence, both dependent upon a concept of transcendency; an essentialist notion of a pre-linguistic, 'given' entity needing protection from all outside threats; and that post-Romantic product, the idea that every individual must be free to develop their selfhood autonomously (an idea with a complex and often contradictory relationship with existentialism, as examined in Chapter 3). Both these paradigms delineate a potent, and potently contradictory, role for the feminine Other. In the first, consolatory paradigm, the congenital, authentic male self confronts the various pressures of technocratisation and consumerism, a Lawrentian primitive defined in opposition to the domesticated inauthenticity of the female. ('We are too mentally domesticated', wrote Lawrence in disgust, in *Psychoanalysis and the Unconsious*, quoted Knights, 94.) This recourse to a neo-pagan masculinity is a reactionary refusal of the concept of gender as a complex cultural construct. Its pitting of (good) wildness against (bad) domesticity deliberately ignores another potent opposition within the collective consciousness, that of primal evil versus civilised morality (itself a legacy lingering from the declining discourse of Empire). In the second paradigm, didactic rather than consoling, the privilege in the gender binary shifts. It is the female who is 'natural', irrational, undefined, and the masculine self which gains its authenticity from sophisticated rational progression and personal dynamism. As the post-war period progresses, however, it is precisely this latter definition of a 'feminine', and fluid, selfhood that is validated within the cultural consensus.

The majority of the novels here refuse to work accelerating contemporaneous theories about the contingency of language into the language of their fiction, and into their conceptions of self. Instead, they tend to make plain a conflation of self and narrative that depends upon an implicit confidence in an empirical link between world, words and self. In the main, what is upheld is a notion of coherent selfhood as contiguous with coherent narrative, despite the fact that this identification to some extent compromises both essentialist and existentialist definitions of self. If the self is a pre-existent entity, it should not require narrative progression, and if it is a series of contingent acts, narrative should logically be its antithesis, yet the importance of narrative coherence prevails. Indeed, in an era of profound social and cultural change, male-authored texts have a tendency to subscribe to narrative consistency and the *Bildungsroman* structure with a vehemence indicative of a conception of it as a vital means of masculine consolidation in a time perceived as one of declining power.

So if selfhood is figured as masculine and identified with narrative unity, can traditional narrative paradigms in fact be nominated as male-orientated? Designating narrative, just as Fetterley designated American literature, to be 'male' seems dismissive of the pleasure it affords readers of any gender. It also tends towards essentialism in its implicit identification of male goal-orientated sexuality with linear, con- clusive narrative. Masculine conceptions of sexuality *do* tend towards images of individual conquest, but linking them to traditional narrative paradigms sets a dangerous precedent for a further identification of the feminine as anti-narrative and unscriptable. My examination of the novels selected here will rather consider how far their narratives might justly be characterised as masculine. To hazard an early definition, a masculine narrative paradigm tells its story for masculine ends, to con- solidate a community founded upon masculine principles of identity, and to console a gender anxious about its instability.

Both these fictional texts and the contemporary critical writing surrounding them determinedly associate the interpretation of narrative fiction with a process of rational cognition by a pre-existent self. The emotional investment required for this process of identification is con- veniently ignored. Texts are couched as *objective* at both their conceived source and their destination, and objectivity, of course, is a strongly gendered concept. In *Feminism and the Politics of Reading*, Lynne Pearce characterises this process as follows:

> Reading has been conceptualized as an act(ivity) of interpretation, and interpretation as a mode of cognitive intellectual application; and the way in which both these concepts are classed and gendered to make sure that 'the reader', whether omnipotent, impotent, or somewhere in between, is, at least, well-educated, respectable and (if only symbolically) male. (7)

For '(symbolically) male', we can read 'masculine': the reader is immas- culated. I examine the ways in which selected texts figure reading as a purely hermeneutic exercise, and consider the ways in which their con- cept of freedom has come to be identified with the unhindered exercise of reason. A narrative quest for freedom, then, and a dedication to the freedom of the reader, becomes contiguous with a striving for successful rational assertion. In this schema, selfhood becomes subject to the same reading process. Linear narrative quests focused upon a unitary self are used repeatedly to reinforce conceptions of self based upon masculinist principles of isolation and relentless rejection of the Other. In other words, unity of text = unity of self = unity of manhood: *real men write coherent narratives.* Real men, of course, are healthy men, and this conception of narrative as curative is firmly founded in a patriarchal psychoanalytical discourse, in which the doctor dispenses explicatory narratives to the weak-of-mind. In a time of accelerated social change, creating the impression of masculine unity and health is a deeply political project. In order to effect a liberation from the limitation of masculine conceptions of selfhood, I argue, English male-authored fiction needed to re-imagine its models both of narrative and of reading, and Chapters 4 and 5 consider ways in which the unity of narrative/self/ rational manhood has been disrupted by certain texts, and the consequences for masculinity of this disruption. Once again, the ultimate goal is to consider the possibility of a mode of narrative in which inclusiveness does not demand this kind of relentlessly rational identification, to which the only response is the complicity and compromise of the reader, or their excommunication; and to assess the extent to which male-authored texts of the period might realise this goal. Such a mode would not proffer some construction of the female or the feminine as antidote, like Stephen Dedalus's glimpse of womanly beauty and fluidity on the beach, but rather involve an attempt at narrative progression beyond the binaries.

2
The Consolations of Conformity

'Well,' she says in a minute, 'how does it feel to be a man?'
I give a laugh. 'Ask me another.'

Stan Barstow, *A Kind of Loving* (1960)

It has become a cliché that the years immediately following the Second World War in Britain witnessed social change at a bewildering pace. The War was a defining experience for more than one generation of men, whether through active or national service, or evacuation. Rather than attempting to assess the impact of these fractured and various effects of combat, however, this chapter will focus upon the more cohesive experience of post-war social conditions of the 1950s and early 1960s. Vast areas of the British Empire were ceded in two spurts; one immediately after the War, the other in the early to mid-1960s: what Salman Rushdie has called 'the Great Pink Age' (130) was over. Domestically, England moved from rationing to affluence in a matter of years. Perceptions of the period tend to combine this sense of profound and dizzying change with one of concurrent political apathy, as the moral fervour of the 1930s and the dynamic purpose of a society at war dissipated into political passivity. Acquiescence, and the unsavoury acquisitiveness generated by a consumer boom, it is assumed, is the inevitable curse of social prosperity. The era is frequently derided for the slightness of its fictional output: Bernard Bergonzi in his 1970 *The Situation of the Novel* calls the English literature of the 1950s and 1960s 'backward- and inward-looking' (56). Tom Maschler's 1957 edited collection of essays, *Declaration*, intended as a crescendo to the angry howls of the young generation, contains little more than ineffectual rants about tepid topics such as the over-privilege of monarchy and the state of the West End stage.

This glaring lack of *Look Back in Anger*'s Jimmy Porter's much-missed 'good, brave causes' (84) is a lack of a good, brave, *public* politics. Templates for a coherent contemporary radical stance seemed lacking. After Stalin, the Marxist agenda had fallen into disrepute. Labour defeat in 1951 reinvested Churchill as Prime Minister, the central figure of what Kenneth O. Morgan describes in *The People's Peace* as 'a paternalistic, cautious, undoctrinaire body of men interpreting their role as maintaining the general lines of Labour's policy' (113). The triumphant ideal of collective responsibility enshrined in the vision of Bevan, Beveridge and Butler, what Marwick calls 'the great symbolic statement of British objectives' (46), was informed by a continuing assumption of national moral superiority, as well as a medieval metaphor of organic unity. Section 31 of Beveridge's 1942 'Report on Social Insurance and Allied Services' makes this plain: 'The scheme proposed here is in some ways a revolution, but in more important ways it is a natural development from the past. It is a British revolution.' Yet the radical social reorganisation effected by the inauguration of the Welfare State is perceived in the male-authored fiction of the period not as an expansion of public and patriarchal morality, but as its ignominious scaling-down. It is simply not radical enough. Rather than a grand civic project, the Welfare State is, as we shall see, apprehended as a nagging interference in the quotidian. The public sphere is compromised by its concern with private matters: Anthony Hartley notes a common sense of increased 'state intervention into the affairs of the individual', which has begun 'to resemble that which all too frequently accompanies the ministrations of a well-meaning but fussy maiden aunt' (147). This is in spite of the fact that, as social work policies placed a new emphasis on prevention, direct state intervention was predominantly targeted at working-class homes judged to have, as Elizabeth Wilson puts it in *Women and the Welfare State*, 'difficulty in caring for their children in a socially acceptable way' (88). Ultimately it is less the case that there was increased intervention by the Welfare State mechanisms into the families of those producing the majority of contemporary fiction, and more that the very concept of welfare undermines two crucial assumptions. These assumptions are characteristically masculine ones: that the authority of the (male) individual is paramount, and the patriarchal family is 'natural', and naturally good.

Jimmy Porter remains infamous for his raging against the influence of women. In an article entitled 'What's Gone Wrong with Women?' in the *Daily Mail*, 14 November 1956, his creator John Osborne blames the loss of male dynamism in a welfare-ridden state upon 'the fact that we are becoming dominated by female values, by the characteristic female indifference to anything but immediate, personal suffering' (1994, 256). Elizabeth Wilson quotes a 1948 article, 'Family Relationships', from the journal *Social Work*. Its author, A. Maberley, ascribes the danger of the welfare system not to the fact that it feminises the members of a society, but that it lures them into childishness, by nurturing:

> A tendency for the man or woman to retain towards society the infantile dependence appropriate in the child, with a demand for maintenance as a right without obligations in return. While the child is justified in this attitude the adult is not. The adult should contribute to society as much or more than he receives back. (1977, 158)

One of the Beveridge Report's most interesting (and, for its detractors, reddest) innovations was the recognition in its system of Social Security of the role of the housewife in maintaining the economy,[1] and the role of (married) women (and only they) in ensuring the continuance of the British race. The Conservative 'caretaker' government in power immediately after the war ensured that, as Beveridge had envisaged, family allowances were paid directly to Mother. Women as vital resource rather than (albeit charming) burden; the concept (though in truth still a means of maintaining traditional patriarchal labour divisions and a breadwinner ideology) was progressive enough to foster fear amidst the male population that an endorsement of the new social structure was in some way an affront to patriarchal authority in its support for a feminised State. Ultimately, whether the threat to masculine authority is couched as feminisation or as infantilisation, a goal has been achieved – the removal of blame from men themselves, crystallised in Osborne's audacious *Daily Mail* headline.

Contrary to this reaction against the Welfare State is a desire to revere it as the enshrinement of values of logic and fairness, and the harbinger of a genuine English meritocracy. Much literary criticism routinely understands the characteristic novels of the English 1950s (the work, for example, of Kingsley Amis, John Braine and John Wain) as a reaction to the political and social realities of the Welfare State, whilst simultaneously labelling them apathetic and apolitical. Conflict within the dominant ideological structure is characterised as altogether less political than would be attempts to envisage alternatives to that structure. Anthony Hartley notes that:

> A great deal of post-war literature has been concerned with producing this sort of mythical virtue out of necessity, with pretending that

Birmingham is as interesting a place to inhabit as Berlin or that the amenities of Manchester compare with those of Milan. For a novelist this can take the form of a praiseworthy preoccupation with the material around him, but the attitude in itself becomes narrow and banal after a while. (48)

Narrow the material might seem to Hartley, but this genre of English fiction conceals beneath its alleged banality a wide-reaching political project. Kaja Silverman defines what she calls 'historical trauma' as a historical occurrence, 'whether socially engineered or of natural occurrence', which causes a large group of men to 'withdraw their belief from the dominant fiction. Suddenly the latter is radically de-realized, and the social formation finds itself without a mechanism for achieving consensus' (55). This chapter takes as its focus a selection of novels that attempt to design such a mechanism within the larger social engineering works of the Welfare State.

An empirical example

In his introduction to the 1969 reprint of William Cooper's 1950 novel *Scenes from Provincial Life*, Malcolm Bradbury quotes approvingly from John Braine's assessment of the book: 'Seminal is not a word I am fond of, [...] nevertheless I am forced to use it. This book was for me – and I suspect many others – a seminal influence' (i). Bradbury goes on to designate *Scenes from Provincial Life* to be 'the novel in its empirical form. It could and did stand for an important swing away from the stylistic backlog of modernism, or what William Cooper calls the "Art Novel": a swing towards an art of reason, an art of lived-out and recognisable values and predicaments' (iii). *Scenes from Provincial Life* might justifiably be nominated a 'seminal' novel, in that its narrative and stylistic techniques are instrumental in establishing a recognisably masculine style both of text and of the selfhood defined within that text. Bradbury's assessment is indicative of a pervasive misreading of this style, in his apprehension of the novel as empirical, with all its assumptions immediately verifiable from the experience of each reader, as well as a conflation of empiricism with rationality. Dominic Head notes how 'Blake Morrison authoritatively defines the sensibility of the Movement, rooted in the qualities of rationalism, realism, and empiricism' (50), yet these three terms do not sit together easily.

Rather than a single view, 'empiricism' is an umbrella term covering a range of differing standpoints: these are, however, united by the assumption that experience has primacy in establishing authentic human thought and belief. 'Rationalism' is traditionally contrasted with this, depending as it does upon the belief that reason has precedence over any other way of acquiring knowledge: that thought is independent of experience. In eliding empiricism and rationality, Bradbury stakes out an inherently (and interestingly) paradoxical philosophical position,[2] one which may be traced to an interpretation of Alfred Jules Ayer's influential contribution to Logical Positivism in the 1936 *Language, Truth and Logic*. An understanding of this position and its contradictions is crucial to the analysis of the panoply of novels considered in this chapter, texts that span the 'Movement' and 'Angry' groupings. The verve of Ayer's polemics drove their influence through into post-war culture – the title of the book's eighth chapter, for example, is the audacious 'Solutions of Outstanding Philosophical Disputes' (133). *Language, Truth and Logic* is, as its author remarked rather ruefully in a new introduction written in 1946, 'in every sense a young man's book' (5), and many of the young men considered here took up its Positivist debate as to what is permissible within scientific and philosophical assertion, and extended it to literature. Ayer claimed:

> It will be shown that all propositions which have factual content are empirical hypotheses; and that the function of an empirical hypothesis is to provide a rule for the anticipation of experience. And this means that every empirical hypothesis must be relevant to some actual, or possible, experience, so that a statement which is not relevant to any experience is not an empirical hypothesis, and accordingly has no factual content. (41)

From this position, authoritative knowledge, or 'truth', is ultimately apprehended through experience, yet it is also rationally hypothesised in advance, as 'a rule for the anticipation of experience'. The experiencing self, then, is simultaneously styled as the objective assessor of that experience. This mode of empiricism thus combines what Ayer nominates approvingly as a 'thoroughgoing phenomenalism' (32) with a reassuringly rational means of predicting results.

In *Language, Meaning and Context*, John Lyons notes how 'British empiricism and Cartesian rationalism [...] both share the intellectualist prejudice that language is essentially an instrument for the expression of propositional thought' (236). He characterizes J. L. Austin's posthumous *How To Do Things With Words* as a specific attack on the verificationist thesis (associated with Logical Positivism) that sentences were only meaningful if they expressed verifiable, or falsifiable, propositions. Austin's analysis centred instead upon what he called constative (descriptive) and performative utterances, the latter involving some sort of act: an utterance which *does* rather than simply *says*. The 'empirical' novel of Bradbury's definition, then, does attempt to recreate the immediacy of its protagonist's experiences whilst spurring recognition in its reader, but it also serves to prompt the expectation of a particular response in future circumstances. It is to some extent performative of an act of camaraderie with a pre-constructed social stance.

As Bradbury makes clear, the movement towards this professed empiricism in fiction is profoundly reactionary, not only to the Modernist undermining of fictional realism through its fracturing of narrative, language and linear time, but also to the experience of the Second World War. A memory for the public's enthusiastic response to Churchill's nationalistic rhetoric was liable to provoke an unsettling debate over degrees of totalitarianism across the European continent. Unsurprisingly, a backlash occurred against grand words and grand gestures. George Orwell, with his prescient distaste of slogans and linguistic conjuring tricks, was an obvious exemplar, his taste for 'common sense' in writing (as well as his suspicion of a lust for power in Left politics of the 1930s and 1940s) an important inspiration. Hartley views him as the source of all contemporary style: 'The "no nonsense" air of an entire generation comes from Orwell. Anyone brought up on his works will try to say what he means as directly as possible, and what he means will often sound less than urbane' (54). Philosophical paradoxes inherent in combining empiricism with rationalism are subsumed beneath an apparently straightforward championing of the realistic and the reasonable, 'a thoroughgoing phenomenalism' (Ayer, 32). The novels considered in this chapter are determined in their demonstration that realism, and in particular the transparency between experience and language that the term implies, had survived all the surreal horrors of the war.

Scenes from Provincial Life is explicit in its bid to focus attention upon the 'lived' experience of its 'ordinary' narrator Joe Lunn. His decision to privilege his personal life is deliberately amplified in its radicalism by the harsh political reality of the novel's 1939 setting:

Sometimes I tried to link the disintegration of our private lives with the disintegration of affairs in the world. I saw us all being carried along into some nameless chaos. Yet it rang false. In spite of what the headlines told me every morning, in spite of what I reasoned must happen in the world, I was really preoccupied most deeply with what was going on between me and Myrtle and between Tom and Steve. People can concentrate on their private lives, I thought, in the middle of anything. (171–2)

Survival under contemporary conditions, he implies, is only assured by maintaining empiricism, that is, by refusing to speculate over universal themes, but rather thinking (and writing) only about that which you have directly experienced. At the novel's opening, Joe is failing to maintain this empirical correspondence in his professional life. He receives a letter from the headmaster of the school in which he is employed, advising him to reconsider his vocation:

> From questioning the headmaster's actions, I went on to question my own. I was soon immersed in serious philosophical doubts. Perhaps the headmaster was right. It might well be that a schoolmaster really ought to behave like a schoolmaster. If I could not behave like a schoolmaster, perhaps I ought not to be one.
>
> This left me faced with the most alarming question of all. 'What *can* I behave like?' (137)

This, of course, is a recognisable tactic of the *Bildungsroman* – the beginning of the philosophical and physical quest for an authentic vocation, in which professional behaviour is a direct translation of the priorities of the inner self. Yet the link between male self-definition and narrative runs deeper than the repetition of a mere plot device.

In her book *Self as Narrative: Subjectivity and Community in Contemporary Fiction*, Kim L. Worthington asserts that: 'Frequently in contemporary theory, textual and personal autonomy are promoted as the refusal to conform to prevailing conventions of value and practice, and as the shattering and dispersal of received, normalised modes of expression – in other words, as the refusal to comply with expectations of narrative followability' (28). *Scenes from Provincial Life*, and the male fictional trope that was to follow its lead, pre-date this assumption, creating and promoting a notion of selfhood the validation of which depends precisely upon conformity with both the contemporary 'conventions of value and practice' and 'expectations of narrative followability'. Joe Lunn's position as hero of the novel is justified in one proclamation: 'In my own behaviour I aimed at some sort of consistency, and until I knew Tom I was under the impression that other people did the same. Not a bit of it! Tom was a revelation to me, and through him others were revealed. Only through observing Tom, I decided, could one understand the human race' (200–1). Tom's qualifications to be nominated a part of that inferior breed 'the human race' will be considered later, but the nature of Joe's heroic superiority is plain: an inner selfhood repeatedly proven in external behaviour consistent with it.

This notion of heroic selfhood as stemming from conformity to rationally ascribed levels of consistency is enshrined in the novel's narrative technique. This hinges upon a retrospective analysis by Joe as the writer of his younger life experiences. This contrivance replicates the traditional hierarchy of patriarchy within one literary character: the adult artist Lunn controls and explains the narrative of his rebellious and boyish self, admonishing him with a comic irony licensed and defused by hindsight. The man is father of the child here, and emphatically not vice versa. In *Writing Masculinities*, Ben Knights notes of the male textual paradigm: 'The normative position of the narrator and of the implied figure of the male author behind him is thus one from which he exercises discriminating power over both subject matter and reader. The pay-off to the reader is membership (at least in fantasy) of a club made up of those who share superior vision' (65). When the narrator is an author himself, the 'pay-off' of the reader's (imagined) proximity to the centre of artistic production, to the site of sense-making, is increased still further. The Agatha Christie mode of narrative – the confused eye-witness version later rationalised and explained by the detective's re-telling – is here pared down to allow only the detective's voice, thus serving the masculine prerogative of portraying existence as aetiological, with an essential self initiating goal-directed action, the cause of evident effects. The Romantic ideal of the artist as tortured solipsist is rejected utterly. The narrative idiom of *Scenes from Provincial Life* further extends this illusion of reader-privilege, both in its simple, reasonable register and in its frequent appeals to, or rather assumptions of, a universal (although explicitly male) code of experience, as in these examples: 'There is nothing makes a man feel so wonderful as a wonderful girl' (34); 'I was faced with an inescapable truth: you cannot have a mistress and read' (40); 'The thought of somebody else [having sex], in the room above, on a Sunday afternoon – the mystery of it! What man can honestly say he does not know what I mean?' (97).

For all the novel's professions of commitment to the personal, the technique of retrospection also allows the narrator tactfully to shirk any description of emotional experience. When Joe's relationship with Myrtle comes to an end, he shares this much with his reader: 'A love affair cannot end without heartbreak. And as I have already told so much, I think the time has come for me to draw a veil' (259). Joe's emotional expression is limited to a letter to Robert articulating his anger at the behaviour of their mutual friend Tom. Despite traditional acceptance of the letter as a sanctioned forum for personal confession, the reader is allowed only a glimpse of its purportedly lengthy contents, and this revelation is immediately followed by an ironic, but nonetheless telling, assertion of manhood: 'After completing it I felt a certain satisfaction at having stated my position. To state one's position is a firm, manly thing to do: it is right that it should give satisfaction' (249–50). Other characters in the novel are frequently discredited with reference to their emotional volubility. In the sexist idiom of the era, in Myrtle's case, this is predictable and swiftly explained with reference to her gender, but Tom's inconsistency is repeatedly attributed to the 'great fund of emotion' (13) that he is uninhibited in spending in public.

This discreditation of all the characters involved in the hero's life is another noteworthy facet of the novel's technique of masculine self-definition. In *The Inward Gaze*, Peter Middleton considers the way in which Hegel grounds the emergence of self-consciousness in an allegorical battle between two men: the master/slave dialectic. He concludes that: 'The masculinity of the model is not incidental' (213).[3] Joe's position as hero and sense-maker, and the reader's complicity with that position, is enforced by means of a programme of comprehensive subaltern-bashing amongst other fictional males. Joe's rival for Myrtle, Haxby, is swiftly dispatched as a serious threat by means of a description of his social circle: 'They had intense black eyes and jerky movements. I thought their appearance was mildly degraded, and I called them the Crows' (145). (Haxby himself has no direct role in the text, and so readers are left unable to assess the validity of this judgement.) As well as being over-emotional, Tom is also homosexual, and although the novel distinguishes itself to a certain degree amongst its contemporaries in deigning to include a significant gay male character, the predominant function of this narrative device is defensive humour. Hearing of Tom's boyfriend Steve's attempts to join the merchant navy, Joe notes wryly: 'I guess you've already received enough training for the Merchant Navy in arithmetic. As in certain other basic subjects, too' (106). Of course, Tom's emotional lability is intended to be conflated with his homosexuality, and, I would suggest, with his Jewishness. The sentence in which this latter defining trait is introduced is instructive: 'With the best will in the world you could not help noticing immediately that Tom was red-haired and Jewish – it fairly knocked you down' (12). Tom's ethnicity has the added plot-device of making his much-discussed move to America in the face of war more urgent, but his red hair? Any doubts we might have over the desirability of this attribute are banished in a later description: 'He straightened his tie, which was wine-coloured – a mistake, in my opinion, since it enhanced the contrast between the gingery redness of his hair and the purplish redness of his face' (108–9). The complexion of the redhead, the reader is instructed, is an undesirable, unattractive one: this shorthand code of petty prejudices, only mildly effective in isolation, runs parallel to the major code of discreditation, echoing and reinforcing it. If the reader is to bask in the masculine privilege of identification with the rational narrator, s/he must also accept complicity in this attendant set of irrational values. A paradox is apparent: the venerated rational and independent masculine self is established only by means of the irrational emotive investment of its readers. The only character in the novel to be unaffected by this process of compulsive subaltern-bashing, and treated to unchecked praise, is the Dean of Joe's Oxford college: 'His name was Robert, and he was a few years older than us. He was clever, gifted and wise; and he had a great personal influence on us. We had appointed him arbiter on all our actions, and anything he cared to say we really accepted as the word of God' (18).[4] The recipient of Joe's epistolary confessions, but always defined by his absence, Robert is sanctioned to enjoy the position of omniscient patriarch, the same position occupied by the narrator looking back on his boyish self.

In *Gendering the Reader*, Sara Mills draws attention not only to narrative modes of direct address, but also to ' "indirect address", where elements of background knowledge are assumed to be shared and where certain information is posed to the reader as if it were self-evident' (26). This auxiliary code of values does not only apply to the description of men in *Scenes from Provincial Life*. The reader's identification with the narrator's decisions and motivations surrounding his relationship with Myrtle depends upon an appreciation of her desirability, and the initial inventory of her physical attributes seeks to inscribe this male heterosexual desire as normative and inescapably sexually arousing:

> Instead of speaking, I glanced at her. What I saw was entirely pleasing. The sooner we reached the cottage the better.
> Myrtle was modestly tall and very slender. She was wearing grey slacks and a cerise woollen sweater. Her breasts and buttocks were quite small, though her hips were not narrow. She was light-boned, smooth and soft. There was nothing energetic or muscular about her. (25)

Fragility, passivity, child-bearing hips – these quintessentially feminine characteristics are firmly designated as 'entirely pleasing' before they are listed. Later Joe notes 'I have described up to date those of her traits which everyone recognizes as essentially feminine' (64). Coerced into desiring femininity, the reader is immasculated again.

While professing its political quietism, *Scenes from Provincial Life* reveals itself to be an intensely political work, engaged as it is with the establishment of a position of rational and artistic privilege which can be achieved only by means of the acceptance of a host of attendant social judgements. In *The English Novel from Dickens to Lawrence*, Raymond Williams sees the novel from the mid-nineteenth century onwards as responding to a crucial need to portray and illicit a sense of 'knowable community' (14) in the midst of social transformation. Cooper's allegedly apathetic text is in fact engaged in a grand project of interpellation focused upon the reassertion and consolidation of communal masculine priorities. It functions in such a way that rooting for the central character's emancipation, a familiar impulse towards a utopian position, is possible only at the expense of a subscription to a profoundly masculine account of self and of others, from an inescapably middle-class viewpoint. This, then, is what I am designating the 'masculine text'. Within it, emotion must be ruthlessly controlled as a response. Desire is only valid if it is uncompromisingly heterosexual and directed towards a feminine ideal. All messy and alternative selfhoods must be discredited for heroic independence fully to be achieved. Bradbury's determination to emphasise the novel's 'empiricism' – that is the coincidence of its fictive world with the experience of the reader – may be read either as unwitting compliance with the novel's narrative and stylistic technique, or a devious complicity with a masculine community aware of its waning influence.

In the essay 'The Modern, the Contemporary, and the Importance of being Amis', David Lodge notes in a discussion of *Room at the Top*, and by implication, its contemporary, 'realist' male-authored novels, that 'the danger with the contemporary [as opposed to "the modern"] – and it is as much a danger for himself as for the critic – is that, seduced by the superficial thrill of recognition, or by the coincidence of the writer's values with our own, we may overestimate him' (44). In 'Is There a Text in This Class?' Stanley Fish shares Lodge's assurance of an easy (though, in Lodge's case, suspect) identification with the normative values of a text: 'These norms are not embedded in the language (where they may be read out by anyone with sufficiently clear, that is, unbiased, eyes) but inhere in an institutional structure within which one hears utterances as already organized with reference to certain assumed purposes and goals' (306). The texts examined in this chapter function precisely so that the 'thrills of recognition' come about not necessarily through a conflation of the reader's experience with the 'reality' of the text, although this may occur on occasion, but rather that thrills of identification and belonging are manufactured and imposed by the texts themselves. Steven Connor has noted the way in which:

> Novels of this period are characteristically driven (and sometimes instructively defeated) by the desire to build anew the ideal reciprocity between text and reader that seems to have been diffused by competing cultural forms and increasingly complex social differentiations. But they are also characteristically aware of how risky and uncertain this ambition is. (13)

Various names have been spawned for this putative reader with a perfect understanding of the text – Iser's 'implied reader', Rimmon-Kenan's 'narratee', Connor's 'addressee', or a member of Stewart's 'conscripted audience'.[5] An appropriation of New Criticism's 'ideal reader' seems most fitting (albeit with very different political motivations), as the adjective echoes Connor's phrase 'ideal reciprocity' above, as well as Habermas's concept of the 'ideal speech situation', defined as a consensual, rational, totalised act of social communication. In these novels, concerned as they are with establishing a masculine consensus, the ideal reader is too important a person to be met merely by chance. The masculine text is an attempt to close down all possibility of the reader being anything less than ideal. As masculinity, and the masculine conception of self, require, in the words of Michael Kimmel, a 'homosocial enactment' (128), the ideal of the masculine text is to make its reader a man.

(Middle-)classless aspirations

John Wain's 1953 novel *Hurry on Down* addresses just this agenda of a masculine construction of selfhood and text, and does it with a heavy dependence upon a particularly middle-class code of recognition in its chronicle of the various life-choices of its hero Charles Lumley. The methods of subaltern-bashing are in evidence again, as a large part of the humour of the early sections of the novel is achieved at the expense of George Hutchins, who, with his Midlands provenance revealed by his parents' 'Birmingham speech' (14), is immediately established within the 'provincial scholar' trope (more usually from Yorkshire) utilised in numerous novels of the immediate post-war period (e.g., Whitbread in Philip Larkin's *Jill* and Johns in Kingsley Amis's *Lucky Jim*). The only homosexual man to appear in *Hurry on Down* is swiftly identifiable to Charles and to the ideal reader and dismissed accordingly: 'Standing beside him was a young man in grey suède shoes; Charles caught sight of those shoes and decided that he now knew all he wished to know about one guest at least. He avoided glancing in his direction again' (111). This provides an instructive example of the development of Cooper's technique of loading seemingly innocuous visual details with moral implications, compressing large numbers of attendant value judgements into a single symbol; here, suède shoes = homosexuality = anti-masculine = anti-rational, and so on.

Elsewhere these codes are less compact but just as striking. The novel articulates a mistrust of the new breed of male professional, the salesman. The chief figure-head for the breed, the successful Mr Braceweight (his name suggesting the strain of his existence) is dangled before the reader for much of the novel as a potential 'fairy-godfather' figure with the ability to rescue Charles from the turmoil of youth, but this possibility is foreclosed with the description of Braceweight's 'colourless persistence' (169). The godfather role is eventually filled for Charles by Mr Blearney, 'who combined a hearty manner with genuine self-confidence' (100). Braceweight's financial and professional success in sales is attributed to the sacrifice of his core of personal identity: he is no role model of authentic selfhood for a young man. Amidst the legions of those willing to make this sacrifice, however, is Stan, Charles's girl-friend's brother, who is introduced as follows:

> At sixty, Stan would have neither the massive good humour nor the genuine dignity of his father, and already he was immersed in learning the technique of cheap smartness. He talked a different language, for one thing; it was demotic English of the mid-twentieth century, rapid, slurred, essentially a city dialect and, in origin, essentially American. (185)

A vast number of social and moral assessments are implicit here: the nobility of the traditional working-class patriarch, the betrayal of (the working-)class inherent in social aspiration, the undesirability of smartness that comes cheap, and of a verbal idiom rooted in the big city, and a transatlantic city at that. Although *Hurry on Down* rejects the 'hero as retrospective narrator' device of *Scenes from Provincial Life* for the omniscient author of conventional realism, the mechanism of the coercion of the reader into an acceptance of these implied principles is still in operation. Mr Blearney's role as patriarchal godfather is finally confirmed when he responds to Charles's question 'What do you think I want?' as follows:

> 'Neutrality,' said Mr Blearney calmly and without pausing to take thought.
>   Charles looked at him in silence.
>   'Go on, partner, tell me it isn't true, if you can,' said Mr Blearney. 'It's the type who wants neutrality who comes into our racket. Doesn't want to take sides in all the silly pettiness that goes on. Doesn't want to spend his time scratching and being scratched. Wants to live his own life.'
>   Charles was humbled. The man understood him perfectly. His very choice of a word was absolutely right. (248)

For 'neutrality' (implying a receptivity to a range of different viewpoints) we can substitute 'authenticity', defined as the external assertion of an essential selfhood, a man who can 'live his own life' without the hindrance of a sensitivity to relativity. Blearney's 'neutrality' is objectivity; it is Joe Lunn's 'consistency', and Worthington's 'narrative followability' (28). An empirical correspondence between self and behaviour requires an emotional neutrality, and *Hurry on Down* may be read as the story of Charles's quest to conquer the irrational passions and jealousies of his love for Veronica ('the knowledge that Veronica was Roderick's mistress had been there all along, in his bones, in his arms and legs, in the blood in his veins', 161–2) with rational control. The novel has a happy ending in this respect: while welcoming her back into his arms, and listening to her speech of regret, 'mentally he translated this into: *You're rich now, you're doing as well as Roderick. And you're fifteen years younger*' (251).

Parallel to this movement from emotion to reason is Charles's gradual rejection of his initial attraction to the mindless communality of working-class professions: he moves instead towards a more 'modern' vision of community, a purportedly 'classless' society, which fosters and supports individual, intellectual advancement. As Elizabeth Wilson has noted, 'The Welfare State is one very important way in which a belief is fostered that our society is in fact "classless", that "we are all middle class now" '(Wilson, 1977, 11). This shift from socialist collective to capitalist meritocracy retains a lingering respect for the working classes (the 'honest labourer' long the pin-up boy of authenticity for middle-class liberalism), while ultimately rejecting their class-specific solidarity for the assumed meritocracy of middle-class intellectualism. Just as a masculine code of judgement is presented as being universal, so being middle class is figured to be class-neutral. At the beginning of *Hurry on Down*, Charles's imminent certainty of vomiting after a bout of heavy drinking is an unlikely prompt towards an epiphany: 'Could he not, just as easily, cast up and be rid of his class, his *milieu*, his insufferable load of presuppositions and reflexes?' (30). His very use of the word '*milieu*' is testament to the fact that Charles will, of course, never leave his middle-class point of view, as his sense of self is so inextricably bound to it. After his success at cleaning windows, Charles rejects a properly working-class celebration and chooses a meal and a nice claret at the Grand Hotel, recognising his actions as 'ritual gestures, to clutch at the rags of his self-respect' (75). His final career choice – competitive masculine bantering as joke-writer for a radio show – neatly combines wit and independence with communal appreciation and validation. The paradox of the masculine self – isolation and rationality recognised and validated only by a community of those with emotional and practical investments in the maintenance of that selfhood – is replicated once again.

Alan Sillitoe's novel *Saturday Night and Sunday Morning* (1958) serves well to emphasise the middle-class nature of this ideal masculine textual community, and the role of the working-class male within its iconography. The novel is striking in its determined use of the universal 'you' idiom; 'You followed the motto of "be drunk and be happy", kept your crafty arms around female waists, and felt the beer going beneficially down into the elastic capacity of your guts' (5);

> At a piecework rate of four-and-six a hundred you could make your money if you knocked-up fourteen hundred a day – possible without grabbing too much – and if you went all out for a thousand in the morning you could dawdle through the afternoon and lark about with the women and talk to your mates now and again (24);

> And in the evening, when admittedly you would be feeling as though your arms and legs had been stretched to breaking point on a torture-rack, you stepped out into a cosy world of pubs and noisy tarts that would one day provide you with the raw material for more pipedreams as you stood at your lathe. (31)

Sillitoe claimed in an interview that the chief difficulty facing him in writing the novel was 'how to write a book about a man who hasn't read a book' (Allsop, 1958, 60). With a middle-class reader as its ideal, the novel's narrative voice works hard to create empathy with an unfamiliar working-class environment, an empathy which stems, it is subtly suggested, both from intellectualism and liberal generosity.[6]

The text demonstrates two modes of narration. The first is a free indirect discourse in its hero Arthur Seaton's brutal idiom, generating the thrill of the unfettered expression of misogyny through a primal mouthpiece: 'Dave got a woman into trouble who had turned out to be the worst kind of tart, a thin, vicious, rat-faced whore who tried to skin him for every penny he'd got – until he threatened to chuck her over Trent Bridge one dark night, and she settled for a quid a week out of court' (65). Misogyny, of course, is as much a middle-class masculine trait as a working-class one, but the distance created by Arthur's subaltern position licences its expression in a more violent way, in what Anthony Hartley recognises in a footnote to be 'that vicarious enjoyment of the bloody by the bloodless' (132). The novel's second mode of narration is a descriptive, controlling narrative voice located as firmly in a middle-class intellectual discourse as Charles Lumley's '*milieu*': 'Arthur was stirred by the sound of breaking glass: it synthesised all the anarchism within him, was the most perfect and suitable noise to accompany the end of the world and himself' (93). This second voice constantly distinguishes itself from its primal partner by reinforcing the idea of male working-class existence as non-intellectual, as when Arthur lies to Jack, whom he is cuckolding: 'It was simple and explicit, because he had not thought about it. If he gave things too much thought they did not turn out so well' (45). Manual labour is explicitly linked with male virility, as Arthur admonishes himself for daydreams about sex with Brenda while working his lathe: 'Only less of this or there'll be another handle on the lathe that I won't know what to do with and another gallon of suds that will jam the works' (31). The novel's portrayal of a traditional working-class masculinity ruled by survival instincts and pleasure principles is designed to provide a rest-cure from contemporary middle-class manhood, as rehabilitating as Lumley's spell cleaning windows. The pain-staking reconstruction of a stereotypical working-class masculinity founded on mindless virility and violence allows the reader the thrill of the wild while reinscribing a sense of the power of essential manhood. The knowing intellectual commentary upon Arthur's primal motivations simultaneously allows membership of the club of 'superior vision' (Knights, 65), providing a sense of rational narrative control.

Rather than expanding male fiction with empathetic heroes drawn from disadvantaged environments, Sillitoe produces another example of middle-class masculine protectionism; as Nigel Gray notes in his discussion of the novel in *The Silent Majority: A Study of the Working-Class in Post-War British Fiction*, 'Sillitoe is too much taken with the working-class hero cult' (113). The terms of this cult allow an unusually appreciative assessment of Arthur's appearance in the controlling narrative, just as they allowed George Orwell in *The Road to Wigan Pier* to lavish description upon the 'small pronounced buttocks and sinewy thighs' of miners below ground (20). These lingering looks are also licensed in the free indirect discourse sections by the narcissism of Arthur's teddy-boy tendencies, which demand an ostentatious cataloguing of his hair styles and outfits. Arthur falls down the stairs of the White Horse after eleven pints of beer and seven gins, and there is a moment of stillness which invites the reader and a nearby observer to dwell on his exterior: 'It was a waiter, towel in one hand and tray in the other, white jacket open from overwork, a face normally blank but now expressing some character because he had begun to worry about this tall, iron-faced, crop-haired youth lying senseless at his feet' (7–8). With one exception, exteriority is the extent of the novel's descriptions of Arthur Seaton. In its project of reinscribing working-class male mindlessness, and an accompanying reluctance to address the nature of an alternative selfhood, the text makes only the vaguest references to Arthur's subjectivity, as here, where Brenda is 'bringing off' her pregnancy in a hot bath: 'Sometimes he was part of the scene, sitting among the two women, warmed by the fire, choked by the steaming bath; then he was looking down on it, like watching the telly with no part in what he was seeing. He was only real inside himself' (75). The only time the novel abandons free indirect discourse for unmediated access to Arthur's interior monologue, he merely reiterates the platitudes of the young working-class rebel that have been explicit in the rest of the text: 'Once a rebel, always a rebel. You can't help being one. You can't deny that. And it's best to be a rebel so as to show 'em it don't pay to try to do you down' (176–7).

Arthur Seaton, established as instinctual rather than rational, is excluded by the masculine text from a privileged position over his own selfhood. This privilege belongs solely to the middle-class reader, who accepts it with an implicit recognition of the superiority of rational control over emotional or impulsive drives; a particularly masculine hierarchical binarism. In *Saturday Night and Sunday Morning*, the class divide between the hero and the narrative voice draws attention to a gulf between the hero and his explanation, and between knowledge and self-knowledge. Though still present, this is not foregrounded in *Scenes from Provincial Life*, with its ubiquitous rational, middle-class register. Yet instability is apparent in the midst of this purported rationality.

In *The English Novel in History: 1950–1995,* Steven Connor attributes this instability to what he terms the 'addressivity' of narrative:

> With this term, I mean to evoke not just the tendency of narratives to surmise or otherwise orientate themselves towards certain receivers or addressees but also the associated effects of recoil and redoubling, whereby the narrative may be seen to acknowledge, or even react against the knowledge of that address. It may be useful here to distinguish between 'address' and 'addressivity'. The addressivity of a text concerns not only the kinds of reader or reading it may seem to imply or require – for this I would employ the term 'address' – but also the manner in which the text may reflect on these acts of address. The analysis of addressivity would thus attempt to describe the recoil and impacting of the conditions of address upon the text itself. (10–11)

This chapter has provided an analysis of the way in which the masculine text addresses (and thereby immasculates) its readers. In uncovering some of the anxiety within that text over the paradox that the essential self should need to be defined and recruited for in this way, it has also begun to address these texts' addressivity. Further anxiety might also be expected over the medium in which this paradigm of selfhood is established – language. In *Sources of the Self: The Making of the Modern Identity,* Charles Taylor acknowledges the referential nature of selfhood in his statement that it 'exists only within what I call "webs of interlocution" ' (36). He claims:

> To know who I am is a species of knowing where I stand. My identity is defined by the commitments and identifications which provide the frame or horizon within which I can try to determine from case to case what is good, or valuable, or what ought to be done, or what I endorse or oppose. In other words, it is the horizon within which I am capable of taking a stand. (27)

Like that of Fish, his definition of self-definition draws attention to the mechanisms of address, to the appeal to a shared (or imposed) sense of 'what is good or valuable' and 'what I endorse or oppose'. It is also interesting to note the way in which his chosen metaphors are so determinedly spatial and situational. If language is the medium of selfhood, then both the rational and empirical standards of that ideal self are compromised.

Addressivity, anxiety and influence

Kingsley Amis's 1954 novel *Lucky Jim*, through the functioning of its plot, its narrative technique, and the critical attention surrounding it, provides another demonstration of the post-war desire for peer recognition and validation of a self constructed upon masculine principles and the manifestation of this desire in a particular mode of address. The novel evinces an awareness of a double selfhood – the 'real I' inside, and the exterior self compromised into civility and sacrifice – years before Laing's diagnosis of the phenomenon in his study of schizophrenia, *The Divided Self* (1960). The extent to which this sham-self/real-self divide is justifiable by contemporary social conditions is portrayed in the novel to be heavily gender-dependent. Jim Dixon's compromised self-awareness is treated with the cheerful fatalism characteristic of Amis's work: 'He'd been drawn into the Margaret business by a combination of virtues he hadn't known he possessed: politeness, friendly interest, ordinary concern, a good-natured willingness to be imposed upon, a desire for unequivocal friendship' (10). Dixon's sham-self is a necessary evil for him to function in his current *milieu*, and the comic dynamo behind the plot; his quest is to discover another, utopian *milieu* in which he will be at liberty to do nice things rather than obliged constantly to do nasty ones. The comedy only occasionally gives way to flashes of regret at his inauthenticity, as when Margaret 'switched back to him with a little smile which he recognized, with self-dislike, as consciously brave' (20). This 'self-dislike', presumably, stems from the recognition of his own reflex to assess the co-ordination in others of their exterior and interior selves, thus emphasising the discrepancies of his own experience. It is certainly not prompted by guilt over thinking ill of Margaret. Her own self-dramatisation is a source of constant annoyance to Jim – 'Don't be fantastic, Margaret. Come off the stage for a moment, do' (159). It represents just another facet of her regrettable adherence to a desiccated, out-dated and inauthentic femininity: 'Her hair had been recently washed; it lay in dry lustreless wisps on the back of her neck. In that condition it struck him as quintessentially feminine, much more feminine than the Callaghan girl's shining fair crop' (76). Musing upon Christine Callaghan's relationship with Bertrand Welch, Jim neatly sums up the double-standard of the double-self: 'All the same, what messes these women got themselves into over nothing. Men got themselves into messes too, and ones that weren't so easily got out of, but their messes arose from attempts to satisfy real and simple needs' (116). Jim's inauthenticity of self, it is stressed here, stems from a deeply authentic need to survive amidst social codes hostile to young men – Christine's (and Margaret's) from a loss of rational control.

This gender divide is emphasised by the narrative technique of the novel itself. In *Kingsley Amis*, Richard Bradford notes how *Lucky Jim* contains a narrative which functions in two modes:

> It is as though there are two Jims: one inside the narrative, struggling with his own impatience, frustration and feelings of contempt; the other controlling and orchestrating the narrative, ensuring that the reader will share his perspective – on the idiocies of the Welches and the pretensions of Bertrand and Margaret. (12)

In a letter of 3 March 1953 to Philip Larkin, Amis fretted of the novel: 'I'm afraid you are very much the ideal reader of the thing and chaps like you don't grow on trees, course not' (Leader, 2000, 310). Yet *Lucky Jim*'s free indirect discourse is doubly compelling for the agenda of creating and recruiting for a community of readers subscribing to idealised masculine principles. The narrative synthesises two positions: Jim's idiom inside the story, frustrated and amusing, and the third-person narrator outside it, controlling ideal reader-responses to characters and events. The reader gets to share all the jokes amidst an atmosphere of bantering camaraderie, sympathising with Jim's entrapment and empathising with his quest. By identifying with the authoritative narrative voice, s/he also takes up a place in the seat of judgement, at the site of sense-making. Like *Scenes from Provincial Life*, *Lucky Jim* is set in an unnamed but obvious Leicester. In his fictional debut, Amis modifies Cooper's template of the retrospective narrative, maintaining the sense of rational control while amplifying the atmosphere of clubby partiality in what Bradford refers to later as a 'shifty alliance' (17). In Amis's essay 'Real and Made-Up People', the author idealises the propensity of this combination of empathy and rationality between writer and character and reader, upholding it as a means of self-revelation for all interested parties:

> By that very act of distancing, by projecting himself into an entity that is part of himself and yet not himself, he may be able to see more clearly, and judge more harshly, his own weaknesses and follies; and, since he must know that no failings are unique, he may be helped to acquire tolerance for them in others. In the second place, if the novel comes off at all, the reader will perhaps accompany the writer in some parallel process of self-discovery. (25)

This neatly incorporates just that blurring of empiricism, with its primacy of experience, and rationalism, with its emphasis upon objective intellectual reasoning, that was noted in Malcolm Bradbury's response to *Scenes from Provincial Life*. It also suggests an emotional honesty and moral judgement in the portrayal of the hero that *Lucky Jim* fails to deliver. On the rare occasions that Jim's emotional state is mentioned, it is with reference to the physical consequences of his emotions, which are always uncomfortable, as here in reaction to his attraction to Christine: 'He wanted to implode his features, to crush air from his mouth, in a way and to a degree that might be set against the mess of feelings she aroused in him: indignation, grief, resentment, peevishness, spite, and sterile anger, all the allotropes of pain' (72). Adhering to a masculine agenda, Jim's 'mess' of feelings appear in the text as anything but messy: their neat list provides, the reader is assured, a comprehensive inventory of a qualifiable elemental experience. Feminine emotion yields to masculine organisation. Elsewhere in the clubby dictatorship of the free indirect discourse, the reader is simultaneously invited and given no option but to share Jim's relief at his avoidance of any participation in feelings: 'He began eating the largest surviving gherkin and thought how lucky he was that so much of the emotional business of the evening had been transacted without involving him directly' (21).

So the interiority of the narrative technique of the novel is notable for its determined avoidance of intimate revelation. Likewise, the 'exterior' element that controls the judgement of the reader towards the female characters and the subaltern males of the plot avoids exercising its assumed rationality upon itself, despite Amis's intimations of self-analysis above. In his examination of the period's novels in *The Movement: English Poetry and Fiction of the 1950s*, Blake Morrison deems a democratic cast of characters to be a necessary fictional response to the prevalent social philosophy: 'What was needed from writers was the suggestion that in a Welfare State democracy everyone was of equal importance, that everyone had an equally vital part to play: "Exit the hero" ' (172). Tempting though it might be to read Jim Dixon and his peers in male-authored novels of the period as part of a universal striving towards a classless meritocracy, the hero has evidently not made his exit in *Lucky Jim*. Though Amis's plots, in *Lucky Jim* and elsewhere, honour the prevalent social philosophy of the Welfare State, transgressing class boundaries, and celebrating hypergamy and the new opportunities afforded by a better education, his fictional form is disposed against it. The novel works hard to ensure that no viewpoint other than Jim's is even momentarily viable without excommunication from the literary text. Christine, gradually proven to be a suitable mate for Jim, is suitable precisely because of her irrational and peachy 'naturalness'. Within the heterosexual codes of masculine desire, this otherness allows her to function as both complementary to Jim's state of necessarily compromised self-awareness, and utterly discredited by it. Apart from Jim's friends, Atkinson and Beesley (identifiable as such because, together with Christine, they are the only characters to address him as 'Jim'), who operate as plot facilitators rather than characters, all subalterns in the novel are ruthlessly bashed.

At one point, Jim's guide to survival is summarised as follows: 'The one indispensable answer to an environment bristling with people and things one thought were bad was to go on finding out new ways in which one could think they were bad' (129). This, too, provides an insight into the novel's technique of the discreditation of supporting characters. A triumphant example comes at the end, when Professor and Bertrand Welch are described as having 'a look of being Gide and Lytton Strachey, represented in waxwork form by a prentice hand' (251). The description contains a quadruply reductive whammy of insults: the two men look out-dated, they look homosexual, they look artificial, and their artifice looks to be of poor craftsmanship.[7] As in *Scenes from Provincial Life*, discreditation on the 'major' counts is enhanced and echoed by a code of superficial but influential judgements on each character's appearance: Margaret wears too much make-up and has lipstick smeared on her teeth, for example; Bertrand Welch wears a beret; and Johns cuts his hair (incompetently) himself. One way in which Christine is encoded as desirable is by a reference to her lack of lipstick, and the longing that this prompts once again results in Jim's physical incapacity: 'She stared at him, her full, dry lips slightly apart. A pang of helpless desire made Dixon feel heavy and immovable' (218).

Lucky Jim also provides an instructive example of the way in which critical and media attention surrounding the work of young male novelists during the 1950s was united in strengthening the sense of a young middle-class masculine-orientated community. Contemporary reviews were quick to point out that Dixon's position as lecturer-on-probation at a provincial university was not dissimilar to that of Amis. 'Contemporary Portraits', the anonymous review of *Lucky Jim* in the *Times Literary Supplement* on 12 February 1954 placed the novel firmly within a specific genre identified by the status and origins of the authors purveying it, saying of Jim:

He is the anti-, or rather, sub-hero who is beginning to figure increasingly as the protagonist of the most promising novels written by young men since the war – in, for example, the work of Mr Ernest Frost, Mr William Cooper, and Mr John Wain – an intelligent provincial who, after getting a scholarship and an Oxford or Cambridge degree, finds his social position both precarious and at odds with his training. (101)

Five decades later there remains a tendency to read the hero as contiguous with the author: in his introduction to *Critical Essays on Kingsley Amis*, editor Robert Bell notes: 'In many of his narratives, Amis seems massively ubiquitous, his characters articulating the author's likes and dislikes' (2). Thus a reference in *Lucky Jim* to 'some skein of untiring facetiousness by filthy Mozart' (63) is repeatedly read not as a hung-over Jim's grumpy response to the whistling of someone he hates from a bathroom he desperately needs to access, but an Amisian rejection of all things high-brow. A similarly avid identification occurred between John Osborne and the hero of his 1956 play *Look Back in Anger*, spearheaded with some determination by Kenneth Tynan in *The Observer*. In *Success Stories: Literature and the Media in England, 1950–1959*, Harry Ritchie notes how the assertions by critics of a direct link between the author, the hero, and the reader become self-fulfilling prophecies: 'Eventually, the very popularity of their books – itself caused by the discussion and controversy inspired by assumptions of their representative status – was taken as clinching proof that these new writers had appealed to, and now represented, a new readership' (209). Ritchie is adamant that *Look Back in Anger*, for example, did not represent a deliberate political statement: in other words, Osborne did not set out to preach a new agenda of anger in response to the apathy engendered by the lack of good, brave causes. Although Amis can similarly be pronounced free from recreating the agenda of a particular political party in *Lucky Jim*, the novel and the hype surrounding it can be interpreted as part of a wider political project.

In an era of accelerated social change, the text of *Lucky Jim* and the other novels examined in this chapter work to reinscribe masculine superiority by inculcating masculine principles of selfhood through their narrative technique. This project is amplified by an interpretative community intent upon reading the literary heroes of contemporary works as in some way 'new' and excitingly realist, when the values they represent are in fact profoundly traditional and protectionist. Further, the dogged identification of hero with author, and reader with both hero and author, increases the communal buzz of belonging. Both *Lucky Jim* and *Look Back in Anger* are profoundly political in their simultaneous dependence upon, and determination to create, a community based upon masculine hierarchical binaries, and in their portrayal of that community as representative of a whole generation. Idealist literary propaganda was advertised as realism by a media loyal to the cause with a vehemence redolent of the inherent instability of the whole project.

The ultimate means of enforcing identification within and surrounding this narrative, though, is language itself, and it is the instability inherent in language that ultimately demonstrates the instability of *Lucky Jim*'s masculine community and its text: its 'addressivity'. Ritchie notes a critical tendency to make 'blithe assumptions about the Movement authors being influenced by Logical Positivism' (176–7). *Lucky Jim* can and has been read in this way: an attempt to banish the mysticism of metaphysical, theological and ethical propositions with a language founded upon experience. Language is imbued with a rational cynicism deemed appropriate for the new, practical social vision: in *In Anger: Culture and the Cold War 1945–60*, Robert Hewison identifies in Philip Larkin's work 'an "oh-now-come-off-it" tone also heard in Kingsley Amis' (121). Jim's retort to Bertrand after knocking him down follows a physical assertion of his vigour with a linguistic one:

> It was clear that Dixon had won this round, and, it then seemed, the whole Bertrand match. He put his glasses on again, feeling good; Bertrand caught his eye with a look of embarrassed recognition. The bloody old towser-faced boot-faced totem-pole on a crap reservation, Dixon thought. 'You bloody old towser-faced boot-faced totem-pole on a crap reservation,' he said. (209)

Having translated a long-seething desire into a physical act, Jim's inner and outer selves coincide, and he finally says exactly what he thinks. Thereafter the plot accelerates towards utopia. Yet what do Jim's divided selves coincide to produce? The insult inarguably provides a rush of comic and linguistic verve, but even amidst this novelistic trope's codes of value judgements occasionally puzzling in their randomness (suède shoes signifying homosexuality, for example), it is deeply obscure – unlikely to mean anything specific to the reader, and least of all to the rarefied Bertrand Welch.

The limits of what Anthony Hartley refers to as Jim's 'technique of limited revolt' (149) become still more conspicuous in the book's comic climax, the Merrie England lecture. This also represents the climax of anxiety over a lack of linguistic control, and the climax, in Harold Bloom's phrase, of an 'anxiety of influence' prompted by the apparent impossibility of the young male rebel escaping the patriarchal establishment. After voicing his elaborate totem-pole insult, Dixon is by this stage of the novel in an enviable state of utter confidence in his selfhood and his own ability to express that selfhood in language, yet at the podium:

> When he'd spoken about half a dozen sentences, Dixon realized that something was still very wrong. The murmuring in the gallery had grown a little louder. Then he realized what it was that was so wrong: he'd gone on using Welch's manner of address. In an effort to make his script sound spontaneous, he'd inserted an 'of course' here, a 'you see' there, an 'as you might call it' somewhere else; nothing so firmly recalled Welch as that sort of thing. (223)

(It is interesting that here the final phrase 'that sort of thing' continues to make the register of the novel complicit with those it seeks to criticise.) Jim carries on:

> He cleared his throat, found his place, and went on in a clipped tone, emphasizing all the consonants and keeping his voice well up at the end of each phase. At any rate, he thought, they'll hear every word now. As he went on, he was for the second time conscious of something being very wrong. It was some moments before he realized that he was now imitating the Principal. (224)

Public discourse has become, in the mouths of the older male generation, utterly inauthentic: Jim is serially possessed by the speech idioms of the professional superiors he holds in such contempt. Rather than his sacking, it is this revelation that will free him to renounce his academic career without regret. Kim L. Worthington notes our contemporary conception in the wake of theorists like Derrida and Lacan that subjectivity derives from intersubjectivity: 'I speak myself, to myself and to others, in the language of others' (5). The model of the masculine self provided in *Lucky Jim* flatly denies this intersubjectivity: it assumes a pre-linguistic, 'finished' self, the authenticity of which is severely compromised by its expression in 'the language of others'.

Revealingly, though, Jim's only alternative to the mimicry of his patriarchs is a slight change of tone: 'No more imitations, they frightened him too much, but he could suggest by his intonation, very subtly of course, what he thought of his subject and the worth of the statements he was making' (225). This is the extent of Jim's rebellion: a sarcastic tone of voice. His future holds a career under Gore-Urquhart, the novel's deeply ambiguous 'fairy-godfather' figure who, although nicely removed from the networks of nepotism of the English upper-classes by virtue of his Scottishness, reveals that his success is based precisely on a technique of verbal manipulation, attempts at which Jim had previously found so repulsive in Margaret:

> I want to influence people so they'll do what I think it's important they should do. I can't get 'em to do that unless I let 'em bore me first, you understand. Then just as they're delighting in having got me punch-drunk with talk I come back at 'em and make 'em do what I've got lined up for 'em. (215)

Dominic Head characterises the novel as dramatising 'the Movement's impotence and incoherence, its inability to mount an effective challenge to existing institutions in the terms it set for itself' (51). Confronted at the novel's conclusion with the two male Welches, both in preposterous hats, and triumphant with Christine on his arm, Jim is still unable to formulate any complete verbal response whatsoever:

> 'You're ...' he said. 'He's ...'
> The Welches withdrew and began getting into their car. Moaning, Dixon allowed Christine to lead him away up the street.
> The whinnying and clanging of Welch's self-starter began behind them, growing fainter and fainter as they walked on until it was altogether overlaid by the other noises of the town and by their own voices. (251)

The couple's voices may be overlaying the noise of the Welches, but the reader cannot hear those voices, and Jim is off to London (the metropolitan centre in opposition to which his heroic credentials were originally defined) to cultivate his sham-self for financial gain. Offered up as the culmination of the quest of a rebellious 'new man', Jim Dixon's utopian ending turns out to be a compromise with patriarchal power-structures and the restrictions of a self fissured with the debilitating paradoxes of masculinity.

Kingsley Amis's 1960 novel *Take a Girl Like You* nicely demonstrates an increasingly confident masculine literary technique of 'othering' all other male characters with reference to clubby codes of discreditation. Jazz is upheld as indicative of the insider-knowledge required to identify with Movement males, and those who reject the art-form are ruthlessly excluded from a number of jokes in the novel: 'The music played. It was East Coast stuff, carphology in sound. After a frugal tune had twice been announced in unison, an alto saxophone offered a sixty-four bar contribution to the permanent overthrow of melody' (269). ' "Give up your masculinity, let yourself be castrated", the eunuchlike sound of the jazz band both mocks and proclaims', claimed Adorno (129), yet in the England of the 1950s jazz's attendant ambience was rather one of beer and blokes, a rebellion that satisfyingly combined machismo with being in-the-know. More striking than this sort of ostentatious clubbiness, though, are the invidious codes of discrimination in *Take a Girl Like You*. Here, for example, Graham McClintoch, friend of the hero Patrick Standish, says of Dick Thompson: 'I shall never forget the time I offered him a packet with two in it and he took one between his ring and little fingers because he'd got a pork pie in that hand and a pint I'd bought him in the other' (75). To share the humour, the ideal reader will extrapolate the following assumptions:

1. The packet contains cigarettes, and cigarettes are desirable, and expensive, commodities.
2. The older Dick's taking the cigarette demonstrates his greed and failure to adhere to the codes of reciprocity of the young male community.
3. The way he holds the cigarette is comically ungainly and also effeminate (the latter charge is to be confirmed later in the novel on the revelation of Dick's inability to father a child).
4. The pork pie is again indicative of Dick's greed and of his lack of sophistication.
5. The pint, again, is desirable, expensive and unreciprocated.

(Graham, although here in the moral ascendancy, is himself neutralised as a potential threat to the superiority of Patrick's viewpoint by discreditation with reference to his red hair, unattractive facial features and Scottish pronunciation, which the novel inscribes as both comical and indicative of a dour attitude stereotypical of his race.)

Good, clean, rational fun

Such codes are becoming familiar to us. *Take a Girl Like You* is notable, however, for its innovations in the Amisian scheme of selfhood, and the relationship between that selfhood and morality. Written on the brink of the decade which was to redefine sexuality as the foundation of the authentic self, rather than an embarrassing primal urge to be ignored, the novel attempts to create a sexual morality for the changing social climate around the essentialist creed that 'What people do doesn't change their nature' (316). The massive intellectual upheaval of the post-war period in Britain – gradual revelation of the reality of the death camps, and the exposure at Suez of the nation's self-nominated position of moral leader as fraudulent – had unsettlingly demonstrated morality to be heavily context-dependent. *Take a Girl Like You* attempts to counteract this doubt by binding its 'new' sexual morality to the notion of an essential selfhood. (A similar priority might be read in the 1960s British literary project to rehabilitate D. H. Lawrence as a revelational moralist.) Philip Oakes's identikit for the Welfare State Englishman in *The Observer*, 1 January 1956, concludes its list of defining characteristics with 'Interests: people, money, sex. Worries: money, sex' (8). For the masculine text, sex is similarly fraught with both fascination and anxiety. Allsop is vociferous in his demands that Osborne fulfil the social obligations necessitated by his literary creativity, and the metaphor he uses (albeit incorporating a disquieting exhibition of his own sexual neuroses) is instructive:

Osborne must accept the situation in which he finds himself – that he has the ear of a generation and, having stirred up their feelings far more excitingly than he could ever have dreamed he would do, he cannot resign from the job and leave it to others to 'fill the void'. Or at least, he can – but that is an abnegation of a writer's responsibility, the kind of sly artistic titillation without orgasm that belongs more to the *Silk Stockings* magazine or a strip-tease show than to the legitimate stage. (1958, 131–2)

The arousal of identification, Allsop asserts, makes narrative fulfilment a moral obligation: this is indicative of a perception that both literary form and sexual desire are inescapably linear. In other words, we might expect this literary trope to portray sexuality, if it does so at all, as compliant with the pre-established narrative paradigm of the masculine text. This is an anxious negotiation. The very inclusion of sexuality within that text is a risk, as sex involves an automatic association with the female. Osborne notes of the degenerate gender in 'What's Gone Wrong with Women?' that 'Her roots are so deep in sexuality that she is the natural enemy of the visionary, the idealist' (257). The traditional binary marks sexuality as feminine and emotional, the antithesis of the rational self. To neutralise, or rather, to masculinise the threat, sex in these novels must be rationalised. In a review of *Take a Girl Like You* in the *Daily Express* on 22 September 1960, Peter Forster renames its author as 'Kinsey Amis' (16), acknowledging the novel's intentions towards the kind of demystification of sexual relationships achieved by the 1948 report. *Take a Girl Like You* determinedly couches sexual urges as 'natural' for men, demonstrated by means of Patrick's cheerful and wordy proclamations that sexual pleasure is simple and simply reciprocated. There are frequent and darker glimpses, however, of a libido that is a primal, and dangerous, masculine force. Able Seaman Jackson delivers one of his regular, drunken news bulletins outside Jenny's window, reporting that modern marriage is no more than 'legalized bloody prostitution' (22). Julian Omerod notes of Patrick's breezy dismissal of the strip club they are patronising as 'good clean fun':

> Exactly. That's the whole idea. Wouldn't do at all if it set a pulse beating in your temple and your knuckles whitening under the strain. [...] Of course, it wouldn't be the thing for most of our fellow-members and guests if there actually were some real nudity here. They want a demonstration of how clean and straightforward and entertaining and part-of-a-spending-spree and good-fun-for-all-concerned sex *really* is, not all those peculiar old other things they're liable to suspect it may possibly be when they read the *News of the World*, or pass a girls' school at playtime, or cut across the common last thing at night. (211–12)

This points up the paradox of the use of the concept of the 'natural' in the service of codes of masculine priority: it can be linked to essential manhood and used in opposition to the inauthenticity of femininity, but it is unable to shake the consequences of its more traditional position within the binary epistemology, that is, man = civilised and rational, woman = natural and chaotic. The chief problem identified in the novel is that sex has become commercialised, fetishised and corrupted. However, the underlying sexual violence functions in a similar way to Arthur Seaton's brutality – a lingering primal thrill in the midst of a contemporary and consensual rationality.

Patrick's sunny approach to sex is also darkened by his repeated tendency, like that of Jim Dixon, to link desire to pain and to oblivion, encouraged by contact with figures like Lord Edgerstoune, a human memento mori, who excuses his lechery as a defence against death: 'When I put my arm round Nancy's waist and give her a little kiss on the ear, or something like that, I'm testing for a tingling, that's all. Seeing if there's any juice left' (242). Patrick's bouts of existential nausea are prompted by desire, or rather by an association of sensuality with irrationality, of sexuality with the surrender of the (rational) self.

The fact that sexuality remains fraught with intimations of the female means that Patrick attempts to argue Jenny into bed using two opposing positions; that sex is natural and fun, and her reluctance towards it stems from the imposition of an 'unnatural' moral code; and that advances in contraception must force her to overcome her 'natural' concerns about pregnancy. He tells her:

> It's because you've had the kind of upbringing – very excellent in its way, I'm not saying anything against it – but it's the kind with the old idea of girls being virgins when they get married behind it. Well, that was perfectly sensible in the days when there wasn't any birth control and they thought they could tell when a girl wasn't a virgin.
>
> Nowadays they know they can't and so everything's changed. You're not running any risk at all. (63)

Yet this traditional code of seduction, which Jenny summarises as '(chap) *I like you and* (girl) *I like you but*' (40), still holds elsewhere in the novel, as Patrick is repulsed by the 'unnaturally' eager Anna (her role as sexual predator later revealed to be a front for a lack of self-confidence), and unable to achieve an erection with the indifferently amenable Joan. Jenny needs to change her celibate instinct to allow her to have sex with Patrick, but other instincts within her are commended for their accuracy. Handed a cup of tea by Dick Thompson, she admits to a 'natural feeling that men should not do things like seeing to the tea when there was a woman at hand to do it' (34). As we have seen, her suspicion that Dick is unmanly is confirmed by the masculine codes of discreditation in the novel. Although the free indirect discourse of the text alternates between the assumed perspectives and speech patterns of Jenny and Patrick, predictably it is the male viewpoint which is shown as closer to absolute truth. The risk to masculine supremacy of an alternative point of view in the novel through Jenny's free indirect discourse sections is repeatedly neutralised by this benevolent compliance with the codes of value of the young male community: 'Now that she was more used to Patrick Standish's appearance and manner they seemed quite attractive, and intellectual rather than sissy – the two were sometimes hard to tell apart' (18). Female sexuality is policed to ensure that it conforms to masculine-dictated hierarchies of heterosexual desirability:

> Most of the time they sat and listened, or perhaps went down to the bar for a drink in more comfort and to play one of their games. In the

smasher-maybe-and-dud one – she had told him how she divided
men up, and he had got very interested straight away – she would
guess the rating of some girl there or that they knew, and he would
say how it stood up to a man's rating, and then he would start with a
man. They hardly ever differed more than one point. (180)

The rape scene is narrated in the idiom of a Jenny semi-comatose with
drink and reliably indulgent towards Patrick, and it is she who later
delivers a dreamy epitaph on the incident: 'I can't help feeling it's rather
a pity' (317). Her position is a familiar one – speculum to masculine
codes of value, in a project to couch a protectionist morality as progressive. Any intention to produce a *Clarissa* with a morally repugnant anti-
hero is not supported by the novel's narrative form. Its very title – *Take
a Girl Like You* – contains a smutty in-joke available only to the ideal,
immasculated reader.[8]

Published in 1960, the same year as *Take a Girl Like You*, Stan Barstow's
A Kind of Loving shares its interest in sex. Its working-class hero Vic
Brown worries at the gulf between the language used to describe male
sexuality and the actual experience of desire. In desiring him, and omit-
ting to say '*I like you but*', his girlfriend Ingrid has reneged upon the traditional heterosexual contract of man as seducer and woman as denier.
Vic counteracts his anxiety by couching their situation in a more contemporary, and transatlantic discourse – the language, if not of pornography, then of pulp-fiction: 'she's a pretty hot bit of stuff. She gave me
the green light okay the way she kissed me that night on the seat down
there, or I'd never have gone as far as I did then' (130); 'A couple of days
later I'm all for it again and feeling quite a lad about it. I feel like a proper
man of the world with a willing bint laid on like this' (187).

In adopting the language of commercialised sex, Vic is deceiving
himself and betraying both reason and realism. Yet before the imposition of this inauthentic discourse, his narration of the loss of his virginity with Ingrid is riddled with romantic (and thus feminine) cliché and
euphemism:

All I can think of is this is what I was born for, this is what I've been
waiting for as long as I can remember. And that's not all, because
later, when my hand moves somewhere else, it's as though she's feeling just the same way as me, as though it's what she's been waiting
for, because she quivers at my touch and sighs and then rests back in
my arm and makes little noises in her throat as I love her like I never
thought was possible except in imagination. (109)

The Consolations of Conformity 47

Crucially, the first-person narration of the novel is in the present tense, and thus focalised through the confused, compromised and youthful Vic. This narrative voice is not completely innocent, however. It does make deliberate appeals for validation to its ideal and middle-class reader through a contempt for mass media's corruption of the working-class environment reminiscent of the disdain evident in Richard Hoggart's *The Uses of Literacy*: ' "Telly". I don't like that word somehow. It always reminds me of fat ignorant pigs of people swilling stout and cackling like hens at the sort of jokes they put on them coloured seaside post-cards' (107). Yet, robbed of rational hindsight by the narrative's present tense, Vic is a subaltern narrator, his confusion over sexual relations appealing for empathy while simultaneously instigating superiority in the masculine reader. This textual tactic may seem risky, but within so powerfully imagined and enforced a community as that of masculine readers, the risk that the actual reader will not recognise their ideal relationship with the narrator is minimal. By the 1966 sequel *The Watchers on the Shore*, however, any risk at all has been eradicated as Vic's voice, though still in the present tense, is tempered by a continual and cynical self-awareness:

> When I say there's no hurry it's not the real reason I give her. The real reason is that a baby would put another chain round us, tie us a bit more firmly, and try as I might I can't help resisting this. There's a part of me under the daily routine, the settled surface of our marriage, that never accepts, that's always holding out against a final surrender to the facts. (22)

David Lodge's novel *The British Museum is Falling Down* functions as a parody of numerous literary modes, one of them the trope of novels examined in this chapter. Its hero, Adam Appleby (his very name, of course, jesting with his everyman status), remarks to his friend Camel of a rich (and portly) American he has extricated from a telephone booth: 'If I was the hero of one of these comic novels [...] he would be the fairy-godfather who would turn up at the end to offer me a job and a girl. Don't suppose I shall ever see him again, actually' (74). (The American, of course, does reappear, and does offer him a job, at a salary that will at least allow him to buy a girl – his wife – a new coat.) When asked by a stranger in a crowded and noisy pub his opinion on 'Kingsley Anus', Adam replies, 'Oh, yes. I like his work. There are times when I think I belong to him more than to any of the others' (118). Lodge notes in his 1980 afterword to the novel how his own 'creative practice' was 'formed by the neo-realist, anti-modernist writing of the 1950s' (170). At a post-graduate sherry party, which Lodge describes as 'a kind of distillation of the post-Amis campus novel' (168), Adam perpetuates the illusion that this neo-realist fiction closes the gap between writing and reality:

> Before the novel emerged as the dominant literary form, narrative literature dealt only with the extraordinary or the allegorical – with kings and queens, giants and dragons, sublime virtue and diabolic evil. There was no risk of confusing that sort of thing with life, of course. But as soon as the novel got going, you might pick up a book at any time and read about an ordinary chap called Joe Smith doing just the sort of things you did yourself. (118)

Published in 1965, the novel's setting, if not quite contemporaneous to its publication date, is set in the midst of Beatlemania (Adam becomes embroiled in a crowd of 'screaming, weeping teenagers' (32) on his way to Bloomsbury), and, by that token, after sexual intercourse, for Philip Larkin, or, for everyone else, the sexual revolution, had begun. Adam is a practising Catholic, at least in the sense that he and his wife Barbara do not practice any artificial methods of contraception. The resultant retrograde nature of the couple's sexual preoccupations allows the narrative paradigm and priorities of the novel's 1950s predecessors still to function, even as they are parodied. *The British Museum is Falling Down* makes manifest the competing conceptions of sexuality as common-sensical requirement and irrational urge. Its epigraph is from Dr Johnson: 'I would be a Papist if I could. I have fear enough, but an obstinate rationality prevents me' (6), and Adam's conclusion over the Catholic rejection of preventative methods is that the use of contraception implies a pre-meditated transgression, contradicting the Catholic require-ment that sex is a spontaneous, violent libidinal desire (and thus an atoneable sin).

Though Adam's appreciation of the potential of contraception to rationalise sexual desire might initially make him seem qualified as a traditional hero of the masculine text, he differs from that typical hero in one important respect: he is married. Dominic Head notes of novels in the *Lucky Jim* style that: 'An interesting aspect of many of these nov-els is how the narrative impetus often colludes with adolescent male desires for sexual gratification or initiation, and a self-advancement that is linked to sexual assertiveness' (56). The 1950s plots of hypergamous seduction and personal advancement ultimately follow a trajectory of trying to take a girl, not continuing to keep a woman as your wife.

The British Museum is Falling Down does imitate masculine hypergamous sexual selection in Adam's refusal of a teenage girl's advances in preference for fidelity to Barbara. Like the use of contraception, however, an established marriage, in its theoretical provision of sex-on-demand from the beginning of the novel, cannot conclude in a traditional masculine happy ending of sexual conquest. Lodge emphasises this impossibility by ending instead with the voice of a woman, Barbara, gratefully not pregnant, uttering a provisional 'perhaps' (161) in the more modern place of Molly Bloom's elated 'yes'.

'Part-of-a-spending-spree and good-fun-for-all-concerned'

In John Braine's 1957 novel *Room at the Top*, masculine codes of value, both explicit and implied, are extended from people to possessions. The consumer boom of the post-war period demanded masculine mastery of a force newly rampant. Like the Welfare State, the consumer market, as a public space rapidly escalating in importance, maintained troubling intimations of the feminine for the men who had no choice but to participate in it. Women (initially in a colonial context) traditionally function as showcases for the material success of their men, and during the boom of the 1950s, the economic mechanism of a housewife spending on the home what her husband left it to earn remained the perceived norm. Male consumption, in other words, had always been predominantly vicarious. In 'Masculinity as Homophobia', Michael S. Kimmel records the embrace by the American male of a masculinity freed by capitalism from privilege and proletarianism: 'It is this notion of manhood – rooted in the sphere of production, the public arena, a masculinity grounded not in landownership or in artisanal republican virtue but in successful participation in marketplace competition – this has been the defining notion of American manhood' (122).

Adopting the ethos of Kimmel's slogan for the self-made man – 'He who has the most toys when he dies wins' (122) – proved an anxious game for Englishmen. *Which?* magazine, first appearing in 1957, attempted to bring some semblance of rational choice to the explosion of the consumer market. *Playboy*, which began publication in Britain in the 1950s, preached a conspicuously transatlantic but nonetheless highly relevant ethic of confidence in conspicuous consumption to the British male, off-setting any accusations of feminised priorities or masculine narcissism by the liberal inter-leaving of consumer articles with opportunities visually to consume the female form. In her book *The Social*

Meaning of Money, Viviana Zelizer notes how in early-twentieth-century America, a concept of 'cashworthiness' was prompted by new systems of relief: if consumer competence could be built through money, then cash dispensed to the poor was a therapeutic means of rehabilitating them back into society. Similarly, a man disorientated by the unfamiliar social conditions of the post-war Welfare State could, it was perceived, regain power through his purse, or rather wallet, by learning to spend and consume both effectively and ostentatiously.

Early in *Room at the Top* the narrator Joe Lampton boasts of his own particular skill in translating status symbols into hard cash: 'I've an instinct like a water-diviner's where money's concerned; I was certain that I was in the presence of at least a thousand a year' (15–16). The style of the earlier sections of the novel seeks to educate the reader in how to achieve this consumer savvy. In his essay on the James Bond series, 'Narrative Structures in Fleming', Umberto Eco notes of Fleming's tendency to catalogue the brand-names of possessions: 'Our credulity is solicited, blandished, directed to the region of possible and desirable things' (175). The same process is evident in Braine's novel: 'I wanted an Aston-Martin, I wanted a three-guinea linen shirt, I wanted a girl with a Riviera suntan – these were my rights, I felt, a signed and sealed legacy' (29). Joe lodges with the Thompsons in a house in Cyprus Avenue in Warley, where:

> The hall smelled of beeswax and fruit and there was a large copper vase of mimosa on a small oak table. Against the cream-painted walls I could see the faint reflection of the mimosa and the vase, chrome-yellow and near-gold; it looked almost too good to be true, like an illustration from *Homes and Gardens*. (10)

Joe says of Susan, the daughter of Warley's rich entrepreneur, that he was immediately attracted to her because she was 'conventionally pretty' (36). The nature of these conventions is immediately made explicit: 'Black shoulder-length hair, large, round hazel eyes, neat nose and mouth, dimples – she was like the girl in the American advertisements who is always being given a Hamilton watch or Cannon Percle (whatever that is) Sheets or Nash Airflyte Eight' (36). Susan is being judged, and the reader is invited to judge her, by the conventions of 'admass', the contemporarily fashionable, and disapproving, term for advertising-driven consumerism. This functions as an oblique comment upon the nature of Joe's desire for her, hinting that his attraction is despicably aspirational rather than admirably authentic. The consumer economy seeks continually to impose and reinforce a code of desirability: the thrill of recognition comes not from the potential consumer's own experience – to want to buy something you perceive a lack of it – but from a dictated impression that the item is to be coveted.

As well as its perceived power to feminise (attributable in part to its previous social unimportance, as well as the central figure of the house-wife in its advertising iconography and economic realities), the post-war rise of consumerism as a social dynamo is negotiated as a threat in male-authored novels of the period precisely because its mechanisms are suspiciously close to those of the masculine self, and the means of por-traying that self in fiction. Readers are coerced into the desirability of cer-tain judgements with the promise of privilege; what are in reality arbitrary symbols (linen shirts, suède shoes, Aston Martins) are loaded with atten-dant values. The media of the consumer market – *Homes and Gardens*, for instance, or the (presumably cinematic) American advertisements – make the means of their coercion, or, in Steven Connor's term, their 'addressiv-ity', blatant. Commodity fetishism interferes with a direct connection between appearance and reality: if, like the Thompsons's entrance hall, things look 'almost too good to be true', then they probably are. *Room at the Top* was produced during an early stage of the cultivation of consumer literacy, and difficulties in reading this new set of signs draws attention not only to individual male incompetence, but also to the relativity of sign systems themselves. Fiction is thereby revealed as an unstable site for establishing an essential masculine selfhood.

Anxiety over this sense of consumer illiteracy is modified, however, by the mode of narration that Braine employs in the novel – the retrospec-tive narrative recognisable from *Scenes from Provincial Life*. In this way, Joe's judgements of desirable possessions can be those not of an inexpe-rienced young man, but a seasoned connoisseur, a successful purchaser empowered with the benefit of hindsight. Narrator-Joe notes of the young Joe's dressing gown: 'The stitching was poor and after one wash-ing it became a shapeless rag. It was a typical example of the stuff turned out for a buyer's market in the early post-war period and I rather think that I was drunk when I bought it' (13). (Intoxication is proffered as an added excuse for poor literacy skills.) In his chapter on the novel in *Writing Men*, Berthold Schoene-Harwood finds in this narrative technique the introduction of 'the perspective of a self-conscious inward gaze hith-erto unprecedented in men's writing' (90), apparent in passages from the novel such as this one:

> I look back at that raw young man sitting miserable in the pub with a
> feeling of genuine regret; I wouldn't, even if I could, change places with

him, but he was indisputably a better person than the smooth character I am now, after ten years of getting almost everything that I ever
wanted. I know the name he'd give me: the Successful Zombie. (123)

Room at the Top is indeed notable for the way in which it foregrounds the
processes of patriarchal and masculine conditioning, and this emphasis
is heavily dependent upon the tool of the retrospective narrative, which
allows the analysis of a boy's initiation into masculine adulthood from
a male adult well-versed in its expectations and dividends. However, any
sense of resistance to patriarchal prerogatives from a man in a position
to rebel against them is dulled to the pervasive sense of malaise of a man
long-since in a state of subservience. This sense of malaise may be unusual
among male-authored novels of the period, but the plot and levels
of rational narratorial control remain identical to the other examples of
peer masculinist protectionism examined in this chapter. Radical tendencies are subsumed and compromised by the narrative mode itself.
The anguish at the irreparable loss of the opportunity of authentic self-
fashioning is effectively neutralised by the narrative tone of resigned
retrospective analysis, and the novel ends just as Joe's agony and anger
at Alice's death and society's refusal to implicate him in it requires full
emotional expression:

> Eva drew my head on to her breast. 'Poor darling, you mustn't take on
> so. You don't see it now, but it was all for the best. She'd have ruined
> your whole life. Nobody blames you, love. Nobody blames you.'
>   I pulled myself away from her abruptly. 'Oh my God,' I said, 'that's
> the trouble.' (235)

Having finally articulated the 'trouble' with contemporary male existence,
Joe's voice is stopped.

The surrender of the possibility of an authentic male selfhood outside
the patriarchal dictates of masculinity results in resigned malaise rather
than anguish precisely because of the impossibility of either expressing
or defining what that selfhood might be. The deepest sense of loss in the
novel surrounds the descriptions of Joe's relationship with Alice, a
communing of equals which allows him to envisage a chance to 'enter
into marriage, not just acquire a licence for sexual intercourse' (173).
The glimpses of human relativity, of the potential in sharing and surrender that his love allows him, is portrayed as an experience of both
relief and pain: 'We're all imprisoned within that selfish dwarf I – we
love someone and we grow so quickly into human beings that it hurts'

(180). A number of revealing assumptions about the nature of the self are apparent here. The self is rigid and constrictive, mean and small. It is 'selfish': inward-looking, isolated, insular. It exists in a state of binary opposition to love and its profoundly human state of messy relativity. By implication, 'that selfish dwarf I' is a masculine I, founded upon masculine codes of value. The novel reinscribes a traditional literary male paradox: the awareness of the inauthenticity of self is sported both as unique to male experience, and at the same time as a facet of universal human experience. Alice both shares in Joe's sense of release from the unnatural codes of identity that her society places upon her, and acts as the antithesis to his experience of selfhood, with her unfettered opinionatedness and sensuality.

As noted previously, the process of masculine self-recognition functions in a similar way to the means by which a consumer is positioned within a particular market. Both systems involve a relinquishing of individual choice and judgement for values dictated by an external influence. Both the consumer and masculine reflexes are dependent upon the correct perception and processing of external signs, and a suitable demonstration that this process has been completed successfully. Both patriarchy and consumerism, as Schoene-Harwood points out, operate by remote control. During the central section of *Room at the Top*, as the relationship between Joe and Alice deepens to a point of reciprocity and mutual satisfaction, so the flurry of consumer judgements of the novel's opening slows. It is as if this glimpse of a past-state of intuition and relativity negates the possibility of expression in metaphors of consumerism. Joe's current selfhood, however, is easily expressed with reference to commodification:

> I'm like a brand-new Cadillac in a poor industrial area, insulated by steel and glass and air-conditioning from the people outside, from the rain and the cold and the shivering ailing bodies. I don't wish to be like the people outside, I don't even wish that I had some weakness, some foolishness to immobilize me amongst the envious coolie faces, to let in the rain and the smell of defeat. But I sometimes wish that I wished it. (124)

Traditional gender divisions dictate that femininity can be defined by its passive acceptance of commodification and masculinity by its championing of individual, independent choice. The post-war acceleration in the growth of consumer markets prompted an uncomfortable awareness in some male-authored fiction that the processes of the consumer marketplace are unsettlingly similar to the long-established processes of locating and recognising the masculine self.

David Storey's 1960 novel *This Sporting Life* charts a movement between a working-class community perceived as 'pure' (and poor), to one infiltrated by the priorities and desires of a more affluent consumer society. Hymned with a tinge of hysteria by Richard Hoggart in his 1957 *The Uses of Literacy*, working-class culture was perceived to be changing from a circulatory space for utilitarian commodities to one of goods the value of which derived primarily from their ascribed prestige. Status symbols were gaining priority over survival methods, as their signifying power was repeatedly reinscribed in the burgeoning mass-media. For Hoggart, the admirable depths of duty and purpose of the working classes were silting up with these phoney values:

> Most mass-entertainments are in the end what D. H. Lawrence described as 'anti-life'. They are full of a corrupt brightness, of improper appeals and moral evasions. To recall instances: they tend towards a view of the world in which progress is conceived as a seeking of material possessions, equality as a moral levelling, and freedom as the grounds for endless irresponsible pleasure. (282)

The appeal to D. H. Lawrence, redolent with a determination to enshrine an essential manhood, is once again instructive here. *This Sporting Life* is rife with anxiety at the perceived dilution of an industrial-strength masculinity with the priorities of a male identity dependent upon the manipulation of signs endowed with significance by effete advertising executives. The novel focuses upon a group of working-class men on the very fault-line of changing social priorities: their lives are split between the harsh reality of employment in mines and factories, and the unreality of a sporting arena within which conflict is stagy, narcissism is sanctioned, and commodification of their bodies at its most blatant.

In her essay 'The Traffic in Women: Notes on the "Political Economy" of Sex', Gayle Rubin notes: 'Men are of course also trafficked – but as slaves, hustlers, athletic stars, serfs, or as some other catastrophic social status, rather than as men' (176). Such categories are easily contained and dismissed in an analysis focused (justifiably, of course) upon women, but what of life on the inside of that catastrophe, for the 'athletic stars' of the City Rugby League Club at Primstone? Arthur Machin's anxieties at the attendant objectification of his stardom – at being 'an ape' (164) – are liberally voiced in the text. Amidst his triumph at holding out for a £500 signing-on fee are frantic personal calculations of his own body's 'cashworthiness' that extend far beyond the confines of the stadium, as he demands of his landlady:

> 'Guess how much I'm worth.'
>   'I don't know. I don't know anything about football.'
>   'I know you don't. So just guess how much you think I'm *worth*. How much solid cash do you think am?' (68)

Throughout the novel, terms like 'worth' and 'value' are routinely fraught with uncertainty. Reckoning men in impersonal units invokes a familiar horror at the interchangeability of the male body in the hands and minds of the men in power. Arthur says of Weaver and Slomer, the owners of the club:

> They were supposed to be the most dangerous people in town – if you could have dangerous people in this town – and Primstone was their mutual toy. They bought and sold players, built them up and dropped them, like a couple of kids with lead soldiers. But that seemed to be the way with any professional sport. (88)

The horror is familiar from the indiscriminate slaughter of war-time, when the soldiers involved were constituted of something still more malleable than lead. It was resurrected in a new strain of social angst: that before the invention of the redemptive concept of consumer choice, the market has the terrifying power to level all its participants to interchangeable consumers, emphasising the disjunction between the ideal of the free market and that of freedom. This is at the root of Hoggart's suspicion: conversely to the optimism ascribed to Macmillan's 1957 phrase, the British people had, in reality, never *been had* so good.[9]

'The ho(m)mo-sexual monopoly'; the phrase was first coined by Luce Irigaray in *This Sex Which Is Not One*, and developed into a literary paradigm in Eve Kosofsky-Sedgwick's *Between Men*. Within a patriarchal society, men act as the exclusive agents of exchange, with women and other goods functioning as conduits for their homosocial desire. It is notable that in Arthur Machin's personal life, the mechanisms for the smooth transferral of women have stalled. He expends enormous effort in attempting to insert himself into the family who own his lodgings, or rather, into the empty space left by Mr Hammond, killed in an industrial accident at Weaver's factory, his body another expendable commodity. Arthur has sex with Mrs Hammond, he takes her and the kids on Sunday outings, he buys them gifts, but ultimately the patriarch is absent, and Mrs Hammond is unwilling, and unable, to give herself. Kinship has malfunctioned. As Irigaray notes in 'Women on the Market':

> All the systems of exchange that organize patriarchal societies and all the modalities of productive work that are recognized, valued and rewarded in these societies are men's business. The production of women, signs and commodities is always referred back to men [...], and they always pass from one man to another, from one group of men to another. (171)

Arthur's impotence amidst these systems of exchange is emphasised repeatedly by his inability to abandon Mrs Hammond's married moniker when he addresses or thinks of her. The traditional patriarchal cash nexus is also disrupted by Arthur's position as a lodger, as it makes the dynamics of market forces within the domestic sphere patently obvious. He says hopelessly to Mrs Hammond after sex: 'You make me feel I'm buying it off you. I'm just buying. And I'm not' (161). As a gift-giver, too, bearer of fur coats and television sets, he voluntarily locates himself within an economy the dynamics of which are noted by David Cheal in *The Gift Economy* to be dictated by 'a feminized ideology of love' (183). Denied the status of patriarch and provider, Arthur confusedly misuses these new-fangled public symbols of status as personal statements of love and intent. The only gift he bestows upon himself, a car, he confidently expects to endow him with the freedom enshrined in the motorised mobility of the heroes of the pulp fictions he avidly consumes. The Northern road system, however, will have no truck with a British Kerouac:

> I thought if only I could break things up like this Stulton [hero of the paperback *Love Tomorrow*], and get on to the next place and leave all these wrecks behind. I even tried driving out of town fast. But the roads were crammed. They twisted and ducked about. And I'd only go a couple of miles, hardly leaving town behind, before I was in the next bloody place. (191)

Elsewhere in Arthur's dealings with women, systems of exchange are also failing: he rejects the advances of the 'sample' Mrs Weaver (107) (the term riddled with the ethos of the travelling salesman) for fear of how sex with her might affect his professional relationship with her husband. Afterwards he regretfully notes of his refusal: 'It's just not an economic proposition. It's so uneconomical that I've to turn down the best thing that ever happened to me. [...] It was so uneconomical that I'd acted like a decent human being' (107). His only glimpse of the dynamics of a 'normal' gender marketplace is through Judith Braithewaite's description of girls on a Saturday night at the Mecca dance-hall: 'It's more or less an auction sale, and they're terrified of going to the wrong bidder' (205).

Why has the ho(m)mo-sexual monopoly broken down in the case of Arthur Machin? In 'Commodities Among Themselves', Irigaray notes that 'there is a price to pay for being the agents of exchange: male subjects have to give up the possibility of serving as commodities themselves' (193). By virtue of his sports-star status, however, Arthur has had to surrender the possibility of this surrender: as noted above, he is only too aware of his status as commodity. As with all patriarchal social mechanisms, the ho(m)mo-sexual monopoly is founded upon the establishing and containment of the Other. Commodities are necessarily feminised. Crucially in this novel, the feminised commodity is simultaneously a hyper-masculine symbol – the working-class rugby league player. This contradiction strikes at the very heart of a masculine economy so intent upon denying the true direction of its desires. If the commodity is masculine, its acquisition and attendant specularisation affords the male purchaser not self-congratulation and increased social standing, but an unavoidable confrontation with the male narcissism that is the concealed crux of the system. Desire between men becomes overt. This rupture leaks out into the novel's manifestations of sensuality, all but one, a lingering over 'the smooth misty curves of the man-cliffs, big and amiable and intimate' (220) at Scarborough, located in the changing rooms at the Club, site of male intimacy, bathing, gazing, and the application of liniment: 'Over on my left Maurice chatted, just his head and lighted cig above the water. Frank, drawing relief from his fag, turned his bull's back to me. I rubbed the soap over his familiar stained skin. I knew it better than my own' (253). The homosexual desire within the novel, cumulative among scenes like this, is as blatant as contemporary censorship would allow. The basic dynamic of the ho(m)mo-sexual monopoly is exposed.

The novel ends as it began, in the changing room. Life goes doggedly on inside and amidst the bruised bodies, but Arthur Machin's body is older, is depreciating, and the span of his earning potential as a commodity drawing to a close. Earlier, rushing towards the hospital to the bedside of the dying Mrs Hammond, his car breaks down and he has to get out and run. He notes later: 'Perhaps I didn't need a car now. It was getting too old, too knocked about, and I'd never afford another' (248–9). Retirement from the pitch looms, but so too does retirement from his limited attempt competently to consume and to display the symbols of his affluent status. Yet men in general cannot afford to withdraw from their attempt to master the consumer sphere, and there are men, like Joe Lampton, whose economic agency is not compromised by the (catastrophic) object status of the rugby star. The novel affords a brief glimpse of the possibility of progress. Having moved into a flat located, in keeping with his commercial status as necessarily feminised commodity, above a 'small women's department store, just off City Centre' (211), Arthur bumps into Mrs Hammond and her son:

> 'Hello, Arthur,' the boy said as if I'd seen him every day of his life. 'There's Arthur, Mam.'
> She grunted and pushed by. I followed her a couple of steps. 'Aren't you going to stop and talk?'
> She didn't say anything, and I followed her again. I knew she'd recognized me, knew who and what I was.
> 'With you in them clothes?' she said. I was in a new lounge suit. Ian put his hand out to touch it and say, 'Suit'. (213)

The next male generation shows a sign that it is learning the language of materialism, and reaches out a hand to feel the fabled quality of a status symbol.

The *male* text?

This chapter concludes with a brief coda, by way of a reiteration of the fact that the narrative techniques and textual practices that I have been tracing in these novels are properly designated 'masculine' and not male, and thus available to authors of both sexes. Lynne Reid Banks's novel *The L-Shaped Room* (1960) was much lauded on its publication as the debut of an authentic female voice. There are elements of the heroine's subjectivity that can be read as a realistic portrayal of the ways in which a contemporary woman has internalised patriarchal principles of womanly virtue. Jane Graham moves into the eponymous, dilapidated room out of a sense of guilt at her pregnancy: 'In some obscure way I wanted to punish myself, I wanted to put myself in the setting that seemed proper to my situation' (42). She notes of her forthcoming child:

> I wanted a son. This was irrational, since obviously I was more nearly capable of rearing a girl by myself than a boy – I knew almost

nothing about little boys except that their need of a father was imperative if they were not to grow into Oedipus-riddled weaklings or even outright homosexuals. (246)

The male characters in the novel that befriend Jane, Toby and John, are coded by their ethnic origins (Jewish and black, respectively), and in John's case, his homosexuality too, as suitably subaltern to also be 'proper' to Jane's degraded situation.

More explicit than this, though, are the ways in which the narratorial voice of the novel seeks to flatter men and their assumptions about female behaviour, as in these examples: 'Shaken, we stood at opposite sides of the room, in separate silences. But I couldn't bear to see him standing there so desolately, face to face with his own failure. I knew how it felt, and it must be worse for a man' (215); '*You darling blackbird*, I thought, yearning for him, my treacherous female arms longing to imprison him for ever' (314); 'My imagination was working overtime. All the womanish terrors which I had always felt myself to be above, came creeping over me as I lay alone. I thought of everything – prowlers, burglars, murderers, maniacs – even ghosts. I was disgusted with myself, but I couldn't help it' (250). A familiar binary opposition is being vehemently reinscribed: man = rationality and progression, woman = emotion and regression. Jane's assessment of her Aunt Addy's 'novel of letters' to a lover provides an insight into the way in which this masculine foundational binary is worked into the narrative technique of *The L-Shaped Room*:

Most of the writer's troubles were self-made, as in real life; they were the self-created hells that a sensitive, emotional woman will always encounter in her everyday dealings with herself and with other people; it was impossible not to believe in them as I read. And I marvelled at the way that explaining them to the recipient of the letters, getting outside them sufficiently to avoid alarming him, yet safe in the knowledge that this was a token act of kindness because he would know quite well how desperately important they seemed to the writer – these factors, together with the vital underlying one that basically nothing mattered too terribly except the fear of losing the one who was loved, made for a sense of balance and light-hearted courage in the face of life which I found so moving and exciting that I kept reading, one letter after another, avid to see how this magic formula would affect the wide range of life-like situations the writer found herself involved in. (242)

The narrative voice of the novel exhibits enough detachment and control to an immasculated reader 'to avoid alarming him', while its occasional emotional expression is explained and excused by being characterised as the product of a feminine, 'womanish' outburst. The heroine herself measures her selfhood with reference to explicitly masculine codes, and the novel's narrative technique again replicates the 'double voice' of superior and rational control and knowing, chummy complicity with a range of attendant values. Aunt Addy insists of the recipient of the letters: 'he doesn't exist [...]. Men like that never do. They always have to be invented' (244). The text of *The L-Shaped Room* uses the narrative techniques of its male-authored peers precisely to reinvent this ideal, immasculated reader.

3
The Contradictions of Philosophy

> I have tried to show in the course of this book, how the Outsider's one need is to discover how to lend a hand to the forces inside him, to help them in their struggle. And obviously if he is only vaguely aware of these interior forces, the sensible thing is to become more aware of them and find out what they are aiming at.
>
> Colin Wilson, *The Outsider* (1956)

'*Existentialism is an attempt at philosophizing from the standpoint of the actor instead of, as has been customary, from that of the spectator*': so reads E. L. Allen's attempt to 'hazard a definition of existentialism in a sentence' in his 1953 *Existentialism from Within* (3). Simplistic though this might be, it does prompt an immediate recognition of the potentially radical implications for the influence of existentialism upon the masculine definitions of selfhood and narrative techniques examined in the previous chapter. The existentialist self, encapsulating as it does the concept of an authenticity continually hard-won by dynamic, individual choice amidst a contingent universe, stands in opposition to a self whose behavioural patterns and values issue from a pre-existent masculine core. As Mark Poster has pointed out, for existentialist thinkers, 'Consciousness existed [...] before it had any particular attributes – before, that is, it had an essence' (82). Identity is won by the constant striving of the individual, not inherited by virtue of solidarity with a group: in fact, existential authenticity is usually apprehended as being inversely proportionate to social conformity. The existential novel should stand in antithesis to the masculine text. The notion of existence as 'being-in-the-world', with its acknowledgement of the subjectivity and instability of each individual viewpoint, provides a marked contrast to Malcolm Bradbury's lauded 'art of reason' (1969, iii), based upon a supposedly objective record of a supposedly recognisable universal experience.

In *Feminism Unmodified*, Catharine MacKinnon claims that 'to look at the world objectively is to objectify it' (50), and that to do so is the quintessential political and epistemological stance under male dominance. The single masculine textual viewpoint, as we have seen, relies upon the valorisation of objectivity and the practice of objectification. The objectification of the Other – 'subaltern-bashing' – should be healthily compromised by the existentialist recognition that your own self exists as a mere object from the point of view of others. The existential hero revels in the isolation of his subjectivity. The recognition of objectification as a false position undermines the device of retrospective narrative as means of gaining control over contingency. A random universe should not be empirically representable in the form of a linear, aetiological narrative. Commitment to an existential philosophy might therefore be expected to effect a radical rethinking of the paradigms of selfhood, gender and narrative traced in Chapter 2. Furthermore, it could herald a break from a male-authored literature riddled with resignation into one which is didactic and dynamic rather than conformist and consolatory.

Allen goes on to note of Jean-Paul Sartre's radical assertion of freedom in *L'Etre et le Néant*, 'Thus, in a certain sense, I *choose* to be born':

> Whatever criticisms one may be disposed to pass on so startling a conclusion, it has at least one great merit, inasmuch as it challenges the contemporary mood of irresponsibility, the couldn't-care-less attitude. It is clear that this ontology involves an ethic. It is indeed as the effort after a new morality that Sartre's existentialism must be judged. (71)

The existentialist philosophy, in other words, is here hailed as a potential antidote to the perceived moral and political apathy of a stalled liberalism. In 'The Existentialist Hero', a radio talk broadcast on the BBC *Third Programme* in March 1950, Iris Murdoch voices her optimism at the philosophy's potential to politicise what she calls the 'cynical frivolity' (109) of the contemporary novel: 'The existentialist shares with the Marxist a feeling of responsibility for the condition of men, a conception of life as perpetual warfare, and a willingness to engage his weapons as a thinker in the battle. Literature, too, must be in the fight, it must be *engagée*' (110). Empiricism rejects detached theorising for experience and observation. Existentialism, Murdoch implies, unites theory with experience and literature with society. In a later essay, 'The Existentialist Political Myth', published in 1952, Murdoch goes so far as to nominate the novelist's aims and strengths as directly convergent with those of the newly emergent brand of philosopher: 'This is the revolution in philosophic method which is showing us its different faces at the present time. It is a move, one might notice, which brings the activity of the philosopher in some ways closer to that of the novelist. The novelist is *par excellence* the unprejudiced describer of *le monde vécu*' (131). The existential viewpoint, she claims, free as it is from dogma and bias, can be conflated in its purity with the ideal novelistic viewpoint.

This chapter will not offer an analysis of the existentialist doctrine in its numerous and varied incarnations, or speculate upon its ideological sources. It will instead consider textual evidence from a number of English male-authored novels of the post-Second World War period selected for their engagement with existentialist thought. The novels will be used to gauge the extent to which these narratives' interpretations of existential tenets serve to liberate them from the oppressive and regressive masculine interpretations of gender and self examined in the previous chapter.

Outside the hero

If the existential stance is that an individual is at large in a contingent universe about which his knowledge is severely limited, his actions redolent with subjective meaning, but the empirical effects of those actions negligible, then the conventions of male literary heroism are under attack. The concept of existential nothingness infers a vacancy for a new type of hero, and those authors averse to the cheerfully compromised popular heroes of the quintessential 1950s English novels were keen to fill it. When his 1957 novel *The Divine and the Decay* was republished as *The Leap* in 1984, Bill Hopkins used the Author's Preface to the new edition to take issue with the swathes of criticism his novel had received at first publication. A good example of this negative reaction occurs in Kenneth Allsop's examination of the 1950s, *The Angry Decade*:

> We seem to be on the edge of a new romantic tradition which is sanctifying the bully as hero. It is exceedingly strange, and profoundly disturbing, if the dissentience (the 'anger') in our present semi-socialised compromise welfare society is going to swing retrogressively to the discredited and hateful system of murder gangs and neurotic mysticism which perished in its own flames. We know that

there is political boredom and apathy in Britain, that the drive seems lost and the blood runs thin. Can it be so intolerable that it is creating an ardour for the corrupt vigour of fascism? (186–7)

Hopkins attempts to counter these accusations of political fascism in his novel with an appeal to a mode of artistic experimentation appreciable only by an elite, claiming: 'To be candid, it was written with the idea of offering a seminal work for a few concerned people who appreciated the need to revitalize the novel, or to create a new form altogether' (1), and going on to refer to it as an 'iconoclastic blare of the trumpet' (2). There is a flaw in Hopkins's defence beyond its wording (which, in denying fascist tendencies, manages to evoke both an elitist hierarchy and the military enforcement of that hierarchy, with its trumpet blast). *The Divine and the Decay* is very far from exploding the traditional novelistic form – and it is precisely for this reason that it was repeatedly read as condoning fascism.

Peter Plowart, the novel's protagonist and a ruthless quester for authenticity, has removed himself to Vachau, off Guernsey – the island's isolation is to act as alibi for an assassination he has organised. His character is established to a great extent by his antithesis to Claremont Capothy, daughter of Vachau's absent owner. Claremont is given the opportunity to deconstruct the masculine literary representation of her gender. She is aware of the conceit of woman as erotic mystery, and equally aware of the incompatibility of this conception with female corporeality. When Plowart breaks into her bedroom one night, she averts his lust by showing him her naked body, explaining: 'You see, while a woman is synonymous with concealment and mystery she's desirable to men. The moment she strips herself the reality is an insult beside the paintings of the imagination. It's the reason men detest wantons; they're too honest to be seductive' (142). However, the text uses Claremont less as an agent of metafictional insight than as a representative of naïve liberal humanism, or, in Plowart's terms, someone 'duped by the world's filthy morality' (230). Confronted with his dramatic and bleak pronouncements, she counters with appeals to basic humanist assumptions, redolent with an enduring horror of the War: 'You can make vileness a virtue so easily! Your kind of thinking can relate eugenics and incinerators and make them part of a perfectly sane argument; isn't that enough to make one suspicious?' (224). This is Allsop's point exactly: that attempts to challenge the populist heroes of what he calls 'our present semi-socialised compromise welfare society' (187) have resulted only in the creation of vile monsters. Hopkins announces in his preface to

The Leap that 'I wanted a suspicious, even a hostile reader, with all the aliveness enmity means' (3). Yet the fact that these counter-arguments emanate from a woman, and a woman already revealed in her corporeality, does little to discourage an equation familiar from the masculine text: Plowart = not feminine = heroic. Plowart's judgement of humanism is as a doctrine that fosters sentiment and inauthenticity, an antirational, 'feminine' doctrine, and even Claremont herself notes sagely that 'a woman usually acts in advance of her reasoning' (218).

Hopkins's ideal readers, presumably, would be cynical and superior enough to reject both Plowart's violent extremism and Claremont's conservative stasis for a middle way, yet his novel's realist narrative and gendered sources of symbolism function to ensure instead the identification of an immasculated reader with a traditionalist masculine exemplar. Rather than allowing that elite interpretive community to infer their own conclusions, the narrative relentlessly positions Plowart as a hero. The third-person narrative is continually focalised through him. The only other character with a substantial role in the novel, Christopher Lumas, is ruthlessly subordinated with reference to his disability (his legs became useless after a fall), his loss of self-control through alcoholism, and his slavish subservience to his cuckolding wife: 'he was mentally, morally, physically and spiritually a ruin of what a man should be' (65). Plowart announces with confidence that 'in the case of men, the greatest in history were those most dynamic in their actions' (48). The picture gallery of inspirational figures that he establishes in his room contains images of Attila and Hitler. The two potential alternative selves in the novel, Claremont and Lumas, are dismissed as female and feminised respectively, and Plowart is the only character whose actions might be construed as dynamic. He drives the plot, and his violence (he arranges the murder of co-leader of his political party, the New Britain League) is part of the same drive as his admirable striving for self-definition. Just as the immanence of Claremont's corporeality is used to discredit her, so his dynamism manifests itself as that traditional demonstration of male heroism (and Cartesianism) – he can submit his bodily instincts to the majesty of his will, as when he meets Claremont's challenge to go to the end of the precipitous White Feather spur:

Looking down he was aware it was for just such ordeals as this that the complicated machinery of his mind had been designed ... just sufficient to drive his body forward where nobody else would go; just harmonious enough to knit his body into an obedient chain of responses; just wilful enough to assume it could be done without the imagination forming pictures of the consequences of a drop. (121)

He has already informed Claremont that: 'even if I fall, I shall not die. Like all great men I've an unconquerable life force, beside which a few rocks are nothing' (121). In the foreword preceding Hopkins's preface to *The Leap*, the author's friend Colin Wilson says of Plowart:

> He feels that imagination is not enough; the answer has to lie in action. The saviour requires a saviour. At the end of the book, he has to learn the hardest of all lessons: that he will never solve his problem while he looks to someone else to provide him with the answer. Claremont is lying when she tells him that the rocks will move if he has enough faith; yet the rocks *do* move, and he is saved. (xii)

Plowart triumphs in subjugating his body to his will, and in the novel's final scene, he succeeds in subjugating the power of the ocean currents too, as the rocks appear to move towards him, saving him from the sea. The hero of a *Bildungsroman*, he is ultimately educated and triumphant, and his final words, 'Indestructible, you fools!' (234) conclude *The Divine and the Decay* on a hectoring note of celebration, rather than pathos at his presumption in the face of a contingent universe. Instead of an isolated existential individual, Plowart becomes the representative of a universal principle, a potential example to and dynamic leader of men.

'Ways Without a Precedent' reveals an ulterior motive behind this professedly radical but effectively conservative hero, as Hopkins claims of the shadowy figure of 'the writer': 'He has conditioned himself to observe everything that happens within his orbit with a steady and remembering eye. As his craft is produced at first-hand, constantly in positions of physical and mental hardship, for him the step towards vision and leadership is not a large one' (148). The nature of this alleged physical hardship constantly endured by this writer is unclear, but Hopkins's intention is obvious: to prompt the conflation of writer and hero similar to that imposed upon Amis and Osborne, and name himself heir to the heroism his novel reasserts. That heroism may profess its existentialist aims, but revels in a traditional, hierarchical glory. It is a glory collectively appreciated rather than individually asserted and legitimised.

Accusations of self-glorification as both a writer and a man were frequently levelled at Colin Wilson, self-styled prophet of what he branded a 'religious existentialism'.[1] By 1972, MacQuarrie is claiming forcefully in *Existentialism* that: 'One cannot [...] link existentialism to Romanticism, except in the sense that they were both opposed to what they took to be a narrow intellectualism. The existentialists have been just as much opposed to aestheticism and sentimentalism as to rationalism' (53). Yet in his 1966 *Introduction to the New Existentialism*, Wilson reveals a similar tendency to Hopkins to elide existentialism into the tenets of a long-established Romantic literary heroism:

> Now the basic impulse behind existentialism is optimistic, very much like the impulse behind all science. Existentialism *is* romanticism, and romanticism is the feeling that man is not the mere creature he has always taken himself for. Romanticism began as a tremendous surge of optimism about the stature of man. (96)

Wilson's earlier philosophical tract, *The Outsider* (1956), an impassioned medley of personal literary preferences, potted biographies and pop-psychological analyses[2] by way of evidence of man's potential for spiritual transcendence, went through nine printings in its first two months of publication. It was read as a despicable effort of self-aggrandisement by Kenneth Allsop in *The Angry Decade*. He judged Wilson and his cohorts to be 'propagating their Religious Existentialism which they say requires a higher type of man, a superman, to thrust humanity through to safety out of civilization's big crash. It is probably unnecessary to add that they see themselves as the super-men, the law-givers' (22). Wilson and his cohorts did initially plan to enforce their ideals of freedom through the founding of a neo-fascist political party, and initiated exploratory talks with Sir Oswald Mosley.

'Religious Existentialism', like 'existentialism *is* romanticism': Wilson is unperturbed by the conflation of terms. For him God does exist, because a man can make himself godlike, and existentialism, as a code for achieving this individual transcendence, *is* a religion. Fashioned in this way, existentialism becomes a means of achieving spiritual security rather than radical uncertainty, and also a way of establishing a new social hierarchy, with super-men (and emphatically *not* super-women) at the head. Wilson notes in 'Beyond the Outsider' that: 'All the great religions were founded by one man, a law-giver: Mahomet, Moses, Zoroaster, Christ, Gautama. That is most important' (45). No contradiction is seen between existentialist aims of individual liberation, and the reassertion of a patriarchal and essentialist social structure. The ultimate goal, as laid out in *The Outsider*, is 'the ultimate restoration of order' (15). Wilson's alleged existentialism involves no Nietzschean disavowal of the doer behind the deed, but rather a race of super-men whose actions are guaranteed authentic by the pre-existing authenticity of their gender, their essence and their intellect. As Jeffner Allen has noted, this kind of 'existential hero intercepts the decline of the rule of essence' (75). Wilson's existential acts are not random, but emanate from a pre-existing central core – a masculine self.

This congenital masculinity is reinforced in Wilson's treatment of sexual relationships. In the groundbreaking essay in feminist film studies, 'Visual Pleasure and Narrative Cinema', published in *Screen* in 1975, Laura Mulvey claims of the voyeurism of the male cinematic gaze that its 'sadistic side fits in well with narrative. Sadism demands a story, depends on making something happen, forcing a change in another person, a battle of will and strength, victory/defeat, all occurring in a linear time with a beginning and an end' (22). Colin Wilson's own fictional works would seem to offer perverse early evidence of this connection between male sadism and narrative. *Ritual in the Dark* centres upon its protagonist Gerard Sorme's fascination with Austin Nunne, who is gradually revealed to be the prolific 'Whitechapel Killer', engaged in murdering prostitutes with increasingly elaborate violence. Sorme, though repulsed to some extent by Nunne's 'combination of coarseness and femininity' (21) – Nunne is homosexual – is determined for the majority of the novel to interpret his crimes as an admirable reaction to the stasis of contemporary society, and his sadism as a vital aspect of male sexual desire. Nunne explains to Gerard:

> The whole point of sadism ... is that it wants to take what someone doesn't want to give. If they want to give it, it's not the same.
>
> But I *do* understand, Sorme contradicted him. I feel the same frequently. Nothing shatters me more than a woman who wants to be made love to. (129)

This points to the philosophical thesis of the novel: modern life has lost its intensity, and there is a possibility for a man to regain that intensity through (heterosexual) sex, but the act must retain its traditional balance of power, with the woman passive and unwilling, and the man active and triumphant. Wilson's attempt to come to terms with the bodily nature of the subject centres upon the portrayal of sex as an enactment of volition, rather than a surrender to 'natural urges'. Sorme's two sexual conquests in the novel, Gertrude and her younger niece, Caroline, are both virgins, and the penetration of Caroline is immediately followed by this effusive burst of Nietzschean yea-saying at the discovery of a means of experiencing the intensity of existence that does not involve murder:

> What was happening now was realler than any of his thoughts about sex, more real than anything except pain: it was an intimation of the reason behind the tireless continuity of life. He felt astonished at his own stupidity for not realising it before. He wanted to make a vow: to accept always, only accept, accept anything, embrace everything with the certainty that all things would yield like this, an engulfing pleasure. (240)

God may be dead, but as John MacInnes argues, 'the fetishism of religion (whereby people projected their existential anxiety onto god and dealt with it through their imagined relationship to Him)' (13) can be replaced with the fetishism of sex.

(Hetero-) Sex plays a similarly crucial philosophical (and religious) role in Wilson's *Man Without a Shadow: The Diary of an Existentialist*. In it, the returning Gerard Sorme explicitly conflates the sexual impulse with an existential impulse toward authenticity: 'I watch my sexual impulse at work with a kind of amazement. I may not know why I'm alive, but something inside me does. Sex is the only power I know that can defeat the awful pressure of the present' (35). However, this is far from a project to incorporate sexuality into the masculine definition of selfhood. Sex is portrayed here as an intensifier of consciousness, a philosophical tool, but one that requires to be wielded by a man, and in the presence of feminine surrender (Gerard has not lost his taste for virgins). Volition in heterosexual intercourse and existential insight are conflated, then ruthlessly policed to exclude the feminine: 'The male confronts his boredom with a need to conquer, to penetrate, to achieve ecstasy by a kind of aggression. The female reacts to freedom with the cry: come and penetrate me. Bring me ecstasy and sensation' (119). The novel upholds orgasm as the model for the apotheosis of human consciousness, but it is a specifically masculine conception of orgasm, a linear quest to an end, a drive to 'conquer' and 'achieve'.

Wilson's work preserves the sanctity of the heroic masculine narrative, and the climax of that narrative becomes a matter of the education of a paradoxically already-complete selfhood. Just such an assumption is replicated in the later work of the philosopher Alasdair MacIntyre in his 1981 *After Virtue*. His argument is made in opposition to that continental existential set-text, Sartre's *Nausea*, in which Roquentin asserts that to present a life as a narrative is to falsify the true lived experience, which is one of fragmentation, alienation and dislocation. MacIntyre's chief concern is to present identity as inextricable from community, but he also makes the assertion that: 'The difference between imaginary characters and real ones is not in the narrative form of what they do; it is in the degree of their authorship of that form and of their own deeds' (200). Authentic identity is a matter of the control of deeds and events by an authoritative pre-existing self. Similarly, in *The Outsider*, itself ostensibly a narrative of self-improvement, Wilson makes the point that:

> The *Bildungsroman* sets out to describe the evolution of the 'hero's soul'; it is fictional biography that is mainly concerned with its hero's reaction to ideas, or the development of his ideas about 'life' from his experience. The *Bildungsroman* is a sort of laboratory in which the hero conducts an experiment in living. For this reason, it is a particularly useful medium for writers whose main concern is a philosophical answer to the practical question: What shall we do with our lives? Moreover, it is an interesting observation that as soon as a writer is seized with the need to treat a problem he feels seriously about in a novel, the novel automatically becomes a sort of *Bildungsroman*. The *Bildungsroman* is the natural form of serious fictional art. (51–2)

This is a tour-de-force for a masculine literary agendum: not only is authentic existence equated with the narrative of the heroic male quest, but this style of narrative is established as the über-form of all literary endeavour, its (male) writers heroes too. Steven Connor notes the frequency with which it is assumed that

> The representative form of the novel is the *Bildungsroman*, the novel of education and development. Such a novel offers the promise of a reciprocal mirroring between the individual and society; in the *Bildungsroman*, society becomes visible as the enabling field of operations for the individual, and the individual as the actualisation of social possibility. (6)

The English novel of education in its most familiar form, a retrospective narrative focused upon a single male protagonist, functions to reinscribe the patriarchal social structure as an arena of personal liberation and fulfillment.[3] Patriarchy is simultaneously normalised and glamorised.

In his introduction to *Man Without a Shadow*, Wilson discusses the problems of producing 'a novel of ideas'. He notes: 'I approached this problem in *Ritual in the Dark*, to which this present novel is a sequel.

There I failed, and contented myself with a compromise – a novel that "told a story", and got in the ideas wherever it could, provided they never held up the action'. *Man Without a Shadow*, he claims, 'cannot be called a novel' (Wilson, 1963, 14), but is rather an attempt at 'an existential realism. Like social realism, its attitude to reality is not passive or pessimistic. In a qualified sense, it might be called practical; it wishes to change things. What it wishes to change I prefer to leave unstated; it can be inferred from this book' (15–16). *Man Without a Shadow* purports to avoid the perceived philosophical compromise of *Ritual in the Dark* by resorting to a diary form, which touts itself as more realistic:

> It may seem that in writing like this I am only indulging in a kind of intellectual onanism; but this would be to miss the point. *There is a point*. I keep trying to break into reality with this crowbar of reason. I don't try a 'systematic' attack, like a philosopher or a theologian; I don't want to 'explain' the world, like Thomas Aquinas. I want to keep *jabbing*, in the hope that the point of my crowbar will find a crack in the stones and be able to lever them apart. In a way, this diary is the ideal way to try and do it. My method of attack is the same as that of Nietzsche, Kierkegaard, Wells; fragmentary. Yet this is necessary. (69)

Wilson denies a charge of onanism (once again, with this metaphor, the intellectual is conflated with the sexual) with a sustained description of striving for penetration, a situation he has previously established as both revelatory and exclusively male. The traditional (and feminine) connotations of the diary form – secrecy, domesticity, emotion and so on – are sidestepped with the concept of 'inductive existentialism': 'All my work is existential in the sense that it badly wants to stick to living experience; but it's inductive because it wants to reason from the *particular* to the general' (25). For all the allegiance sworn to existential thought, Wilson's aesthetic philosophy has come full circle – affirming Bradbury's desire for 'the novel in its empirical form' (iii). Claims for the universality of the masculine, it seems, are inextricably linked to narrative in its realist, contiguous form. In *Introduction to the New Existentialism*, Wilson, rejecting what he identifies as the '*cul de sac*' of pessimism that is part of 'traditional' existentialism, announces:

> My purpose is to outline a new form of existentialism that avoids this *cul de sac*, and that can continue to develop. It rejects Sartre's notion of man's contingency – for reasons which I shall discuss in detail.

Its bias is therefore distinctly optimistic, and its atmosphere is as different from that of the 'old existentialism' as the atmosphere of G. K. Chesterton's novels differ from *Waiting for Godot*. Its methods might be described as Anglo-Saxon and empirical rather than as 'continental' and metaphysical. (18)

A masculine philosophy?

The novels examined so far in this analysis have been read as demonstrative of a compromise of the implications of existentialist doctrine in order to allow a more traditional definition of selfhood, and one compliant with patriarchal priorities. The masculine self is an essentialist one, its gender identity a given rather than a performance, and its actions an imposition of that self onto the world, not a means of achieving its essence. The epistemological and social structure disseminating from this ideal self is one of purportedly 'natural' male superiority. Yet could it be the case that, rather than being a compromise of existentialism, this reinforcement of masculine conceptions of self and society is intrinsic to the philosophy itself? Albert Camus's *The Outsider*, first translated into English in 1946, ends thus:

> As if this great outburst of anger had purged all my ills, killed all my hopes, I looked up at the mass of signs and stars in the night sky and laid myself open for the first time to the benign indifference of the world. And finding it so much like myself, in fact so *fraternal*, I realized that I'd been happy, and that I was still happy. (117, my emphasis)

Contingency here has become a source of comfort, and this comfort stems from self-identification with a random universe, and a resulting 'fraternal' kinship: reality, and revelation, are coded as male. In her *SCUM Manifesto*, Valerie Solanas propounds just this case with characteristic verve and viciousness, albeit with a different motive:

> Most men, utterly cowardly, project their inherent weaknesses onto women, label them female weaknesses and believe themselves to have female strengths; most philosophers, not quite so cowardly, face the fact that male lacks exist in men, but still can't face the fact that they exist in men only. So they label the male condition the Human Condition, pose their nothingness problem, which horrifies them, as a philosophical dilemma, thereby giving stature to their animalism, grandiloquently label their nothingness their 'Identity Problem', and

proceed to prattle on pompously about the 'Crisis of the Individual', the 'Essence of Being', 'Existence preceding Essence', 'Existential Modes of Being', etc., etc. (18–19)

Existentialism, she claims, is an aggrandising ideology for inherent, and abhorrent, male characteristics. In the essay 'An Introduction to Patriarchal Existentialism', Jeffner Allen too is uncompromising in her judgement of the philosophy: 'Existentialism is, in principle, patriarchal existentialism' (78). The philosophy, in other words, is the product not of intrinsic male mania (as it is for Solanas), but rather of a society organised under the auspices of male superiority.

Judith Butler extends the critique of existentialism from the level of the social to the epistemological. In her analysis of the philosophical work of Simone de Beauvoir in *Gender Trouble* she sees Beauvoir's feminist aims as antithetical to those of existentialism, suggesting that the doctrine does not need to be misread in order to be appropriated by masculine priorities; rather, it inherently rehearses and enforces these priorities. Beauvoir's project of existential feminism – to reinscribe gender as a developing engagement with situations, structures and responsibilities – is, according to Butler, doomed to failure due to a fundamental clash between feminism and existentialism. In contrast to Irigaray's thesis of the feminine self as a point of linguistic absence, outside all established epistemological systems, Beauvoir's interpretation of the female sex is that it exists within signification as a *marked* concept, while the male sex remains unmarked. It is precisely this 'purity' of the male sex that assures its positioning as universal:

For Beauvoir, the 'subject' within the existential analytic of misogyny is always already masculine, conflated with the universal, differentiating itself from a feminine 'Other' outside the universalizing norms of personhood, hopelessly 'particular', embodied, condemned to immanence. Although Beauvoir is often understood to be calling for the right of women, in effect, to become existential subjects and, hence, for inclusion within the terms of an abstract universality, her position also implies a fundamental critique of the very disembodiment of the abstract masculine epistemological subject. (11)

Beauvoir argues in *The Second Sex* that a woman's body has come to be interpreted as her essence, but should become instead a site of freedom rather than imprisonment. Butler takes issue with this assumption, arguing that it merely perpetuates the radical (and masculine) ontological distinction of mind and body (and man and woman) passed through the patriarchy from Plato to Descartes to Husserl to Sartre. Beauvoir's feminist ambitions are thus conceived to be a betrayal of the Third Wave, post-structuralist feminist aim precisely to defuse and abandon such binary hierarchies.

During the 1970s, as the Anglo-American Woman's Movement developed, Sartre was much criticised by feminists for the 'sexism' of the imagery employed in his philosophical texts (the standard piece being Margery Collins and Christine Pierce's 1973 article 'Holes and Slime: Sexism in Sartre's Psychoanalysis'). This accusation of Sartre followed an earlier and similar charge against William Barrett for his popular book *Irrational Man* (1962), in which Barrett claimed that Sartre's psychology of Being-in-Itself (*en-soi*) and Being-For-Itself (*pour-soi*) was implicitly aligned with established gender roles; that is, femininity as immanence and masculinity as volition. The debates surrounding existentialism that we have considered, then, have placed it in the dock under three distinct charges related to gender: it is a male philosophy, a patriarchal philosophy, or a philosophy riddled with the misogynist assumptions of a pervading masculine epistemology. In this context, we will interrupt our examination of male-authored fictional selves to consider Iris Murdoch's 1954 novel *Under the Net*, to assess how her novel's engagement with existentialism negotiates the philosophy's association with these various misogynist systems of value. *Under the Net* plays explicitly with two recognisable contemporary heroes, the 1950s Welfare State male of Chapter 2, with his hapless love affairs, mistrust of money and class, and a well-meaning job in a hospital, and the timeless, lone, existential hero. The confrontation of these two tropes is manifested in the relationship between Jake and Hugo, but also within the character of Jake himself, whose narration displays characteristics of both: 'A strange light, cast back over our friendship, brought new things into relief, and I tried in an instant to grasp the whole essence of my need of her. I took a deep breath, however, and followed my rule of never speaking frankly to women in moments of emotion' (12). Jake's statement jokily juxtaposes a philosophical quest for the truth about his relationship with Madge and a knowing, clubby, witticism.

These two modes of heroism are used to defuse and undermine each other, pointing up the practical inadequacy of both. Hugo combines an empiricist's respect for situational particularity with Wittgenstein's scepticism over the ability of language to capture the truth of existence. Yet crucially, his ideas are only available to us through Jake's representation of them in his published tract *The Silencer* (in which Hugo appears as

'Annandine'). (The publication of Jake Donaghue's pseudo-existential tome, extracted in *Under the Net*, preceded Wilson's startlingly reminiscent *The Outsider* by two years.) In *The Silencer*, Annandine[4] proclaims: 'It is in silence that the human spirit touches the divine' (81). Hugo ends the novel by embracing contingency to the point that he abandons all his wealth to become a watchmaker in Nottingham, the nonentity of his chosen location terrifying to a narrator who considers those parts of London that are west of Earls Court to define nothingness: 'There are some parts of London which are necessary and others which are contingent. Everywhere west of Earls Court is contingent, except for a few places along the river. I hate contingency. I want everything in my life to have a sufficient reason' (24). Horology is a worthy occupation, but though the precision it requires might be admirably empirical, it is not the aspirational stuff of 1950s novels. As a writer, Jake himself cannot abandon the possibility of an engaged negotiation of existence communicable in literature. By the end of *Under the Net* he has rejected the translation of novels for writing his own, and recognised his need to respect the authenticity of the selves of others such as his friend Finn. After Jake's repeated and flippant assertions that Finn would never return to Dublin, Finn has returned to Dublin: 'I felt ashamed, ashamed of being parted from Finn, of having known so little about Finn, of having conceived things as I pleased and not as they were' (247). Jake comes to a practical personal and political compromise: he will work part-time in a hospital (as in *Hurry on Down*, the venue serves as microcosm of the new reality), and write part-time, combining direct social engagement with indirect (but still engaged) literary production. This 'middle way' between the individualist and community-minded literary male heroes evidently emphasises the inadequacy of both figures before their compromise.

Why, though, does Murdoch's hero need to be male? A number of possible reasons spring to mind. One reinforces the case of those who claim existentialism to be inherently misogynist: a novel about an epistemological quest needs a male hero in order to be recognisable as such, as women, mired in their immanence, do not traditionally ask the universe for meaning. Would the philosophical musings of Jake or Hugo be received less seriously by a conditioned contemporary audience if they came from the mouth of a woman? In his examination of her work, *Iris Murdoch: The Saint and The Artist*, Peter Conradi notes of the novel: 'It is the first and least disquieting of her brilliant first-person male narrations. She has called her identification with the male voice "instinctive"; I know nothing quite like them. There are male novelists who can persuade you into the minds of young women [...]; the reverse feat seems rarer' (28). The same process of conflation is at work both in Murdoch's claim that her attraction to the male narrative is instinctive, and Conradi's that this instinct is both exceptional and laudable – that of masculinity with volition and philosophical clout. Philosophy, Conradi implies, as a rational business, requires the male instinct to run it; hence his determination here to make Murdoch mentally male.

Under the Net never resorts to the petty machinations of subaltern-bashing apparent in, say, *Scenes from Provincial Life*, but its exclusion of the female characters from its philosophical discussions and conclusions does seem a valid topic for consideration due to the gender of its presiding author/philosopher. The Parisian episode in which Jake loses Anna in the Tuileries gardens at night, and is then confronted by a similarly dressed woman seeking a lover amongst the trees (192–6), might initially be interpreted to function as a metaphor for essential feminine mystery. However, on the removal of the comforts of Finn from Jake as punishment for his stubborn misreading of his friend, it becomes apparent that the park scene symbolises the otherness of Anna for the man who claims to love her utterly. Is it possible then, that Murdoch's motivation for choosing a male protagonist might be predominantly deflationary, allowing a critique of contemporary literary male heroism, in both its tropes as posturing existential adolescent and quietist adult conformist? If so, it is unclear why the novel conforms so closely to traditional patterns of masculine realist narrative, with an omniscient, retrospective narrator who is apparently unable to apply the self-irony he has allegedly discovered before the point of telling his story. Frustratingly, rather than making a mockery of Conradi's misogynist assertions, the narrative form of *Under the Net* perpetuates the implicit gendering of philosophy as a masculine pursuit.

Choosing to be born

Vinson, a character in Nigel Dennis' 1955 novel *Cards of Identity*, attempts a definition of the post-war English self in terms too Sartrean to be merely coincidental: 'The nearest I can get to defining the new identity is to say that the one I lacked previously is now lacking on a much higher level. It's as if with a single leap I had mounted a full flight closer to the Realization of Nothingness' (167). Through its scenario of the annual conference of the mysterious Identity Club, the novel provides numerous case-studies of inauthentic human existence. Initially, the basic supposition seems to be anti-existentialist: that human identity issues from an individual's past. That past, however, is then shown to be infinitely alterable, thus removing the possibility of a contiguous self-hood. In *An Eye for an 'I': Attrition of the Self in the Existential Novel*, Roseline Intrater notes how 'Dennis uses this indeterminacy much as Sartre does, as a construct of Nothingness, as if it were an amniotic fluidity from which all identities emerge and to which they periodically return' (111). *Cards of Identity* is conspicuous in its existential mistrust of rigid theoretical reasoning ruthlessly applied to this fluidity of individual human experience. The members of the Identity Club range from a Freudian psychiatrist to a dialectical materialist to a cleric, but they are united across their many disciplines by their interest in documenting their imposition of new identities upon unwitting members of the public. The intellectual unity of this common interest, however, is acknowledged by their own president to be as contingent as all other identities. He, it is noted, has 'even given the impression that all theories are pretty much alike as far as he is concerned, and that the Theory of Identity is not only not the only true theory but merely one of the many plausible ideas which are floating about nowadays' (288).

In its stipulation of theoretical reasoning as just another interchangeable system, Dennis's novel demonstrates affiliation with the texts of Chapter 2. The antidote to effete Mandarin intellectualism in, say, *Lucky Jim*, was an empirical demonstration of selfhood – a fist and a heartfelt insult into the face of Bertrand Welch. Existential authenticity involves the exercise of choice rather than muscle. Vinson, a case-study in Dr Bitterling's conference paper 'The Case of the Co-Warden of the Badgeries', initiates a new identity for himself:

> As I watched, Vinson suddenly stiffened his limbs and groaned; his eyes rolled upwards and he began to twitch with convulsive shudders. I said gently, but with excitement: 'Vinson! Are you being reborn?'
>
> He nodded tersely, reluctant to be distracted, and reached his hands backwards as if grasping a pair of bed-posts. A few seconds later he again groaned, shuddered, slapped himself sharply on the buttocks and let out a high wail. Then, all at once, he became himself again, and lit a Craven A. (166)

Vinson is sovereign of his own birth – in Sartre's phrase he *chooses* to be born – and here combines the roles of a mother in the throes of labour, a screaming baby, a slapping midwife and a smoking father: a man creating, delivering and celebrating himself. Jeffner Allen, referring to Nietzsche's *Thus Spoke Zarathustra*, has claimed that:

> The existentialist voices the belief that birthing is 'sick' and 'unclean', and comes himself miraculously into existence, seemingly without nurturance of any kind. Just as God created the world *ex nihilo*, the existentialist attempts to create himself out of nothing. By separating himself from 'the given', the existential hero is omnipotently what he makes himself. (76)

This male usurpation of human creation is a key gambit in the context within which the novel was produced. Ten years after the end of conflict, the Second World War could now unhesitatingly be nominated as some sort of fracture in the progression of Western character and history. The narrator of Dr Bitterling's paper provides a vivid picture of what he considers to be a 'natural' progression of male identity: 'There is the father, still leaning backwards towards the world of *his* father, and beside him a son following exactly the same bent. They are thus together recreating the identity of the young man's grandfather and binding the vague present to an identifiable past' (170). The war has made absent an entire generation of supplicant sons and potential fathers and grandfathers, compromising the possibility of an inherited patriarchal identity and demanding a new, instantaneous means of male reproduction. Despite its existential ambitions, as we will see, solace for this disruption is found in the novel in a familiar concept – congenital gender identities.

Existential awareness in the novel is not only gender-specific, but also distinguished by a specific nationality. The instability of identity is diagnosed as symptomatic of a particular time in a particular place. In the paper he presents to the Identity Club, Dr Shubunkin remarks of the British post-war nation that 'we are in what is always called a transitional period – and nothing disgusts me more than the transitional' (221). The loss of a stable national and personal identity in the novels is directly linked to the decline of the class system and its hierarchical structure of reference. By 1972, John MacQuarrie is categorising existentialism as inherently antithetical to Britishness:

> The existentialist style of thought seems to emerge whenever man finds his securities threatened, when he becomes aware of the ambiguities of the world and knows his pilgrim status in it. This also helps to explain why existentialism has flourished in those lands where the social structures have been turned upside down and all the values

transvalued, whereas relatively stable countries (including the Anglo-Saxon lands) have not experienced this poignancy and so have not developed the philosophizing that flows from it. (60)

In *Cards of Identity*, however, the continental metaphysical vertigo resulting from military occupation and total devastation are equated with and subsumed by English uncertainties arising from a destabilisation of the class system. The Club meet in a dilapidated country pile, of which it is remarked:

> This sort of house was once a heart and centre of the national identity. A whole world lived in relation to it. Millions knew who they were by reference to it. Hundreds of thousands look back to it, and not only grieve for its passing but still depend on it, non-existent though it is, to tell them who they are. Thousands who never knew it are taught every day to cherish its memory and to believe that without it no man will be able to tell his whereabouts again. It hangs on men's necks like a millstone of memory; carrying it, and looking back on its associations, they stumble indignantly backwards into the future, confident that man's self-knowledge is gone forever. (119)

This epitaph is, of course, in part parodic of a literature and a way of life no longer possible in the modern state. As Robert Hewison claims in *In Anger*:

> Mandarin values can be seen most clearly in relation to the values of a secure social order represented by the English country house, a regular setting for plays and novels, of which *Brideshead Revisited* [...] is the most significant. Yet the celebration of the country house was more an attempt to retrieve the shreds of the institution's former glories, than to use its values as a source of imagination or inspiration. (xiii)

Similarly, *Cards of Identity*, for all its aspirations towards mockery, is riddled with a sense of loss rather than liberation in reaction to the allegedly classless society. The paper 'The Case of the Co-Warden of the Badgeries' provides a vivid, and comic, demonstration in its parody of English ceremonial ritual:

> The stuffed, or token, boar-badger is inserted into a symbolic den and then eased out with your official emblem, a symbolical gold spade. In this way, there is no need actually to disturb any living

badger: the whole ceremony is performed quietly in London. [...] Once you start letting your symbolic acts overlap, each tends to deny the significance of the other. That's what's wrong with the Health Service, of course. One minute people think they're getting it free, the next that it is an intolerable burden. They don't know if they're giving or receiving. (152)

The criticism here is aimed at symbolism *per se*, though there is a lingering sense of nostalgia for the pomp of former circumstances. In a 1959 article entitled 'Class and Conflict in British Foreign Policy' in the journal *Foreign Affairs*, Peregrine Worsthorne remarked how 'everything about the British class system begins to look foolish and tacky when related to a second class power on the decline' (quoted Cannadine, 159). Badgers and golden spades are obviously, and deliberately, 'foolish and tacky', but they are still preferable to the mundane muddle of the new symbolism. This replaces the country house with the urban hospital as preferred national microcosm, but it is unclear as to whether that Health Service is celebratory of individual responsibility for the collective, or collective support of each individual.

Dennis's interpretation of existential thought is becoming clearer, and it refutes the philosophy's most basic tenets. The nostalgia that pervades the novel cannot be attributed to an existential recognition of the eternal nothingness surrounding the self and a regretful longing for the blissful ignorance before the realisation. Rather, it stems from the recognition of the loss of a once unquestionably stable selfhood and 'natural' social order. In other words, existential angst is not the enlightened recognition of the reality of the human condition, but inspired by contemporary, and potentially temporary, circumstances. The compromise of selfhood is marked as the affliction of a particular generation – the young adults of a 'classless' society – and a particular gender. It is explicitly linked not to the male experience of war itself, but to the implications of the War for the male post-war population. In post-war Britain, by necessity, women were evident in the public sphere: they had power in the work-place and ambitions of their own. A good part of the novel's horror lies in the perceived emasculation of the Englishman: 'The pallor of the young post-war husbands, out to furnish the hard-won cottage or flat, was in no way as terrifying as the cold-steel ferocity in the faces of their wives' (144). The stable, pre-war self that has been lost is an essentialist, masculine self. A monstrous reversal of gender roles is portrayed as having taken place: men are pale and disorientated, women crazed by their new-found power. Freudian psychology and its reckless talk of the fluidity of sexuality have only increased the gender confusion. Dr Shubunkin claims that 'there is no such thing as pure male or pure female. Some wear skirts and some wear pants, but this is only convention. Every man is stuffed with womanly characteristics, every woman is fraught with man. The gap between the powder-puff and the cavalry moustache appears wide but is really a hair's-breadth' (206). The phantasmagoric descriptions that accompany Dr Shubunkin's assertions, of Violet the gigantic lesbian balancing policemen atop oaken tables on her broad back, leave the reader with no option other than to treat his conclusions with suspicion.

The character of Shubunkin does not constitute an existentialist mocking of over-intellectualised theory, but rather the use of an ironically exaggerated Freudian psychology in order to mock the exaggerated tenets of existential thought. The doctor is ridiculous because he does not appreciate the 'natural' essence of personal and gender identities: Sartre *et al* are ridiculous for precisely the same reason. If existence precedes essence, the essential male self cannot exist, yet for the nation to survive, it *must* exist, and it must be reasserted. This is a transitional period of national identity, but a means of ending the transition is proffered, and it is not the morality forged amidst the actions of each individual, but a reassertion of a traditional morality in which men are the holders of power. If the self is inherently masculine, and masculinity is under threat, then that threat will be interpreted as a threat to selfhood, as it is here. If national identity is also conceived of as masculine, the nation too is in danger. Similarly, if received conceptions of selfhood are threatened, as existentialism seeks to do, that threat will be interpreted as a threat to masculinity. Just as it was in the Burgess and MacLean affair of 1951, stable masculinity has been conflated with a state of both national and ontological security.[5]

In the preface of *Two Plays and a Preface*, which contains a theatrical version of *Cards of Identity*, Dennis levels the following criticism at both T. S. Eliot and Jean-Paul Sartre:

> The theoretician decides that existence consists in action, from which he concludes that any sort of action confers existence and any sort of inaction abolishes it. And that is all. Those who are to be the victims of the evil actions are not consulted: they belong to the world outside the library and are therefore excluded from its considerations. (49)

Existentialist action is firmly rejected as being anti-community, antisocial. Sartre and the philosophy that he was instrumental in shaping are branded Mandarin. Existentialism and socialism are notoriously uneasy bed-fellows. Murdoch makes the claim in 'The Existentialist Political Myth' that Sartre's 'more Fabian *persona*' (139) is forced into feigning the conclusion that social equality is deducible from existentialism, when in fact, she adjudges, it necessitates the assumption of a pre-existent human nature: humanity as absolute. For Sartre, and his ideological ingénues of the 1960s, an emphasis upon individual freedom self-evidently required attendant political freedoms to allow its development. When, like Dennis, your concealed political agendum involves the reassertion of a patriarchal social hierarchy, the assumption of a pre-existent human identity is necessary, and that identity must be gendered. His reluctance to entertain the notion of existence preceding essence might be attributed to the fact that such a gambit removes the possibility of a guaranteed patriarchal dividend: a male individual forging his essence alone loses his right to traditional masculine social superiority. The essential self is once again upheld as paradigmatic, and as masculine. The masculine gender, and identity itself, is ultimately defined as innate rather than dynamic and performative.

The essentialist existentialist

The dynamism of the existential self may initially appear as antithetical to, and redemptive of, personal and political stasis. Yet existentialism may also conceivably be adopted as a glamorous label which conveniently removes its bearer from the demands of active political engagement precisely so as to deliver him into the covert conservatism revealed in *Cards of Identity*. A rejection of *mauvais foi*, to use the Sartrean term, can leave no *foi* at all. Murdoch, for all her initial optimism over the revolutionary implications of the philosophy, recognises its potential in practice for political apathy in 'The Existentialist Political Myth':

> I have been suggesting that existentialism can be seen as a mythological representation of our present political dilemma. I think the Marxists are right when they say that a powerful reason for the popularity of existentialism is that it makes a universal myth of the plight of those who reject capitalism but who cannot adjust themselves to the idea of socialism, and who seek a middle way. They seek it, the Marxists might add, in doubt and despair, finding no genuine political road in the centre, but only turnings away to the left and the right. (141)

Existentialism can be misappropriated as a noncommittal compromise between capitalist isolationism and a herd-like socialist collective.

The 'doubt' and 'despair' she mentions here is with reference to writers such as Sartre and Camus, committed to unflinchingly intense dramatisations of existential angst in their fiction. In the chapter 'Identity and the Existential' in his *Postwar British Fiction*, James Gindin identifies in the post-war period a continental compromise of radical existential tenets into a less dramatic 'existential attitude':

This attitude seems particularly relevant for the western European since 1945. It offers him the possibilities of freedom and responsible choice, possibilities valuable to the man both bored and frightened by the implications of Marxist determinism. At the same time the existential attitude prevents man from regarding his truths as sacrosanct, his government as the fount of all wisdom and virtue, and his own nature as a pattern for universal emulation, for the intelligent man can recognize the obvious existence of other fountains and other patterns. Yet, within the plethora of patterns, the responsible man can make distinctions and choices, can prefer quasi-rational muddles to Nazi bestiality simply because the muddles (and what the responsible man prefers is always less clear than what he hates) allow for more free choices than do the zealous brutalities. (236–7)

Couched in Gindin's terms, existentialism begins to take on the air of a happy, if messy, compromise between Marxism and Fascism, allowing its English practitioner a justified conformity with patriarchal society as it stands, together with a simultaneous, and stylish, self-deprecating cynicism. The troublingly political dynamics of Sartre's thinking tended to be rejected by the English literary establishment in favour of an interpretation of Camus's work that read its angst as universal and politically neutral. Sir Herbert Read's foreword to the 1953 first English translation of *L'Homme Révolté*, *The Rebel*, makes the claim that:

The nature of revolt has changed radically in our times. It is no longer the revolt of the slave against the master, nor even the revolt of the poor against the rich; it is a metaphysical revolt, the revolt of man against the conditions of life, against creation itself. At the same time, it is an aspiration towards clarity and unity of thought – even, paradoxically, towards order. That, at least, is what it becomes under the intellectual guidance of Camus. (7–8)

This foreword, to a book which marked a decisive split between the two great existentialist thinkers of the era, fails to mention Sartre at all.

As we have seen so far, existentialism reinterpreted in English male-authored fiction is still likely to emphasise selected truths as sacrosanct, and a selected gender and nation as a universal template. Contingency is qualified by gender and by imperialism, as the Cold War functioned to redeem patriotism. The enormously popular novel *The Spy Who Came in From the Cold* (1963) replicates this particular compromised version of existentialist doctrine. Iris Murdoch makes reference to the 'universal myth' offered by existentialism, and Christopher Booker in *The Neophiliacs* reads the contemporaneous popularity of spy stories as a 'subtle reflection of the *Zeitgeist*' (179). In *Metafiction*, Patricia Waugh's explication of the appeal of the spy thriller also assumes the 'universal' (and thus implicitly trans-gender) attraction of its existential dilemma, emphasising this with meticulous equal-opportunities phrasing:

> The [spy] thriller is based not upon the same faith in human reason as the detective story but much more upon the fear of anomie, of disorder, of the insecurity of human life. It is much closer to what appears to be the experience of living in the contemporary world. The spy, unlike the detective, but like contemporary men and women, does not know who he or she is looking for. The spy moves in a Kafkaesque world whose laws remain unknown. He or she is forced continually to shift identity, donning one disguise after another. The existential boundary situations that recur frequently in the thriller are experienced vicariously by the reader, who is thus allowed to play through the uncertainties of his or her own existence. (84–5)

An examination of Le Carré's spy thriller, however, reveals that its narrative functions in such a way as to ensure that its conclusion is only compellingly heroic and tragic after the reader's adoption of masculine tenets of belief, together with a nationalistic zeal. The novel's narrative voice is that extra-diegetic third-person narrative that Dorrit Cohn nominates 'psycho-narration' (46), noting the form's potential for rendering verbally a character's thoughts and emotions with a clarity that would seem inauthentic in a first-person account. Yet in *The Spy Who Came in From the Cold*, the narrator frequently and stubbornly refuses to psycho-narrate, remaining instead in a strange limbo of cognitive privilege in relation to the hero, Alex Leamas, as in this example: 'Fawley didn't like Leamas, and if Leamas knew he didn't care' (16). Leamas's heroism, however, is not compromised by this documentary uncertainty surrounding his interior life. Rather, his identity derives precisely from this refusal of self-revelation. His masculinity is unreflective and unemotional, setting him impressively apart from his fellow prisoners whilst in jail:

> He was contemptuous of his cell mates, and they hated him. They hated him because he succeeded in being what each in his heart longed to be: a mystery. He preserved from collectivisation some discernible part of his personality; he could not be drawn at moments of sentiment to talk of his girl, his family or his children. (46–7)

When he finally succumbs to Liz, a co-worker at his cover-story job at the Bayswater Library for Psychic Research, their intimacy is indicative of professional and personal failure on his part. Leamas recognises this immediately: 'She made him stay that night and they became lovers. He left at five in the morning. She couldn't understand it; she was so proud and he seemed ashamed' (37). Leamas's act of love makes him vulnerable to feminine weakness and a failure of control. Liz, long susceptible to the dogmatic charms of Marxist doctrine (this being tantamount to weakness), is lured behind the Iron Curtain and eventually shot attempting to escape over the Berlin Wall. Having failed in his duty to rescue her, Leamas delivers himself back into danger on the side of the wall at which she fell, where 'he stood glaring round him like a blinded bull in the arena' (240), before he too is killed. The metaphor employed here is instructive. The bull incorporates strength and virility even amidst its confusion, of course, but the arena in which it demonstrates these qualities is built and controlled by a greater power.

Waugh's depiction of the function of the spy thriller couches it as some sort of existential playground: a world beyond morality, where existence precedes essence, all belief systems are pointed up as interchangeable, and choice is unfettered. Rather than providing an opportunity to play through existential experiences of contingency, though, the intelligence world of *The Spy Who Came in From the Cold* is enclosed within a 'boundary' that is anything but existentialist. The narrative does emphasise the purely subjective nature of one mortal's viewpoint – the reader is unaware for a portion of the novel that Leamas is merely faking treachery so as to achieve the goal of his mission. However, the incomplete nature of this subjectivity is revealed to be characteristic of a position lower down the intelligence hierarchy, for, as Peters confirms with Leamas: 'it's part of our work only to know pieces of the whole set-up' (97). The radical possibilities of admitting the instability of subjectivity are countered by the conviction of an absolute, male-controlled morality. Leamas's universe is wholly logocentric and ultimately whole: somewhere, someone knows the truth. That truth, too, is perceived to have a strongly nationalistic stamp – the guarantee of English rational behaviour, the imperial moral high ground. Leamas's Control stresses in his 'donnish bray' (17): 'The ethic of our work, as I understand it, is based on a single assumption. That is, we are never going to be aggressors' (20). Leamas's allegedly existential activity is ultimately directed at maintaining a colonial, logocentric, patriarchal status-quo.

In his 1950 pamphlet *What is Existentialism? The Creed of Commitment and Action*, Roland Bailey, ignoring the realist narrative structures and reasonable registers of the fiction of Sartre and Camus, asserts: 'For the most part, existentialists make no effort to be understood. They are inclined to use difficult or obscure language, nor do they set out to be rational in their philosophy. Indeed they state: "Existentialist thought cannot be communicated" ' (10). Existentialism as antithetical to communication; this may be a misreading, but it is a pervasive one, and is supported and strengthened by a traditional masculine binary, words versus action, or, in terms of the masculine hero, loquacious sissiness versus silent strength. Colin Wilson's influential existential-ish *The Outsider* reiterates this same point: 'The Outsider problem is essentially a living problem; to write about it in terms of literature is to falsify it. [...] The reason is simple: beyond a certain point, the Outsider's problems will not submit to mere thought; *they must be lived*' (70). Hugh J. Silverman's article 'Sartre's Words on the Self' recognises this concept of a self that is impossible to express in words (as words make the *pour-soi*, *en-soi*) to be symptomatic of an early stage in Sartre's on-going development of a more complex relationship between self and verbal expression:

> When Sartre claims that this true self is entirely for-itself (*pour-soi*), he means that it cannot be an object for itself and still be itself. So he calls the true self, this being for-itself, *nothingness*. As *nothingness* (*le néant*), the self is a meaning with no referent, an existence with no essence, a consciousness with no object that is other. (89)[6]

To those keen to interpret it as such, this concept of the 'true self' dovetails neatly with an essentialist view. Rather than being nothingness without referent, the self becomes a something with no referent except itself: a pre-existent essence, powerful, pure and beyond expression. If that self is masculine, then masculinity will thereby be enshrined as pre-verbal and primal.

Thomas Hinde's *Happy as Larry* (1957) nicely demonstrates this manipulation of existentialism for essentialist purposes. At the opening of the novel, Larry Vincent, miserable amidst the stasis of post-war society, demonstrates a nascent awareness of the inauthenticity of his existence. Authentic existence is once again couched as antithetical to contemporary society:

> All his life he had been failing because he had not honestly tried, because duty had been something forced on him by relations without his consent – or something selfish, performed because he wanted approval and at the same time despised himself for wanting it. Now for the first time he honestly wanted to try. Now, at last he understood that the first essential for starting to be a real person was to cease to be a person. (11)

Being a 'real person' is set in opposition to social interaction and subjectivity. Larry's anxiety over this intuition manifests itself in a profound gulf between what he says and what he really is: 'It left so little time to be alone and discover why he said things. From morning to evening he went from one lie to the next. There was no chance to stop and decide what he thought, and arrange with himself to start saying it' (108–9). For all Larry's talk of 'persons', however, this allegedly human condition is identified throughout the novel as a male one. Larry's failure at modern masculinity, it is implied, began with his failure to conform to life under National Service:

> The whole of that time seemed to have been lived under disapproval. The uncles and aunts he had visited on leave had disapproved. His commanding officers had disapproved. It had become clear that he was no good. So he had ceased to try to be any good in the way they wanted. The trouble, of course, was that he was failing to be much good in any other way. (108)

The failure, however, is actually admirable, as it is contemporary masculinity that is inauthentic and incompatible with true manhood.

In so far as the novel can be said to have a plot beyond the inexorable progression of Larry's decline, it centres upon Larry's quest to gain possession of an incriminating photograph of his friend Matthew Broom, a lawyer and parliamentary candidate. Matthew's ample money comes, instructively, from his verbosity. Exactly what the photograph depicts is never made clear (although there are hints that it involves some sort of homosexual encounter), but it is apparent that its circulation in the public world would end Matthew's successful and conformist professional life. The photograph, however unsavoury, connotes the 'truth', and all those in Larry's circle are complicit in one way or another in concealing it from him. Exemplary contemporary masculinity like Matthew's is a sham, and not masculine enough, with Matthew's implied homosexuality as proof positive. Larry's yearning for an authentic selfhood is directed not towards an existential ideal of freedom, but a recognisably traditional masculine stereotype, nominated by the American sociologist Michael Kimmel as 'the Heroic Artisan' (1996, 9):

> It was impossible not to think that things had once been different. The money had gone on beer, not the hire-purchase, and occasionally one had felt a man. There had been work in clean air with some rustic tool and at moments in the fourteen-hour day it had been good to feel strong and warm from exercise not central heating. That was the real trouble. It wasn't safe to feel good. You might step backwards into a passing car. (241)

This idealised image of man/selfhood is a long way from the existential hero, but derived instead from nostalgia for an imaginary unreflective, proletarian, presumably uncommunicative idyll. The novel redesigns the existential quest for self as the hunt for an authentic, essential masculinity. It is not the existential self that is betrayed by language, but this essential male one.

The masculine gaze[7]

In 1964, John Fowles published *The Aristos*, a collection of philosophical aphorisms issued on the back of the success of *The Collector*, though written during the previous decade. The seventy-eighth assertion in the section entitled 'Other Philosophies' reads as follows:

> It is to me impossible to reject existentialism though it is possible to reject this or that existentialist action. Existentialism is not a philosophy, but a way of looking at, and utilizing, other philosophies. It is a theory of relativity among theories of absolute truth. (116)

This opposition between a practical awareness of relativity and the artificial imposition of a rational absolutism extends to the Fowlesian scheme of gender roles. In his essay 'Notes on an Unfinished Novel', Fowles makes the claim that: 'My female characters tend to dominate the male. I see man as a kind of artifice, and woman as a kind of reality.

The one is cold idea, the other warm fact' (146). *The Magus*, published in 1966, but largely written, and set, during the previous decade, reinforces this Cartesian dualism and its attendant hierarchical assumptions amidst a dedicatedly existential framework of thought. In an interview with James Campbell, Fowles identified the novel's hero Nicholas Urfe as 'a typical inauthentic man of the 1945–50 period' (466). The novel centres upon the confrontation of Self and Other, pupil and teacher, the 'inauthentic' Nicholas and the mysterious Conchis. In 'Notes on an Unfinished Novel' – a documentary of the creative process written alongside *The French Lieutenant's Woman* – Fowles remarks: 'If the technical problems hadn't been so great, I should have liked to make Conchis in *The Magus* a woman' (146). These potential 'technical problems' (presumably involving Conchis's role during Phraxos's occupation), however, do not interfere with Conchis being used to represent what the novel encodes as a 'female principle' of multiplicity, relativity and emotion. In *The Collector* (1963), it is a female character, Miranda, who is used to represent the principles of relativism and existentialism, and to whom the reader has exclusive cognitive privilege via her diary entries. The diary form allows Miranda's expression of her self as a work-in-progress, rather than the static passivity that excites her captor Clegg. He can summon sexual excitement only for the pornographic pictures that he takes of her, not for her presence itself. Miranda's quest for authenticity is bound to her realisation of her essential femaleness, the discovery of what she calls her 'woman-me he can never touch' (258).

In *The Magus*, in a long speech preceding his description of the Nazi torture that took place on Phraxos, Conchis asserts:

These events could have taken place only in a world where man considered himself superior to woman. In what the Americans call 'a man's world'. That is, a world governed by brute force, humourless arrogance, illusory prestige, and primeval stupidity. [...] Men love war because it allows them to look serious. Because it is the one thing that stops women laughing at them. In it they can reduce women to the status of objects. That is the great distinction between the sexes. Men see objects, women see the relationship between objects. Whether the objects need each other, love each other, match each other. It is an extra dimension of feeling that we men are without and one that makes war abhorrent to all real women – and absurd. I will tell you what war is. War is a psychosis caused by an inability to see relationships. Our relationship with our fellow-men. Our relationship with our economic and historical situation. And above all our relationship to nothingness, to death. (378)

Initially this seems to be a radical philosophical assumption – woman as intellectually (if instinctively) aware, man bogged down amidst the material. However, the novel's focalisation through Urfe draws the reader towards other conclusions. The retrospective first-person narrative allows a certain amount of criticism to be directed towards the inauthentic Nicholas, but as Bruce Woodcock notes in his *Male Mythologies: John Fowles and Masculinity*, any critique of his compromised selfhood is complicated by the narrative itself:

> The book itself acts to seduce the reader – perhaps we should specify the male reader – into an imaginary pursuit of the very fantasies it exposes. It repeatedly suggests the promise of imaginative access to women figures, real or fantastic, who are part of the basic idea of the book as Fowles has crucially described it – 'a secret world, whose penetration involved ordeal and whose final reward was self-knowledge'. (63)

Nicholas is able to recognise that his attraction towards the pure, chaste, Edwardian Lily is based upon a longing for a time of more simplistic gender roles and more clearly defined binary hierarchisms:

> Perhaps it was partly a nostalgia for that extinct Lawrentian woman of the past, the woman inferior to man in everything but that one great power of female dark mystery and beauty; the brilliant, virile male and the dark, swooning female. The essences of the two sexes had become so confused in my androgynous twentieth-century mind that this reversion to a situation where a woman was a woman and I was obliged to be fully a man had all the fascination of an old house after a cramped, anonymous modern flat. (227)

Lily functions, of course, as the antithesis to her less inhibited sister Rose (the quaint imagery of their names increasing the sense of nostalgia), but more importantly in opposition to Alison, whose antipodean origin emphasises her identity as the novel's New Woman.

Alison is far from providing 'imaginary access' to 'a secret world': she flaunts a sexual availability contemporary to the date of the novel's publication rather than its setting. The essence of her 'female dark mystery' is utterly compromised by her enthusiasm for sex. Yet a solution to Nicholas's inauthenticity must be fashioned from his contemporary environment. His revelation is couched in explicitly existential terms:

> But now I *felt* it; and by 'feel' I mean that I knew I *had* to choose it, every day, even though I went on failing to keep it, had every day to choose it, every day to try to live by it. And I knew that it was all bound up with Alison; with choosing Alison, and having to go on choosing her every day. (601)

Alison's symbolic function has, however, become hopelessly confused by this point. On the one hand, she is chosen because her sex allows her to see 'the relationships between objects', the uncertainty and relativity of existence; on the other because she has been 'cast as Reality' (608) by virtue of the 'warm fact' of her body. She is forced into two enduring but antithetical feminine roles simultaneously: she represents both unknowable mystery and honestly available corporeality. This confusion permeates the novel's conclusion. That this conclusion represents a didactic climax is inarguable: Nicholas finally realises that Conchis is not watching him, that he is free and that God is only a game ('the theatre was empty', 617), and so becomes an authentic subject. His liberation, though, is demonstrated by a gesture that is far from progressive: he slaps Alison across the face, rebelling against his choice of her and against Conchis and all the 'female principles' enveloped in the Magus. He achieves heroism by his rejection of the feminine, and by the assertion of his gloriously isolated selfhood, the former a necessary step to achieving the latter. The intended symbolic power of his liberation is derived from the establishing of the Other as feminine in order for him triumphantly to reject that other and choose himself: authentic existential selfhood established with a traditional masculine gambit.

In the 1969 novel *The French Lieutenant's Woman*, the conflation of existentialist principles with enduring masculine archetypes and traditional structures of narrative and textual authority is still more explicit. In 'Notes on an Unfinished Novel' Fowles claims that in it he is 'trying to show an existential awareness before it was chronologically possible. [...] It has always seemed to me that the Victorian Age, especially from 1850 on, was highly existentialist in many of its personal dilemmas' (140). Nowhere, in 'Notes on an Unfinished Novel', or elsewhere, does Fowles explicitly state exactly what he understands this 'existential awareness' to involve. In the interview with James Campbell, Fowles was asked if he was aware that all his male heroes 'come to a greater awareness of their real selves in the arms of women?' He replied: 'Yes, especially in *The French Lieutenant's Woman*. This is the sort of existential thesis of the books – that one has to discover one's feelings' (466). The vagaries of his response here, in references to 'the sort of existential thesis', and the blurring of existentialism into a definition of emotional literacy ('one has to discover one's feelings'), are revealing. A later assertion in *The Aristos* demonstrates a more distinct determination to code existentialism as inherently female, as well as providing a good indication of the mythic and dualistic nature of Fowles's feminism:

> Adam is stasis or conservatism; Eve is kinesis, or progress. Adam societies are ones in which the man and the father, male gods, exact strict obedience to established institutions and norms of behaviour, as during a majority of the periods of history in our era. The Victorian is a typical such period. Eve Societies are those in which the woman and the mother, female gods, encourage innovation and experiment, and fresh definitions, aims, modes of feeling. The Renaissance and our own are typical such ages. (157)

Woman is associated with creativity, with innovation, with *freedom*. Rather than destroying the binary organisation of gender identities or changing the traditional connotations of femaleness, Fowles attempts to make them positive, in much the same way that D. H. Lawrence, another hero of Sixties liberation, does in the opposition of darkness and light.

In this supposedly 'unstyled' work, however, negative implications and traditional archetypes still linger in the reference to Eve. Woman is simultaneously figured as symbolic of existential relativity, yet prized for and envied her essence, her desirable facticity against Man's detached rationality. Towards the end of the novel, Sarah is referred to as 'the protagonist' (348), but the basis for such a judgement is unclear. She is patently the catalyst for Charles's journey towards an authentic self, precisely because, in pop-psychology phraseology, she is 'in touch with her feelings', and with those of others: the narrator refers to 'that fused rare power that was her essence – understanding and emotion' (54). She is more emotionally and sexually aware than Charles, free from repressive convention. She represents corporeality, she represents 'warm fact'.

Yet this particular feminine essentialist ideal is contradicted in the novel's narrative by its adoption of another, contradictory representation of its purported protagonist. The narrative denies all cognitive and psychological access to Sarah. Descriptions of her throughout the book, but particularly when Charles meets her on the Undercliff, are peppered with noncommittal phrases like 'seems', 'as if', and 'looks as though'.

(In this way, of course, her culpability in Charles's social downfall is complicated.) Such a portrayal provides a marked contrast with the narrative authority exerted over Ernestina, whose most fleeting 'sexual thought' (30) while writing her diary is recorded by the narrator. To put it brutally, Ernestina the virgin is the narrative's whore, and Sarah the whore the narrative's impenetrable virgin.[8] Of course, the fifth chapter, which contains the diary scene, functions to poke fun at the simplistic omniscience of Victorian novelistic conventions, so the denial of rational access to Sarah might be interpreted as the logical move of a didactic existential fiction – fostering respect for the individual's freedom despite the impossibility of knowing the nature of that freedom – were it not riddled with appeals to such a recognisable role.

'Who is Sarah?' asks the narrator, thereby ushering in all the postmodern self-reflexivity of the succeeding chapter, chapter 13. 'Out of what shadows does she come?' (84). The answer can be unhesitating: she comes direct from the Romantic feminine – from an image of woman as shadowy mystery. Sarah's symbolic role in the existential condition is utterly contradictory. On one hand, her corporeality qualifies her as existential agent, as authentic, embodied existence rather than abstract theory. On the other, her intangible mystery makes her a demonstration of existential contingency. Nothing is something in this novel, and that something is Sarah: she is contingency made sexy. Her role as hazard, as the uncertainty principle, becomes increasingly identified with her sexuality, as the novel dares to play with the disruptive potential of female desire. Hidden in the jungle of the Undercliff, privy to the lovemaking of Mary and Sam, Charles interprets Sarah's smile to say: 'Where are your pretensions now, those eyes and gently curving lips seemed to say; where is your birth, your science, your etiquette, your social order?' (162). Making his escape, 'Charles's thoughts on his own eventual way back to Lyme were all variations on that agelessly popular male theme: "You've been playing with fire, my boy" ' (164), and it is exactly this theme that forms the novel's textual thrill, as the unpredictable nature of the universe is identified with the female and with female sexuality. In 'Hardy and the Hag', Fowles provides a considerably less delicate summation with regard to Thomas Hardy's female characters: the 'endlessly repeated luring-denying nature of his heroines is not too far removed from what our more vulgar age calls the cock-tease' (170).

As with the case of Alison in *The Magus*, the existential Other in *The French Lieutenant's Woman* comes to be represented by a confusing mixture of feminine stereotypes: Sarah is simultaneously accessible through her body (as woman = corporeality) and yet beyond it (as woman = mystery). The angst surrounding this unstable symbolic construction reaches a climax in the sex between Charles and Sarah, with the reader's awareness that her hobbled and helpless situation is a constructed pose, and the discovery that the French Lieutenant's 'whore' is in reality a virgin. Sarah is revealed as active in her own passivity (she has bought the bandage to bind the 'damaged' ankle that makes her so delectably immobile for Charles in advance), innocent in her wantonness. This scene does to some extent deconstruct the artificial nature of the Madonna/whore dichotomy, but it also demonstrates the anxiety and confusion that results in the destruction of that binary opposition. The existential nothingness that she is employed to represent is not empty, but full of this terrifying confusion of feminine roles. This ambiguity of status may be compared with another way in which Sarah's existential authenticity is undermined by a traditional feminine role. The novel's intertextual use of the Marie de Morell story encourages the textual confusion of Sarah and her relationship with Charles, with Marie and *her* French lieutenant, a confusion that leaks into the novel's title.

In her essay 'The Look in Sartre and Rich', Julien S. Murphy notes the potential violence of the look:

> From a Sartrian perspective, the look of the other can rob us of our possibilities, alienate us from ourselves and our options for choice, and make us feel in the service of the other. The impact of the look can be so devastating that it reduces us, at a glance, to powerlessness, to the status of a thing. The recognition that we are always under the gaze of the other evidences that our freedom is held in constant check. We live, to varying degrees, as objects in the world of others. (102)

In *The French Lieutenant's Woman*, Charles's first meeting with Sarah on the quay is self-consciously Sartrean:

> She turned to look at him – or as it seemed to Charles, through him. It was not so much what was positively in that face which remained with him after that first meeting, but all that was not as he had expected; for theirs was an age when the favoured feminine look was the demure, the obedient, the shy. [...]
>
> Again and again, afterwards, Charles thought of that look as a lance; and to think so is of course not merely to describe an object but the effect it has. He felt himself in that brief instant an unjust enemy; both pierced and deservedly diminished. (13)

Her look is likened to a lance, with all the phallic and penetrative implications of that simile, and this is an image that is used repeatedly in the novel for Sarah's looking. She looks at Charles as if he were an object; she makes him aware of his object-status within her subjectivity. Her gaze, a female gaze, is, at this point, active. In 'Sartre on Objectification', Phyllis Sutton Morris makes a point that has resounding implications for a consideration of the relationship between existentialist and masculine principles:

> According to the standard Cartesian view, the human subject is a nonphysical mental substance separable from, but interacting with, the nonconscious bodily machine. However, for many existential phenomenologists, including Sartre, the continuing subject of conscious experience and action is the human body. A nonphysical, invisible, intangible subject would be hidden from public view. To be a *bodily* subject, however, is *necessarily* to be experientially accessible to others – that is, to be a possible object of others' perception. (65)

To be aware of yourself as the object of another's look is simultaneously to be aware of yourself as bodily subject. It is also to be aware of the other's self, both as existent and inaccessible to your own perception. In 1975, Laura Mulvey's 'Visual Pleasure and Narrative Cinema' announced its initial intention as the use of psychoanalytic theory as a political weapon. Aspects of her argument have been regularly and comprehensively criticised since, primarily by means of accusations of essentialism and over-simplification, but its basic tenets remain relevant in this examination of the literary representation of subjectivity. To hazard a brief summation; the essay classified the tradition of Hollywood narrative cinema by means of the fact that its gaze (of the camera, and by implication, of the audience) was 'male'. The male gaze is defined by the fact that it is active, and to achieve this power, the female object in film is routinely styled to connote passivity, to constitute '*to-be-looked-at-ness*' (19), rather than an active, looking, subject position. Mulvey's political assertion, then, is that the construction of looking in Hollywood cinema establishes limits on women's agency. The spectator sees through the eye of the camera which in turn 'sees' through the eye (and the 'I') of the character who does the looking. Through this privileged gaze, film viewers, regardless of their actual gender, are treated (and hence re-constructed) as masculine subjects:

> As the spectator identifies with the main male protagonist, he projects his look onto that of his like, his screen surrogate, so that the

power of the male protagonist as he controls events coincides with the active power of the erotic look, both giving a satisfying sense of omnipotence. (20)

The threat of the female Other is met with two distinct responses. Mulvey distinguishes between the voyeuristic look, which wants to know its object, and by knowing her is able to control and explain her. The fetishistic look, in contrast, does *not* want to know, its bearer is happily captivated by what he sees, comforted, delighted with the symbolic and reluctant to see beyond it.

There is a great deal at stake for masculinity within these two distinctive looks: Mulvey's has profound political implications, and Sartre's profound ontological ones. The Sartrean look, precisely because it is defined by lack (inability to know the other), is rejected in the narrative of *The French Lieutenant's Woman* for the masculine gaze, objectifying the woman, eroticising the object, and suppressing the possibility of difference in the reader. As E. Ann Kaplan points out in 'Is the Gaze Male?': 'The gaze is not necessarily male (literally), but to own and activate the gaze, given our language and the structure of the unconscious, is to be in the masculine position' (331). The narrative's contentment 'not to know' Sarah turns her into what Mulvey describes as a fetish: it objectifies her. Later in the novel, the narrator says of Charles:

He perceived that her directness of look was matched by a directness of thought and language – that what had on occasion struck him before as a presumption of intellectual equality (therefore a suspect resentment against man) was less an equality than a proximity, a proximity like a nakedness, an intimacy of thought and feeling hitherto unimaginable to him in the context of a relationship with a woman. (159)

With the reflex reference to 'nakedness', Sarah's intellectual challenge to Charles is immediately sexualised. In this way, the radical potential of Sarah's apparent early control of the gaze is denied. The narrative makes her a fetish, not a feminist, dealing with its 'existential anxiety', as John MacInnes puts it, 'by projecting it onto sexual difference, imagined as gender' (13).

In his Foreword to the 1977 revised edition of *The Magus*, Fowles claims the new version to be predominantly 'a stylistic revision' (1997: 5), although 'the erotic element is stronger in two scenes' (7).[9] Fowles admits of the novel published in 1966: 'I might have declared a preferred aftermath less ambiguously ... and now have done so' (7). Interestingly, in the light of the preceding discussion of *The French Lieutenant's Woman*, this 'preferred aftermath', one of an on-going relationship of love and equality between Nicholas and Alison, is made less ambiguous in part by means of a more active role for Alison in the dynamics of looking in the final chapter. In the revised version, Nicholas has learned to see 'the relationships between objects', and his looking at Alison is no longer gazing, unlike the man in the tea pavilion in both versions, whose 'eyes follow her out through the door' (1967: 608, 1997: 647).[10] His look at Alison has become fully Sartrean, making him aware of his own status as object, and his love and need of her. Alison, for her part, aware of the vulnerability inherent in looking (and thus showing lack) to a man who has betrayed her, determinedly refuses to look at Nicholas. Phrases in the 1966 original text which convey her sub-servience to him through her continual surrender to looking at him: 'She was looking down, then up, straight at me' (1967: 607); 'as I stared at her, unable to speak, at her steady, bright look' (607); are systemati-cally altered in the 1977 reissue; 'She was looking down at the table, not at me' (1997: 647); 'I stared at her, unable to speak, at her refusal to return my look' (647). Alison, aware of the reciprocity of need that she requires from Nicholas's look, is loathe to risk meeting his eyes, and autonomous enough to resist doing so. Nicholas, rather than exhibiting the petulant, bullying rage towards Alison of the end of the 1966 ver-sion, confesses secretly to the reader only that 'it infuriated me that she would not look at me' (648). Alison initially allows herself 'a little, lancing look' (647) (as with 'cryptic colouring' just below this phrase, the language of *The French Lieutenant's Woman* is leaking into this revised encounter), before her emotion overrides control:

> 'I hate you. I *hate* you.'
> I said nothing, made no move to touch her. After a moment she looked up and everything in her expression was as it had been in her voice and words: hatred, pain, every female resentment since time began. But I clung to something, the something I had never seen, or always feared to see, in those intense grey eyes, the quintessential something behind all the hating, the hurtness, the tears. A small step poised, a shattered crystal waiting to be reborn. She spoke again, as if to kill what I was looking at.
> 'I *do*.' (655)

Nicholas, now, is looking, not gazing, and this epiphany is prompted, as in the 1966 novel, by his realisation that 'there were no watching eyes'

(1967: 617, 1997: 654). Freedom, the couple's mutual freedom, is a refusal of the gaze – of giving, or enduring it. Existential freedom, in other words, has become more clearly defined as a different kind of seeing: 'A hundred yards away a blind man was walking, freely, not like a blind man; only the white stick showed he had no eyes' (1967: 616, 1997: 654).[11]

As if in direct response to Mulvey's 1975 essay, the eponymous protagonist of Fowles's 1977 novel *Daniel Martin* writes film scripts for Hollywood narrative films, and the novel sets out explicitly to interrogate the links between masculinity, literary form and ways of seeing. This later novel, schooled perhaps by Mulvey, but certainly by a burgeoning feminist rhetoric as the 1970s progressed, exhibits a much deeper awareness of the sexual politics of looking. The American film industry is identified throughout the novel as both symbol and agent of capitalism and reification. Daniel himself harbours a profound mistrust of first-person narration:

> In his already rather low valuation of the novel [...] he reserved an especially, and symptomatically, dark corner for first-person narration; and the closer the narrative *I* approximated to what one could deduce of the authorial *I*, the more murky this corner grew. The truth was that the objectivity of the camera corresponded to some deep psychological need in him; much more to that than to the fundamental principle of aesthetic (and even quasi-moral) good taste that he sometimes pretended lay behind his instinct here. (72)

The text dramatises the reflex masculine association of first-person narration with the subjective and thus the unreliable. An 'I' is manipulated to appear subject to emotion, whim and change in a way that a 'he' is not. When Daniel narrates in the first-person his spontaneous (and sentimental) decision to invite Jane to Egypt with him, a reactionary pronoun-shift occurs immediately afterwards: 'Then he began to wonder what he had done' (448). Dan's room at Oxford is noted to have 'had at least fifteen mirrors on its walls' (61), an affectation his fellow students took to indicate a jest-worthy self-love, but, 'Perhaps that ancient jibe about him, Mr Specula Speculans, had not been quite fair: a love of mirrors may appear to be only too literally *prima facie* evidence of narcissism, but it can also be symbolic of an attempt to see oneself as others see one – to escape the first person, and become one's own third' (72). Bruce Woodcock has noted how Dan's trait is extended into a metafictional comment upon the gendered workings of the text:

> In order to indicate his *own* attention to this process of male bias
> active in fiction, Fowles focuses our attention on the ambivalent
> slippage between 'I' and 'he' which keeps entering Dan's novel, a pre-
> varication of pronouns which counterpoints the deviousness of Dan's
> male persona and his attempts to distance or escape it. (124)

Authorial complicity in the male viewpoint, and the awareness of that
complicity, is emphasised by Dan's speculative name for his putative
hero, 'S. Wolfe': this is, of course, an anagram of 'Fowles'. The third-
person narrator notes of Dan: 'He didn't like the name and knew he
would never use it, but this instinctive rejection gave it a useful kind of
otherness, an objectivity, when it came to distinguishing between his
actual self and a hypothetical fictional projection of himself' (449).
This distinction between the subjectivity of the first-person and the
objectivity of the third is an illusion. Fowles conveys his knowing col-
laboration in the illusion by means of this 'prevarication of pronouns' to
heighten the metafictional demonstration of literary artifice. As it is for
Dan, this clash between the objective and the subjective is portrayed
beyond a 'fundamental principle of aesthetic' into a 'deep psychological
need'. This need, tellingly, is presented as a universal, one: the debate
between 'I' and 'he' slips into one over 'we' and 'I':

> He argued about it with Jane one evening: whether the acute new
> awareness of self – its demands, its privileges, its rights – that had
> invaded the Western psyche since the First World War was a good
> thing or a largely evil consequence of capitalist free enterprise ...
> whether people had been media-gulled into self-awareness to
> increase the puppet-master's profits or whether it was an essentially
> liberalizing new force in human society. Predictably Jane took the
> first, and Dan the second view. (555)

The gendered source of these arguments about individualism and
collectivism is recognisable from other novels considered in this chapter
(Marxism was branded feminine in Le Carré's novel) and relates once
more to Fowles's overriding ethos, that women relate to others, and
embrace relativity, more 'naturally' than men.

In addition to its 'prevarication of pronouns', *Daniel Martin* draws
attention to the tense of traditional masculine narration, quibbling with

the favoured retrospective mode as antithetical to lived experience:

> A novel is written in the two past tenses: the present perfect of the
> writer's mind, the concluded past of fictional convention. But in
> terms of the cramped and myopic fictional present ... if Jenny
> accuses Dan (has still, of course, in the chronology of this recon-
> struction, hardly put pencil to paper, let alone had Dan read the
> result) of a love of loss, she is being disingenuous, since she knows he
> likes her too much to hurt her; that if she insists, they continue. (269)

With these complex metafictional machinations, we are back in familiar
existentialist literary territory, with a worrying at the gulf between the
tenets of existence and of literature. Dan sleeps with Jane, his fiancée's
sister, while at university: 'Our surrender to existentialism and each
other was also, of course, fraught with evil. It defiled the printed text of
life; broke codes with a vengeance; and it gave Dan a fatal taste for adul-
tery, for seducing, for playing Jane's part that day' (104). Predictably, sex
is here used to symbolise a reality that cannot be fettered within literary
artifice: the sex act is an existential one. Ironically, of course, the passage
cannot help but prompt aesthetic associations – Eve may not be mentioned by name, as she is in *The Aristos*, but Dan's existential epiphany
still occurs within a tradition of female seduction and original sin. The
gulf between action and words is understood as an essentially English
dilemma:

> Perhaps all this is getting near the heart of Englishness: being happier
> at being unhappy than doing something constructive about it. We
> boast of our genius for compromise, which is really a refusal to
> choose; and that in turn contains a large part of cowardice, apathy,
> selfish laziness – but it is also, I grow increasingly certain of this as
> I grow older, a function of our peculiar imagination, of our racial and
> individual gift for metaphor; for allowing hypotheses about our-
> selves, and our pasts and futures, almost as much reality as the true
> events and destinies. (83)

Narrative is diagnosed as the cause of national stasis. Englishness
is assumed to be antithetical to existentialist action, and its literary
tradition, realist or otherwise, is exposed as unreal. It is worth pausing at
this point to assess the magnitude of the associations being made in this
novel. First-person narration has been conflated with emotion, solipsism and subjectivity; third-person narration with control, reification

and objectivity. Dan has been conflated with Fowles, and by implication, all male authors, in his problems of self-expression. These problems are linked to a long-standing Western cultural confrontation between the principles of individualism and those of community. Masculinity and selfhood are in crisis. Just as literary practices are shown to mirror lived experience, however, the ultimate incompatibility of words and life is emphasised, and the stasis caused by story-telling is characterised as a quintessentially English one.

Despite making this radical connection between masculinity, self-hood, nationality and narrative, however, the novel's relationships and conclusions are disappointingly traditionalist. The ultimate vision of community occurs to Dan while part of a naked ring waist-deep in the Mediterranean: Nell, his fiancée, and her sister Jane are present, but Dan has eyes for only one link in the circular chain:

> The profound difference between Anthony and myself – and our types of mankind – is that I did for a few moments there feel unaccountably happy; yet I could see that for him, the supposedly religious man, this was no more than a faintly embarrassing midnight jape. Or I can put it like this: he saw me as the brother-in-law he liked, I saw him as the brother I loved. It was a moment that had both an infinity and an evanescence – an intense closeness, yet not more durable than the tiny shimmering organisms in the water around us. (125)

Jane's femaleness and her Marxism are conflated, and her traces of individualism are characterised, like Murdoch's by Conradi, as non-female: 'She remained different; she reminded me slightly of one or two women writers I had known – of a withholding, not exactly male, but springing from an independence of feeling that was also not female' (337). Other female characters are also loaded with symbolism by Dan, from his childhood peasant-girl love Nancy, from whom he learnt that women are 'much, much nicer, softer, more mysterious' (412), and Jenny, who like Alison in *The Magus*, is attractive for 'her franknesses and simplicities, her presentness' (177). This tendency to make symbols of women may be mocked in Dan, but *Daniel Martin* provides no alternative model for male fiction to follow. Fowles's feminism falls short: so short that its central tenet brings to mind a couplet from Kingsley Amis's poem 'A Bookshop Idyll': 'Women are really much nicer than men: / No wonder we like them' (57). This novel about an existential quest for an authentic selfhood that merges individual integrity with communal care, for 'whole sight' (7), ends in a statement of peculiarly cheerful despair that the questions it raises can never be answered:

> That evening, in Oxford, leaning beside Jane in her kitchen while she cooked supper for them, Dan told her with suitable irony that at least he had found a last sentence for the novel he was never going to write. She laughed at such fragrant Irishry; which is perhaps why, in the end, and in the knowledge that Dan's novel can never be read, lies eternally in the future, his ill-concealed ghost has made that impossible last his own impossible first. (704)

The irony is, of course, that Fowles's own novel has just been read, and replicates and perpetuates the very masculine fictional mores that it mocks in its fictional writer.

This chapter began with a quotation from E. L. Allen that suggested the potential of existentialism to revolutionise masculine conceptions of self and narrative: '*Existentialism is an attempt at philosophizing from the standpoint of the actor instead of, as has been customary, from that of the spectator*' (3). Yet purely by virtue of its status as a philosophy, and the apprehension of philosophy (an intellectual pursuit) as inherently male, existentialism provides for many of the male authors considered here an attractive means of masculine consolation. Though existentialism might have been conceived to achieve the valorisation of human subjectivity, relativity and interaction, its apprehension from within a system of thought which bases its definition of self on the antithesis to others confuses these tenets with pervasive and contradictory systems of value. Existentialism is upheld as a creed of rational decision, ensuing action and repeated self-imposition on to the world. Acting pour-soi is more commonly represented as 'acting upon': acts of heterosexual inter-course which require female unwillingness in order to be existentially 'authentic' are a case in point. The novels under consideration have demonstrated the way in which the existential action-man can simulta-neously spectate or observe. In its interpretation of existentialism, mas-culine epistemology confuses the cultural imposition of its own terms of value with naturally given traits both of gender and of race.

The patriarchal pay-off within this covert system is a dual one. Dynamic existentialist selfhood is stabilised by the traditional ontologi-cal security of manhood, while masculinity is elevated from a matter of passive inheritance to a dynamic, heroic achievement of essence. The masculine self becomes more gloriously isolated, achieved in the individual mind, as well as inherited by virtue of certain bodily characteristics. Such duality is indicative of the doublethink of gender, which requires the concept to be both intrinsic and natural, and dynamic and mutable. To resurrect John MacInnes's apposite and arresting phrase once again, 'we are left swinging from penis to phallus' (78). When existentialism is examined in masculine narrative, its radical implications will always be subsumed by the paradox of this mode of thinking. To effect an authentic liberation from the limitations of masculine conceptions of selfhood, male-authored fiction needs the motivation to reimagine its narrative models.

4
Non-Conformity and the Sixties

> In general, generalization is to lie, to tell lies.
>
> B. S. Johnson, *The Unfortunates* (1969)

Popular iconography of the 1960s in Britain immortalises a decade triumphant in its counter-culture, a sustained rebellion with effects more far-reaching and far more real than the conservative rantings of the Angries and the Outsiders of the English of the fifties. As Alan Sinfield puts it in *Literature, Politics and Culture in Postwar Britain*, 'the "1960s" is of course a myth; but that is an important thing to be, since what we think and do depends on the stories we tell ourselves' (283). We are encouraged to retain a dominant fiction of an era liberated by satire, chemical stimulants and contraception, its audaciously won freedoms enshrined in the national culture by a rush of liberal legal reforms at the end of the decade.[1] Paul Johnson's farewell editorial for *New Statesman* on 26 June 1970 serves as a summation of the achievements of the period: 'We no longer terrorise homosexuals. We do not force mothers to bring unwanted children into the world. We have made it easier to end wrecked marriages. We have begun the true liberation of women. Children by and large get a better deal. [...] We do not murder by the rope' (quoted in Morgan, 315–16). In his cultural commentary *The Seventies*, Christopher Booker tracks a British impetus towards what he calls 'individual self-realization' from the end of the 1950s onwards, and is decisive in his nomination of the two areas in which this change was at its most dynamic:

> In essence this mighty impulse, first appearing in the form of the Romantic Movement, was a revolt against structure, order, discipline – a reaction in the name of 'life' against the dehumanization of an

increasingly machine-dominated, money-conscious, bureaucratic civilization. And it showed itself nowhere more than in the arts and in the realm of sexual morality. (31)

This chapter does not attempt an exclusive periodisation of the 1960s, as it omits novels falling within the era and includes novels written outside it. Such periodisation is notoriously difficult anyway, involving as it does so many competing categories; the 1960s as an international political entity, for example, from John F. Kennedy's election in 1960 to Richard M. Nixon's resignation in 1974; or less clearly demarked periods of political rebellion and social experimentation. Instead, this chapter will seek to engage with the concept of 'the Sixties' touched on above, and particularly with the perception that its innovations were most notable in the realms of Art and Sex. Reimagining (heterosexual) gender relationships outwith the spawning patriarchal family, as we have seen, has the potential radically to disrupt the masculine textual paradigm, resulting in a change in novelistic form.

The dates of the era referred to here as 'the Sixties', then, are skewed from the decimal, beginning around 1964 with the election of Harold Wilson and his resurrection of Kennedy-esque rhetoric in proclamations of new frontiers and revolutions, and ending during the early years of the 1970s. In *Too Much: Art and Society in the Sixties 1960–75*, Robert Hewison is sure in his judgement upon the nebulous nature of the Sixties *zeitgeist*:

> Youth, classlessness and a third factor which might be loosely summarized as 'sex, drugs and rock'n'roll', formed the ideological underpinnings of what has become identified as the Sixties style. Since these words suggest images, values or states of being rather than concrete ideas, it is not surprising that we have to talk of style, rather than anything as coherent as a philosophy. (61)

As we have seen in our consideration of the concept of masculinity thus far, a lack of 'concrete' foundations does not exclude an idea from enormous social and artistic influence (just as the idea of 'a philosophy' does not guarantee coherence, or a lack of contradiction). The male-authored novels considered here are chosen for their formal innovation,[2] for their engagement with those received Sixties themes of moral and behavioural revolution (freedom from class, freedom of sex and of youth, and of personal expression for the artist), and with familiar expectations of the Sixties as a time of liberated artistic experimentation. Holes are sliced into pages, sexual encounters are elaborated rather than implied, and the easy identifications between readers, heroes and authors we saw elicited and fostered in Chapters 2 and 3, are thereby complicated and compromised.

Of course, this narrative of a communal progression of literary expression and human liberation, is, like all narratives, to some extent contrived. In *Harvest of the Sixties*, Patricia Waugh reads the pervading mood of the decade in England as one of the culmination of prolonged economic and political pessimism. Kenneth O. Morgan nominates it a time at which 'Britain embarked on a traumatic process of self-examination, self-doubt, and declining morale, a perception of external weakness and internal decay from which it had yet fully to recover in the late 1980s' (197), characterising the Sixties politically as a time of dissolution and indiscipline, with the economy out of control, and a total loss of energy, vision or drive. President Kennedy's 1962 ultimatum to First Secretary Khrushchev to withdraw Soviet missiles from Cuba underscored the nation's demotion within the hierarchy of global power. As David Cannadine notes of the three decades following the Second World War in *Class in Britain*: 'Internationally, Britain gradually but inexorably declined from being a first-ranking world power, the Empire was dismantled with astonishing rapidity between 1947 and 1968, and the pound sterling was twice devalued' (145–6).

In previous chapters we saw the pessimism surrounding the lack of cohesive social and international dominance of English men to be expressed and repulsed in their fiction in two distinct ways. Some authors chose to reassert the cohesion of the male community by championing an empiricism established in advance as a masculine trait, some to assert individualism through a compromised version of continental existentialism. Either way, rational decision, and the actions resulting from it, were gendered male and upheld as eminent. The Welfare State, however its mechanisms might be mistrusted for their interference with class hierarchies and paternal control of the family, was for the most part accepted as the inevitable apotheosis of rational and patriarchal statehood. In contrast, Waugh notes a marked shift in the mid-60s towards a view that enlightened reason, and the social planning emanating from it, is in fact a mode of technocratic instrumentalism that reaches its gory climax in the arms race. A counter-cultural response to this realisation was simple and extreme: a rejection of all reason as oppressive and debilitating. For the cultural majority, however, anti-rationalism was disturbingly difficult to distinguish from the uncompromising capitalist individualism asserted by the extreme right. Thus,

Waugh claims, 'from the sixties onwards [...] there was a growing intellectual rejection of the extreme countercultural abandonment of rationality and a concomitant concern to find ways to redefine reason in non-instrumental or in other than narrowly functionalist ways' (121).

The redefinition of rationality so as to place emphasis elsewhere than on its empirical results – a severance of reason and action; such a desired step can be assumed to involve seismic disturbances in the previously delineated masculine paradigms of selfhood, the essential and the existential. Previously, the masculine had routinely been defined in opposition to feminine irrationality, and its credentials paraded in public, instrumental demonstration. One of the prevailing concerns of the 1960s, according to Robert Hewison, was to reverse the flow of this outward self-assertion: 'The convention was to ignore all boundaries and conventions, and as far as possible to escape the imposed definitions of material reality by exploring inner space' (86). The valorisation of inner space does not involve ignoring boundaries, of course, but rather a reversal of binary hierarchies, so that the public corresponds to conflict and oppression, and the private a fabled space of sanctuary. Established definitions of masculine selfhood are thereby placed in jeopardy.

Alongside this renegotiation of reason, another legacy of the decade might be heralded as its initiation of new modes of public and political discourse, and of new ways of locating each person culturally and relatively within those discourses. In a self-fulfilling cycle, encouraged by the rising prominence of various social groups – immigrants, students, Hippies – people began to envisage themselves not within the traditional vertical (and phallic?) hierarchies of class and attendant privilege, but rather upon horizontal social scales of race, gender, age-group, and sexual object-choice, and embarked upon an articulation of these newly perceived locations. A parallel impulse can be traced in John A. T. Robinson, Bishop of Woolwich's controversial *Honest to God* (1963), which argued that the sense of God should be relocated from 'up there', the untouchable, to 'in here', the personal, making prayer an engagement with the world, rather than a withdrawal from it. In 'Periodizing the Sixties', Fredric Jameson understands this proliferation of voices and diversification of dialects as the emergence of a multiplicity of increasingly legitimate subjects, in opposition to the imperial sectioning of the world's population into 'men', and 'natives' or Others: 'The 60s was, then, the period when all these "natives" became human beings, and this internally as well as externally: those inner colonized of the First World – "minorities", marginals, and women – fully as much as its external subjects and official "natives" ' (128). For the traditional masculine subject, both the participation in this project of the liberation of the Other and the failure effectively to react against it amount to the same thing – complicity in your own downfall. This chapter seeks to determine how far male novelists in the post-war, pre-Women's Liberation period are willing and radical accomplices in this dissipation of the self: in recognising a means of exploring selfhood beyond a consideration of its public and empirical effectiveness, and of maleness beyond its repressive, hegemonic definitions.

'The personal is political'; despite the proliferation of sexual and political scandals in the mid-60s, the slogan is yet to come to prominence in the era under consideration, but this anachronism may perhaps be excused after a consideration of the importance of this succinct phrase to masculine definitions of self and their repercussions in fictional narrative. Close analysis of the phrase reveals an inherent doublethink already delineated as characteristic of the concept of gender: does it mean that politics is founded upon personal identities and desires, or that personal identities are dictated by their social context? The feminist point, of course, is that private (female) experience should be voiced and validated in a public arena in order to secure permanent social change. The implications of such a move for that masculine binary, the Public/Private divide, are enormous. Once the personal is political, the binary dissolves, and private becomes public. Hierarchical distinctions dissolve too, and the Public can no longer be solely good or solely male. A variety of subject positions – black, gay, and female – become tenable. Though a post-structuralist move would be to embrace this dissolution of binaries, the Sixties cultural consensus is different. Rather than granting the subjective and the objective, or the particular and the universal, equal status, the assumption is that the subjective is now charged positive against the negative status of rationality and objectivity.

A predictable patriarchal move has always been to appropriate the positive. In the essay 'Any Theory of the "Subject" Has Always Been Appropriated by the "Masculine" ', Luce Irigaray is fatalistic, if lyrical, in the face of such appropriation:

> When the Other falls out of the starry sky into the chasms of the psyche, the 'subject' is obviously obliged to stake out new boundaries for his field of implantation and to re-ensure – otherwise, elsewhere – his dominance. Where once he was on the heights, he is now entreated to go down into the depths. These changes in position are still postulated in terms of verticality, of course. Are phallic, therefore.

But how to tame these uncharted territories, these dark continents, these worlds through the looking glass? How to master these devilries, these moving phantoms of the unconscious, when a long history has taught you to seek out and desire only clarity, the clear perception of (fixed) ideas? Perhaps this is the time to stress *technique* again? To renounce for the time being the sovereignty of thought in order to forge *tools* which will permit the exploitation of these resources, these unexplored mines. Perhaps for the time being the serene contemplation of empire must be abandoned in favour of taming those forces which, once unleashed, might explode the very concept of empire. A detour into *strategy, tactics, and practice* is called for, at least as long as it takes to gain vision, self-knowledge, self-possession, even in one's decenteredness. (136)

This passage provides a near-perfect epigraph to our concerns here, weaving together as it does images of the rational male self confronted with the need to explore the dark depths of the unconscious (both darkness and the unconscious being traditionally coded as Other) in order to re-establish a centre of selfhood, and, if not an Empire (the colonies now long lost), then at least an imperial means of defining that selfhood. Vital to this exploration will be a consideration of the '*strategy, tactics, and practice*' employed in male-authored writing, its narratives, heroes, and assumptions regarding the relationship between reader and text. It is a *near*-perfect epigraph in the sense that around Irigaray's study of the category of 'female' hovers the assumption that the category of 'male', culpable of the negative definition and subsequent oppression of the feminine, is negative itself and beyond redemption. Once again, it seems necessary to assert that this movement to appropriate the revelatory, liberatory processes of the decade should be attributed to the *masculine*, not the male. These texts are chosen as representative of genuine attempts to expand and alter male fictional self-definition outwith patriarchal paradigms, albeit to varying degrees. Our experience of the contradictions of the masculine subject, the ways in which these contradictions fissure the fiction in which he appears and asserts himself, and the contradictions of our own experience as readers, suggest that male fiction's negotiation of the new expectations of selfhood will resist simplistic categorisation.

It came from inner space

The gender assumptions of traditional modes of autobiography have become increasingly prominent as feminist literary criticism has developed. As subject matter for gynocritical studies, autobiography has been invaluable as a means of asserting the political nature of the personal in print. The insertion of the subjective into the traditionally objective register of critical writing (Jane Tompkins's deferred trip to the toilet in 'Me and My Shadow' being a controversial example) has proved a powerful tool in the disruption of masculine authority and its designation of the acceptable modes of public expression. The deflationary potential of self-revelation ensures autobiography is an anxious genre in which to display traditional masculine tenets of distance and control. In her essay 'Authorizing the Autobiographical', Shari Benstock unpicks the assumptions behind what she identifies as a masculine style of autobiographical writing:

> In definitions of autobiography that stress self-disclosure and narrative account, that posit a self called to witness (as an authority) to 'his' own being, that propose a double referent for the first-person narrative (the present 'I' and the past 'I'), or that conceive of autobiography as 'recapitulation and recall' [...], the Subject is made an Object of investigation (the first-person actually masks the third person) and is further divided between the present moment of the narration and the past on which the narration is focused. These gaps in the temporal and spatial dimensions of the text itself are often successfully hidden from reader and writer, so that the fabric of the narrative appears seamless, spun of whole cloth. The effect is magical – the self appears organic, the present the sum total of the past, the past an accurate predictor of the future. This conception of the autobiographical rests on a firm belief in the *conscious* control of artist over subject matter; this view of the life of history is grounded in authority. It is perhaps not surprising that those who cling to such a definition are those whose assignment under the Symbolic law is to *represent* authority, to represent the phallic power that drives inexorably toward unity, identity, sameness. (1047)

Masculine autobiography, she suggests, seeks to deliver the same level of authority and cognitive privilege to the narrating self (and, by implication, to the reader) as was apparent in our consideration of the first-person dissonant narration of *Scenes From Provincial Life* in Chapter 2. The older, wiser narrator and his peer the reader enjoy a unity of vision that welds together temporal and spatial fragments into aetiological narrative progression and the impression of an essential, organic self.

Such a masculine method of writing autobiographically is conceived of as generating more authority for its author by means of its empirical credentials – the fact that the text is the product of personal experience, of the 'real'. Benstock lays emphasis upon the unreal, or fictional, nature of this reality and the constant sleight of hand required to maintain it. In 'writing autobiography', bell hooks claims that during the eponymous exercise she 'was compelled to face the fiction that is a part of all retelling, remembering' (1038). The fictional nature of fiction, autobiographical or otherwise, as we have seen, generates more anxiety than celebration in the work of male authors. In *The Situation of the Novel*, Bernard Bergonzi quotes from a 1967 BBC radio interview with B. S. Johnson, in which the writer claimed: 'I'm certainly not interested in the slightest in writing fiction. Where the difficulty comes in is that "novel" and "fiction" are not synonymous. Certainly I write autobiography, and I write it in the form of a novel. What I don't write is fiction' (207). Apparently conscious of its lowly artistic status, Johnson seeks to resurrect autobiography precisely by distinguishing it *from* 'fiction', the artificial, contrived processes expounded by Benstock. In claiming the novel as an autobiographical non-fictional form, Johnson makes a bold claim for a direct (and empirical) link between text and selfhood. The reliably experimental nature of his narrative form makes Johnson's work a crucial case-study.

B. S. Johnson's intention to renegotiate the status of autobiography within the novel form, and the form of the novel itself, is apparent from his first publication, *Albert Angelo* (1964). The novel's claim to speak from any coherent source of authority is faltering by the end of its epigraph, a quotation from Samuel Beckett's beleaguered monologue *The Unnamable*, a text which foregrounds its fictionality and unreliability at every opportunity. The 'Prologue' begins as a script with a cast of three characters, 'Joseph', 'Luke' and 'Albert', then continues into a description of Albert's residence written in the third-person. The 'Exposition' section, narrated in the first-person, then immediately disrupts the rational authority of that narration with its tone of mild disinterest in traditional autobiographical factual data:

> I think I shall visit my parents every Saturday, as a rule, as a habit. Occasionally Sundays: instead, though, not as well. But usually Saturdays, as a rule, as a habit almost. Yes.
> I think that they are my parents, at least, yes. (19)

Shifting pronouns, alterations in typographical layout, a hole cut in page 149 that gives the reader a preview of a disturbing death on page 153; all these ensure the text can never allow a vision of a whole self, fictional or autobiographical, but worries constantly at the eye and the I. This tactic of altering pronouns (though not typography) is famil-iar from Fowles's *Daniel Martin*, which for all its gestures towards surren-dering narrative authority, remains a traditional *Bildungsroman*, based upon masculine tenets of self and fictional narrative. The most striking attempt to denounce fiction comes later in Johnson's novel, with the (now infamous) interjection: '– OH, FUCK ALL THIS LYING! [...] – fuck all this lying look what im really trying to write about is writing not all this stuff about architecture trying to say something about writing about my writing' (163–7). This is an explicit denouncement of the 'fictional' for the 'autobiographical', which, it is implied, is more 'real', and more of a risk.

It is telling that this risky, vehement and capitalised outburst is followed by a ranting exposition of authorial intention, which, para-doxically, aims to re-establish in far more certain terms the presence of a unifying controlling identity both within and without the text: '– Im trying to say something not tell a story telling stories is telling lies and I want to tell the truth about me about my experience about my truth about my truth to reality' (167). The 'i' has quickly become capi-talised, and the rules of written grammar are reinstated just after this passage. It is telling, too, that the breakdown in any semblance of fic-tional character-identity comes immediately after that section of the novel which testifies most convincingly to the pain of the hero's self-exposure. Pain at this level, it seems, merits being made personal and it can then be claimed as a means of legitimisation, as a badge of bravery. In his position as supply teacher at a turbulent inner-London school, Albert attempts to purge the mounting student resentment at his term's teaching by allowing his class to 'write down exactly what they feel about me, with a guarantee that there will be no complaints or recrimi-nations from me, whatever they say' (149).[3] The students' detached, vicious, semi-literate accounts undermine Albert's fictive attempts at subjective truth to such an extent that his character is usurped by the authorial ('autobiographical') voice in the immediate aftermath. Remembering the start of a love affair, Albert has been described as Jenny's 'equal, right for her, big, hard, everything physically about him was big and hard' (48). There is barely a student essay which fails to con-tain a physical description of the teacher as some variation on 'big fat over fed fool' (159) or 'fat, porky selfish drip' (161). Descriptions of Albert's teaching experience, in both the third- and first-person, have represented him restraining himself at the brink of violence, yet most of the children make reference to the fact that he hits the boys repeatedly around their heads. Albert is revealed as a liar immediately prior to being 'revealed' (and denounced by the narrator) as fictional. Any cognitive privilege granted to the reader so far is thereby revealed to be a sham. This sense of a swindle, coupled with the reader's distress at Albert's masochism in inviting this student assessment, makes the interjection of 'OH, FUCK' at the end of the 'Development' section easy to read as a heroic rescue, both of Albert and the reader. The reader is thankful to leave the masochistic and helpless Albert for the authority of a 'real' person telling the 'truth', surreptitiously enforcing the impression that autobiography is in opposition to fiction, and superior to it, by virtue of its direct linguistic communication between author and reader. Autobiography, it is implied, functions to announce and impose the identity of its author rather than constructing it.

Albert's authority has been severely compromised even before he is denounced by the autobiographical narrator. He keeps his teaching temporary in the belief that his true profession, referred to variously as 'real work, my work, real work, vocation' (103), and 'this essential myself, my identity, my character' (115), is architecture. Apart from the fact that he does not work as an architect, Albert is content to admit this 'vocation' is still more immaterial, in that its

> Real satisfaction, even with success, whatever that means, would be in the work itself, as it is now, the real satisfaction, in the work. When I've done something, hewn it from my mind, then when it's actually built does not seem to matter, really, it's an accident, a commercial or economic accident, quite beyond my control. (103)

The confession in 'Disintegration' that 'what im really trying to write about is writing not all this stuff about architecture' (167) prompts interrogation of the selection of architecture as Albert's non-profession for the unsuccessful analogy. Arthur Marwick has called the profession 'the most socially determined of the plastic arts' (87), and architecture, in its requirement for practical limitations upon artistic design, might be considered a compromised art-form. Johnson's probing of the limits of truth amidst traditional narrative techniques foregrounds writing as similarly, and necessarily, compromised. Albert's hangdog acceptance of the impossibility ever of converting his scribbles into concrete parallels fiction's failure to make firm claims upon reality. Albert's buildings are never built, his supply teaching is by definition fragmented, and any semblance of a fictional narrative is ultimately untenable.

In the article 'B. S. Johnson' in *The Review of Contemporary Fiction*, Philip Tew notes of the setting of *Albert Angelo* that 'London is narrowed to the mundane consciousness of various inter-subjectivities rather than any grand narrative' (24). His nomination of subjective consciousness as 'mundane', though clearly intended in part to chime with the 'grand' of 'grand narrative', hints at a recurrent supposition noted above, that subjectivity lies on the negative pole of an opposition with the objective: the very supposition Johnson himself opposes. Tew goes on to argue that, though Johnson's novels, when they are considered critically at all, are considered from a textual viewpoint, their *con*text too, should be accounted for: 'Johnson's novels balance the personal reflection with a sociological account of urban living' (26). *Albert Angelo* generates a powerful proportion of its sense of alterity from the wanderings of its hero ('what a useless appellation', Johnson, 1987, 167) in the dives of a post-colonial, post-war capital city. Albert attempts to bring out his silent Greek Cypriot students with his vague recollection of classical Greek, and the culinary tastes he shares with his friend Terry are not in the least mundane: 'There must be cafés for ten or a dozen nationalities – Maltese, West Indians, Somalis, West Africans, Turkish and Greek Cypriots, and so on – and we usually go in a West Indian or a Somali one' (51). Tew concludes that 'Johnson [...] seems acutely attuned to recognizing and critiquing the power and hegemony of the imperial/colonial narrative and its collapse in the postwar world, rather than its narrativization' (27). In its maintenance of hierarchies and marked refusal to let the subaltern speak, of course, the imperial/colonial narrative functions in the same way as the masculine narrative. In his exploration of issues of authority in autobiographical writing, Johnson is inevitably involved in deconstructing the gender implications of confessing the self.

Yet just as an examination of the work of John Fowles revealed that a feminist sensibility need not necessarily undermine a masculine narrative, so Johnson's novels may be used to demonstrate that the deconstruction of a masculine narrative need not prompt an empathy with the aims of feminism. Johnson's 1969 'book in a box' *The Unfortunates* represents a professed attempt to keep a promise to Tony Tillinghast, dead from cancer aged 29, to 'get it all down, mate' ('So he came to his parents at Brighton',[4] 5). Despite its unusualness as a physical literary object, the novel seems immediately less experimental than *Albert Angelo* in its uninterrupted adherence to a mode of autobiographical confession. In his introduction to Picador's 1999 reprint of the novel, Jonathan Coe demonstrates the affinity noted by Tew towards a view of

Johnson's work as valuable for its subjective, rather than contextual, revelations:

> *The Unfortunates* offers thin pickings as a social document. Johnson
> was a highly politicized writer in the sense that he was very active in
> a number of writers' and filmmakers' unions, but the novels them-
> selves are for the most part apolitical, gravitating instead towards the
> personal and the interior. (ix)

This affinity was in fact encouraged by Johnson himself, who claimed in an interview, 'outside writing I'm a very political animal' (Burns, 88). Such a claim is immediately denounced by a gynocritical consideration of the glaring absence of women in the text, who, as the Women's Liberation Movement accelerated during the time of the book's writing, appear only to serve tea to those participating in the pivotal male bond, or to fail to reach orgasm despite the narrator's best, bemused attempts. More interesting for this discussion, though, is the further light Coe's comment throws upon the received relationship between the political and the personal. Like the narrator of *The Unfortunates*, who claims to be 'not really interested in motives, actions are what are important' ('Then he was doing research', 5), Coe persists in limiting the definition of 'politics' to a public display of action, refusing to acknowledge the power relationships at work within the interior of any person, or any text. His assumption here, albeit astonishing in the context of 1999, is that the personal is apolitical, or at least private.

The exact tone of the novel's first-person narration is initially difficult to determine. Here, the narrator is speaking of his friend Tony:

> That vacation, I remember he told us at tea, or in a letter, which was
> it, both probably, that he had been selling rugs door-to-door down
> workingclass streets in this city, yes, which later came in very useful,
> the knowledge, to him, when there were race-riots in the city, he was
> interviewed by reporters, or something, I don't remember, why
> should I, it doesn't matter, nothing does, it's all chaos, look at his
> death, why?   Why not? ('His dog, or his parents' dog', 2–3)

Dorrit Cohn's categorisation of narrative voice in *Transparent Minds* includes the 'autonomous monologue' (217), defined as that mode of narration in which the figural voice of the speaking 'I' totally obliterates the authorial narrative voice. The 'Penelope' chapter of *Ulysses* is commonly upheld as the ultimate example. The proliferation of its yeses makes it tempting to classify *The Unfortunates* narrative mode in the same way. However, a comparison of Molly Bloom's 'yes', accumulating more positive charge with every repetition, makes Johnson's seem negative in comparison, followed as it is in the extract above by a breakdown in recall and a cancellation of its dynamism. In *The Unfortunates*, 'yes' means 'momentarily, I'm asserting that I've remembered something correctly'. It is a 'yes' to celebrate recall and its inscription on paper as successful. It marks the recognition, and recording of truth. This success however, is fleeting. In *The Politics of Experience and the Bird of Paradise*, R. D. Laing, in one of his tellingly gendered explicatory scenarios, examines the ordinary ways in which a speaker's authority over their material can be undermined. He posits a situation in which Jill keeps returning to a subject which Jack wants to forget:

> Jack may act upon Jill in many ways. He may make her feel guilty for keeping on 'bringing it up'. He may *invalidate* her experience. This can be done more or less radically. He can indicate merely that it is unimportant or trivial, whereas it is important and significant to her. Going further, he can shift the *modality* of her experience from memory to imagination: 'It's all in your imagination.' Further still, he can invalidate the *content*. 'It never happened that way.' Finally, he can invalidate not only the significance, modality and content, but her very capacity to remember at all, and make her feel guilty for doing so into the bargain.
>
> This is not unusual. People are doing such things to each other all the time. (31)

The male narrative voice of *The Unfortunates* turns all the weapons listed by Laing – guilt, invalidation, a shift of modality, and a rejection of the reliability of memory – upon itself.

Yet, as a textual male confession, *The Unfortunates* is not without defences against such weapons. As noted at the beginning of this chapter, much feminist critical writing has made striking use of autobiography as 'shock-tactic' in exploding the myth of authorial objectivity. In *The Inward Gaze*, Peter Middleton, considering the autobiographical nature of much writing in the still-forming field of masculinity studies, notices the presence of a confessional narrative in much of the work. In contrast to its original purpose in female critical writing, in which it is intended precisely to undermine patriarchal standards of objectivity, he claims that 'this imposes on the story a subsequent, more informed, more worked-out viewpoint. Indeed the more self-critical the tone of such writing, paradoxically the more virtuous the writer will appear' (21). In *The History of Sexuality, Volume One: An Introduction*, Michel Foucault recognises a recent 'metamorphosis in literature' with regard to the confessional mode:

> We have passed from a pleasure to be recounted and heard, centering on the heroic or marvelous (sic) narration of 'trials' of bravery or sainthood, to a literature ordered according to the infinite task of extracting from the depths of oneself, in between the words, a truth which the very form of the confession holds out like a shimmering mirage. (59)

The ideal reader of male-authored confessional texts, or male-narrated ones, however, retains to the present day an appreciation of the chivalric heroism of truth-telling. David Goldknopf, quoted by Dorrit Cohn, refers to 'the "confessional increment" ' (15) of first-person narration, both autobiographical and fictional, and in 'The Masculine Mode', Peter Schwenger, anxious to defend confessional writing against any charge of passivity, contests that 'to write about certain aspects of one's life is to change that life. The writing becomes not a passive reflection but an act in itself, full of risk and consequence' (106).

Expectation of this 'confessional increment' to the inflation of narratorial heroism is demonstrated in *The Unfortunates* at the confrontation with Tony's weight-loss: 'this diminution made features stand out more, which were not that noticeable before, his eyes stood out, stared, fixed you, I slip into the second person, in defence, stared for longer moments than you wanted, than I did want, yes' ('So he came to his parents at Brighton', 2). The second-person, like the third-person, is figured as refuge from the demands of the first-person. The increment stems from a traditional masculine apprehension of the personal as a risk. In female-authored texts – for example, *The L-Shaped Room*, and even *The Golden Notebook* – women's confessions of weakness and confusion are ritualised, habitualised, naturalised and seem relatively ordinary. Male confession, and the voice of *The Unfortunates*, is posited as extraordinary. The familiar artifice of the stream-of-consciousness mode and the constant reminders of the narrator's authorial presence ensure that the narrative of *The Unfortunates* is better included under Cohn's category of 'memory narrative', an a-chronological form organised by memory as a narrative principle (182), and that (as in *Albert Angelo*) its authorial voice as well as its figural one is calling for a confessional increment. Narration as expiation – guilt is measured out to match the expected amount of forgiveness, as here, when Tony's cancer is advancing:

> That it was serious, the first thing that brought it home to me, was that he was too ill to come down to London for the publication party of my novel, in my flat, the novel which was so much better for his work on it, for his attention to it. It was dedicated to them! This shocked me, I was annoyed, angry even, that he, that both of them, should find any excuse whatsoever for missing something so important, that its importance to me should not be shared by them, it made me think almost that he was backing out of his support for the book, my paranoia again, yes. ('Just as it seemed things were going his way', 4)

Albert's pedagogical tactic is brought to mind – he assumes that his students' resentment will be overtaken by admiration at the risk he is taking in allowing them to write what they think about him. Self-flagellation fails to pay off for Albert, because the children, being childish, fail to understand the dividends he should be paid for his risk. The narrator of *The Unfortunates* confesses to an adult-only Sixties audience, educated to admire attempts at personal analysis. If the reader is moved by his confession, it is on the basis of a number of assumptions about the 'risk and consequence' of that confession, and these assumptions depend in turn upon a gendered concept of subjectivity. In other words, if consequentially the reader grants Johnson and his narrator heroism for getting personal, s/he does so *because* they are both men and the personal is understood as Other to them. If confession assumes this concession, if it pleads its special case, then its actual risks are greatly diminished.

Suspicion is escalating with regard to the integrity of the confessional risk. Can a narrative fraught with masculine assumptions escape them with a genuine plea for the personal? Or does such a narrative inescapably plead instead for the recognition of a failing universality? Is a reader experiencing empathy for the narrator's loss of his friend inevitably committed via that empathy to a host of insidious, gendered, epistemological hierarchies? The reader-response work of Stanley Fish can be, and has been, criticised for its failure to address the gender of the readers in the interpretive communities it posits.[5] It is precisely due to this gender-blindness that one of Fish's key points is useful here. Defending his focus upon the reader against accusations of relativism, Fish asserts that 'while relativism is a position one can entertain, it is not a position one can occupy' (319). Everyone is always already situated *somewhere*, he goes on to argue, and 'an individual's assumptions and opinions are not "his own" in any sense that would give body to the fear of solipsism' (320). Subjectivity and solipsism, relativism and chaos – the personal is still to be feared here, but that fear can be quelled by the sense of (an interpretive) community. Johnson's mode of narration in *The Unfortunates* may be seen as subject to the same assumptions of communal mores and values, and these values, and this community, are frequently masculine ones. In such a professedly 'personal' novel, the narrator refers repeatedly not to *his* mind, but instead to the fact that 'the mind is confused, was it this visit, or another, the mind has telescoped time here' ('Again the house at the end of a bus-route', 5). The factual and temporal vagaries of memory are here marked, then, not as personal failure, but as a universal trait. The narrator speaks highly of Tony's skill in suggesting revisions of the manuscripts of his novels, believing that Tony's comments gave his work 'some sort of objective, or at least collective-subjective, value' (1). 'Collective-subjective' – the phrase nicely maintains a sense of the independent choice of a single agent happily coinciding with that of other single agents and resonates with Fish's notion of the 'interpretive community'. Tew, in his determined attempt to reclaim Johnson's work for realism in *B. S. Johnson*, preserves Fish's gender-blindness with regard to this communal recognition: 'He appeals to a wider context of socially understood factors and dimensions of power that dominate even the most simplistic account of the nature of the real and encountered relations in the world' (52). What is difficult, however, is to distinguish between this collective-subjective and the 'objective' (itself a collective, and masculine, agreement upon how to perceive) Johnson rejects as untenable.

A 'collective-subjective' perspective has further claims towards the traditional stability of the objective, universal viewpoint. Previous chapters have emphasised a theoretical dissonance between traditional linear narratives and the competing concepts of the essentialist or existentialist self. A pre-existent, essential self, it was argued, should not need to rely upon narrative development as a demonstration of existence. An existential self, mindful of contingency, should exist in antithesis to linear plot progression. Thus it might be assumed that a fragmented narrative is a more 'realistic' demonstration of self in an increasingly heterogeneous, divisive environment. Ronald Hayman makes such an argument in *The Novel Today 1967–1975*: 'Far from being antithetical to realism in the novel, formal invention is indispensable to it. If the novelist carries his realism far enough, he finds that the formal relationship he has set up between the component parts of his fiction is making a statement about external reality' (5–6). Fragmented form is apprehended as a statement of the reality of contemporary experience, which is contrasted with a lost or utopian existence of unity and wholeness. In other words, narrative, even when fragmented to the point of anti-narrative, is always understood structurally. This structure always incorporates the pervading values of the dominant epistemology.

In her queering of narratology, *Come as You Are: Sexuality and Narrative*, Judith Roof makes just this assertion in relation to post modern fiction:

> Although various metanarratives of knowledge, according to Lyotard, might be disrupted, the structuralist character of narrative with its adherent binarisms and presumed productivity still holds sway not only as a comforting relic of more certain times but also as a thriving defence against poststructuralist skepticism, systemic failures, and grandiose multiplicity. (32)

Though *The Unfortunates* expounds and demonstrates the elastic temporality and mutable reliability of memory through its unbound structure, its narrative limits are set by the sections marked 'FIRST' and 'LAST', and those limits are in turn set by those of a (male) human life. Empathy for the gaps that cancer has forced in Tony's speech (his saliva glands destroyed by chemotherapy, he has to sip continually from a glass of water) and in his reading (the illness 'deprived him of his ability to read', 'Just as it seemed', 7) is expressed in the text by failing sentence structures and textual gaps. The physical form of the book itself provides a tangible metaphor, not just for the contingency of human memory, but also for the contingency of human suffering, and cancer itself. Yet here it is Tony who dies, not the Author, in spite of Roland Barthes's death knoll, published the year before the novel. Tony's illness may silence him, but it paradoxically prompts the narrator to seek and attempt both meaning and a meaningful means of elegy:

> That this thing could just come from nowhere, from inside himself, of his very self, to attack him, to put his self in danger, I still do not understand. Perhaps there is nothing to be understood, perhaps understanding is simply not to be found, is not applicable to such a thing. But it is hard, hard, not to try to understand, even for me, who accept that all is nothing, that sense does not exist. ('For recuperation', 2)

The meaninglessness of cancer is interpreted as a challenge, not a conclusion, and its oncological absolute prompts a quest by the narrator for an ontological one. Just as the novel itself is bound by the nomination of its first and last sections, so its fragmented interior text preserves the sanctity of narrative progression. The narrator notes at one point of Tony that:

> He had successfully kept from [his parents] what it was, until then, though they knew it was very serious, but not that serious, he had kept it from them, what nature of deception is that, I wonder, what are the morals of that?   I should try to work that out some time, I should try to understand. ('So he came to his parents at Brighton', 1)

The responsibility of placing some sort of narrative of morality, a causality, upon the contingency of cancer, preys upon the narrator, and 'the mind' still seeks for chains of logic stretching back into the past. The narrator professes a hatred for the sub-editors that hack all the lyrical touches from his football match-report: his stint as a football journalist is described by Nicolas Tredell in 'Telling Life, Telling Death: *The Unfortunates*' as an ' "anti-portrait" of the artist' (36). Linguistic parsimony, however, is exactly what he admires in Tony's editing of his novels: 'it was good to have him to bounce ideas off, to learn from, to have him pull me up when I committed wild excesses, made a fool of myself, in my work' ('Then he was doing research', 4). In her 1984 article 'The Trojan Horse', Monique Wittig upheld that 'one must assume both a particular *and* a universal point of view, at least to be part of literature' (68). The Sixties masculine mindset still held these two terms to be mutually exclusive, linking them with another lingering polarisation: that of Reason and Emotion. In this professedly subjective novel, rational progression is still upheld to be the ultimate, if elusive, goal. This perceivedly paradoxical commitment to the personal and the public, the subjective and the objective, is nicely encapsulated in the novel's conclusion:

> The difficulty is to understand without generalization, to see each piece of received truth, or generalization, as true only if it is true for me, solipsism again, I come back to it again, and for no other reason.   In general, generalization is to lie, to tell lies.

> Not how he died, not what he died of, even less why he died, are of concern, to me, only the fact that he did die, he is dead, is important: the loss to me, to us (LAST, 6)

Paramount here, of course, is empathy for and duty to Tony, and a value placed upon knowledge stemming from interpersonal relationships which denies the binary of Self and Others. Yet, 'in general, generalization is to lie, to tell lies': the contradiction inherent in a generalising statement that refutes the possibility of generalisation provides a fitting epitaph to a narrative that attempts to valorise subjectivity by constructing an objective framework for that valorisation.

In sickness, not in health

It is appropriate, perhaps, that the text of *The Unfortunates* is haunted by cancer and its contingent nature, for in a masculine epistemology, the subjective always carries with it intimations of femininity, and thus negativity, and so illness. 'The root of sanity is in the balls', claims Mellors in Lawrence's *Lady Chatterley's Lover* (227), making mental stability a male preserve. Within this epistemology, Johnson's attempt to redefine the relationship between subjective and objective, solipsism and generalisation, is similarly sick. Third-person narration, too, is not immune. For the masculine mindset, there is a danger of infection during any foray into the personal. Dorrit Cohn traces the emergence of Free Indirect Discourse, or what she calls 'narrated monologue' (99), to a specific moment in the development of the novel, that is, the point at which third-person narration entered the domain previously reserved for first-person texts of epistolary or confessional fiction. The mode had Jane Austen as one of its first pioneers, of course, and this tarnishing with femininity further explains the effort of the FID texts considered in Chapter 2 both to immasculate their readers and to exhibit the empirical masculine credentials of their heroes.

One of the tools of textual immasculation, as we have seen, is a linear narrative, driving the reader to accept a host of implicit assumptions in her or his anticipation of utopia. A coherent narrative is vital to masculine health. Peter Brooks, in his essay 'Changes in the Margins: Construction, Transference, and Narrative', notes that modern psychoanalysis is now recognised to be 'a narrative discipline' (47), and that patients are defined, rather than those without balls, as people with incoherent personal narrative discourses:

> *Mens sana in fabula sana:* mental health is a coherent life story, neurosis is a faulty narrative. [...] The narrative chain, with each event connected to the next by reasoned causal links, marks the victory of reason over chaos, of society over the aberrancy of crime, and

restitutes a world in which aetiological histories offer the best solution to the apparently unexplainable. (49)

The 'aetiological history', as we have seen, is coded masculine in its logical progression, as against the fragmentation and confusion of feminine irrationality. Causal narrative, like the patriarchy, is couched as 'natural'.

Such an assumption, however, was undermined during the Sixties by the pervasive influence of the new (anti-) psychiatry, which preached precisely that mental health (and by implication, healthy narrative) was *not* a given or a natural state, but rather an artificial and precarious construction. In his 1960 book *The Divided Self*, R. D. Laing developed the idea of insanity as an intelligible, even sane, response to the dissipated demands of contemporary society. In *The Politics of Experience and The Bird of Paradise* (1967), he remarked upon the pervasive cultural tendency to regard the contemplation of the private self as disreputable, and even diseased: 'We are socially conditioned to regard total immersion in outer space and time as normal and healthy. Immersion in inner space and time tends to be regarded as anti-social withdrawal, a deviancy, invalid, pathological *per se*, in some sense discreditable' (103). As R. W. Connell notes in his essay 'Psychoanalysis and Masculinity', Laing never developed the clues his own work offered to a radical analysis of gender. Rather, *The Divided Self*, for example, continually utilises resolutely male metaphors to describe the ontological insecurity in predominantly female case-studies: 'We may approach this rather difficult psychotic material by comparing the fear of loss of the "self" to a more familiar neurotic anxiety that may lie behind a complaint of impotence' (149). Pathological selfhood (schizophrenia) is described like a pathological case of masculinity: it shows all the symptoms (the mind/body split; fear of engulfing relationships; pathological attempts at self-sufficiency; use of fantasy and stereotypes in the contemplation of others; repulsion/narcissistic attraction of homosexuality; depersonalisation; creation of false-self system and so on) diagnosed in this study so far.

Laing's theory of madness as intelligible and even intelligent under contemporary conditions offers a potentially disruptive challenge to the traditional paradigm of healthy self = healthy narrative, not least because madness is always coded as feminine. David Storey's 1963 novel *Radcliffe* provides an interesting demonstration of these competing value systems. If, as we have seen, masculinity couches and values the reading process as a rational, hermeneutic exercise, then it is a radical step by a male author to make both the fictional male self, and the narrative in which it appears, ambiguous. Though the novel's form as a realist narrative may initially suggest that it sits uncomfortably with the selection criteria of the novels in this chapter, dependent as they are upon formal innovation, its disso- lution of that genre from within will be used to justify its inclusion. In *David Storey*, John Russell Taylor assesses the novel as follows:

> A powerful, disturbing book – many would say his most powerful and disturbing – but a lot of its power comes from the sense we have of not quite grasping what it is about and our feeling that the author does not either: that it represents an almost uncontrollable boiling up of violent emotions which are shaped and forged – but only just – on the anvil of art. (20)

As well as a profoundly Romantic vision of the artist, this assessment may be attributed to a weird atmosphere in *Radcliffe* that all modes of perception are breaking down, with a constant fog hanging over the landscape, the darkness of the shuttered rooms in the Place, Leonard's home, and his own fluctuating levels of deafness. This failure of percep- tion is not only visual and aural, but mental too. It is frequently impos- sible to deduce what someone in the novel is thinking or meaning, and the text is peppered with retractions and obfuscations:

> Tolson stood gazing in at the barren interior with *a kind of stifled* curiosity, *half*-embarrassed. He *seemed neither to hear nor to see* John who, *as though* recognising *some sort of* threat in Tolson's attitude, had suddenly leaned against the wall in a *vague gesture* of appeal. (236; emphases added)

Apparently unconnected facts are placed together in the same para- graph, and the reader struggles to connect them but frequently fails:

> It was into this void that the Place had seemed to fit. It was as if the building itself represented a complete abdication; and to the extent that [John Radcliffe] struggled now to preserve and secure it from out- side interference. During this period, now almost a year since his arrival, he had begun to see an increasing amount of his brother. (24)

Cognitive privilege is constantly proffered, then snatched away from the reader. Here, Leonard and Victor Tolson are camping on the Show Ground, and we are momentarily inside Leonard's mind:

> Moonlight filtered through the canvas above his head. The lamp had gone out. Tolson was kneeling beside him, stooped forward and

apparently gazing at his body moulded in the thick texture of the blankets. Leonard closed his eyes. He lay perfectly still. It seemed only a few seconds, yet when he looked again he saw that Tolson was in fact lying in his bed on the other side of the bike. (61)

The description juxtaposes an 'apparent' occurrence with a factual situation, but the fact that Tolson is first located close to Leonard, and only then designated 'in fact' to be on the other side of the tent, ensures Leonard's hallucination takes preference over the report of his empirical observation. Two pages later, we are outside the tent and Leonard's mind is once again utterly opaque: 'He lifted the hammer and swung it down on a boulder. He glanced up once more at the tent. He brought the hammer down again, more fiercely' (63). Cognitive access, it seems, is granted only when the deductions possible from it are obscure; that is, when Leonard is confused, fantasising, or merely mistaken.

Perception in the novel, and subsequently the process of interpretation of that novel, are unwell. The reasons for this sickness are numerous, but all involve a dissolution of hierarchical (and profoundly masculine) value-sets. The class system is one of these: through its consideration of the degenerating squirearchy of the Radcliffes, the novel (like Fowles's *The Collector*) explores the subjective consequences of class transition. Aristocratic property, once a symbol of affluence and security (as fetishised in Evelyn Waugh's *Brideshead*), is now a debilitating, draining responsibility. The Place, hunched upon its hilltop, is rocked by the train services in the tunnels beneath it, and glared at by the council housing that has encroached upon every acre of the valley. Of the trinity of men at the centre of the novel, Leonard Radcliffe represents this compromised aristocracy, Tolson, the physical working-class, and Blakeley functions as a bridging figure between the rarefied environment of Leonard's home and Tolson's estate – he is a self-educated man living in a council flat. This tripartite relationship (already the number of people involved is in excess of the sacred binary) is disruptive of other hierarchies too. In his book *All Bull: The National Servicemen*, B. S. Johnson quotes Jeff Nuttall on the military concept of 'over-identification', defined as 'army jargon for not sticking to your rank socially, for being too friendly with the lads' (24). Leonard would be 'over-identifying' with Tolson merely through associating with a working-class man, but his identification goes further: he is in love.

Homosexuality is at the centre of the 'sickness' degenerating the novel's narrative and interpretive processes. *Radcliffe* may initially seem laudable for its determined foregrounding of a homosexual relationship in an era of continuing censorship,[6] and its obfuscation of interpretation may in part be attributed to the threat of that censorship. Yet it is impossible not to see the novel's plot and fictional technique reflected in Judith Roof's diagnosis of homosexuality's negative narrative connotations:

> The bourgeois need for the correct narrative, one effected by proper heterosexual, reproductive sexuality, and good timing, positions sexuality as itself causal: perverted sexuality is the cause of the bad narrative, familial disfunction, low production; and good, reproductive sexuality is the cause of profit, continuity, and increase. (35)

The heterosexually perceived narcissism of homosexual love disrupts the primacy of binary thinking and prevents Othering, as well as wrecking the structure of the patriarchal family and the placement of that family within a hierarchy of class. This judgement is borne out by the plot of *Radcliffe*, which is one of warped reproductive processes: Tolson's father is absent, and he has a much older wife; Kathleen has three children by her own father Blakeley; and Elizabeth, Leonard's sister, gives birth to Tolson's illegitimate son.

In focusing on a homosexual love affair, Storey has committed himself to competing and paradoxical demands upon the text he will publish in an era of censorship, for as Judith Butler notes in *Gender Trouble*: 'for heterosexuality to remain intact as a distinct social form, it *requires* an intelligible conception of homosexuality and also requires the prohibition of that conception in rendering it culturally unintelligible' (77). Heterosexuality depends for its ultimate coherence upon the clear delineation of the 'bad' example of homosexuality, at the same time that its social organisation requires the concealment of that bad example. Homosexuality is still more threatening in that attempts at its definition involve an unrationalised coexistence of pre-existing, competing explanations. In *Epistemology of the Closet*, Eve Kosofsky Sedgewick notes how:

> Foucault among other historians locates in about the nineteenth century a shift in European thought from viewing same-sex sexuality as a matter of prohibited and isolated genital *acts* (acts to which, in that view, anyone might be liable who did not have their appetites in general under close control) to viewing it as a function of stable definitions of *identity* (so that one's personality structure might mark one as *a homosexual*, even, perhaps, in the absence of any genital activity at all). (82–3)

Radcliffe's dissonance as a narrative structure may in part be attributed to its inclusion in the central triptych of its characters of both of these competing methods of understanding. It can be noted how these tropes mirror the now-familiar split between the masculine paradigms of selfhood: the existentialist and the essentialist. Tolson can be nominated 'homosexual' within one patriarchal psychoanalytic discourse in that he chooses to participate in sexual acts with other men. Choosing to act is, of course, masculine. Blakeley is marked a number of times during the novel as feminine, as when Leonard 'saw Blakeley's face close to his and the anxious, vaguely feminine look, inquisitive and almost sensitive' (152). Blakeley, evidenced not only by his homosexual desire for Tolson, but also his incestuous relationship with his daughter, is unethical, illogical and thus feminine in his desires. Male homosexuality as a feminised identity is, of course, a familiar misapprehension, but here this is complicated by the simultaneous demonstration of Tolson's sexuality as a series of willed acts perpetrated by a man with all the attributes of primal manhood. Tolson's physicality is emphatically *not* feminine, characterised as it is by acts (digging, lifting, hammering) rather than innate facticity.

Leonard's case is still more complex and contradictory. In *The Divided Self*, R. D. Laing quotes approvingly from a 1949 case-study by Boss:

> When his progressing schizophrenia 'depleted his masculinity', when most of his own male feelings 'had run out', he suddenly and for the first time in his life felt driven to 'open himself' to a certain form of homosexual love. He described most vividly how in this homosexual love he succeeded in experiencing at least half of the fullness of existence. He did not have to 'exert' himself very much to attain this semi-fullness, there was little danger of 'losing himself' and of 'running out' into boundlessness in this limited extent and depth. On the contrary, the homosexual love could 'replenish' his existence 'to a whole man'. [...] We, however, see in both phenomena, in this sort of homosexuality and in the persecution ideas, nothing but two parallel forms of expression of the same schizophrenic shrinkage and destruction of human existence, namely two different attempts at regaining the lost parts of one's personality. (146–7)

Homosexuality is an attempt (albeit misguided) at self-completion in a society in which depletion is endemic. Julian Mitchell's 1963 novel *As Far As You Can Go* contains an unstable American youth, Eddie Jackson, who demands of the hero: 'You know why there are so many queers about these days? Because the race is beginning to get the idea. If we were all cut in half, way back there at the beginning, we've got to be looking for somebody of the same sex, right?' (226). Leonard Radcliffe holds a theory which, though less flippant, similarly attempts to take authority from antiquity. At Leonard's trial for the murder of Tolson, it is a shock to read, after a number of vague but fevered descriptions of the two men's love-making, that the Prosecution's report states 'there was no physical evidence of homosexual practices' (344).

This rational, simplistic rebuttal to a complex and passionate emotional and physical reality would seem to confirm Laing's stated need for a revolt against the depersonalising rhetoric of the establishment and psychiatry in particular. Yet Leonard, like Eddie Jackson, and Boss in the case-study of homosexual tendencies above, is himself determined to understand homosexual desire as symptomatic of a universal psychosis rather than an emotional and physical reality. This atmosphere of rational depersonalisation is increased in the narration of the courtroom scene by its determined denial of cognitive privilege over Leonard's subjectivity in favour of journalistic reportage:

> Then later, when he was trying to describe the relationship that had existed between Tolson and himself, he said, almost in tears, 'The battle was so intense between us because we could see something beyond it. It was the split between us that tormented us; the split in the whole of Western society.'
>
> When it was suggested that he was trying to obscure something which was intensely personal and distasteful to him by giving it an air of objectivity, by disguising it in terms of some general theory, he stated vehemently, 'You've got to *accept* that there is a love that exists between men which is neither obscene nor degrading, but is as powerful and as profound, and as fruitful, as that love which bears children. The love that men have for other men, as *men*, may be beyond some people's powers of comprehension. But it has a subtlety and a flexibility, a power that creates order. Politics, art, religion: these things are the products of men's loving. And by that I mean their hatred, their antagonism, their affection, as *men*, and their curiosity in one another as men. It isn't that women have been deprived of these things, but simply that they can't love *in this way*. They have been given something less abstract, more physical, something more easily understood. Law, art, politics, religion: these are the creation of men as *men*'. (345)

Leonard's love for Tolson, he asserts, was an intelligible attempt to blend his intellectuality, his rationality, with Tolson's primal purity of physical awareness, and thus reunite his divided self. In their attempt to make the concept of homosexuality culturally intelligible, both Leonard and Storey subjugate the concept to the binary hierarchisms of the dominant epistemology. Despite his efforts, Leonard's justification of instinctive love rings insincere in its attempts to intellectualise physical desire and sexual object-choice. Homosexuality may here have been dignified from a physical disease to a universal symptom, but it is still redolent with madness and sickness, and the novel's confusing and obfuscatory descriptive practices are symptomatic of this. Homosexuality, in its disruption of binary definitions, has wrecked narrative realism and corrupted the masculine text.

Writing the male body

It is not only homosexuality that can disrupt traditional narrative paradigms. A burgeoning frankness about heterosexual practices was apparent in Britain since the 1948 publication of the first Kinsey Report, *Sexual Behaviour in the Human Male*. Conducted in the United States, its revelations were nevertheless widely read and very influential in Britain, most notoriously, that of the incidence of homosexual experience amongst its sample of 5300 white males.[7] The Sixties, too, saw a new ubiquity of contraception, most notably in oral form: in Britain, Conovid became available in 1961, and by 1964 nearly half a million British women were taking a high-dose contraceptive pill. Sex could now occur more frequently outside the patriarchal, reproductive framework we saw to be so dominant in the preceding chapters.

The British equivalent of Kinsey, Masters and Johnson, published their research, *The Human Sexual Response*, in 1966, but by this time heterosexual psychosexual liberation had already become synonymous with the liberation of human expression, thanks in no small part to the obscenity trial surrounding the publication of D. H. Lawrence's *Lady Chatterley's Lover* (*Regina* versus *Penguin Books Ltd*, 1960). The fact that such a synonymity could and did occur within the popular consciousness speaks volumes about the gendering of that consciousness. Future feminist scholarship, particularly that of the French variety, sought to write the (female) body in order to inscribe opposition to the symbolic (and overwhelmingly phallic) systems of the presiding epistemology. For Irigaray and Cixous in particular, self-expression and liberation necessarily began with the expression of bodily experience. During the

Sixties, the liberation of the body from the repressive restraints of Western thinking was still officially to be dubbed a feminist project by the academy. However, as sexuality's traditional definition placed it in opposition to reason and language, and thus to received definitions of selfhood, it is already, by default, marked a *feminine* project. The concept of the body, saturated with its own materiality, as quintessentially feminine, and the mind as masculine, like nature versus culture, and private versus public, is a polarisation lingering from the Enlightenment. Yet if female sexuality can be considered to contain the potential to deconstruct and destroy phallic and symbolic patterns through an exploration of physical and libidinal difference, male sexuality too should have similar liberational potential in its authentic expression. As this book repeatedly stresses, male ≠ masculine, and penis ≠ phallus. 'Masculine' writing, as we have seen, characteristically effaces the body, making the expression of bodily reality and physical desire a potentially radical step for male literary liberation. This is emphatically not because sexuality is somehow more authentic than other human experience, for as Foucault concludes strongly in his introduction to *The History of Sexuality*: 'Sexuality must not be thought of as a kind of natural given which power tries to hold in check, or as an obscure domain which knowledge tries gradually to uncover. It is the name that can be given to a historical construct' (105). Sexuality is not innate, but as a construct it is in a potent position of opposition to masculinity.

During the allegedly 'permissive' Sixties, masculine defensive action against the accusation of feminisation in writing about sex frequently takes predictable forms. For the first time, almost totally reliable contraceptive methods offered both men and women the opportunity to explore (at least in theory) sex on both a quantitative and qualitative scale.[8] For men so minded, the unfettered nature of that sexuality could be couched as the unleashing of the primal force of male desire from its cultural fetters. Lawrentian literature, and *Chatterley* in particular (both text and court case), provided a perfect template for the conflation of the expression of the essential, sexual male with the liberation of all humanity. Foucault, with his (or his translator's) reference to the hypnotic cultural power of sex in contemporary society as 'the dark shimmer of sex' (157), illustrates the persistent power of Lawrentian sexual terminology. Just as female and male readers can be immasculated by the attendant principles they are obliged to accept in order to gain utopian narrative satisfaction, so a population striving for psychic and sexual liberation is encouraged to seek that liberation amidst the pages of a novel which transfigures male heterosexuality into religious might.

Masculine epistemology masquerades both as ontology and theology. John Thomas, his nomenclature marking his independence from Mellors the appendage, is a principle, a phallus, a godhead – not a penis. Feminised physicality is overridden by masculine power, the congenital by the dynamic. Kate Millett concludes of the novel that it is 'sexual politics in its most overpowering form' (238).

The dedication of John Berger's 1972 novel *G.* reads: 'For Anya and for her sisters in Women's Liberation' (5). Berger's reworking of the Don Juan myth shows sisterly solidarity in cherishing female knowledge (portrayed to be predominantly bodily rather than intellectual) as profoundly authentic and liberatory. As a child, G.'s crush on Miss Helen, his governess, leads him to consider her the fount of all the answers to his questions. G.'s child-like, unadulterated assessment of Miss Helen is vindicated by the narrative of his life and the novel: 'He senses or feels that she – by being all that is opposite and therefore complementary to him – can make the world complete for him. In adults sexual passion reconstitutes this sense. In a five-year-old it does not have to be reconstituted: it is still part of his inheritance' (49). 'Opposite and therefore complementary': though radical in respect of the gender hierarchies we have encountered in the novels considered so far, it is notable how Berger's sexual utopia remains a site of ruthlessly maintained sexual difference. This pattern of (without exception, hetero-) sexual attraction revealing truth is replicated in the description and effect of all G.'s adult sexual encounters, as the women he selects are utilised by the text to represent a purer mode of physical being, uncorrupted by public mores and expectations. His lover Marika, for example, 'made very little distinction between the idea of an action and the action itself; the words which expressed the idea tended to translate themselves straight away into messages to her limbs' (288). Such women, it would seem, by virtue of their social exclusion, are already liberated from the artificial constrictions of public mores and moralities. Wanting and being with liberated women is, for men, a means both of sexual and personal liberation.

The politics of heterosexual experience, the novel argues, have enormous potential. Following Marcuse, an adopted prophet of the Sixties counter-culture, in *G.* authentic sex is the antithesis of the capitalist socio-economic order and the encroachment of that order upon heterosexual relationships. Sex, in other words, can be socialist. As a heterosexual male outsider, G., like Don Juan, defines himself in opposition to a bourgeois world of inauthentic sexuality, where the male majority uses sex as a means of ownership. G. silently accuses Monsieur Hennequin and the businessman Harry Schuwey of believing that 'to touch is to claim as property. To fuck is to possess. And you take possession either by paying rent or by buying outright' (197). 'To fuck is to possess'; in the anti-utopia, power is empirically demonstrated by means of sex. In the introduction to *The History of Sexuality*, Foucault notes how, (in an age of repression), 'the sexual cause – the demand for sexual freedom, but also for the knowledge to be gained from sex and the right to speak about it – becomes legitimately associated with the honor of a political cause' (6). Berger's novel revels in the Second Wave's advantage over its matriarchs: Laura, G.'s mother, must, in the nineteenth century, necessarily reject the innate knowledge of her own body for an effective engagement with the body politic: 'In London she became more and more involved in her political interests. The secret of life, she considered, was no longer hidden in her own body but in the evolutionary process' (36). 'The knowledge to be gained from sex and the right to speak about it': as in much of the male-authored work we have considered, *G.* as a manifesto lies caught between these distinct concepts of sex as both primal knowledge and political dynamism, essential and existential.

G. merits his repeated nomination as 'principle protagonist' (9, 11, 27) because he chooses to act, randomly and sexually, disrupting class- and race-ridden Europe with his indiscrimination in female sexual partners. He finds fulfilment with servants and society sophisticates alike. In contrast, contemporary and capitalist masculinity remains static amidst his dynamic trajectories:

A man's presence was dependent upon the promise of power which he embodied. If the promise was large and credible, his presence was striking. If it was small or incredible, he was found to have little presence. There were men, even many men, who were devoid of presence altogether. The promised power may have been moral, physical, temperamental, economic, social, sexual – but its object was always exterior to the man. A man's presence suggested what he was capable of doing to you or for you. (166)

These men have relinquished action for the symbolisation of the potential to do, and contemporary manhood is existentialism stalled. Yet, as well as an existential hero, G. also functions as an agent of primal desires. In 'Marxist Fictions: The Novels of John Berger', Joseph H. McMahon notes how the First World War, about to begin as the novel ends, is also properly designated a 'libidinal monster' (220). G.'s similarly 'ungoverned libidinal force' (220), he argues, is distinguished from the bad male primal of mindless destruction by virtue of the hero's intellectual choices, however paltry the context in which they are made. The choice to channel the primal (male) libido into authentic political rebellion becomes conflated with an existential assertion against nothingness. Once again, here, the essential and the existential interplay to bolster the heroism of a male protagonist.

The critique in *G.* of contemporary history and the History it produces depends upon the then still revolutionary recognition of a now familiar opposition – that of History and herstory, the artificial masculine grand narrative and the earthy feminine mundane, or what the young G. identifies as the 'horse and harness smell' as opposed to 'the cowshed smell' (43). The novel explores whether history and historiography might be made to incorporate individual sexual experience, and there is an attempt to combine these perspectives (History/herstory) in an inclusive narrative idiom (as opposed to exclusionary objectivity). Its form is constructed around a narrator who alternates between first-person metaphysical and metafictional discussions on the one hand, and the third-person narration of the novel's plot on the other. As a text, *G.* attempts to prevent either the objectivity of the narrator or the subjectivity of the protagonist from dictating its viewpoint. It does this by repeatedly declaring the fallibility of the narrator's cognitive privilege – 'What the old man says I do not know. What the boy says in reply I do not know. To pretend would be to schematize' (61) – and by focalising its third-person portions through a variety of different characters, both male and female.

The template for this gender-reciprocity of voice is provided in the text when the young *G.* overhears his uncle and aunt, Jocelyn and Beatrice, siblings, and, it is revealed later, sexual partners:

> The boy listens on the stairs to their talking in the bedroom. Later he will realize that the cadence of their two voices is like that of a couple talking in bed: not amorously but calmly, reflectively, with pauses and ease. [...] Their words are not decipherable to the boy on the stairs. But the manner in which the male voice and the feminine voice overlap, provoke and receive each other, the two complementary substances of their voices, as distinct from one another as metal and stone, or as wood and leather, yet combining by rubbing together or chipping or scraping to make the noise of their dialogue – this is more eloquent than precise over-heard words could ever be, eloquent of the power of the decisions being taken. Against these decisions no third person, no listener, can appeal. (42)

This moment is instructive, too, in its valorisation of cadence over vocabulary. G. is frequently critically perceived to be an utterly anonymous hero, yet large portions of the text are emotionally focalised through him, particularly at the beginning and end of the novel. His forest encounter with the dead dray-horses (56–9), for example, is powerfully and emotively described, and his nausea rises again in response to Monsieur Hennequin's sophisticated gentleman's agreement over access to the body of his wife (303), the experiences linked with a common smell of paraffin. Yet still Geoff Dyer can remark in *Ways of Telling: The Work of John Berger*:

> What of G.? We know his history but almost nothing about him. There is probably no novel of comparable length in which the principal protagonist speaks so few lines (what few lines there are amount to little more than blank expressions of politeness.) He is felt as a powerful physical presence but communicates nothing about himself. (89)

G., in other words, is a troubling hero as he does not speak, and speaking is conflated, by Dyer and by the traditional tenets of masculinity, with protagonism. He is a radical hero not because he is anonymous, but rather because we as readers know frequently how he feels, though infrequently what he has to say. The tone of the first-person narrative is innovative, too, and stands in contrast to the 'I' of, say, *The Unfortunates*. It is open and confessional without expectation of a confessional increment. In the process of describing a dream, the narrator asserts of his chosen personal pronoun: 'I keep on saying "we" because I wasn't by myself, but I wasn't with any other specific people either, I was in the first person plural' (136). This resonates with Johnson's ideal of the 'collective-subjective', and the multiple-focalisations of Berger's novel ensure that *G.* is closer to achieving this bilateral narrative ideal than *The Unfortunates*.

The ultimate refutation both of objectivity and solipsism in the novel, however, is specifically sexual. More specifically, it is the orgasm, the moment when the equation 'the experience = I + life' (125) holds fleetingly absolute. This utopia, however, is antithetical to narrative, as to language itself:

> How to write about this? This equation is inexpressible in the third person and in narrative form. The third person and the narrative form are clauses in a contract agreed between writer and reader, on

the basis that the two of them can understand the third person more fully than he can understand himself; and this destroys the very terms of the equation.

Applied to the central moment of sex, all written nouns denote their objects in such a way that they reject the meaning of the experience to which they are meant to apply. [...] They are foreign, not because they are unfamiliar to reader or writer, but precisely because they are their third-person nouns. (125–6)

Language, in other words, is always to a certain extent objective, inevitably placing both its writer and its reader in an elevated 'seat of sense-making' which here, in contrast to the novels of Chapter 2, is undesirable and unfulfilling. Sex in *G.* is supposedly supremely natural, a repository of real, immanent experience for its heterosexual participants. Ann Rosalind Jones is able to note by 1981 that: 'All in all, at this point in history, most of us perceive our bodies through a jumpy, contradictory mesh of hoary sexual symbolization and political counter-response' (363). In *G.* in 1972, however, sex is celebrated as resoundingly pre-cultural, and as such, has the potential to liberate not just humanity, but also the traditional construction of narrative from its constricting cultural limitations. Heterosex demands that its narrator enters into a direct and immediate confrontation with reality:

All generalizations are opposed to sexuality.
   Every feature that makes her desirable asserts its contingency – here, here, here, here, here.
   That is the only poem to be written about sex – here, here, here, here – now. (124)

Literary sex is redemptive, in other words, because its immediacy refuses the possibility of objective description. Writing the body is understood as involving its writer and its reader in a redemptive confrontation with the inauthenticity of traditional writing: 'why does writing about sexual experience reveal so strikingly what may be a general limitation of literature in relation to aspects of all experience?' (124), the narrator asks. Yet this places the narrator of *G.* in a paradoxical position in relation to the characters he narrates. A third person, or the third-person, is associated throughout the novel with ignorance and exclusion, as when the young Giovanni witnesses his mother looking at his father: 'It is a look which confesses a secret common interest deriving from some past experience from which, by its nature rather than by its timing, he is conscious of being inevitably excluded. It is a look which makes him conscious of being the third person' (76). G., when older, receives such a look himself from his aunt just before losing his virginity:

> The look in Beatrice's eyes being in equal measure appealing and grateful is not the result of these two feelings co-existing. There is only one feeling. She has only one thing to say with her uncontrollable eyes. Nothing exists for her beyond this single feeling. She is grateful for what she appeals for; she appeals for what she is already grateful for. (128)

Beatrice's look is no gaze, and unlike Sartre's and Silverman's look, it does not lack, but is complete. Simply put, this is a look of desire, and true heterosexual desire in G. mends the flaws in heterosexual relationships (in which women are forced, 'unnaturally', to be both 'surveyor and surveyed', 167) and supplements the lack in looking. Yet if existential authenticity is concomitant with authentic sexual intimacy, then three within the textual relationship becomes a crowd. The reader or narrator of a sex scene written in the third-person are textual gooseberries, unfulfilled, embarrassed and embarrassing.

A solution to this problem is wrought within the narrative of G., but it is a solution that ultimately undermines the careful gender-reciprocity of the novel's focalisation. It contains a number of slippages between first- and third-person narration, and, tellingly, these occur at the moments of G.'s seduction of a varied portfolio of women. Declarations of love for these women in the first-person are attributed to G., if at all, only as an afterthought:

> Why do I want to describe her experience exhaustively, definitively, when I fully recognize the impossibility of doing so? Because I love her. I love you, Leonie. You are beautiful. You are gentle. You can feel pain and pleasure. You are tiny and I take you in my hand. You are large as the sky and I walk under you. It was he who said this (150–1);

> Marika, how I love you! Your smile is more complete than any last judgement. When you take off your clothes you are pure will. We make each other bodiless. All the rest are talkers or sensualists. Marika! When will G. say this? (291).

When it comes to the physical and metaphysical appreciation of women, G. can provide only one perspective, and it is male. It is also, of course, heterosexual. In a novel that makes the claim for sexual desire to revolutionise narrative, there remain scrupulous limitations upon the permitted origins and directions of that desire.

These limitations are still more apparent within the descriptions of sex themselves. There is one example of an attempt to relocate male desire away from the penis, which begins in a description of the taste of sugar:

> This is a taste whose effects are not confined to the mouth.
>
> Sweetness is like Eurydice's thread: it leads from the tongue down the throat and then, mysteriously, through the stomach to the sexual centre, to the tiny region (distinct in a male from the sexual organs themselves) where sexual pleasure accumulates before extending outwards in waves. (51–2)

Otherwise, however, the text makes no attempt to diffuse male sexual pleasure. The difficulty of writing the male body is that, thanks for the most part to masculinity's eternal metonymic project to conflate manhood with universality, biology with destiny, the penis as liberatory symbol is supremely difficult to distinguish from the phallus, instrument of patriarchal oppression. Writing the penis, of course, could be construed as a means of demystifying the phallus, and *G.* addresses itself to the possibilities of using the penis (as opposed to the phallus) as a vision of physical beauty:

> Formerly [Camille] has been aware of men wanting to choose her to satisfy desires already rooted in them, her and not another, because among the women available she has approximated the closest to what they need. Whereas he appears to have no needs. [...] The taste of his foreskin and of a single tear of transparent first sperm which has broken over the cyclamen head making its surface even softer to the touch than before, is the taste of herself made flesh in another. (226–7)

The reference to a cyclamen echoes *G.*'s loss of virginity with Beatrice: 'thus a cyclamen opening' (129). In its first appearance, the image of the flower is used to convey a fresh naturalness, and here it hearkens back to that firstness. The apprehension of this vision of unity is placed, significantly (and following *Lady Chatterley's Lover*), within a female consciousness, thus crediting and legitimating it with the natural instinct previously established to be innate in women. Throughout the novel, descriptions of G.'s penis remain femalely focalised:

> It did not astound Marika that she saw him naked as he danced. What astounded her was that she saw his penis. She had never before seen a man on his feet with his penis erect. It changed the whole body of a man. [...] In bed, seen from above or from the side, a penis looks like an object or a vegetable or a fish. His, during the waltz, was indefinable. It was red. It was thrust forward in the direction of its own progress. Its head shifted a little from side to side, as a horse's head when galloping. Often it was so acutely foreshortened that its body became invisible. All she saw was a darkness with a glowing ember at the entrance to it. She could smell the sulphur, she told herself, and it was making her feel giddy. (325–6)

'An erection is the beginning of a process of total idealization' (124), claims the narrator, but his narrative allows for an exclusively female idealisation of the erection. Desire for the penis has to be female desire; a description by the narrator in the first-person would disrupt the narrator/protagonist relationship. This relationship, then, is ultimately less innovative than might at first be supposed – it is homosocial and homophobic. The desiring look, though alleged to be free from society's enforcement of gender roles, is systematically coded as either masculine or feminine in opposition to its sexual object choice. The longed-for dissolution of culture can only take place, paradoxically, amidst culturally imposed binary oppositions: gender.

In its examination of heterosexual relationships and the writing of those sexual relationships, *G.* has a valid agenda: imagining a male freedom, in tandem with women's liberation, which is unbound from patriarchal and capitalist standards of objectivity and objectification. Yet, in its apprehension of gender at least, *G.* has flaws as a revolutionised *Bildungsroman*, as ultimately it reads like an all too familiar narrative. Geoff Dyer reasserts G.'s existential credentials in the following way: 'G.'s actions, then, are indistinguishable from the philanderer, but his determination to pursue his own ends in the face of social convention is disruptive, subversive; his consciousness is revolutionary' (91). Dyer's and Berger's shifting of the means of the legitimisation of G. from the libidinal to the existential make it difficult to distinguish G.'s penis from the phallus and his revolutionary sexual work from the comforting and continual conquest of Colin Wilson's Gerard Sorme. It is a temptation to view G.'s career as a philanderer, albeit an existentialist one, as a proffered means for men to fend off accusations of the contemporary male as '*castrati*' (88) amidst burgeoning female self-expression.

More tangibly, although the focalisation of the narrative may shift, the narrator of *G.* is always male, and his identification with G. at its strongest during the hero's fulfilment of heterosexual desire, when their characters become indistinguishable. The fact that this strong male identification occurs at the events in the text which its ideology upholds as both politically and spiritually vital for self-discovery, ensures that its narrative idiom finally denies inclusiveness. As this slippage between first- and third-person never occurs with any female, or any other, characters in the novel, the crucial and gender-specific relationship between the narrator and the protagonist, so prevalent in the masculine text, is maintained. After Chavez the heroic adventurer has crashed on the far side of the Alps, Mathilde tells her friend Camille of their prolonged stay in an unprepossessing Alpine town: 'I believe we are waiting, my dear, for the hero to die' (207). The narrator, from his privileged position, can note that 'next day, Chavez' last words, whose meaning cannot be interpreted, were: *Non, non, je ne meurs pas ... meurs pas*' (232). G. is indisputably a different kind of protagonist, but despite the novel's prolonged and innovative interrogation of traditional narrative, a vital tenet of his masculine textual credentials, the homosocial bond with a male narrator, is ultimately preserved. Such a bond, here proffering shares in the narrator's omniscience (he may not hear all, but he does see it), as well as the liberationist potential of sex with G.'s women, can thus be extended to the reader, provided they adopt the male, heterosexual viewpoint. The traditional hero, it would seem, is yet to die. Even with the best intentions, his mould is difficult to break.

A teenage ball

The final, and twenty-first, chapter of Anthony Burgess's novel *A Clockwork Orange*, published in 1962, concludes that Youth, portrayed throughout as a violent challenge to contemporary society, is actually a passing phase before real priorities kick in with an equilibrium of the hormones.[9] With the inclusion of this chapter, the novel retains its integrity as a *Bildungsroman*, charting moral growth as well as, as Morrison points out (xx), its numerological patterning of three sections with seven chapters. Alex grows up on the occasion of the twenty-first. The identification of this novel with the sanctioned rebellion of the Angry Young Men of the 1950s is invitingly easy: indeed, Jimmy Porter's anti-battle cry is echoed by Alex as he remarks: 'myself, I couldn't help a bit of disappointment at things as they were those days. Nothing to fight against really. Everything as easy as kiss-my-sharries. Still, the night was still very young' (14). The only good, brave cause may lie in bemoaning the lack of such a cause, but male individualistic assertion in a society which privileges male individual assertion still remains an act of conformity rather than rebellion.

The droogs' assault upon adulthood is conveyed by means of an attack upon traditional linguistic and literary values. Nadsat, the esoteric idiolect of Alex and his 'droogs' is conceived, both in the novel and the minds of its teenage inventors, as a threat. Despite the recognisable influence of the comic-book upon its turns of phrase, it does not function, as so many comics of the era did, as a linguistic education in traditional masculine imperatives. Morrison reports Burgess's disapproval of the inclusion in the original American version of a nadsat glossary (x), and we can speculate that this is because such a tool of objective definition contradicts the intended emotionality and instability of the idiom. It undermines too, of course, the reader's experience of its *foreignness*: the word 'nadsat' is etymologically 'a transliteration of the Russian suffix for "teen" ' (iii).

In *The Neophiliacs*, Booker notes how, after the election of J. F. Kennedy, a 'mechanically make-believe use of language, indiscriminately transforming the commonplace into a preconceived image of the remarkable, was, particularly in *The Observer*, *The Sunday Times* and their respective colour supplements, to become the most distinctive journalistic reflection of the spirit of the age' (151). In *A Clockwork Orange*, masculine tenets of belief dictate suspicion of a language used not necessarily to convey meaning, but dependent for communication upon sounds and associations instead. Alex notes of his cell-mate's incoherent speech: 'It was all this very old-time real criminal's slang he spoke' (68). The proliferation of such idiolects, in other words, is used as indicative of the dissolution of community in general, when it is in fact indicative of a threat to masculine linguistic rationality. At Alex's 'Reclamation Treatment' (75), a bitter parody of aversion therapy, he is asked his opinion of the cause of the nausea he has come to feel when watching violent films:

> 'These grahzny sodding veshches that come out of my gulliver and my plott,' I said, 'that's what it is.'
> 'Quaint,' said Dr Brodksy, like smiling, 'the dialect of the tribe. Do you know anything of its provenance, Branom?'
> 'Odd bits of old rhyming slang,' said Dr Branom, who did not look quite so much like a friend any more. 'A bit of gipsy talk, too. But most of the roots are Slav. Propaganda. Subliminal penetration.' (91)

Dr Branom's diagnosis involves a series of reductive judgments: Alex's dialect is tarnished by its association with the lower classes (rhyming slang), with gypsies, with the Eastern block (Slavs, and thus communism), and with the manipulation assumed to be endemic in communist politics. In John Wain's *Hurry on Down*, a young, working-class man was excluded from that novel's utopian masculine community on the basis that 'he talked a different language, for one thing; it was demotic English of the mid-twentieth century, rapid, slurred, essentially a city dialect and, in origin, essentially American' (175). It is a nice twist here, in the midst of the Cold War, that Burgess's demotic dialect is, in effect, 'essentially Russian', but still indicative of a betrayal of the core values of masculine selfhood and nation: still foreign.

Youth is portrayed as a threat in its antipathy to capitalist acquisition, as Alex argues against his droog Georgie's proposal of setting up a serious robbery:

> 'And what will you do,' I said, 'with the big big big deng or money as you so highfaluting call it? Have you not every veshch you need? If you need an auto you pluck it from the trees. If you need pretty polly you take it. Yes? Why this sudden shilarny for being the big bloated capitalist?' (43)

Alex's rehabilitation, as well as promising the reproduction of the patriarchal, capitalist family (by the end of the twenty-first chapter he is clipping pictures of laughing babies from glossy magazines and carrying them in his wallet), reasserts the authority of omniscient narration and universal cognitive privilege. The novel achieves this on a number of levels. As the novel's narrator, Alex has retrospective authority over his material, and his demonstrations of this control are frequent; 'So it was important to me, O my brothers, to get out of this stinking grahzny zoo as soon as I could. And, as you will viddy if you keep reading on, it was not long before I did' (63); 'I jumped, O my brothers, and I fell on the sidewalk hard, but I did not snuff it, oh no. If I had snuffed it I would not be here to write what I written have' (132). Both the selected quotations emphasise the fact that Alex's story is explicitly *written*, rather than told. The fact that he is in a position to write the story provides some reassurance from the very beginning of the novel that his rehabilitation will have been achieved by its end. Narrative, as we have seen throughout this chapter, is conceived to be curative, healthy. The cover of the 1983 Penguin edition of the novel bills its contents as the 'confessions' of Alex, calling for readers to grant a confessional increment to the narrator before they have opened the book.

The novel's creation of such a distinctive narrative voice (or rather, as the text is so emphatically a written one, a distinctive literary narrator) is further emblematic of the fact that the Author, though badly beaten towards the start of the novel, is not dead. Alex notes of the writer of A CLOCKWORK ORANGE and his wife, as the droogs are ready to leave the cottage called HOME, that 'the writer veck and his zheena were not really there, bloody and torn and making noises. But they'd live' (22). Staying at HOME after his 'Reclamation Treatment' is complete, Alex finds a copy of A CLOCKWORK ORANGE on the writer's bookshelf and notes of his name 'F. Alexander', 'Good bog, [...] he is another Alex' (124). Indeed, while undergoing the treatment, his sudden realisation of its true and brutal purpose, and the documentary integrity of the films he took to be cleverly edited, is signalled by the involuntary plea: 'Am I just to be like a clockwork orange?' (100). Like Jim Dixon's 'totem-pole epiphany' in *Lucky Jim*, when he finally says out loud what he thinks, individual authenticity is signalled by the coincidence of imaginative, literary language and public self-expression. Intimations of Alex's immanent surrender to adulthood come during the visit of the Minister of the Interior to his cell at the end of his treatment. Alex writes:

> You could viddy who was the real important veck right way, very tall and with blue glazzies and with real horrorshow platties on him, the most lovely suit, brothers, I had ever viddied, absolutely in the heighth of fashion. He just sort of looked right through us poor plennies, saying, in a very beautiful real educated goloss: 'The Government cannot be concerned any longer with outmoded penological theories.' (73)

His word ordering and lack of punctuation in the phrase 'real educated goloss' prevents a definitive decision as to whether 'real' is intended to qualify 'educated' or 'goloss': however, the novel's conclusion, which leaves Alex on the brink of developing the voice he has been using in his narration, suggests the latter. Initially, Alex has mocked an article 'about how Modern youth would be better off if A Lively Appreciation of the Arts could be like encouraged' (35), as classical music routinely functions as foreplay to his bouts of ultraviolence. By the novel's close, however, he has been rehabilitated by the form of the novel itself. He is educated in the 'Three Rs' of masculinity: rationality, realism and retrospection.

Yet although Alex's retrospective narration is some demonstration of his eventual conformity with masculine-prescribed standards of rationality and narrative coherence, his self-narration is not entirely dissonant with the priorities of his younger incarnation. Though not his rational,

Alex's *emotional* identification is with his boyish self. Rather than urging a similarly emotional identification in the reader and a concomitant recognition of the cruelty of the treatment, however, the text implies that boys are emotional precisely because emotion is childish. Describing himself strapped to a chair in the Institute with his eyelids prized and clamped open, Alex plaintively writes: 'And then the lights went out and there was Your Humble Narrator and Friend sitting alone in the dark, all on his frightened oddy knocky, not able to move nor shut his glazzies nor anything' (81). Rather than fear, the reader is, in contrast, allowed to share the superior adult understanding of one of the doctors when Alex remarks to him:

> 'This must be a real horrorshow film if you're so keen on my viddying it.' And one of the white-coat vecks said, smecking:
> 'Horrorshow is right, friend. A real show of horrors.' (81)

Alex's 'clockwork orange epiphany' is here pre-empted by a 'horror-show' epiphany of the reader's own, as the word 'horrorshow' is reinstated in its adult, literal (and English[10]) meaning, over and above its nadsat association with pleasure. An 'anxiety of influence' over the infection of rational language with a superficial discourse, dependent upon association and dictated by the young, is dispelled. Alex ends the final chapter by writing:

> Yes yes yes, there it was. Youth must go, ah yes. But youth is only being in a way like it might be an animal. No, it is not just like being an animal so much as being like one of these malenky toys you viddy being sold in the streets, like little chellovecks made out of tin and with a spring inside and then a winding handle on the outside and you wind it up grrr grrr grrr and off it itties, like walking, O my brothers. But it itties in a straight line and bangs straight into things bang bang and it cannot help what it is doing. Being young is like being like one of these malenky machines. (148)

Booker's fear of a youth-inspired, media-adopted 'mechanically make-believe use of language' (1969, 61) is quelled by a reassertion of linguistic and artistic rationality, by implication a reassertion of an adult and essential(ist) masculinity. As *A Clockwork Orange*'s narrator concludes of himself, 'Alex like groweth up, oh yes' (148).

In its examination of white English youth, Colin MacInnes's 1959 *Absolute Beginners* affords a more radical disruption of masculine narrative.

In his introduction to the 1969 MacInnes anthology *Visions of London*, Francis Wyndham reads the novel's narrative voice as doubled by the kind of retrospective analysis familiar from our consideration of *Scenes from Provincial Life* and *A Clockwork Orange*:

> The author has taken a flying leap into the heart of the 'teen-age thing', allowing himself no opportunity for withdrawal and comparative detachment. This results in a slight falsification: the narrator seems too good to be true, for not only does he have the charms, originality and *insouciance* of a symptom, but also the wit, wisdom and experience of the diagnosis. (viii)

Wyndham's use of the phrase 'wit, wisdom and experience' with reference to the omniscience of retrospective analysis leaves no doubt as to its privilege over 'charms, originality and *insouciance*', but if further proof were necessary, it is present in the diagnosis of illness. Subjectivity is a *symptom* of sickness, and objectivity its cure. In contrast, Steven Connor attributes the radical nature of the narration to its deliberate refusal to 'concede to the novel's tendency to typify the particular' (90). Rather, he claims, it may be distinguished by the way it relates incidents without any apparent plot development of the narrative. The young narrator remains an 'absolute beginner' throughout, untransformed by the benefits of hindsight and adulthood. Connor claims that the novel is anti-realist in its refusal of two crucial aspects of the social 'condition of England' novel: it simplifies the conventional dialectic of character and context, by making the unnamed narrator the period of history through which he lives, and it thwarts the expectations of development and growth, by its narrative stasis and by its invention of a linguistic register which emphasises an 'incommensurability of narrator and readership' (91).

Such incommensurability is occasionally signalled in the text by dissonant narratorial comment, as here: 'I should explain (and I hope you'll believe it, even though it's true)' (288). The more general technique of such a register may be exemplified by its merry incorporation of a lengthy description of the functioning of canal locks, born of the assumption that the reader, like the narrator, has never been outside London:

> This is the spiel. You form up in a queue, just like at the Odeon, then, when it's your turn, sail in at one end, into a sort of square concrete well, and they shut two big doors behind you, as if you were going

away inside the nick, and there you are, like pussy at the bottom of
the drain. Then the lock-keeper product – with a peaked cap, and an
Albert watch-chain, and rubber boots – throws some switches or
other, and the water gushes in, and you'd hardly credit it, but you
start going up yourself! (397)

Elsewhere – in *A Clockwork Orange* for example – the innocence of the
narrator's experiencing self has been utilised to increase the reader's
sense of rational superiority. *Absolute Beginners* is different. Not only
does the child-like exuberance of the description make the experience
new (or at least newer) for the reader, but the narrator's assumption of
consonance implicitly critiques a stance that much of contemporary
fiction portrays to be 'natural', that is, the reader shares its point of view.
The text's lyricism is increased by its distance from empiricism, by its
dissonance with the adult reader's experience:

So I went out of the Dubious to catch the summer evening breeze.
The night was glorious, out there. The air was sweet as a cool bath,
the stars were peeping nosily beyond the neons, and the citizens
of the Queendom, in their jeans and separates, were floating down
the Shaftesbury avenue canals, like gondolas. Everyone had loot to
spend, everyone a bath with verbena salts behind them, and nobody
had broken hearts, because they were all ripe for the easy summer
evening. (322)

With his teenage dialect, the novel's narrator, then, begins to take on the
characteristics of Connor's conception of self as a question of style:

Absolute Beginners seems to suggest an abandonment of the large,
assimilative perspective of the nation-novel and the novel-nation in
favour of the self-inventing and self-legitimating communities of
style that were increasingly generated by the explosion of pop and
youth culture in Britain from the 1950s on. (91)

The novel achieves its assertion of the new values of teenage style while
simultaneously mocking the empty signifiers by which the youth phenomenon is distinguished by adults. MacInnes's narrator shares
Hewison's disgust, noted earlier in this chapter, at the thought of an
identity sketched from media sound-bites:

'I dunno about the trouble with *me*,' my oafo brother finally declared,
'but *your* trouble is, you have no social conscience.'

'No what?'

'No social conscience.'

He'd come up close, and I looked into his narrow, meanie eyes.

'That sounds to me,' I said, 'like a parrot-cry pre-packaged for you by your fellow squalids of the Ernie Bevin club.'

'Who put you where you are.'

'Which who? And put me where?'

And now this dear 50 per cent relative of mine came up and prodded my pectorals with a stubby, grubby digit.

'It was the Attlee administrations,' said my bro., in his whining, complaining, platform voice, 'who emancipated the working-man, and gave the teenagers their economic privileges.' (283)

Wyndham's judgement on the novel's nameless narrator, though intended as praise, is riddled with a similar assumption, that 'wit, wisdom and experience' are antithetical to youth, yet the novel's narrator, like the Spades in MacInnes's preceding novel, *City of Spades*, possesses them *in* spades. This subaltern narratorial authority is what makes the novel radical, rather than the stasis of its narrative, or the gap between that narrative and its readers.

Just as *A Clockwork Orange*'s final narrative conclusion comes from Alex's acceptance of the ideal of reproductive sexuality within a patriarchal, capitalist framework, so the refusal of the narrator of *Absolute Beginners* to provide narrative progression may be linked with his refusal to conform to such a compromised standard of humanity and sexuality. Not that the narrator opposes capitalism. Randall Stevenson notes how 'by 1962, young people were spending £850 million annually on themselves' (22), and one of the radical characteristics of the narrator's male teenage-hood is his easy, guilt-free adoption and exploitation of the principles of the consumer market. Symbolically, he is a photographer, his living earned immortalising the superficial on a shiny surface, and he is as comfortable blurring the boundaries between art and pornography as he is blurring those between genders and stylistic influences in his dress code:

I had on precisely my full teenage drag that would enrage [Vernon] – the grey pointed alligator casuals, the pink neon pair of ankle crêpe nylon-stretch, my Cambridge blue glove-fit jeans, a vertical-striped happy shirt revealing my lucky neck-charm on its chain, and the Roman-cut short-arse jacket just referred to ... not to mention my wrist identity jewel, and my Spartan warrior hair-do, which everyone thinks costs me 17/6d. in Gerrard Street, Soho, but which I, as a matter of fact, do myself with a pair of nail-scissors and a three-sided mirror that Suzette's got, when I visit her flatlet up in Bayswater, w.2. (278)

The narrator's golden rule for a morally acceptable negotiation of the consumer market, however, is to ensure that the only objects of exchange it involves should be consumer goods. Money is desirable only in that it can be exchanged freely for such goods. Hoarding and fetishising money itself marks you out as a 'conscript', one of the narrator's habitual terms of moral criticism:

> This teenage ball had had a real splendour in the days when the kids discovered that, for the first time since centuries of kingdom-come, they'd money, which hitherto had always been denied to us at the best time in life to use it, namely, when you're young and strong, and also before the newspapers and telly got hold of this teenage fable and prostituted it as conscripts seem to do to everything they touch. Yes, I tell you, it had a real savage splendour in the days when we found that no one couldn't sit on our faces any more because we'd loot to spend at last, and our world was to be our world, the one we wanted and not standing on the doorstep of somebody else's waiting for honey, perhaps. (258)

A strong distinction is made between exploitation of the market (which the narrator's friend Wiz, 'the number one hustler of the capital' (260), used to do in his conveyancing work, 'introducing A to B, or *vice versa*' (260) so that they might exchange their goods and cut him in) and the exploitation of people within a market framework. Wiz himself is somewhat bemused by the narrator's outburst at his move into pimping: ' "And this," he said gently, "comes from a kiddo known around the town for flogging pornographic photos" ' (320). Another habitual term to convey disapprobation in the novel is the narrator's application of the word 'product' to people: he distinguishes between 'real' teenagers and those sucked in by media exploitation of the phenomenon by referring to the latter as 'teenage products' (311). The prostitute who supports Wiz is discredited by a note of the fact that she 'had a way of *looking* at you as if you were a possibly valuable product' (383).

The novel does offer up an antidote to the corruption of human relations by consumerism, and, predictably, it is a heterosexual relationship. Yet the narrator distinguishes himself by a telling description of his love for Suzette in his declaration that 'I swear the thought of her was more me then than I was' (338) – she is part of his subjectivity, rather than his desired sexual object. When the couple finally have sex, he is careful to distinguish it *from* sex, to avoid a negative context of exploitation, as after rescuing her from race riots in the city, he 'went and got the bowl and things, and washed her all over, and I kissed her between, and there in my place at Napoli we made it at last, but honest, you couldn't say that it was sexy – it was just love' (442).

It is telling, though, that this allegedly 'new' code of heterosexual relationships bears a strong resemblance to the ancient one of chivalry. Telling, too, that one of the only times in the novel that the word 'product' is used to describe a person without condemning them is in a reference to his friends' son, whom he calls 'their youthful warrior product, Saul' (328). *This* particular brand has integrity and is desirable. Wiz is quick to diagnose a traditionalist trait in his friend: 'I paid for him, and Wiz didn't mind my paying, only laughed that little ha-ha laugh of his as we walked down the white and silver metal stair. "Boy," he said, "you're a born adult number. With your conventional outlook, you just can't wait to be a family man" ' (259–60). After sex, and after making a meal which the reader sees them 'scoffing like some old married couple' (442), the narrator leaves Suzette in his bed, vowing that they will leave the riots of Napoli the following day on their honeymoon. Though the novel never reaches this resolution, the fact that it is established as a future event, and one which we are given no reason to doubt *will* occur happily ever after, gives the lie to Steven Connor's characterisation of the novel as a narrative without progression.

MacInnes' novel is just as serious as *G.* in its project to rewrite the terms of History, although it does explicitly reject the Marxist model precisely on the basis of its narrative stasis:

But I saw I was breaking one of my golden rules, which is not to argue with Marxist kiddies, because they *know*. And not only do they know, they're not *responsible* – which is the exact opposite of what they think they are. I mean, this is their thing, if I dig it correctly. You're *in* history, yes, because you're budding here and now, but you're *outside* it, also, because you're living in the Marxist future. And so, when you look around, and see a hundred horrors, and not only musical, you're not responsible for them, because you're beyond them already, in the kingdom of K. Marx. But for me, I must say, all the horrors I see around me, especially the English ones, I feel responsible for, the lot, just as much as for the few nice things I dig. (373)

The title of the novel itself contains a complex joke about the outmoded nature of Marxist divisions of class. Outside a dance academy the narrator passes, the sign reads:

CURRENT CLASSES
MEDALLISTS CLASS
BEGINNERS PROGRESSIVE CLASS
BEGINNERS PRACTICE
ABSOLUTE BEGINNERS

and I said out loud, 'Boy, that one's us! Although me, after my experiences, maybe I'm going to move up a category or two!' (409)

Self-identification is no longer with reference to a traditional, static class structure, but instead to a dynamic meritocracy. *Absolute Beginners* contains two historiographers – the narrator and his father: ' "And how's the book going?" I asked my poor old ancestor. Which is a reference to a *History of Pimlico* Dad's said to be composing, but nobody's ever seen it, though it gives him the excuse for getting out of the house, and chatting to people, and visiting public libraries, and reading books' (280). On his father's death, the narrator is given a dog-eared package by his half-brother Vernon and opens it to find 'hundreds of sheets all grubby and altered and corrected, except for the first one, where he'd written on a single page, *"History of Pimlico. For my one and only son"* ' (445). The text of that particular History is not made available to the reader; it does not need to be, for what it represents, a blend of history and History, the personal and the objective, is realised in the text of the novel itself.

The tactic of appeal to the solidarity of a masculine community in any analysis of the state-of-the-nation is explicitly rejected. In fact, it is equated with a *loss* of manhood. At Big Jill's house, the narrator throws down the local newspaper after reading Amberley Drove's column on the race riots in anger: ' "What's the matter with our men?" I said to her. "Can't they hold their own women? Do they have to get this pronk (and I bashed the Dale daily on to the chair back) to help them and protect them?" ' (418). Confronted with the reality of the riots, however, the narrator is unable to record it in his customary way: 'I took up my Rolleiflex, but put it down again, because it didn't seem useful any longer' (435). Unlike marriage and a family, a conclusion that is only promised to the reader, the promise of the narrator's decision to abandon his camera is fulfilled in the text itself: he has stopped taking pictures, and started to write.[11] Youth has produced a new type of text, a text that proffers a traditional conclusion without conclusively closing its narrative and achieves a subjective authority without making claims to objectivity. The liberational and cultural potential of this new young masculine narrative, however, is to be severely compromised by events at the end of the Sixties. The absolute beginners, it seems, were never to make it to the medallists' class. The eruption into violence that began with the Parisian student/worker strikes of May 1968, in Christopher Booker's words, 'provided a jolt to that adulation of Youth for its own sake that since the middle Fifties had become perhaps the predominant characteristic of societies all over the world, from the affluent West to Mao-Tse-Tung's China: a final tragic-comic disproof of the belief in young people's innate "individuality" and "originality" ' (296). That year was the most seismic of the Sixties internationally, seeing the événements in Paris, the assassinations of Robert Kennedy and Martin Luther King, the Baader-Meinhof terrorist outrages in Germany, and Russian tanks crushing the Czech Revolution during the Prague Spring. In England's case these events had the potential to provoke a realisation that the youthful rebellions of the domestic permissive era ultimately had no political implications at all, as their fervour failed to provide coherent social and political alternatives to those structures they rebuked. Morgan concludes that Sixties culture in Britain 'posed no questions and operated within familiar social and economic parameters' (262).

A rational rebellion

The novels considered in this chapter, with the notable exceptions of *Absolute Beginners* and *G.*, tend towards a reassertion of traditional masculine values of rationalism even as they purport to explode such values. Even the innovative narration of *Absolute Beginners* gestures towards the traditionalist narrative closure of marriage, and *G.* maintains its narrator as male and heterosexual. Just as young male rebels rebel only within the limits sanctioned by their elders, so too are these male writers confusingly complicit with policing the limits of their own innovation. Sexual liberation and youth, apparently in opposition to patriarchal authority, are in fact designated as worthy of literary consideration by the standards of that very authority itself. This chapter has shown how the incorporation of such topics into the fictional output of male authors is less a concerted process of appropriation than a piecemeal attempt fraught with some genuine aspiration, debilitating reflexes and intense anxiety. Subjectivity is coming to be recognised as a political space. Crucially, though, it is also a *gendered* space, and further, a *feminine* space. A long-established epistemology marks the subjective as irrational, fraught with relativity, sick, and even mad. We have seen how masculine values tend to conflate writing with rational, realist, linear narratives and with an identification between character and author and reader. An aetiological narrative, a story-chain of cause and effect, is crucial both to an essentialist and an existential conception of the masculine self. In owning up to its subjectivity, then, the existence of writing itself is considered to be under threat. This threat results in a contradiction: texts professing the intention to surrender narrative authority end in a reflex reassertion of that authority itself. The assumed assurance of a confessional increment ensures that authorial presence is increased rather than abandoned. Writing pertaining to these 'masculine' values is upheld as rehabilitation for droogs and drop-outs alike.

5
Credit for Confession – Gendered Addressivity in the Contemporary Male-Authored Novel

> Was he being inadequate, or was he being English?
>
> Malcolm Bradbury, *Stepping Westward* (1965)

The year 1956 is routinely characterised by historical commentators as something of a seismic year for Britain with regard to its international and imperial reputation. In *The People's Peace*, Kenneth O. Morgan characterises it to be the year that saw:

> Almost the last British independent military venture in the twentieth century, and amongst the most humiliating. It tore apart the Anglo-American relationship and damaged the unity of the Commonwealth. It made Britain a pariah at the United Nations and brought its economic stability into grave question.
>
> [...] Worst of all, the British stood branded as offenders against international law, if not plain liars. (153–4)

The various vainglorious and increasingly isolating decisions of the British government played out after the announcement on 19 July by both Britain and the United States that they were unable to participate in financing the construction of the Aswan High Dam due to enduring Egyptian connections with the Soviet Union. A week later, President Nasser seized the Suez Canal under a nationalisation decree, intending to use revenues from the waterway to fund the project. The invasion and bombardment of Egypt by British and French troops, wreathed in anachronistic rhetoric by Prime Minister Eden (he likened Nasser to Hitler), culminated in a ceasefire demanded by the US and the United Nations at the beginning of November. The last Anglo-British troops departed on 22 December, leaving UN salvage crews to clear the Canal of their debris, a task which took two months to complete.

Kazuo Ishiguro's 1989 novel *The Remains of the Day* takes as its setting this final, post-Indian, summer of British pretensions to global political influence. Its narrator is Mr Stevens (the formality of his address never drops to reveal his first name), the ageing butler of England's Darlington Hall. One of the ways in which the redundancy of Stevens's professional and interior life is signalled is by means of his unstinting and syco-phantic national confidence, as when he notes:

A quality that will mark out the English landscape to any objective observer as the most deeply satisfying in the world, and this quality is probably best summed up by the term 'greatness'. [...] We call this land of ours *Great* Britain, and there may be those who believe this a somewhat immodest practice. Yet I would venture that the landscape of our country alone would justify the use of this lofty adjective. (28)

Stevens's national pride rests heavily upon a sense of an organic superiority and beauty that is superior and beautiful precisely due to its understated nature: 'In comparison', he claims on the authority of his excursions into the *National Geographic Magazine*, 'the sorts of sights offered in such places as Africa and America, though undoubtedly very exciting, would, I am sure, strike the objective viewer as inferior on account of their unseemly demonstrativeness' (29).

As one of the increasingly influential group of 'international' writers (both he and Salman Rushdie use the term approvingly), Kazuo Ishiguro, born in Japan and arriving in Britain at the age of six, lies outwith the pro-claimed scope of this study. Yet though his motives for the projection of a quintessentially English male psyche may be distinct from many of the authors considered here, the fact that *The Remains of the Day* stands as a revealing testimony to the changing priorities and techniques of English male-authored narrative over the second half of the twentieth century justifies its consideration here. In *The Modern British Novel* Malcolm Bradbury seems determined to place the oriental origins of the novel's author at its hermeneutic heart; he identifies him as following 'a historic (and near-Japanese) code of deference, obedience and reticence', and its narrative as one 'in which Jamesian precision and Japanese aesthetic economy merge' (475).[1] Stevens himself would be affronted at the sug-gestion that any other race might excel at reticence or precision, though the cultural comparisons he selects are considerably closer to home:

Continentals are unable to be butlers because they are as a breed incapable of the emotional restraint which only the English race is capable of. [...] In a word, 'dignity' is beyond such persons. We English have an important advantage over foreigners in this respect and it is for this reason that when you think of a great butler, he is bound, almost by definition, to be an Englishman. (43)

Ironically, of course, Stevens's proud characterisation of Englishmen as a 'natural' race of butlers (and his own post-war position in service to the American Mr Farraday) unwittingly naturalises Britain's enforced position in the post-Suez political world: one of subservience to the United States, albeit disguised, in the post-Suez 1957 conference in Bermuda between Macmillan and Eisenhower at least, as one of parity.

We have noted how issues of English masculinity are intertwined with those of contemporaneous national identity and Britain's international role. Ishiguro's novel parodies and rejects two templates for the male gender. The first is exemplified by Stevens's inter-war employer, Lord Darlington, who, in choosing to devote his time to ameliorating relations between Germany and the rest of Europe, unwittingly becomes, as his young godson claims, 'the single most useful pawn Herr Hitler has had in this country for his propaganda tricks' (224). His Lordship's 1923 informal conference reaches a fraught climax with the speech of the American senator Mr Lewis, who identifies Darlington as '*an amateur*', adding that 'international affairs today are no longer for gentlemen amateurs. The sooner you here in Europe realize that the better' (102). His host appears to secure a traditional moral victory as he counters: 'Let me say this. What you describe as "amateurism", sir, is what I think most of us here still prefer to call "honour" ' (103). That this kind of victory, however, was no longer valid nor achievable in 1956, was neatly demonstrated in the collapsed career and health of Prime Minister Anthony Eden, admired pre-Suez, Morgan notes, as 'the stylish prince of international diplomacy' (153).[2]

The second mode of masculine behaviour to be deconstructed within the novel is the 'emotional restraint' of the narrator himself. In an essay entitled 'The Unreliable Narrator', David Lodge says of what he calls Stevens's 'butlerspeak' that 'viewed objectively, the style has no literary merit whatsoever. It is completely lacking in wit, sensuousness and originality. Its effectiveness as a medium for this novel resides precisely in our growing perception of its inadequacy for what it describes' (155). This dearth of cadence is fully established within the novel's opening sentence, with its ridiculous and immediately redundant attempt to calibrate a state of non-assertion: 'It seems increasingly likely that I really will undertake the expedition that has been preoccupying my imagination now for some days' (3). Stevens's voice speaks from the year, and possibly even the month, that the first staging of *Look Back in Anger* sounded Jimmy Porter's call to rebel against the patriarchal Establishment.[3] He recounts his (butler) father's favourite, and probably apocryphal, tale of a butler who dealt with a tiger under the table of his master's mansion in India by means of a shot-gun, sang-froid, and the understated announcement that, come dinner-time, 'there will be no discernible traces left of the recent occurrence' (36). Stevens claims generational superiority over his father's peer group, claiming it 'was not one accustomed to discussing and analysing in the way ours is and I believe the telling and retelling of this story was as close as my father ever came to reflecting critically on the profession he practised' (36). Yet he goes on to narrate his own equivalent of the tiger-under-the-table story: the 1923 pro-Fascist conference he professes the 'turning point in my professional development' (110). There, he served seamlessly downstairs while his father passed away in an attic room. Beyond registering a professional pride, Stevens proves himself unable to discuss or analyse (in our contemporary, psychoanalytical sense of the word) that occurrence in any meaningful way, thus paradoxically reinforcing his uncritical commitment to his father's principles whilst betraying the man in the most profound personal way.

Two of the novel's supporting male cast offer alternative models for masculinity, each characterised by a very vocal rejection of the perceived presiding values of their father's generation, particularly that of ossified class divisions. Reggie Cardinal, Darlington's aristocratic godson, earns a living as a morally engaged, morally outraged newspaper columnist, who attempts to spur Stevens into a response to his employer's political affiliations with the Nazi party: 'Are you content [...] to watch his lordship go over the precipice just like that?' (224). He does not succeed, of course, and Stevens is later to register Cardinal's destruction by the very forces that endangered his godfather: 'I was then obliged to inform Miss Kenton of the gentleman's being killed in Belgium during the war' (234). Stevens's unscheduled stop in the village of Moscombe in Devon, enforced by his American employer's mighty Ford running out of fuel, confronts him with a certain Harry Smith. Stevens's utterances are characterised by a determination not to be 'presumptuous' (4), but Smith is shamelessly unfettered in this regard:

> The way I see it, England's a democracy, and we in this village have suffered as much as anyone fighting to keep it that way. Now it's up to us to exercise our rights, every one of us. Some fine young lads

from this village gave their lives to give us that privilege, and the way I see it, each one of us here now owes it to them to play our part. (189)

His speech is distinguished within the diegesis by means of its marked self-assertion; its determination to register itself as personal with the repetition of 'the way I see it'. Amidst the stilted calibrations of Stevens's self-expression, the direct nature of Smith's rant is a relief.

At the close of *The Remains of the Day*, Stevens sits at dusk on Weymouth Pier, where a man strikes up a conversation with him. He mentions that, until his retirement three years previously, he was the butler (and sole full-time employee) of a nearby house. When Stevens reveals his own position, the man responds, laughing, 'And here I was trying to explain it all to you. [...] Good job you told me when you did before I made a right fool of myself. Just shows you never know who you're addressing when you start talking to a stranger' (242). The masculine texts of the 1950s, we have seen, attempt to create and enforce a certain ideal reader precisely in response to this strangeness of the addressee. Much of the interwoven pathos and comedy of Ishiguro's novel comes from the fact that there is no possibility of an ideal recipient of Stevens's narrative. He repeatedly utilises a second-person mode of address, which functions each time as a pathetically empty signifier, with no possible reference in an audience contemporary to the novel's publication, or even to the novel's setting. 'You will not dispute, I presume', Stevens asserts, 'that Mr Marshall of Charleville House and Mr Lane of Bridewood have been the two great butlers of recent times. Perhaps you might be persuaded that Mr Henderson of Branbury Castle also falls into this rare category' (34). Passing a sign as he drives deeper into the West Country, he opines to his non-existent confidant, 'Perhaps "Mursden" will ring a bell for you, as it did for me upon my first spotting it on the road atlas yesterday. [...] Mursden, Somerset, was where the firm of Giffen and Co. was once situated, and it was to Mursden one was required to dispatch one's order for a supply of Giffen's dark candles of polish, "to be flaked, mixed into wax, and applied by hand" ' (133).

This 'you' is of a very different character to that used in the narrative, say, of *Saturday Night and Sunday Morning*: a 'you' which attempts to coax the reader into an imaginative leap into identification, a dynamic idiom provoking a homosocial character in its audience. Stevens's 'you', in contrast, is inherently solipsistic. It naively assumes a 'natural' and immediate shared viewpoint, similar to the effect we observed in

Absolute Beginners, as when the teenage narrator gives 'the spiel' on the functioning of canal locks (397). This mode of address in the voice of a young man is endearingly innocent and optimistic, but in the voice of an old man, with fewer days remaining, it engenders only pathos.

Stevens relates the visit of some American acquaintances of Mr Farraday's to Darlington Hall. In response to their questions about the history of the house, the butler denies having been in the employ of the eponymous Lord. He attempts to justify this lie as follows:

> It seems to me that my odd conduct can be very plausibly explained in terms of my wish to avoid any possibility of hearing any further such nonsense concerning his lordship; that is to say, I have chosen to tell white lies in both instances as the simplest means of avoiding unpleasantness. This does seem a very plausible explanation the more I think about it. (126)

We noted a propensity in the purportedly 'Angry' genre of male-authored fifties fiction (and the criticism surrounding it) to elide the empirical with the rational. The obvious unreliability of Stevens's account, however, is foregrounded precisely by a sharp distinction between these two methods for the acquisition of knowledge. In his search for a 'plausible explanation', Stevens utterly ignores the evidence of his own experience, constructing instead a perfectly rational, yet fundamentally fallacious, justificatory narrative for his actions and reactions. The impossibility and inauthenticity of a position as 'objective observer' is demonstrated throughout the novel. Stevens's doomed desire for such a viewpoint is parodied in his recourse to the outmoded 'one' idiom in times of heightened emotional experience. He approaches Miss Kenton, for example, ostensibly to offer his condolences at the news she has that day received of the death of her aunt, and yet is able only to voice a criticism of Miss Kenton's newly employed maids:

> Naturally, when one looks back to such instances today, they may indeed take the appearance of being crucial, precious moments in one's life; but of course, at the time, this was not the impression one had. Rather, it was as though one had available a never-ending number of days, months, years in which to sort out the vagaries of one's relationship with Miss Kenton. (179)

Though Stevens does appeal regularly to a notional shared experience through his use of the 'you' idiom, his attempted empiricism, as we have seen, is utterly invalidated by the fact that no addressee could plausibly have had that experience.

In contrast to the earnest honesty of novels of the 1950s like *Room at the Top*, then, Stevens's narrative is characterised by its unreliability. He repeatedly conceals his own motives, as here, where his self-interest as an employee of a businessman in denouncing the credibility of the Hayes Society, is not acknowledged:

> It was made clear, furthermore, that the Society did not regard the houses of businessmen or the 'newly rich' as 'distinguished', and in my opinion this piece of out-dated thinking crucially undermined any serious authority the Society may have achieved to arbitrate on standards in our profession. (32)

Yet as we shall see in our consideration in this chapter of the characteristic mode of male narration in popular English fiction spanning the turn of the century, the contrast of Stevens's narrative with what we may loosely term 'Ladlit', is *not* necessarily this unreliability. This contemporary genre might in fact be considered to be distinguished precisely by its acceptance of the possibility of perceptual inconsistency, and occasional, emotionally motivated self-delusion. Rather, Stevens's narrative anachronism, his crime against the contemporary male mode, is his emotional denial, his betrayal of the terms of narrative confession and of his chosen diary form.[4] Returning once again to the question of his stilted collusion in the politics of his former employer, Stevens is unrepentant (almost) to the end:

> How can one possibly be held to blame in any sense because, say, the passage of time has shown that Lord Darlington's efforts were misguided, even foolish? [...] It is hardly my fault if his lordship's life and work have turned out today to look, at best, a sad waste – and it is quite illogical that I should feel any regret or shame on my own account. (201)

In concealing his guilt, Stevens once again makes use of the distancing effect of the 'one' idiom, coupled with an appeal to logic.

Interestingly, the novel does not seek to uphold women as an antidote to masculine emotional repression or unreliable narration. Miss Kenton, considering her own culpability in the sacking of two Jewish housemaids in 1932, admits her failure to resign to be attributable only to a fear that, on leaving Darlington Hall, she would be 'going out there and finding nobody who knew or cared about me' (153). Miss Kenton may be more aware of her emotional and moral impulses, but she does not authentically enact them either. Yet the most serious condemnation placed by the text upon Miss Kenton is the point at which the unreliability of her own testimony overrides that of Stevens. He quotes her recent letter as containing the line 'the rest of my life stretches out like an emptiness before me'. On Stevens's insistence, she alters her assertion that she 'couldn't have written any such thing' to the confession that 'there are some days when I feel like that' (236). This is the only moment where we accept Stevens's version of events as being entirely trustworthy – and her retraction emphasises that we are right to do so.

Miss Kenton's mode of expression is never upheld as some kind of touchstone of authenticity – her appeals against Stevens's emotional repression, couched as they are in a kind of verbal excess, are almost as embarrassing to a reader immersed in the narrative's characteristic formality as they are to Stevens: 'Why, Mr Stevens, why, why, why, do you always have to *pretend*?' (154). Yet she is routinely able to confess. In his essay on Stevens's unreliable narrative, David Lodge nominates it 'a kind of confession, but it is riddled with devious self-justification and special pleading, and only at the very end does he arrive at an understanding of himself – too late to profit by it' (155). Leaving aside, temporarily, the question of Stevens's 'profit', *The Remains of the Day* both concludes and climaxes with Stevens's confessing his personal shortcomings, anxieties and regrets to an amiable man on Weymouth pier:

> Lord Darlington wasn't a bad man. He wasn't a bad man at all. And at least he had the privilege of being able to say at the end of his life that he made his own mistakes. His lordship was a courageous man. He chose a certain path in life, it proved to be a misguided one, but there, he chose it, he can say that at least. As for myself, I cannot even claim that. You see, I *trusted*. I trusted in his lordship's wisdom. All those years I served him, I trusted I was doing something worthwhile. I can't even say I made my own mistakes. Really – one has to ask oneself – what dignity is there in that? (243)

Stevens performs this confession, crucially, in a public space and to a total stranger, performing his grief still more publicly through his tears: 'Oh dear, mate', says his companion, 'Here, you want a hankie?' (243).

It is a significant feature that, when it finally arrives, Stevens's confession is spoken rather than written. In contrast to the rehabilitation of the droog Alex, achieved by means of the curative powers of literary authorship, Stevens finds his liberation into a more authentic manhood outwith the conventions of textual expression. In fact it has been his writing, with the attendant considerations of appropriate register and potential posterity, that is shown to have been inhibiting his self-examination and expression. Through the negative example of the vast majority of its narrative, the novel validates an alternative means of address, inaugurated upon an idea of non-literary, 'unmediated' male communication. Dorrit Cohn notes of Samuel Beckett's novelistic narrators that they ' "sound" more like monologists than like authors' (177), and this trait will be posited as crucial in a new generation of male fiction emerging in the decade after Ishiguro's novel. In a move that Jacques Derrida nominated as characteristic of modern Western culture, 'speech', or rather the textual illusion of unmediated verbal communication, is placed upon the privileged side of a hierarchical binary in opposition to writing. That Stevens avoids confessing directly to his addressee, that pseudo-person indexed by his use of the pronoun 'you', is vital in conferring authenticity upon his self-revelation on the pier. By directing his confession to a stranger, albeit one established as both sympathetic and genial, Stevens to some extent embraces the instability of address that his companion has already pointed out ('Just shows you never know who you're addressing when you start talking to a stranger', 242).

Though David Lodge might judge Stevens 'too late to profit' by his epiphany, *The Remains of the Day* may, in fact, justly be deemed a *Bildungsroman*, and its exercise in discrediting Stevens's original mode of narration successful and redemptive. The novel ends with him deciding 'that bantering is hardly an unreasonable duty for an employer to expect a professional to perform' (245), and his resolve to practice and improve his skills is an indication of a nascent appreciation of a changing professional and social world. Watching the laughing crowd gathered at dusk on Weymouth Pier, Stevens is able to concur that 'it is not such a foolish thing to indulge in – particularly if it is the case that in bantering lies the key to human warmth' (245). Lodge's ultimate pessimism, and our own, with regard to Stevens's ability to change, might be motivated by the butler's apparent inability to appreciate the element of spontaneity in this mode of communication. Our forthcoming investigation of the bantering tone of much recent popular male-authored literature, however, dependent as it is upon a kind of cultivated unmediation or crafted immediacy, may lead to other conclusions. The allegedly spontaneous self-expression of the 'Lad' will be examined as a context-specific form of idiolect every bit as elaborate as Stevens's outdated own.

The anti-masculine text

Magnus Mills's 1999 novel *All Quiet on the Orient Express* parodies precisely the conventions and motivations of address observed to be characteristic of the 'masculine text' in preceding chapters. His motor-bike having broken down, its nameless narrator stays on in a northern lakeside village long after the tourist season is over, taking on a widening portfolio of odd jobs for the owner of the campsite, Mr Parker. Parker himself holds his community in an unexplained but powerful sway, the front of his house commanding such views that, as he says with a hint of menace, 'We don't miss much from our window' (3). Surveillance of the stranger extends beyond the sightlines of Parker's Panopticon to the gazes and gossip of all the village folk: as the narrator says, 'it struck me that there was very little you could do around here without somebody else knowing about it' (52). Ordering baked beans or pints of beer; spilling green paint; playing on the darts team – such actions are subject to conventions of labyrinthine complexity to rival any Japanese system of deference.

The novel makes apparent the possibility of influencing the reader through carefully calibrated modes of address. One of the many duties the narrator assumes, always without actively volunteering, is the homework of Gail, Mr Parker's nymphet daughter: 'I watched her walk to the door and go out,' he tells us, 'and had to remind myself not for the first time that she was only fifteen' (172). Gail's grades are soon soaring, because:

> I'd discovered over the past few weeks [...] that her geography teacher was very interested in limestone. Questions about stalactites, stalag-mites and swallow holes cropped up regularly, and any answers which included the words 'sediment' and 'precipitation' were sure to receive favourable marks. Meanwhile, the English teacher had a fasci-nation with the concept of irony. Questions about the ironic condi-tion seemed to be his or her stock-in-trade. I only had to suggest in an essay that such-and-such a fictional character seemed to be mocked by fate or circumstance, and I'd be rewarded with a red star and 'v.g.' beneath my final paragraph. (127)

Yet the tone of the narration and the nature of the rural community described encourages the reader to ignore this warning of a text's poten-tial to exercise manipulation. The first-person account of the unfamiliar environment with its alien expectations and conventions aligns readers with the outsider-narrator, as he receives another stream of Mr Parker's characteristic blend of entreaty, threat and criticism: 'While he was telling me all this I stood beside the boats nodding vaguely. I wasn't sure what it was supposed to be leading up to, but it seemed interesting enough in its own way' (87). Descriptions of the village and its inhabitants are routinely riddled with uncertainty, as when the locals enter the 'bottom bar' of The Packhorse pub, empty of its summer clientele of tourists: 'As they drifted in they gave the impression that it was their first visit to the bottom bar for some time. It was almost as if they were reclaiming lost territory' (25).

The constancy of this tone of speculation prompts the reader to adhere to signs of intimacy and affability in the narrator's address more quickly and vehemently than might be the case in a more homely fictional diegesis. The narrator is quick and frequent in calling attention to his own honesty: 'That was the trouble with this place: the scenery was great and everything, but there was nothing to do except "take it in", and, to tell the truth, I'd already had enough of that' (4). Inverted commas appear regularly in his narrative, delineating and emphasising a particular idiolect founded in a complex and context-dependent arrangement of assumptions. For example, he says of the junior barmen at The Packhorse: 'They each seemed the type who would probably have been expected to do something "better" than just work in a pub, and I liked to imagine they were only doing this until something else turned up' (25). 'Better' implies a received hierarchical assessment of admirable (male) career choices, along with a self-deprecating sense of irony at the traditional nature of that hierarchy that does nothing ultimately to undermine it. 'I liked to imagine' is similarly self-mocking, yet similarly assertive of the need for these men to advance themselves. Overall, the narrator's point is indicative of a point-of-view that is resolutely urban – that is, it assumes a model of job opportunities and aspirations that may not be applicable within this rural environment.

Yet for all its covert metropolitan credentials, the narrator's mode of address is frequently quaint. Its liberal use of the unfashionable exclamation mark, for example, is both nostalgic for and parodic of a kind of Enid Blytonesque wholesomeness: 'With a sudden shock I remembered I had some grammar to hand in by tomorrow morning! I'd been having a bath for the last hour and gone and forgotten all about it!' (108). So enclosing is this register, that the rude intervention of Marco, the narrator's considerably less conscientious predecessor in Mr Parker's casual employ, comes as a genuine linguistic shock. The narrator is attempting to reason with the belligerent Marco's cavalier attitude towards credit accounts at the local shops:

> 'But you've got to pay them off eventually, haven't you?'
> Marco gave me a long look of disbelief, slowly exhaling as a smirk developed on his face. Then he laughed at me, directly and unashamedly.
> 'Don't be a cunt all your life,' he said. 'Have a day off.' (200)

Marco's sarcasm and casual obscenity represents no more than the default speech idiom of the contemporary 'lad', so the distaste that it generates is testimony to the ideologically encompassing influence of the narrator's register and viewpoint.

The narrator is witness to, and partially responsible for, the drowning of a local, Deakin, who becomes entangled in the chain of a concrete mooring weight and is dragged to the depths of the lake. The suddenness of his death, and the narrator's failure to alter his register from its now familiar combination of bemused speculation and affable appeal to values shared with the reader, is extremely disorientating. Expelled on the grounds of moral protest from the intimacy of the text's address, the reader is forced to review the enforced homosociability of the established relationship with the narrator, and catalogue all the benefits of doubts engendered by the narrative to date. After Deakin's death, the camaraderie of the first-person narrative takes on precisely the exquisitely sinister tone that has pervaded Mr Parker's pronouncements. The narrator takes over Deakin's milk delivery round, and the recurrent image of a pint of homogenized milk (49, 59, 149) hints, to a now paranoid reader, of the disturbing nature of homogeneity, be this in dairy or gender form: white, bottled-up, imperishable. *All Quiet on the Orient Express* is a masculine text that enacts its own discreditation as a democratic fictional form, suturing the readers and then cutting them out.

The women's decades?

'After the swinging Sixties,' claims Malcolm Bradbury in *The Modern British Novel*, come 'the sagging Seventies' (416). Dispiriting political events punctuated a decade of deserved national and Western pessimism: the ignominious US withdrawal from Vietnam; Watergate and Nixon's resultant resignation; an international oil crisis that effected a global economic recession; and, at home, increasingly fraught industrial relations and escalating conflict in Northern Ireland. Britain's primary industries were in free fall – a comparison of the 1971 and 1981 censuses confirms that the 1970s saw the largest national decline in the proportion of manual workers in the twentieth century.[5] Morgan's phrasing nicely captures the misogynistic ethos of the opinions of Oxford economists Bacon and Eltis in the wake of the winter of discontent, 'Rather than being the workshop of the world,' he claims, 'Britain was becoming one of the world's secretarial colleges, with priority given to non-manual clerical and service occupations' (428).

The 1970s are routinely characterised as the 'Me' decade, the period in which communalist beliefs in general declined into disrepute. Gentle consensus, altruistic rebellion – these were at an end. In the face of a turbulent global political situation, it seemed preferable to contemplate only the fuel in your own hearth and petrol-tank at the end of a three-day week, rather than that in wells far to the East. The prevailing political mood was incorporated into the figure of 'Selsdon Man', made animate by Harold Wilson on 6 February 1970 in an attack on the Conservative Party's apparent move to the far right. Heath, groping for something to tell an unexpected throng of journalists that turned up to his working-party at Selsdon Park Hotel that January, had emphasised an immanent new Tory toughness on crime. Selsdon Man's lumbering frame was intended to encapsulate the primitivism of Conservative instincts, as well as deriding a scope limited to the suburbia of the South East of England.

A proliferation of 'India books' on the Booker Prize shortlists during these years, of Empire trilogies (J. D. Farrell) and Raj Quartets (Paul Scott), testifies to an indifference not to history *per se*, but only to the inglorious wrangles and retributions of contemporary history. English fiction of the period saw a notable expansion in female self-representation and female-orientated fiction, with the emergence or consolidation of reputations for novelists like Angela Carter, Fay Weldon, Margaret Drabble and A. S. Byatt. Ian McEwan, who, along with Martin Amis, might be nominated one of the very few significant male authors to debut during the decade, confessed to the editor of *Granta* that his fame in the fiction market of the 1970s was relatively easy, as 'the horizon was uncluttered' (quoted Showalter, 66). His early work, like that of Amis *fils*, preferred to explore changing political and social realities obliquely, in psychic and sexual inner spaces.

Selsdon Man, for all his enduring symbolic power, failed to make his affiliations felt at the ballot box until 1979, when the Conservative Party, with Margaret Thatcher at its head, was elected by a narrow margin. The era of post-war consensus was finally over, and the concept of parliamentary democracy as a means of undoing the class divisions and social inequalities produced by capitalism – as potentially and ideally independent from the market – lost currency. Instead, whole sets of ideological and social practices – the arts, healthcare, transport policy – *became* currency, or at least riddled with private investment. 'Tomorrow', says John Self, narrator of Martin Amis's 1984 novel *Money: A Suicide Note*, 'we go to the big new show by Monet or Manet or Money or some such guy' (327). Under Thatcher, the dominant discourse of the 1980s was founded upon money, upon acquisition rather than production. It was a different kind of money, too, from the 'solid cash' Arthur Machin uses to calculate his self-worth: now money was plastic, or it was share-portfolio money, stock-market money – invisible but culturally pervasive. In *Sacred Cows: Is Feminism Relevant to the New Millenium?*, Rosalind Coward confirms the cliché of the 1980s as the 'women's decade', reading it as a time of momentous change in women's positions within society, due both to feminism and to economic transformation. She also acknowledges how easy it was, and is, to underestimate this change on the evidence of the decade's dominant narratives – Margaret Thatcher's overt hostility to feminism and intimations of a 'nanny state', for example, and the presiding of another male political icon, the 'yuppie'.

John Self himself is chafing against a perceived feminisation of 1980s society. *Money* is set in 1981, chosen, its author told John Haffenden, because of the year's 'conjunction of the Royal Wedding and the riots' (3). Flicking through a tabloid in the pub, Self summarises its contents, emphasising the culpability of women in the disintegration of the nation, and replicating some of the misogynistic verve of John Osborne:

> Another pussy-whipped judge has given some broad a ten-bob fine for murdering the milkman – premenstrual tension, PMT. The Western Alliance is in poor shape, I'm told. Well what do you expect? They've got an actor, and we've got a chick. More riots in Liverpool, Birmingham, Manchester, the inner cities left to rot or burn. Sorry, boys, but the PM has PMT. (155)

In Self's life, in a country he claims is 'pussy-whipped by money' (270), 'Butch' is the name of a woman. A long way from the pin-striped, stock-selling yuppie, the working-class Self nonetheless devotes himself to the ethos of the new economy, consuming continually. 'Unless I specifically inform you otherwise', we are informed in the opening pages, 'I'm always smoking another cigarette' (8). (The twist of this anti-/capitalist fable, of course, is that Self is consuming only himself: Bad Money Ltd, the company financing the film he is producing, derives all its money from Self's bank account.) Acquisitiveness, he movingly pledges, is a labour of love: 'I truly love money. Truly I do. Oh, money, I love you. You're so democratic: you've got no favourites. You even things out for me and my kind' (238). Self has already been explicit about his social positioning: by 'me and my kind' he means those of 'the criminal classes' (167). John Brannigan has noted of the character Keith Talent in Amis's later novel *London Fields* (1989) that as well as a comic treatment, 'there is also a great deal of contempt, which is channelled through the American narrator in order to construct the appearance of coming from an external, anthropological perspective' (76). The narration of *Money*, however, strives for no such objectivity, consisting as it does of the relentless, riffing, first-person monologue of Self himself.

The hyper-addressivity of *Money* may be characterised as an audacious paradox: it relies upon, and achieves, a sensation of unmediated communication at the same time as it emphasises the sensational impossibility, and fraught deficiency, of the terms of that communication. Surrounding the narrative voice is Amis's own, frequently updated, extra-diagetic commentary on his aesthetic processes (in a 1990 interview with Susan Morrison in *Rolling Stone* he encapsulated his stylistics, with rock 'n' roll aplomb, as all 'under the main heading of "Fucking around with my reader" ' (98). Personal prominence is to a degree inevitable in the contemporary literary industry, yet has been courted in particular by Amis, conspicuously embracing the various reputes and notorieties surrounding his family name. This level of discourse only heightens the states of self-awareness surrounding the text: the consciousness of narrator, author and reader, and of the involutional Martin Amis character, of each other's presence and influence. Self's confessional monologue makes frequent appeals to the reader for understanding and absolution, yet is meticulous in its neediness to maintain a bi-lateral gender address: 'I'm touched by your sympathy (and want much, much more of it: I want sympathy, even though I find it so very hard to behave sympathetically). But you're wrong, brother. Sister, you slipped' (29). Yet the nature of the equal opportunities offered by the narrative's address may come to seem rather less opportune. Self says of his middle-class, sometime-lover Martina Twain (another agent of involution) that 'she knew everything. She knew far more than me. But then, who doesn't? *You* do' (301), prompting pathos with reference to his lack of a clear, class-specific cognitive superiority. On occasion, this class hierarchy is exploited for a regressive kick familiar from *Saturday Night and Sunday Morning*, the thrill of a 'primal' masculine ethos that breaches the terms of conventional literary expression: 'The first thing I wonder about a woman is: will I fuck it? Similarly, the first thing I wonder about a man is: will I fight it?' (238). Only some sort of animal, the text prompts the reader to think, could read *Animal Farm* as a story about animals (205). Kiernan Ryan characterises the textual dynamics of the novel as an exploitative and debauched pact made between author and reader:

> The delinquent, the demented, the vain, the lecherous and the vile are *authorized* in a manner that confirms normality upon them and compels us to wonder whether they may not be the rule rather than the exception. The author is seized by a self who licences a blissful indulgence in what one is not supposed to feel and think and want – an indulgence which the reader is invited to share. The writer's and the reader's deepest pleasure consists less in their sense of ironic superiority to the benighted narrator than in the vicarious delight of identification, which is rooted in finding the scandalous secretly seductive and its apologists convincing. (207)

As confirmation, both manifestations of the author figure exhibit relish at the sadistic potential of narrative itself. The intradiegetic Martin Amis of *Money* says of the figure of the hero, 'The further down the scale he is, the more liberties you can take with him. You can do what the hell you like to him, really. This creates an appetite for punishment. The author is not free of sadistic impulses' (247). Extradiegetic Martin Amis tells John Haffenden, 'Every character in this book dupes the narrator and yet I am the one who has actually done it all to him' (7).

Were this imperious sadism unrelenting, the novel's mode of address would be extremely morally problematic. Yet Self's monologue ultimately denies the possibility of interpretation as an internally coherent, unmediated monologue. This is a voice that proclaims its own illiteracy ('Not reading – that's where I put my money', 42), yet describes the experience of being 'bopped by a mad guy' with a Jamesian exactitude: 'like no blow I have ever felt – qualitatively different, full of an atrocious, a limitless rectitude' (38). These conflicting voices ringing in the reader's ears provoke an intimate empathy with John Self's suffering of 'this fresh disease I have called tinnitus', for they too 'have started hearing things recently, things that aren't strictly auditory' (1), voices hymning self-indulgence and self-abuse ('the jabber of money', 'the voice of pornography') in a chorus with other voices of self-rebuke, self-pity and self-loathing:

> Third, the voice of ageing and weather, of time travel through days and days, the ever-weakening voice of stung shame, sad boredom and futile protest ... .

> Number four is the real intruder. I don't want any of these voices but I especially don't want this one. It is the most recent. It has to do with quitting work and needing to think about things I never used to think about. (108)

Self's own self is unrecognisable within the tenets of the masculine self (well defined, well-defended, whole), and the narrative makes a mockery of causal progression in Fielding Goodney's elaborate, motiveless, unexplained destruction of the narrator's life and livelihood. Intradiegetic Amis's epitaph to aetiology ('as a controlling force in human affairs, motivation is pretty well shagged out by now', 359) is authenticated in the echo-chamber of the novel's paratexts by extradiegetic Amis, who tells John Haffenden: 'motivation has become depleted, a shagged-out force in modern life' (6). Karl Miller concludes 'that Self is not a person but a part, a burlesqued proclivity', and *Money* a novel in which 'bad habits are being made endlessly delightful, by an unending author' (414).

We saw how Robert Bell, editor of the 1998 collection *Critical Essays on Kingsley Amis* saw the elder Amis as 'massively ubiquitous' in 'many of his narratives' (2): the younger, it seems, inherits a similar interpretation. This is effected, however, not by immasculation as it is in, say, *Lucky Jim*, but as a complex postmodern stance. In an essay on 'the intrusive author', Richard Todd, conspicuously concerned with foregrounding the subjectivity of his own address, concludes that:

> In devising a voice for John Self, the extra-fictional Martin Amis has, it seems to me, quite explicitly chosen to use his own, a voice that is clearly recognizable from his own other published fiction. I am convinced that we should see Amis's strategy as a deliberate choice that illustrates a self-conscious confrontation of the problem of solipsistic 'closure' and not – instead – as illustrating any kind of limitation of which no awareness has been shown. (73)

The high-pitched hypermediation of the narrative voice of *Money*, its relentless self-reflexivity, is here interpreted as an 'authentic' communication between the reader and the author himself, the narrator being merely its conduit.

There are those who denounce the proffered membership into this literary community. Laura Doan's determinedly resistant reading of the novel accuses its author of a comprehensive failure to address the way in which 'the economic system works as a paradigm of other power systems', that is, gender:

> The first thing Self asks himself when he meets a woman is 'will I fuck it?' [...] By substituting 'it' for 'her', Self, like the pornography he devours, denies woman personhood, placing her in the ultimate state of disempowerment and disembodiment. In fact, Self's dependence on pornography suggests the crucial nexus between the woman as pornographic image and his own objectification of women. (77)

She selects to ignore the companion sentence to Self's professed approach to women. His reflex reaction to meeting a man – 'will I fight it?' (238) – confirms his equal opportunity approach to objectification. Since in any critique of Martin Amis's work, an impassioned speculation as to his authorial motivation seems *de rigeur*, it might be supposed that, at a time when his father's fiction (*Jake's Thing*, published in 1978, and *Stanley and the Women*, in the same year as *Money*) was generating a maelstrom of accusations of misogyny,[6] the machinations of gender equality might be uppermost in his mind. Certainly the ultimate anathema to the pornography of money in *Money* is a reclamation of (elaborately) natural heterosexual relations, achievable with Martina Twain:

> At last I saw what her nakedness was saying, I saw its plain content, which was – Here, I lay it all before you. Yes, gently does it, I thought, with these violent hands ... . And in the morning, as I awoke, Christ (and don't laugh – no, don't laugh), I felt like a *flower*. (336)

(It is appropriate, perhaps, that a novel that seethes with the psychic implications of Thatcherite policy should offer the solution of a more recent Conservative slogan, 'Back to Basics'.) 'Women,' Self says just before his temporary sexual redemption, 'they're very different from us, about as different as the French are, say' (331), breaking with his usual blatantly bilateral address to herald this simple 'truth'. Vindicating Laura Doan's critique, one of the first-person narration's most obvious appeals to poignancy is Self's optimistic location of an atavistic (gender) identity within the nuclear family, that most sustained instrument of patriarchal and economic policy: 'Having kids! That's what takes real balls. To become a husband and a father: no you can't get much butcher than that' (173).

The relatively short revolution in working practices in Britain during the 1990s might be expected to intensify this need to relocate an authentic source of masculine identity outside the professional world and its traditional definitions of what constituted 'manly' work. The 'butch' arena of direct production was replaced by an economy based upon the finance and service sectors. Heavy industry all but closed down, or was itself relocated, to the Third World. The unilinear career path met a dead-end, replaced by part-time, short-term employment patterns that favoured, or at least were more familiar to, women and not men. Socially, Britain was apprehending itself as disintegrating in other ways too. The papers catalogued stories of increasing lawlessness, immorality and violence, a dark nadir occurring in February 1993, when two ten-year-old boys abducted, tortured and murdered the two-year-old James Bulger on a rubbish-strewn train-track outside Liverpool. The discourse of the media may have tempered slightly since the vitriolic outpourings of John Osborne in 'What's Gone Wrong With Women?' in 1956, but newspapers were pervaded with articles that worried instead at the question, 'What's gone wrong with men and/or boys?' Debate was divided as to whether men *were* a problem or rather *had* a problem. Football violence, joy-riding and escalating suicide rates were evoked in support of the former thesis. As for the latter; as Rosalind Coward puts it, 'the days of genial masochism were over' (10), and a body of male-authored fiction and non-fiction began directly to address the nature of the alleged male 'crisis'. Neil Spencer, interviewing Robert Bly, noted in *The Observer* in 1995 that 'being a bloke it seems is big business; "business as usual", some women might say' (7).

Confessional increments

In a 1983 piece on Saul Bellow in *The Observer*, Martin Amis characterises contemporary Western literature as being in a phase that 'is inescapably one of "higher autobiography", intensely self-inspecting. [...] No more stories', he claimed, 'the author is increasingly committed to the private being' (quoted Amis, 2000, 175). In *Experience*, his own contribution to the genre of 'higher autobiography', Amis goes on to muse that:

> One of the assumptions behind HA, I think, went as follows: in a world becoming more and more this and more and more that, but above all becoming more and more *mediated*, the direct line to your own experience was the only thing you could trust. So the focus moved inward, with that slow zoom a writer feels when he switches from the third person to the first. In 1983 I was finishing a novel, *Money*, which was narrated in the first person by a character called John Self. It would be a ferocious slander of Martin Amis (who was,

incidentally, a minor character in the book) if I called *Money* autobiographical. It certainly wasn't the *higher* autobiography. But I see now
that the story turned on my own preoccupations: it is about tiring of
being single; it is about the fear that childlessness will condemn you
to childishness. (176–7)

It would be similarly excessive to nominate Nick Hornby's 1992 debut
Fever Pitch as 'HA', yet this confessional memoir can justly be considered
a vital influence upon the most prominent genre of male fictional self-
expression in the 1990s – that of 'Ladlit'. *Fever Pitch*, its author/narrator
states, 'is about the consumption of football, rather than football itself'
(44), and this consumption, or rather Hornby's obsessive brand of it, is
set repeatedly in opposition to a female view-point. Hornby claims in
the introduction:

> *Fever Pitch* is about being a fan. I have read books written by people
> who obviously love *football*, but that's a different thing entirely; and
> I have read books written, for want of a better word, by hooligans, but
> at least 95 per cent of the millions who watch games every year have
> never hit anyone in their lives. So this is for the rest of us, and for
> anyone who has wondered what it might be like to be this way. While
> the details here are unique to me, I hope that they will strike a chord
> with anyone who has ever found themselves drifting off, in the
> middle of a working day or a film or a conversation, towards a left-
> foot volley into a top right-hand corner ten or fifteen or twenty-five
> years ago. (11–12)

The preceding paragraphs of the book, in which he and his partner sip
cups of tea in their bed, have already established him as the mental
drifter ('PENALTY! DIXON SCORES! 2–0!' 9), her as someone who has
'wondered what it might be like to be this way'. At Highbury, Arsenal's
ground, with a girlfriend in 1977, Hornby finds her 'shaking with laughter' at various points of the match. ' "It's so *funny*," she said by way of
explanation' (101), unable to get the seriousness of the event.

Football fanaticism is repeatedly gendered in *Fever Pitch*, but it is also
rooted firmly in a particular childhood trauma, or 'Freudian drama' as
Hornby puts it (17). In 1968, when Hornby was 11, his parents separated
after his father began an affair; Hornby contracted a serious case of
jaundice; and he began a new school. 'I would have to be extraordinarily
literal', he writes, 'to believe that the Arsenal fever about to grip me had
nothing to do with all this mess' (17). His fevered interest, simmering

into adulthood, is characterised both as a 'natural' response and an artificial crutch during a tumultuous emotional period: simultaneously 'healthy' and 'sick'. The memoir repeatedly makes appeals on both counts. Football is described as a 'retardant' (106), making its devotee reprehensibly childish, but concurrently childlike, a positive attribute in an era that fetishises the 'inner child' and his potential for liberation. The book's epistemology may be seen to strive to extend this elision of the artificial/natural binary with regard to the male gender. 'Masculinity', Hornby claims, 'has somehow acquired a more specific, less abstract meaning than femininity. Many people seem to regard femininity as a quality; but according to a large number of both men and women, masculinity is a shared set of assumptions and values that men can either accept or reject' (79–80). He has the sense that, for contemporary culture, femininity has become a quality, whilst masculinity is appre-hended only as performance. An effort is apparent throughout *Fever Pitch* to reclaim selected masculine 'assumptions and values' as indisputably, if regrettably, *male*, to couch them as at best biological, at worst patho-logical, but always in some way 'natural'. Hornby states in a 1978 entry that he 'had recently read *The Female Eunuch*, a book which made a deep and lasting impression on me', adding with an oft-used dash of devil's advocacy, 'yet how was I supposed to get excited about the oppression of females if they couldn't be trusted to stay upright during the final minutes of a desperately close promotion campaign?' (105). His gender campaign throughout the book might be aligned (albeit schematically) with the Second Wave's aims, whose feminists had a tendency, as Claire Colebrook puts it, to flirt 'with the idea of a sexual essence which demanded women's difference' (82), whilst their Third Wave colleagues, gathering intellectual momentum as Hornby's book was published, advanced the critique of patriarchal essentialism to deconstruct all forms of alleged 'naturalness'.

Hornby's abiding memory of the first football match he attended is 'the overwhelming *maleness* of it all – cigar and pipe smoke, foul language [...], and only years later did it occur to me that this was bound to have an effect on a boy who lived with his mother and his sister' (19). In the narration of his childhood, attendance on the terraces is repeat-edly analysed as an artificial means of attaining gender- and self-identity, its attraction and ultimate failure directly linked to the broken nature of the Hornby home. From the first time they are together amidst the smoke and the swearing, his father uses football as a means of filial bond-ing that, paradoxically, prevents any potentially painful confrontation occurring. It is only when he is in his twenties that Hornby can make the claim that: 'My father and I, almost imperceptibly, had reached the stage where football was no longer the chief method of discourse between us' (137). For the 'sporadically fatherless' son at this time, Hornby confesses, Arsenal provides 'a quick way to fill a previously empty trolley in the Masculinity Supermarket' (80), as well as a series of older male role-models – George Graham haunts his dreams as disapproving patriarch (169). His mother's efforts and economising to procure tickets for her teenage son are diagnosed as 'supposed to be for my benefit', but actually 'for hers', as her Saturday routine of giving lifts to the station and eliciting a post-match report while his tea is on the table allowed her 'a weird little parody of a sitcom married couple' (53). Paradoxically, his father's tactic to ameliorate awkwardness when used more recently by Hornby himself, reveals not self-delusion or gender artifice but a biological affinity between him and his young half-brother Jonathan: 'how odd [...] that my peculiar kink should have been transferred on to him, like a genetic flaw' (132).

Fever Pitch, as already stated, is 'about the consumption of football' (44). Hornby's consumption, self-professedly, is on the level of addiction, a fan for whom 'consumption is all; the quality of the product is immaterial' (150). Yet his self-analysis concurrently maintains what he calls 'this theory of fandom as therapy' (17). Hornby reveals he has received clinical therapy in the past: 'There was a part of me that was afraid to write all this down in a book, just as a part of me was afraid to explain to a therapist precisely what it had all come to mean: I was worried that by so doing it would all go, and I'd be left with this great big hole where football used to be' (245). A complicated identification is underway here: the act of writing autobiography is likened to the process of psychoanalysis, and as fandom too has been nominated a form of therapy, autobiography, therapy and football are absorbed into the same process. Writing itself, and writing your self, in a first-person confessional form, is elided with the 'talking cure'. An addiction becomes paradoxically 'healthy', the genesis of its own antidote. As football fanaticism has been portrayed throughout to be a male pathology, like a parasite on the Y chromosome, this identification serves to cast a set of masculine behaviour patterns (obsession, childishness, inability to maintain perspective) as some sort of 'natural' or necessary indulgence, provided they are acknowledged as part of a therapeutic demonstration of self-awareness. The memoir relies upon its ideal reader to grant a 'confessional increment' great enough to overcome its unsavoury revelations, on the basis that the confessor's self-awareness is admirable enough to compensate for his flaws. Praying that no one will direct a racist insult at a visiting black player, Hornby writes how he begs under his breath for the crowd's silence: ' "Please don't ruin it all for me" (for *me*, please note, not for the poor bastard who has to play just feet away from some evil fascist stormtrooper – such is the indulgent self-pity of the modern free-thinker)' (190). The address of this autobiography may be characterised by its intriguing combination of appeal and defiance, shame and justification, defence and attack. This is a tone that will be revoked and reworked by the male-authored genre that was to follow in its wake.

In the introduction to the 1999 reissue of B. S. Johnson's 1969 novel *The Unfortunates*, Jonathan Coe was upbeat as to the author's prospects in the contemporary literary market, because, he explained:

> Times change: and it may be that B. S. Johnson's moment has come at last. Since the early 1990s, in the wake of books by Blake Morrison, Nick Hornby [...] and others, new life has been breathed into a con-fessional genre of which *The Unfortunates* can now be seen as a great example, and emotional directness has become something we expect, even demand, of our male authors. (xiv)

The revival of the confessional mode in the work of English male authors is worthy of further consideration, and there is something satis-fyingly serendipitous in referring to a series of lectures given in 1955, near the beginning of this study's historical span, to analyse an influen-tial genre towards its end. In *How to Do Things With Words* J. L. Austin showed himself well aware of the addressivity of verbal communication, making the point that 'the occasion of an utterance matters seriously, and [...] the words used are to some extent to be "explained" by the - "context" in which they are designed to be or have actually been spoken in a linguistic interchange' (100). Austin distinguished what he called the 'locutionary act', or the act *of* saying something, from the 'illocutionary act', defined as 'the performance of an act *in* saying some-thing [...]; I call the act performed an "illocution" and shall refer to the doctrine of the different types of function of language here in question as the doctrine of "illocutionary forces" ' (99–100). He draws a further division between illocutionary acts, which he categories as necessarily conventional, and 'perlocutionary' acts, or 'what we bring about or achieve *by* saying something, such as convincing, persuading, deterring, and even, say, surprising or misleading' (109). These are *not* conven-tional nor necessarily rationally predictable, predicated as they are upon the emotional state of both speaker and listener. The category may include 'either the achievement of a perlocutionary object (convince, persuade) or the production of a perlocutionary sequel. Thus the act of warning may achieve its perlocutionary object of alerting and also have the perlocutionary sequel of alarming' (118).

The concept of confession in male-authored English fiction of the 1990s and beyond, tends to differ tellingly from the two presiding definitions of the word, while combining elements of both. According to the modern, psychoanalytic concept of the confessional act, it is by the fact of saying something in the presence of another that you can ameliorate your psychic and emotional state, or 'heal thyself'. Verbalising the repressed in a clinical 'safe space' allows the controlled release of the transgressive psychic energies that would otherwise disrupt sociality.[7] In the ancient, religious concept, you say these things to God, or to God's representative, thus placing yourself in a position of humility in the hope of effecting forgiveness or redemption. In the former, the illocutionary force of the speech act is healing, in the latter, it is absolution. In other words, both the therapeutic and religious acts of confession are illocutionary: it is the act *of* saying that counts. In *Fever Pitch*, and in the Ladlit genre that followed it, confession is intended and apprehended rather as perlocutionary: its importance lies in the effect achieved *by* saying something. Ideally, it brings about the effect of forgiveness, or at least a sizeable degree of sympathetic licence from the ideal reader/listener. In his study of the Japanese literary genre most commonly (if imperfectly) translated as 'the I-novel', *The Rhetoric of Confession: Shishōsetsu in Early Twentieth-Century Japanese Fiction*, Edward Fowler notes that:

> Confessional autobiography [...] like most traditional fiction in the west, is informed by what might be described as a secular teleology whereby personal disclosures are made with a specific formal as well as moral end in mind. Confession in the interest of atonement or self-analysis or even self-aggrandizement is the catalyst for some resolution or action that gives the work its shape and direction. In short, fiction and auto-biography in the west have as one of their formal properties a sense of forward movement and purpose. (xx)

The expectation and achievement of this perlocutionary sequel of licence, if not necessarily forgiveness in the reader, I would suggest, is heavily influenced by gender, that is, by a presiding and pervasive cultural understanding that for a man to verbalise his emotions is a demanding and heroic act.

The preceding chapter charted selected attempts in male-authored fiction of the Sixties to reconcile new cultural validations of the subjective and the self-revelatory with the traditional tenets of masculinity: objectivity and emotional restraint. Distance and control no longer remain as the objectives of men's self expression in the years spanning the turn of the millennium. Following R. D. Laing, a degree of psychic fragmentation, of moral and emotional inconsistency is now expected. Further, it is accepted as that which makes a fictional character 'convincing'. In Chapter 2 we examined a particularly English philosophy that elided rationalism and empiricism. In the novels considered in this final chapter, a confession of irrationalism (albeit occasional, rather than pervasive) has become a necessary part of an empirical representation of male selfhood. Provoking, perhaps, a Bergonzian despair at an English reluctance to experiment with fictional form, the genre of Ladlit reacts with reservation to the concept of the performativity of gender, and to postmodern conceptions of the self. *Fever Pitch* posits a response to the contemporary interrogation of male identity that hinges upon sincere confession and the narrative progression of the *Bildungsroman*. The interpretive community surrounding these texts, though, is not masculine: far from it, as it is assumed to valorise and desired to exercise empathy, a traditionally feminine quality. Austin's theories remain prescient, too, in their insistence upon the notion of a speech *act*: if a confessional increment is granted by the reader, it is in part on the basis of a recognition of the existential credibility and heroism of that confession. Confession, in Schwenger's phrase, is 'full of risk and consequence' (106). In contrast to the Sixties' trajectory into inner space, the contemporary dynamic of these texts' appeal is outwards: now it is up to others to validate and vindicate the self. That the personal has become public in male fiction undoubtedly represents a revolution, but, as we shall see, it is a revolution still qualified by regressive tendencies.

Hitting and telling

Steve Redhead's 2004 article 'Hit and Tell: a Review Essay on the Soccer Hooligan Memoir' sees Hornby's autobiography as initiating a distinct subgenre in the male-authored confessional literature of the twentieth century's last decade:

> After Nick Hornby's early 1990s bestselling memoir *Fever Pitch*, there has been a seemingly inexorable output of a new genre, what I call here 'hit and tell', especially devoted to revealing confessional soccer

hooligan stories. [...] Originally what was once referred to as the new football writing eschewed hooligan stories but as the 1990s wore on a market was created for the hit and tell accounts which were often 'fictionalized' (certainly in form if not in content). (394)

As with a large volume of the criticism surrounding the contemporary male confessional text, Redhead's comment engages in a debate as to the validity of these first-person accounts that may be characterised by its anxiety to police the boundary between fiction and autobiography. The implication of nominating these 'hooligan' texts as '"fictionalized" (certainly in form if not in content)' is that a mode of expression exists which is able to convey content in a pure form, without fictionalisation. This debate about the authenticity of the male confessional text is, like the debate surrounding the commodification of football, heavily inflected by class. In *Writing Masculinities*, Ben Knights remarks upon 'a deep-seated belief that maleness is more authentic, more straightforwardly instantiated in some sections of society than others. To write this down is to be aware what a preposterous belief it is. But its subliminal ideological attraction is a useful reminder of the importance of social icons to any understanding of what masculinity means' (181). Working-class male characters have figured repeatedly in the novels considered here as repositories of traditional masculine values, like literary Bevin boys,[8] staying close to the dirt and providing basic energy.

Redhead notes how the *Glasgow Herald* review of John King's 1996 novel *The Football Factory* pitched it as '*Fever Pitch* with testosterone and eight pints of lager' (quoted 395), setting it implicitly against middle-class masculinity and the mannered mode of self-examination the autobiography had established. The 1992 break-away from the Football League of twenty-two top English clubs heralded a new era of repackaging football for the profit-driven FA Premier League (its Frenchified title hinting at the aspirational consumer base it sought to attract). Yet for all the macho marketing surrounding it, *The Football Factory* functions more accurately as a bridging text between the bourgeoise and the so-called 'hoolie' books, reasserting 'primal' male characteristics in a highly-structured 'fictionalized' form. Just as *Fever Pitch*, in Hornby's claim, is about 'the consumption of football, rather than football itself' (44), so Tom Johnson, the sole first-person narrator amongst King's varied cast, is careful to distinguish his central concerns from the game itself: 'Makes me laugh the cunts calling it football violence when it's nothing to do with football. Nothing at all' (260). For all his atavistic proclamations – 'Real Stone Age society where the biggest lump of rock wins' (64) – Tom and his fellow Chelsea hooligans uphold a set of rules of engagement as elaborate as any military. Random and drunken violence is despised, as are attacks with knives: rather 'it's all about calculation' (24), forward planning, even-odds and a dignified acceptance in the face of defeat. 'You get a handful of decent rucks a season,' says Tom, 'but Millwall was something else, and though I got a kicking it gives me a bit of respect from the other lads' (256). Tom professes to despise the English soldiers of the First World War: 'there's no way I'd have gone over in the First World War because some stuck-up cunts ruling the country thought it was a good idea [...]. Beats me how they could let themselves get conned' (104). Yet, hospitalised after the Millwall fight, Tom's pleasant dreams are precisely those of heroic sacrifice for a distant ideal, and the state-sanctioned pomp of a traditional memorial, a gold plaque which 'says I died for my country and have been buried where I fell' (247).

Tom's narration is characterised by a hyper-awareness of the gaze and the way in which it functions in contemporary society in relation to the male working-class and to football hooligans specifically. His disenfranchisement is generated by the way he perceives his image, and that of those with similar interests, to be altered and manipulated in a society that is 'one big fucking peepshow' (103). Violence provides purification, in part as it must necessarily take place outwith the gaze of surveillance cameras (and thus some distance from the football stadium) if it is to achieve a satisfactory level of intensity before state intervention:

> Cameras have a lot of power, but they won't stop anything. If you've got the urge to do something then it takes a special kind of strength to resist the desire. You don't have to get caught just because London's turning into a surveillance arcade. Not if you're clever. (25)

Yet the very mediation Tom strives to avoid is apparent in his accounts of these allegedly purgative events: 'There's a few bottles bouncing off shields and snatch squads running out to pick off young lads who look the business but are just caught up in the *spectacle*' (my emphasis, 32).

This internalisation of modes of social surveillance, like the self-policing prisoners in Foucault's Panopticon in *Discipline and Punish*, is replicated in paranoiac form in the other activity which the novel characterises as a potentially pure, primal experience. Underlining his essentialist conception of self, Tom tells us 'You can't change human nature. Men are always going to kick fuck out of each other then go off and shaft some bird. That's life' (2). Like violence, heterosex is similarly portrayed as being under threat from a surveillance society, with Tom bemoaning 'the cunts who watch life through their videos and TVs and clips of porn', aligning them with 'the old bill with their surveillance gear and Marshall with his soldier gang rape show. [...] The whole fucking game recorded and examined' (261). The video of a group of 'squaddies' raping a woman is summoned repeatedly by Tom during the novel as an archetypal 'bad' example, involving as it does a mixing of sex and violence that he considers reprehensible ('there's a time for shagging and a time for fighting', 69), as well as the degraded ethic of voyeurism. Within Tom's moral scheme, this aligns the watcher with the state, as well as emphasising a perceived gulf between the immaculate violence of the Chelsea militia, and the contaminated codes of the military. Yet Tom's practice of the pure sexual encounter he preaches is frequently compromised; by the rubbery mediation of barrier methods of contraception, and by his own titillating specular fantasies: 'She has me out within seconds and has a grip like a pro. I can see us in a big wood trimmed mirror and imagine a camera on the other side with MI5 agents recording the details' (189).

Despite his occasional tendency to replicate the very codes he rejects, however, it is ultimately Tom's creed of primal purity that is enforced and enhanced by the language and structure of the novel's narrative itself. The corruptness of the media-driven surveillance society is conveyed by the repeated demonstrations that public language has become nothing more than an apathetic assemblage of clichés. In the stadium press box, a male journalist educates 'a rather attractive [female] young hopeful' (52) in the tricks of the trade, 'listing the buzz-words and phrases which made for a good hooligan article – "scum", "mindless yobs", "thugs", "ashamed to be English", "not true fans", "bring back the birch", "give them a good thrashing" and "now is the time for the courts to hand down tough custodial sentences" ' (58). In the service of its project to identify Tom's working-class male, first-person narration as an authentic ideal, the novel serially feminises and degrades what it characterises as inherently hypocritical, middle-class liberal opinions. Tom sleeps with Chrissie, who videos herself having sex with black men and then, he sneers, 'starts lecturing me on racial equality and sexual freedom in her pinched upper-class voice' (191). A one-off section takes as its focus a certain Michelle Watson who works in a Social Security office, its third-person narration fraught with a contemptuous irony aligned with Tom's suspicion of the middle-class: 'Michelle's great hope, as a radical socialist raised in deepest Hampshire but now living and thriving in London, was the black population. [...] With the help of left-wing, educated whites such as herself the blacks would gradually fight their way up the scale' (114).

The Football Factory is interesting for the way that it enacts and validates the contemporary sanctification of male confession, despite an explicit rejection of the received middle-class register of the genre. Tom's is the only first-person narration made available to the reader, and he seeks to generate more intimacy with the reader through sections narrated in the 'you' idiom ('Doing a Runner', 11–21) and the 'we' idiom ('Millwall Away', 222–32, which switches back to the first-person when Tom receives the punch that floors him). The illusion of unmediated communication is strengthened by the fact that Tom himself is non-literary; his narration what Cohn calls 'emphatically oratorial' (179). Direct speech is upheld as a means of counteracting the mediation and manipulation of experience so rife in a mass-media society. In contrast to, say, Burgess's *A Clockwork Orange*, where it is precisely the act of writing that is crucial to the final judgement upon Alex, the practicalities of how Tom's story could persist without being written down are simply ignored. As in the case of Michelle Watson, third-person omniscient narration in the novel tends to be heavily inflected with irony, and used comically and morally to undermine the personality to which it is privy. For other sympathetic characters (they are rare and always socially excluded), that favoured empathy-generator of the Angries, Free Indirect Discourse, is utilised. Albert Moss is an ailing pensioner whose non-appearance represents just another niggle in Michelle Watson's day:

> Albert was too old to fight angry young men. His heart wasn't what it was and the doctor had told him to take things easy. His nerves weren't as strong as they used to be, and his thoughts had started turning inward. Confusion built up and he was a bit worried about the future. (112)

FID, rather than a means of radicalising literary narrative by its incorporation of a specific and informal idiolect into literary narration, becomes, in contrast to Tom's direct address, an endearingly old-fashioned written register for a dignified but dying man.

Dynamic though Tom's point-of-view may appear, drawing as it does upon a myth of unmediated, untextualised communication, it offers no political radicalism beyond its mindful bouts of rebellious violence. The only character to enact any kind of liberation in (and from) *The Football Factory* is Vince, who saves his manual wage to travel and embrace hybridity and a (qualified) multiculturalism (it is the Commonwealth, rather than the Continental, influence that is celebrated, for after all, 'What have the frogs ever done for the English?' 13). This ability to accept diversity is consistently characterised as being a trait of the (white) English male working-class, itself predicated on empathy because, Tom claims, the reality is that they are 'white niggers' (155).[9] On his home-coming, Vince finds work at *No Exceptions*, a new Chelsea fanzine with impressive initial sales, and a grasp of precisely that dynamic vision of the English working-class that distinguishes the novel's narration as a whole:

> The editorial team believed that football more than any other area of society, with the possible exception of popular music, had accepted the shifting make-up of England's working-class population. It had done this without the help of any of the latter-day interest groups which, now that they felt safe to get involved in football following a middle-class media-inspired acceptance of the game as something other than the domain of Neanderthals, had jumped on the gravy train ten years after the event. (235)

No Exceptions, like Tom's narration, seems to provide a template for a more authentic expression of English male experience; unlike Tom's narration, which requires a constant obfuscation of its textual nature, it is of course written. A fanzine, it is assumed, is not subject to the demands of commercialism that have so corrupted the cliché-churning journalists who cram the hospitality boxes, but issues straight from purer, working-class, unreified roots. Paradoxically, however, authority is ultimately conferred upon the viewpoint both of Vince and the fanzine through a resolutely non-idiomatic, omniscient third-person register, traditionally the most surveillant (and thus, in the schema of the novel, bourgeois) of all modes of narrative.

Ladlit

In a definition deemed current from 1986 onwards, the *Oxford English Dictionary Online* expounds the word 'lad' as follows:

> *Brit. colloq.* A young man characterized by his enjoyment of social drinking, sport, and other activities considered to be male-oriented, his engagement in casual sexual relationships, and often by attitudes or behaviour regarded as irresponsible, sexist, or boorish; (usually) one belonging to a close-knit social group. [...] Cf. later NEW LAD *n.*

In the essay 'Ladlit' in *On Modern British Fiction*, Elaine Showalter reads this contemporary concept of both the lad and his definitive literary genre as spanning the survey of this study:

> From 1950 to 1999, the fictional genre of Ladlit provided British readers with a romantic, comic, popular male confessional literature. Stretching from Kingsley to Martin Amis, Ladlit was comic in the traditional sense that it had a happy ending. It was romantic in the modern sense that it confronted men's fear and final embrace of marriage, and adult responsibilities. It was confessional in the post-modern sense that the male protagonists and unreliable first-person narrators betrayed beneath their bravado the story of their insecurities, panic, cold sweats, performance anxieties, and phobias. At the low end of the market, Ladlit was the masculine equivalent of the Bridget Jones phenomenon; at the high end of the high street, it was a masterly examination of male identity in contemporary Britain. (60)

Bernard Bergonzi's prolonged refutation of creativity in contemporaneous English fiction, *The Situation of the Novel* (1970), would seem to bear Showalter out, though his focus is exclusively on that section she designates the 'low end of the market'. His lament over the repetitive formulas of the allegedly 'new' fiction rings familiarly in the ears of the present-day literary observer: 'Fey, mixed-up Joanna, in Earls Court bedsitter, has trouble with boy – *and* girl friends'; and the 'lightly written tale of nice young adman with scruples. He overcomes them, sleeps with the boss's wife, but marries the girl from back home' (24). Critical claims of innovation are always susceptible to rebuttal, and swathes of Ladlit and its pastel-clad sister genre Chick-lit may well justify nominations of a tired formula more aggressively marketed. Yet, as Dominic Head has claimed, 'the principal novels of Nick Hornby and Helen Fielding reveal something more interesting about the social function of the novel than the generic straitjacket was soon to allow. With the false claims of newness put in perspective, both writers can be seen to have afforded a revealing insight into the social moment' (248–9). A selective investigation of Ladlit's assumptions and modes of address can be expected to yield some conclusions over the nature of English literary masculinity, and gender more widely, in the new millennium.

Nick Hornby's first novel, *High Fidelity*, was published in 1995. Like *Fever Pitch*, its central dynamic is a process of prolonged self-examination and self-assessment on the part of its protagonist, being in this case thirty-five-year-old Rob Fleming, in an (ultimately successful, if delayed) attempt to understand and confront the roots of his emotional immaturity. Rob eludes the *OED* definition of a lad by means of an avowed disinterest in sport: the answers he provides as exemplary in response to his co-worker Barry's questionnaire for prospective partners, 'Nanci Griffith and Kurt Vonnegut, the Cowboy Junkies and hip-hop, *My Life as a Dog* and *A Fish Called Wanda*, Pee-Wee Herman and *Wayne's World*, sport and Mexican food' read 'yes, yes, yes, no, yes, no, no, yes, no, yes' (99). Yet this, it would seem, is not sufficient to prompt reliable reader discrimination between Rob's first-person mode of address and the narrative voice of the autobiographical work that preceded it. It is obliteration of the distinction between fact and fiction that Suzanne Moore values in the novel; her review 'Slipped Discs' celebrates the fact that 'Hornby, thankfully, doesn't want to be American or aimlessly clever. But in fact, as Amis himself said in a recent interview of one of his own fictional authors, he has a purchase on "the universal" ' (7). The associations generated in this succinct judgement are multifold. Hornby's work is prized for the fact that it rejects an 'American' template for fiction, this template, we can assume, being precisely the one that Bergonzi, back in 1970, envied for its dynamic stylistic experimentation. The assonance of (Martin) 'Amis' (not previously mentioned in the piece) and 'aimlessly' subtly codes that author's work as aspiring to be (distastefully) American, as well as suffering from an invalid and infuriating intellectual arrogance. In contradistinction, Hornby's work is coded as sincere, the 'universal' on which he is congratulated for having 'purchase' (itself a 'clever' pun in relation to a novel of sceptical consumerism) presumably being therefore that of a comfortingly *English* universe. *High Fidelity*, Moore implies, speaks to a reader well grounded in the undesirability of transatlantic aspirations and excessive stylistic tendencies in fiction.

Rob himself, in some of the finest comic moments of the novel, draws upon a binary opposition divided by the Atlantic Ocean: despairing over his loss of Laura, he feels, he says, at 'the end of the line', adding, 'I don't mean that in the American rock'n'roll suicide sense; I mean it in the English Thomas the Tank Engine sense' (179). Yet though the nationality requirements might be quite clear, the required gender of Rob's ideal reader/listener is thrown into disarray by the complex and contradictory mode of address of the novel itself. The opening section, subtitled 'then ...' (7), makes frequent use of the 'you' idiom, the referent of which, if Moore and many fellow reviewers are to be believed, is as full of the sensibilities of the average contemporary English person as the narrative address of Ishiguro's Stevens is empty. Yet for all the tempting universality of phraseology like 'if you know what I mean' (25), this section is in actuality addressed to Laura, Rob's former partner, and its primary purpose is to hurt her because she has left him: 'See, Laura? You won't change everything around like Jackie could. It's happened too many times, to both of us; we'll just go back to the friends and the pubs and the life we had before, and leave it at that, and nobody will notice the difference, probably' (22–3). In *Language, Meaning and Context*, John Lyons introduces the idea of 'deixis', deriving from the Greek meaning 'pointing' or 'showing', and originating in the notion of gestural reference. The 'deictic context', he states, operates as an integral part of the context of speech:

> Every act of utterance – every locutionary act – occurs in a spatio-temporal context whose centre, or zero-point, can be referred to as here-and-now. But how do we identify the here-and-now on particular occasions of utterance? A moment's reflection will convince us that there is no other way of defining the demonstrative adverbs 'here' and 'now' [...] than by relating them to the place and time of utterance. [...] The deictic context, then, is centered upon the speaker's here-and-now. It is characterized, in fact, by a particular kind of speaker-based egocentricity. (230)

'Deictic context' – gesturing towards a second-person addressee, for example, while 'centered upon the speaker's here-and-now' – represents a crucial component in Ladlit's insistent verbal evocation of direct presence and its attempts to suture its readers. However, in *High Fidelity* the 'speaker-based egocentricity' is characteristically, and ostentatiously, compromised by appeals to a female moral authority. In the opening section and beyond, Laura is used as a touchstone for morality, and a channel for Rob's self-examination and self-censuring: 'You'd say that this was childish, Laura. You'd say that it is stupid of me to compare Rob and Jackie with Rob and Laura who are in their mid-thirties, established, living together' (20). Rob does mock this propensity in himself, noting wryly how: 'I always think that women are going to save me, lead me through to a better life, that they can change and redeem me' (58). Yet its validity is confirmed, in a pseudo-Shakespearean flourish, by the ramblings of the drunken Johnny on one of his customarily quick entrances and exits at Rob's shop. Rowdy, itinerant, drunken, foul-mouthed; Johnny is laddishness gone rotten, rotten because he is too old and too poor to sustain its properly postmodern pose. His exiled status, however, is intended to inject authenticity into his succinct observation of heterosexual gender relationships: 'You think I'd be in this fucking state if I had a wife?' (53).

In the opening section, then, the 'you' idiom is utilised to address Laura directly (placed, in this case, in proximity to her name) but also to hail a less specific, though ideal reader, a figure who 'knows what Rob means'. The perlocutionary object of Rob's address of Laura may initially be punishment, but this blends from the outset with the appeal for empathy characteristic of this brand of confession. Rob's, and the text's, desired outcome is forgiveness: that Laura grants it to him at the end of the novel is a strong indicator that the reader, co-recipient of the 'you' address with her, should do the same. Yet if the deictic context of 'you' is complicated in the novel's establishing section, that of the indicator 'we' is more fluid still. In the space of a couple of pages, it moves from a referent of a community of adolescent boys ('We were twelve or thirteen, and had recently discovered irony', 10) that is explicitly set in opposition to 'them' (girls, 11) to the mixed-gender unit of the short-lived couple that was Rob and Alison Ashworth: 'So what was the significance of the snog? The truth is that there was no significance; we were just lost in the dark.' Immediately, however, Rob muses retrospectively that 'we were little animals, which is not to imply that by the end of the week we were tearing our tank tops off; just that, metaphorically speaking, we had begun to sniff each other's bottoms, and we did not find the odour entirely repellent' (12). The 'we' of his and Alison's experience has slipped into that of an (imagined) universal community of shared early sexual experiences. The rest of *High Fidelity* extends this fluidity of address to the second-person, which moves repeatedly from a gender-specific, hierarchical referent – 'I never remember their birthdays – you don't, do you, unless you are of the female persuasion?' (170) – to a gender-neutral one:

> You spend Christmas at somebody's house, you worry about their operations, you give them hugs and kisses and flowers, you see them in their dressing gown ... and then, bang, that's it. Gone forever. And sooner or later there will be another mum, another Christmas, more varicose veins. (49)

This shifting mode of address is underscored not by a postmodern acceptance of the multiplicity of subject positions and points of view in an audience, but rather by an assumption of that audience's communal values, predicated upon empathy.

As Joanne Knowles has pointed out, *High Fidelity* replicates the structure of the *Bildungsroman* while simultaneously ironising it through Rob's determination to delay the process of his development. He both recognises his need to grow up while upholding the awareness of his inner child(-ishness) as valuable and endearing. This childishness is most frequently manifested in Rob's confrontations with women; with Laura, his mother, and Liz, 'one of those *paranoid* feminists who see evil in everything you say' (156). Yet it is Laura (her female voice, as we have seen, able 'naturally' to authenticate the statement) who confirms the inner child as a vital and universal symptom of adulthood: 'We're all like Tom Hanks in *Big*. Little boys and girls trapped in adult bodies and forced to get on with it. And it's much worse in real life, because it's not just snogging and bunk beds, is it?' (199). As in *Fever Pitch*, failings diagnosed in the mass media as symptomatic of the parlous state of contemporary masculinity are firmly rooted in childhood in order to effect exoneration with reference to the 'natural':

> Read any woman's magazine and you'll see the same complaint over and over again: men – those little boys ten or twenty or thirty years on – are hopeless in bed. They are not interested in 'foreplay'; they have no desire to stimulate the erogenous zones of the opposite sex; they are selfish, greedy, clumsy, unsophisticated. These complaints, you can't help feeling, are kind of ironic. Back then, all we wanted was foreplay, and girls weren't interested. They didn't want to be touched, caressed, stimulated, aroused; in fact, they used to thump us if we tried. (16)

High Fidelity gestures towards a gender-universal (though unfalteringly heterosexist) address, but its register slips continually into a *male* imagined community of a specific age and nationality, in a gambit familiar from this study's consideration of the novel's male-authored fictional predecessors. As Martin Amis pointed out in a 2000 interview with Alan Rusbridger in *The Guardian*: 'A lad is not a lad by himself, he's only a lad when he's with the lads. You can't walk around in your house being a lad, can you? It's a communal activity' (2). For all its hard-sold newness, Hornby's brand of Ladlit espouses some notably traditional conceptions of women as redemptive, but above all as *different*. The theoretical riskiness of its confessional tone, self-exposing narrative and direct appeal for forgiveness is lessened in practice by its calculated appeal to a contemporary communal value of empathy, as well as that of the heroism of male confession, and by its attempt to naturalise and thus excuse socially prescribed 'masculine' faults by situating their founding impulses in childhood.

By the time Tim Lott's first novel, *White City Blue*, was published in 1999, Ladlit had become a reflex means of generic classification – James Hopkin's review in *The Guardian* claimed: 'Literature for the lads has never been in such rude and raucous health, and the honest guv confessional, dedicated to promoting the sensitivities of ordinary males, is just one of the many sub-genres to prosper' (10). Rather than replicating the shifting referent of address apparent in *High Fidelity*, however, Lott's narrator Frankie Blue tends to enforce a close and gender-specific identification between the first- and second-person idiom: 'nothing against fatties, mind you. Tony loves 'em. Fair play for the chubby chasers. But I felt slightness, smallness made them more different from *me*. When *you* held them. *I* loved that difference' (17, my emphasis). In this way, the narration enacts an honesty and intimacy between men (the male narrator and his ideal reader) that is repeatedly demonstrated as lacking in Frankie's 'real' life. In contrast to Hornby's monologues, too, Frankie's confession may more properly be characterised as illocutionary rather than perlocutionary: its process enacts a gradual self-healing by the systematic revelation of progressively deeper layers of repressed memories. It is an amelioration effected in the act *of* saying, rather an effect generated *by* saying it. The reader is eventually privy to two crucial truths about Frankie. The first is a recognition that his relationship with his father, non-physical and emotionally stilted, has set the tenor for his relationships with men ever since. Remembering the scene surrounding an old photograph, Frankie says:

> I can remember that moment on my sofa so clearly. Mum standing in front of us, telling us to get closer together, Dad getting more and more bluff and irritated. You can see it there in his face, in the already-fading smile. I could feel the waves of embarrassment coming from Dad, and it made me blush. The birthmark on my face seems flushed, livid. I shrank into myself. You can see that too: I'm sort of pulled inwards, arms pressed against chest, neck retracted, torso stiff. The arm never reached the shoulder. That's the story of me and my dad, in a nutshell. The arm never made it. (37)

This childhood memory is proffered early in the novel as a means of understanding Frankie's fraught friendship with 'the Lads' Tony, Nodge and Colin, their inter-relationships characterised by patterns of emotional dishonesty established during their shared childhood. Yet ultimately the novel's primal scene is revealed as non-parental, involving a more aggressively repressed memory from adolescence:

> It is then that I see Nodge, eyes closed, breathing gently, in the bed
> with me. [...] I notice, at first, quite neutrally, that he too is topless,
> that the soft pressure on my back is in fact his chest, and I realize that
> beneath that he has one of his hands down the front of my trousers.
> It is gripping, quite firmly, my half-erect cock. (171)

At this point, homosexuality, or at least the homosexual act, comes to
take up a place of ambiguity in the novel. It is validated to a certain
extent as representing Frankie's supreme self-realisation, and as an
empirical fact that stands in contrast to the dishonest and laddish
euphemisms that characterise the speech-patterns of their unsatisfactory friendship, patterns that Nodge parodies as he finally comes out to
Tony and Colin:

> *That's right!* Says Nodge. *I **am** a fucking pansy. I've been a fucking pansy
> for fifteen years. I'm as camp as a row of tents, as bent as a nine-bob note.
> I'm a fudge-packer, a chocolate-stabber, a nance, a poo-jabber. I like it right
> up the Gary Glitter. I'm a big fucking girl. I've liked it ever since Frankie did
> it to me, on 14 May 1982.* (231–2)

The indisputable emotional and physical truth of the act, and of Nodge's
stating it, partially instates Nodge as Frankie's *true* best friend. His other
crucial credential in this regard is the fact of his 'low, neutral, classless,
slightly sinussy voice' (155) – classlessness being something to which
the working-class Frankie, unable to wear his education with any comfort, aspires: 'Nothing fits the world any more. Me with my degree, Tony
with his thousand pound suits, Nodge and his unreadable books. A cab
driver with his nose in Rohinton Mistry, for fuck's sake. It's all hybrid,
atomized' (25).

Frankie sets the stereotypical 'laddish' behaviour he enacts in the
company of his three friends in opposition to authentic acts and
emotions. Meeting self-styled Tony Diamonte, owner of a successful
chain of hair salons, unexpectedly in the street, Frankie confesses that:
'Immediately I re-present myself. It occurs to me that this is something
I always do before I meet my friends. I arrange to become cocky,
tough, knowing, wry, all with a shrug of the muscles of my face' (123).
Laddishness itself is re-presented as a simulacrum, an exhausting, chat-
tering, unrelenting performance. With Veronica, his fiancée (it is this
commitment that has prompted the self-audit of his confession), he is

able to sit comfortably in silence, but, he says, 'You can't do that with men only, with mates. You have to do something to establish yourself as amusing or interesting. Too much silence itches' (34). Direct speech in the novel is always italicised, emphasising its artifice in comparison to the 'unmediated' communication of confession to the reader. As the enervating verbal theatrics of his male friendships continue, Frankie claims, 'Each phrase uttered, each sentence delivered, is part of a continuum, a larger, three dimensional pattern that occupies the present, but stretches back deep into the past and contains an array of threatening implications for the future' (156). The futility of this superficial (and masculine) communication, in a method familiar from John Braine's *Room at the Top*, is aligned with the ultimate emptiness of the arbitrary sign-system of the consumer market – Frankie, struggling to escape its inauthenticities can still seamlessly catalogue the brands of Tony's outfit: 'The Mulberry Black Cavalry Twill coat draped over his quarter-back shoulders, the bespoke suit, the Patrick Cox shoes, the Oris Big Crown Commander watch' (24).

Veronica herself is to some extent upheld as a potential model of authenticity. On their first meeting, Frankie remarks upon her air of 'self-possession, something I find greatly attractive for some reason' (8), and in their relationship she is intent upon liberating him from his childhood nickname, '*Frank the Fib*' (43). This admirable faculty is inextricably, if understatedly, linked to her ability daily to confront the reality of mortality in her job as a pathologist. Yet the female viewpoint is ultimately rejected as a template for Frankie's future development with reference to Veronica's attraction to the metaphysical – an attraction of which Frankie, following A. J. Ayer, strongly disapproves. Veronica, he says, 'thinks the world talks to you through what appear to be random events. She sees meanings everywhere' (176). She initiates a group-outing to see Christopher Crowley (his surname presumably intended to invoke a hokey occultism) of 'The World Spiritual University' speak on 'Power of Symbol: Call of Myth' (115) which ends when a drunken Tony head-butts the guru after demanding a refund of the money he has just burnt to demonstrate '*the destruction of a symbol*' (128). As Crowley's transatlantic smoothness curdles into 'thick, gasping Brummie vowels' (132), Tony's violent physical defence of the only symbol he invests with meaning is not vindicated, but it is certainly elevated above the phoney spiritualism to which Veronica is attracted.

Frankie's sense of masculine community and emotional honesty is predicated upon an understanding of consumer materialism (enacted by Tony) as directly opposed to a 'realistic' and materialist understanding of the relationship between body and mind:

> A packet of muscle, fat, bone, water, memory, shit, hair, feeling, loss, rage, hope. Sometimes I think I'm Superman, sometimes I think I'm nothing. But I'm neither. I'm just a bloke, among millions of other blokes. Not more, not less. (267)

Yet the potential radicalism of this Ladlit novel's central secret – that Frankie has had sex with Nodge – is denied, not just by Frankie's forthcoming marriage to Veronica (which in its positioning as a conventionally comic ending contradicts the homosexual act as an expression of his 'real' sexual identity), but by a suspicion lingering throughout that Frankie's birthmark, which he recognises as announcing 'my difference, my seemingly inescapable role as misfit' (104), is a mark of shame or of Cain, a branding for an act ultimately judged to be wrongful. The only friend that the text upholds as worthy of Frankie's adult friendship is 'you', the ideal male reader, bound to Frankie by means of the authenticity of his confession. This friend's intentions are strictly homosocial.

The daddy of Ladlit

If sales figures are to be reckoned with, then by far the most successful authorial purveyor of the Ladlit form is Tony Parsons, whose 1999 debut in the genre[10] is approaching a million copies sold. In the essay 'Lucky Jim Revisited', David Lodge suggests that Amis Senior's novel functions as a 'comic inversion' of Graham Greene's *The Heart of the Matter*, reversing the Catholic emphasis on guilt and pity. Harry Silver, narrator of *Man and Boy*, has a one night stand, prompting his wife to take a job in Tokyo and leave him to care for their four-year-old son Patrick. Harry's confession toys with pity, or the invocation of it, with an appeal to the emasculatory nature of involvement in the family home:

> You can get tired of always being the man who pays the mortgage and calls the plumber and can't put together the self-assembly furniture. You get tired of being that man because in the end you don't feel like much of a man at all, more of a domestic appliance. (43–4)

This defence is made somewhat half-hearted, though, by Harry's acute awareness of the way in which his various modes of domophobic rebellion amount to no more than simulacra of late-century masculine stereotypes: he registers his pre-thirtieth birthday purchase of a red sports car as 'blatant macho corn' (7), and winces in recognition at his wife Gina's perception of him as 'just another sad salary man who got caught fucking around' (64). The solicitor that Harry hires is far more determined in his efforts to effect a backlash against what Rosalind Coward has styled 'womanism': 'a sort of popularized version of feminism which acclaims everything women do and disparages men. Womanism is', she continues:

> Feminism's vulgate. It asserts that women are the oppressed or the victims and never the collaborators in the 'bad' things that men do. It entails a double standard around sexuality where women's sexual self-expression is seen as necessary and even desirable, but men's is seen as dangerous or even disgusting. Womanism is by no means confined to a tiny, politically motivated bunch of man-hating feminists, but is a regular feature of mainstream culture. It fuels the tabloids and the broad-sheets alike. Womanism is a convenient response to many of the uglier aspects of the great convulsions shaking modern society; the very convulsions that are, in other aspects, delivering what feminism demanded. (11–12)

The divorced divorce-specialist perpetuates precisely this idea of men as the contemporary social dupes:

> 'Men die younger than women,' said my new solicitor. 'We catch cancer more often than women. We commit suicide with greater frequency than women. We are more likely to be unemployed than women.' His smooth, pudgy face creased into a grin, as though it were all a huge joke. 'But for some reason I have never been able to fathom, Mr Silver, women are considered the victims.' (282)

Yet despite his indulgence in a few short-lived and satisfyingly petulant outbursts about injustice, Harry generally rejects the options of victimhood, guilt or self-pity for a practical acceptance of responsibility in his new situation as (temporarily) single parent.

The symbol of a medal becomes, throughout the text, a grindingly insistent means of signifying a contemporaneous alteration in the constitution of 'good, brave causes' (Osborne 1989, 84). Harry's very surname (Silver) references his thrall to a paternal exemplar of battle-tested mettle and metal: 'My father really was a hero. He had a medal to prove it and everything' (47). In Harry's peacetime environment, wars are limited to those between estranged husbands and wives, and military decoration a cruel taunt in a domestic argument: 'You've done a good job over the last few months, Harry', Gina tells him. 'But what do you want? A medal?' (307). It is Harry's mother who explicitly states the need to redefine the heroic:

> I think you've got a lot of fight in you, Harry. But you beat yourself up sometimes. You can't be the same man your father was – it's a different world. Almost a different century. You have to fight different battles and not expect anyone to pin a medal on your chest. Looking after a child alone – you think your father could have done that? I love him more than my life, but that would have been beyond him. You have to be strong in a different way. You have to be a different kind of tough guy. (296–7)

Coward notes approvingly that 'increasingly, the only convincing contemporary representation of heroism is that of an inner struggle towards greater awareness and deeper relationships; that is, a struggle towards a more "feminine" position. This is one of feminism's most important legacies' (110). Studiously conforming to this contemporary trope, Harry's brief experience of raising Pat alone prompts a supermarket-aisle epiphany: 'I was secretly watching all the women I took to be single mothers. I had never even thought about them before, but now I saw that these women were heroes. Real heroes' (80). Yet the real 'real hero' of the novel, of course, is Harry, completing the *Bildungsroman Man and Boy* in a state of greater self-awareness and near-martyr status as he condones Gina's custody of their son on her eventual return to England.

Harry's working life as producer of *The Marty Mann Show*, a vehicle progressing during the plot's course from the status of radio cult to televisual notoriety, operates in part to underline the plight of the contemporary father who attempts to garner child-care time in a macho professional environment. Marty Mann himself provides an exemplary model of how not to perform modern manhood, in his hysterical, serial sexual conquering, and his violent response to a guest Green activist: 'Cliff cradled his crushed nose. Someone in the audience started booing. And that's when I knew we were stuffed. Marty had done the one thing he wasn't allowed to do on our kind of show. He had lost the audience' (37). In its own attempt to prevent this very taboo, the novel's stylistics demonstrate a heavy reliance upon the 'you' idiom we have found to be instrumental in Ladlit's mode of address and myth of immediacy. Harry himself is alive to the artificial conventions of the speech patterns of the men who surround him (the women he knows he routinely credits with impeccable verbal sincerity). When Barry, an executive at the television studio, issues his reprimand for Marty's assault on the eco-warrior, Harry notes mockingly how 'his conversation was full of stuff like "big boys' rules", as though working in television was a lot like running an under-cover SAS unit in South Armagh' (59). His skills of stylistic analysis are, however, most often directed towards his father, holding up expressions like 'not really my scene' (48), 'skylarking' (109), 'getting spruced up' (110) and 'kip' (142) as verbal curiosities for the amusement of his audience. Harry claims that:

> Sometimes it felt like my old man was the curator of the English language. As well as his love for outmoded hipster jive, another pecu-liarity of his speech was his use of expressions from his youth that everyone else had thrown out with their ration books. (109)

More amusing, perhaps, and certainly most revealing, is Harry's inability to recognise the elaborate conventions upon which his own, allegedly unmediated, communication depends. His father ties up two teenagers who have broken into the house, finally putting the two silk ties his son bought him for Christmas to practical use. Harry confesses that:

> I was angry with him for taking on the two little goons, although I knew he was more than capable of handling them. [...] But there was also something else. I was jealous.
> What would I have done if I had found these two yobs – or any of the million like them – in my home? Would I have had the sheer guts and the bloody-minded stupidity to take them on? Or would I have run a mile? (111)

Terms like 'goons' and 'yobs', themselves sounding somewhat out-dated by 2005, call into play a complex system of reference and deixis – the former towards American gangster-speak, the latter to English media cliché. The phrase 'sheer guts' draws on the macho vernacular of the first-person account of battle, a male-authored genre spearheaded by ex-military men such as Andy McNab that, for all Harry's contention that 'real' heroism occurs in the supermarket, maintain phenomenal popularity amongst male British readers. The language of Harry's con-fession is revealed to be a context-specific idiolect just as studied as Stevens the butler's attempts to 'banter'.

In the preamble to his archetypal work of Western literary confession, Rousseau pledges that his 'purpose is to display to my kind a portrait in every way true to nature, and the man I shall portray will be myself. Simply myself' (17). His autobiography, he is claiming, will not be subject to the mediation of literary form or the observance of various conventions of idiolect. Ladlit's exemplary style, exhibited in *Man and Boy*, is predicated precisely upon this tactic of suppressing the textual nature of the literary act in order to uphold what Fowler calls 'the myth of "sincerity", in which the totally accessible author relates his experiences through the totally transparent text' (41). For, as Fowler concludes, 'sincerity [...] is the *product* of style, not its generator' (68). Approaches to the genre are characterised by precisely that affinity in press and readership to elide the voice of narrator and author that we witnessed in the public response to the fiction of the Angry Young Men of the 1950s. To fail to support this identification is critically identified as heresy. In a 2002 interview with Tony Parsons, 'Meet The Parent', Lynn Barber focuses a lengthy piece on precisely a sense of the betrayal of this confidence:

> Why am I so suspicious of Tony Parsons? Mainly because I find it strange that someone can build a career writing smart-aleck stuff for NME and the men's magazines, and mouthing off on *Late Review*, and then suddenly, in his mid-40s, make a 180° turn and write sentimental guff about father–son relationships. (16)

Barber's vehemence, interestingly, leads us back to where we began this study: a critical insistence upon a novel that directly communicates the experience of its male author, and a fiction the subjectivity of which is predicated upon an objective truth. Empiricism, it would seem, remains a benchmark for English male literary self-expression.

6
Conclusions – Reading to Belie the Binary

His ruler coming down and measuring them. Why all this criticism of other people? Why not some system that includes the good? What a discovery that would be – a system that did not shut out.

Virginia Woolf, diary entry on the publication of
D. H. Lawrence's letters (2 October 1932)

In her 1971 book *Woman's Estate*, Juliet Mitchell notes how the liberationist potential of the existentialism considered in Chapter 3 and the designated 'Sixties themes' in Chapter 4 had yet to be politically realised at her time of writing. The influx of cultural value into feminine qualities such as subjectivity and empathy, she claims, promised feminists much towards a social re-evaluation of women themselves: 'that these female values were appropriated by male radicals initially gave women hope within these movements. But when they found even here, where their oppressed characteristics seemed to be the order of the day, they played a secondary (to be generous) role, righteous resentment was rampant' (175). For all their aspiration, the male-authored texts of the English 1950s, 60s and 70s considered in this study confirm that such resentment was justifiably rampant. It was, of course, to a great extent, the 'righteous resentment' at this arrested cultural and social development that fuelled feminism in the following years. Its radical and comprehensive deconstruction of masculine epistemology, and the misogynist ontology that sought to naturalise it, both inspired and was inspired by the simultaneous development of critiques of its colonialism, racism and heterosexism. Together, these critiques systematically deconstructed that most grandiose of masculine narratives – History.

This book has sought to undermine the enduring conception of the English 1950s as a time of apathetic stasis. Its typifying fictions have been characterised as being engaged within a covert and conservative politics, and complex and enlightening from a literary standpoint as well as a contextual one. The concept of the Sixties as a burst of jubilant change, characterised by the unfettered discovery of selves and of sex, has been revealed as similarly problematic from a literary, and gender, perspective. The English male fictional response to the initial development of Second Wave feminism was decidedly muted: muted, that is, until a vociferous regrouping in the 1980s, in and after which consumerism, paternity and sexuality endure as crucial themes. The Ladlit of the turn of the century is proof of feminism's success in influencing the values our society now upholds as sacrosanct. The (qualified) empiricism of the masculine text of the 1950s sought the coincidence of the fictional world with the experience of the reader to such an extent that it functioned to manufacture and impose that coincidence through its mode of address. In contrast, Ladlit's relationship with its reader, whatever their gender, depends upon a bilateral assumption of shared social and moral priorities, rather than a hermeneutic correspondence. Ideal identification is predicated not necessarily upon the adoption of the viewpoint and values of the narrator/protagonist, but rather on an empathy generated by an appreciation of the contemporary hero's ability to articulate his experiences and emotions. Confession has become a reliable generator of existential authenticity, the speech act a heroic one. The structure of this textual community, then, is no longer patriarchal, but based upon the inter-recognition of individuals. As Sartre recognised, enhanced individual and existential freedom only increases communal responsibility and reliance. Yet still regressive tendencies endure, as the crucial 'confessional increment' inveigled by Ladlit depends upon a tacit recognition that emotional honesty, for men, is 'unnatural'.

The two conceptions of selfhood that have been outlined in this post-war period (themselves representing an ancient philosophical divide) retain their significance in contemporary culture. We continue to negotiate between existentialist and essentialist understandings of identity, frequently, as in the novels considered here, conflating these identities with those of gender. Though the acknowledgement and exploration of linguistic contingency was noticeably absent as a mode of expressing angst in male fiction of the immediate post-Second World War period, an explicitly existentialist understanding of selfhood has now been incorporated into the post-structuralist radical uncertainty inherent in a belief that linguistic operation is the only means of self-conception. Ladlit as a genre invests heavily in a mythic register of immediate, unmediated speech, its intimacy with the reader dependent upon the performance of presence. Yet the lingering link between masculinity, maleness and the male body that I have criticised throughout this book indicates that the essentialism of the masculine side of the gender binary has not been banished from contemporary consciousness. Gender, as a mutable cultural concept, might be expected to have long surrendered all appeals to the primal and the transcendent, yet the *Iron John* school of the Men's Movement continues to cash in. This appeal to nature is resurrected for the familiar patriarchal purpose of normalising a particular power relation, but also for more insidious motives swathed in blame and guilt.

Such essentialism is allowed to endure because masculinity has still to be interrogated to the extent undergone by femininity. The gender remains in danger of becoming a kind of conceptual scapegoat, conveniently encompassing every mode of behaviour or expression that is technocratic, bullying or violent. Feminism has striven to claim numerous purportedly 'feminine', or womanly, attributes for bilateral good, so we should not be too hasty in rejecting everything properly designated 'masculine' to be beyond redemption. This study has framed the textual process by which male fiction of a particular era manipulates its reader, by formal and by philosophical means, into complicity with a masculine epistemology of hierarchical binarisms. The process of reading is neither purely hermeneutic nor purely emotive: as Judith Kegan Gardiner notes, it is 'cognitive as well as affective' (2). In its appeal to a 'universal' male experience, the masculine text understands the identification of its ideal reader to be entirely hermeneutic, denying both its provisional and emotional nature: a tactic we have seen to be outmoded in contemporary discourse. Yet its primary function, through the process of 'suture', or the enmeshment of the reader within its structures of power and meaning, is to create a community.

Readers will always want to belong. As Germaine Greer put it whilst the Second Wave swelled:

> Half the point in reading novels and seeing plays and films is to exercise the faculty of sympathy with our own kind, so often obliterated in the multifarious controls and compulsions of actual social existence. For once we are not contemptuous of Camille or jealous of Juliet we might even understand the regicide or the motherfucker. That is love. (144)

The experience of belonging, as we have seen in our examination of a multi-layered process of recognition, emotional investment and compromise in response to the fiction here, is not passive. Neither is it necessarily regressive. Recreating an experience as if it were a shared one, no matter how divergent from the reader's own context it might be, bridges the boundary of self and Other. Empathic reading (where the concept is understood to involve, as for Gardiner, both cognitive and affective responses) refutes both the binary of gender, and gendered conceptions of the processes of reading and writing. Though rejected as an oppressive normative standard, the masculine narrative remains a source both of stylistic ideas and political and textual tactics available for pillaging by both male and female writers and readers. Gender, however unstable as a concept, will continue to retain a powerful cultural and personal influence. Its ability to inspire identification with a broad church of people is potentially positive, particularly in comparison, for example, with the impossibly diffuse 'identity politics' of later feminism. Yet a reader's empathic response to gender should remain just one of many potential and provisional empathies within multiple valid codes of reader-identification.

Narratives will always address an ideal reader, even if that reader's identity changes amidst multiple textual viewpoints. Yet it is the text's response to its own addressivity that is vital in eliciting reader empathy. For the fiction considered here, addressivity is frequently a shameful business, as its awareness of necessary contextual specifics interferes with a sacred absolute: the universality of knowledge organised upon masculine principles. The function of narrative, as we have seen, is inextricably involved with conceptions of selfhood. Between essence and existence is an understanding of selfhood as a form of narrative itself, or, as Worthington puts it, 'a creative narrative process achieved within a plurality of intersubjective communicative protocols' (12). The narrative of this contemporary self is coherent but provisional, and by necessity retrospective, where this insinuates not total authorial control, as in the masculine text, but rather the unavoidable recognition of provisionality. This conception of self as a provisional narrative, and of textual identification as similarly provisional, removes the possibility of *enforcing* an ideal reader; rather, that reader, if willing, is self-appointed, and self-aware. Reading to belie the masculine binarisms of selfhood and of text removes many enduring contradictions within our understanding of the reading process. It allows me to laugh with Jim Dixon while understanding (and ideologically rejecting) the way in which that laughter is generated. It rejects the gaze for a celebration of the look. It elicits empathy with an Absolute Beginner even as he deliberately excludes you from the innocent optimism of his youth. It allows insight into Nick Hornby's

Arsenal obsession while maintaining scepticism surrounding his susceptibility to a special pleading. It refuses to allow textual manipulation to remain unknowing. It values both a male response to feminism, and a female response to masculinity. This sort of multi-layered critical reader-response is eminently possible. Both men and women have been negotiating it for years in their engagements with the masculine text.

Notes

1   Introduction

1. Their conclusions acknowledge a debt to Elizabeth Wilson's 1980 study *Only Halfway to Paradise: Women in Postwar Britain 1945–1968*.
2. Jackie Stacey in her essay 'Desperately Seeking Difference' similarly balks at the thought of only three available options for the female spectator of narrative cinema: 'masculinisation, masochism, or marginality' (120).
3. As it is figured in Nancy Chodorow's *The Reproduction of Mothering*: 'Men defend themselves against the threat posed by love, but needs for love do not disappear through repression. Their training for masculinity and repression of affective relational needs, and their primarily nonemotional and impersonal relationships in the public world make deep primary relationships with other men hard to come by' (196).

2   The Consolations of Conformity

1. Under 'Unified Social Security and the Changes involved', Section 30, the report reads:

   > 6. Recognition of housewives as a distinct insurance class of occupied persons with benefits adjusted to their special needs, including (a) in all cases [marriage grant], maternity grant, widowhood and separation provisions and retirement pensions; (b) if not gainfully occupied, benefit during husband's unemployment or disability; (c) if gainfully occupied, special maternity benefit in addition to grant, and lower unemployment and disability benefits, accompanied by abolition of the Anomalies Regulations for Married Women. (paragraphs 107–17)

2. Such a standpoint is nicely demonstrated in an entry in *The Cambridge Dictionary of Philosophy*: 'empiricism, British. See RATIONALISM' (225).
3. The fact that this dynamic lingers today as a means of understanding identity is a telling indication of the way in which theories of selfhood remain dominated by masculine priorities.
4. Bradbury points out in *The Modern British Novel* that Robert is 'plainly C. P. Snow' (320).
5. Wolfgang Iser, *The Implied Reader*; Shlomith Rimon-Kenan, *Narrative Fiction, Contemporary Poetics* (104); Steven Connor, *The English Novel in History: 1950–1995* (9); Garrett Stewart, *Dear Reader: The Conscripted Audience in Nineteenth Century British Fiction* (5–6).
6. The successful creation of this empathy was vital to the success of the novel at a time when working-class literature was emerging as an unfamiliar and exciting category within contemporary English literature. Alan Sinfield has noted how, during the 1950s in England, 'There were writers of lower-class origin, it

was acknowledged, but in the very act of becoming writers they were co-opted to middle-class forms. As Orwell put it, the educated working-class person "writes in the bourgeois manner, in the middle-class dialect ... So long as the bourgeoisie are the dominant class, literature must be bourgeois" ' (58).

7. It is, of course, important to stress that the process of reader immasculation in *Lucky Jim* is not solely conducted at the level of narrative structure. Alan Sinfield has pointed out the text's other rudimentary attempts to 'sneer at the queer' in references to Professor Welch's second son, 'the effeminate writing Michel', the three-fold repetition of the description implying 'this were a set collocation in the manner of Anglo-Saxon verse' (79, 80).

8. Far more troubling than this, perhaps, is the title's 'you' idiom: does 'taking a girl like you' constitute the opening gambit in an objective argument that assumes intellectual equality in its female addressee, or, bearing in mind the novel's deeply unsatisfactory conclusion, is it actually a veiled threat?

9. Kenneth Morgan has pointed out how the entry of Macmillan's phrase into the iconography of the period is actually the result of routine misinterpretation: 'Macmillan is popularly supposed to have told a Bedford heckler in 1957 that "You've never had it so good", when in fact he was giving a warning about possible inflation' (176).

3 The Contradictions of Philosophy

1. The phrase echoes Graham Greene's idea, quoted by Bradbury in *The Modern British Novel*, that 'with the religious sense went the importance of the human act' (Bradbury, 2001, 293).

2. And containing, as John Carswell in a letter to *The Times Literary Supplement* pointed out on 14 December 1956, '86 major errors [...] and 203 minor errors' in the quotations of other works (749).

3. The British *Bildungsroman* was of course pioneered to a great extent by female writers (Dorothy Richardson, George Eliot). However the form lends itself to masculine textual appropriation by virtue of its aetiological progression and configuration of the subject as both active and rational.

4. His name provides a tantalising echo of 'anodyne': are such sphinx-like proclamations thereby mocked for being soothing but noncommittal?

5. Though the British spy scandals of the 1950s and 1960s cannot of course be considered on a par with the vertigo inspired on the continent surrounding issues of intellectual (and intellectuals') betrayal, they nonetheless amplified unease surrounding ideas of national loyalty, identity and continuity.

   The concept of 'nation' provides an interesting comparison to that of 'gender'. It would be controversial to suggest that the concept of nationhood has any essential link to geographical territory. 'Nation' is now accepted as being, in Benedict Anderson's phrase, an 'imagined community'. Homi K. Bhabha's work further analyses this community as inextricably linked with narrative, as the concept of a 'nation' is constructed via the isolation of origins, the building and sustaining of continuity through time, summoning of difference and so on, to form the illusion of an 'organic' synthesis. Yet the concept of 'gender' still stubbornly retains its association with a sexed body and an essential identity.

6. Silverman goes on to trace a movement in Sartre's work from a concept of language as a medium of freedom, to a final concept of a self that is directly communicable in linguistic terms.

7. This section draws upon ideas which were reworked in my article 'The Gaze of the Magus: Sexual/Scopic Politics in the Novels of John Fowles' in *Journal of Narrative Theory* 34.2 (Summer 204), 207–25. My thanks to the editor for permission to include them here.

8. Peter J. Conradi makes this point in '*The French Lieutenant's Woman*: novel, screenplay, film': 'Whatever their sexual experience or lack of it, his women divide into narrational virgins, secret, impenetrable and unavailable for focalisation; and whores, whose secrecy is violated and whom, thus devalued, the action then rejects' (47).

9. Both of these involve Nicholas's encounters with Lily/Julie – chapters 49 and 58 in the 1977 version – and not with Alison, unique in the first novel in her sexual availability to him. As Urfe's ultimate Romantic destiny, intimacy with Alison, though acknowledged to include shadowy men on the verges of the plot, like Pete, must exclude the immasculated reader.

10. In the 1977 revised edition, 'out' is omitted from the phrase.

11. In the 1977 text, this description is punctuated slightly differently: 'A hundred yards away a blind man was walking, freely, not like a blind man. Only the white stick showed he had no eyes' (Fowles, 1997, 654).

4   Non-Conformity and the Sixties

1. Examples being the abolition of Capital Punishment (1965), the Wolfendon Report on homosexuality (1967), the Abortion Act (1967), and the end of theatre censorship (1968).

2. This is, though, admittedly limited amongst English fiction of the period, with the bulk of the experimentation of this period contained in the work of women (Christine Brooke-Rose, Brigid Brophy, Eva Figes, Ann Quin), 'outsiders' such as the Scot Alan Burns, or in the surge of dramatic writing for the stage and television.

3. It is tempting, too, to fuel this suspicion of a personal claim upon pain with the fact that, as Johnson's biographer Jonathan Coe revealed to Philip Tew, Johnson himself, driven to supply-teaching for economic reasons, commissioned and collected the essays appearing in the novel from his own pupils. Only the pupils' names have been altered (Tew, 2002, note 6, 54).

4. *The Unfortunates*, though unbound, is divided into 27 sections, all unnamed apart from the 'FIRST' and 'LAST'. Following Tew, the sections from which quotations have been taken are identified by their initial phrases.

5. Mary Jacobus in *Reading Woman*, for example, claims that Fish ignores gender as a constitutive element in the interpretive communities he posits, as well as, in the essay 'Is There a Text in This Class?', in his crucial opening 'anec-joke' (83).

6. Though the Government-commissioned Wolfenden Committee's report proposing the decriminalisation of homosexual acts between consenting adult men was published in 1957, it was not until the 1967 Sexual Offences Act that this was passed into law.

7. 'Homosexual activity in the human male is much more frequent than is ordinarily realized [...]. In the youngest unmarried group, more than a quarter (27.3%) of the males have had some homosexual activity to the point of orgasm [...]. The incidence among these single males rises in successive age groups until it reaches a maximum of 38.7 per cent between 36 and 40 years of age' (Kinsey, 1948, 259).

8. It is crucial to remember, of course, that this liberation of female sexuality from conception was a complicated and compromised process, experienced by a generation of women raised in the main not as feminists but as those duty-bound to put the needs and priorities of men first. Dominic Head notes the way in which 'the images of female sexuality in the 1960s were contradictory, [...] "communicating blatantly opposing messages of freedom and subordination". There was a "double oppression" of women in the libertarian talk of the 1960s, where sexual liberation and freedom were a convenient way of facilitating predatory male desires' (2002, 91).

9. Blake Morrison's introduction to the 1996 Penguin revised edition of the novel notes how this final chapter was dropped upon publication in the US in 1962, and only restored on its reprinting there in 1988. That edition included a preface by Burgess entitled 'A Clockwork Orange Resucked', in which he claimed of the abridgement: 'My book was Kennedyan and accepted the notion of moral progress. What was really wanted was a Nixonian book with no shred of optimism in it' (quoted xvii). Morrison wryly notes that Burgess was therefore 'perhaps the first author ever, if his version of events is to be believed, to suffer from an American need for pessimism' (xvii).

10. 'Horrorshow' is a corruption of 'kharashó', the neuter form of the Russian for 'good'.

11. In 1964, B. S. Johnson published a short story entitled 'Perhaps it's these Hormones', a pastiche of the MacInnes mode of teenage narration centring upon Johnno, the 17-year-old manager of his school-friend and teen pop sensation 'Terry Livid'. The story ends: 'And that's about all I can tell you, mate. I suppose you'll bloody well alter it for your paper. Leave out the dirty bits, like. Nothing I ever said to you boys was ever printed just like I said it. Still, this is my last. Any chance of it coming out this Sunday? I need the loot, mate. Bad' (38–9). Crucially, and in contradiction to MacInnes's narrator, Johnno does not write his own story.

5 Credit for Confession – Gendered Addressivity in the Contemporary Male-Authored Novel

1. Steven Connor has noted a tendency in many critical considerations of the novel towards what he calls an act of 'cultural repatriation' (107).

2. On 23 November 1956 Eden announced that, on medical advice, he had to take an immediate holiday, and departed for the West Indies to recuperate. He returned to Britain the following month, but tendered his resignation to the Queen on 9 January 1957, citing ill health. The following day, Harold Macmillan accepted the Queen's offer of the post.

3. The first performance of the play was given at the Royal Court Theatre, London on 8 May 1956.

4. Barry Lewis has noted how the novel's central theme of denial is both paro-died and enforced by the multiple allusions to the biblical Peter. Stevens denies Lord Darlington on three occasions, and allusions to the crowing of cocks occur throughout the text (98).

5. Morgan quotes the 1971 census record of a proportion of 44.3 per cent non-manual workers to 55.7 per cent manual workers, compared to 52.3 per cent non-manual workers to 47.7 per cent manual workers a decade later (425, footnote).

6. The former novel ends with its hero's renunciation of the possibility of the medical restoration of his libido after a lengthy summation of the utter untenability of the female point of view (285), the latter Martin Amis describes in the autobiographical *Experience* as 'a book of such programmatic gynophobia that for quite a while it was unable to find any American publisher' (177).

7. It is Michel Foucault's work, of course, that has shown so convincingly how these notions of repression and threat are constructed and maintained within various psychiatric, criminological and sociological discourses.

8. Nickname for the young men directed to work in coal mines under the Emergency Powers (Defence) Act, 1940. Ernest Bevin was Minister of Labour and National Service, and under this edict one in ten men called up between the ages of 18 and 25 were sent down the mines.

9. David Savran opens his study of the motif of white male victimhood in recent American fiction, *Taking It Like A Man* (1998), with an epigraph from a 1995 speech by Tom Metzgar, leader of the White Aryan Resistance, which makes the claim: 'As social power decreases faster and faster, state power increases faster and faster. And we see ourselves, if you will pardon the expression, as the new niggers' (3).

10. *Man and Boy* is in fact Parsons's fifth novel – the first, *The Kids*, written while he was still a teenager, was a 'skinhead novel', a genre as fashionably shocking as the 'hoolie novel' around the time of its publication in 1976.

Bibliography

Allen, E. L. *Existentialism from Within*. London: Routledge & Kegan Paul Ltd., 1953.

Allen, Jeffner. 'An Introduction to Patriarchal Existentialism'. *The Thinking Muse: Feminism and Modern French Philosophy*. Eds Jeffner Allen and Iris Marion Young. Bloomington: Indiana University Press, 1989. 71–84.

Allsop, Kenneth. *Scan*. London: Hodder & Stoughton, 1965.

——. *The Angry Decade*. London: Peter Owen Ltd., 1958.

Amis, Kingsley. 'A Bookshop Idyll'. *Collected Poems, 1944–1979*. London: Hutchinson, 1979. 56–7.

——. *Jake's Thing*. London: Hutchinson, 1978.

——. *Lucky Jim*. 1954. Harmondsworth: Penguin, 1961.

——. 'Real and Made-Up People'. *Critical Essays on Kingsley Amis*. Ed. Robert H. Bell. New York: G.K. Hall & Co., 1998. 23–7.

——. *Stanley and the Women*. London: Hutchinson, 1984.

——. *Take a Girl Like You*. 1960. Harmondsworth: Penguin, 1970.

Amis, Martin. *Experience*. 2000. London: Vintage, 2001.

——. Interview. 'All about my Father'. Alan Rusbridger. *The Guardian*, 8 May 2000. 2.

——. Interview. 'The Wit and Fury of Martin Amis'. Susan Morrison. *Rolling Stone*. 17 May 1990. 98.

——. *Money: A Suicide Note*. 1984. Harmondsworth: Penguin, 1985.

——. *London Fields*. London: Jonathan Cape, 1989.

Anderson, Benedict. *Imagined Communities*. London: Verso, 1983.

Audi, Robert, General Ed. *The Cambridge Dictionary of Philosophy*. Cambridge: Cambridge University Press, 1995.

Austin, John Langshaw. *How to Do Things With Words*. Eds J. O. Urmison and Marina Sbisà. 1962. Oxford: Oxford University Press, 1976.

Ayer, Alfred Jules. *Language, Truth and Logic*. 1936. London: Victor Gollancz Ltd., 1970.

Bailey, Roland. *What is Existentialism? The Creed of Commitment and Action*. London: SPCK, 1950.

Banks, Lynne Reid. *The L-Shaped Room*. 1960. London: The Reprint Society, 1961.

Barrett, William. *Irrational Man*. New York: Doubleday, 1962.

Barstow, Stan. *A Kind of Loving*. 1960. Harmondsworth: Penguin, 1963.

——. *The Watchers on the Shore*. 1966. London: Black Swan, 1986.

Barthes, Roland. 'The Death of the Author'. 1968. *Modern Criticism and Theory: A Reader*. Ed. David Lodge. Harlow: Longman, 1988. 167–72.

Bell, Robert H. ed. *Critical Essays on Kingsley Amis*. New York: G.K. Hall & Co., 1998.

Benstock, Shari. 'Authorizing the Autobiographical'. 1988. *Feminisms*. Eds Robyn R. Warhol and Diane Price Herndl. New Brunswick, NJ: Rutgers University Press, 1991. 1040–57.

Berger, John. *G*. 1972. London: Bloomsbury, 1996.

Bergonzi, Bernard. *The Situation of the Novel*. 1970. London: Macmillan, 1971.

Beveridge, William Henry. 'Report on Social Insurance and Allied Services'. 1942. *Internet Modern History Sourcebook*. Ed. Paul Halsall. 1997. Fordham University,

New York. 15 February 2005. <http://www.fordham.edu/halsall/mod/1942beveridge.html>

Bhabha, Homi K., ed. *Nation and Narration*. London: Routledge, 1990.

Bloom, Harold. *The Anxiety of Influence*. Oxford: Oxford University Press, 1973.

Bly, Robert. *Iron John: A Book About Men*. 1990. Shaftesbury, Dorset: Element Books Ltd, 1999.

Booker, Christopher. *The Neophiliacs*. London: Collins, 1969.

——. *The Seventies*. Harmondsworth: Penguin, 1980.

Bradbury, Malcolm. 'Introduction'. *Scenes From Provincial Life*. By William Cooper. 1950. Houndmills: Macmillan, 1969. i–xiv.

——. *Stepping Westward*. 1965. London: Arrow, 1979.

——. *The Modern British Novel 1878–2001*. 1993. Harmondsworth: Penguin, 2001.

Bradford, Richard. *Kingsley Amis*. Plymouth: Northcote House, 1998.

Braine, John. *Room at the Top*. 1957. London: Arrow, 1997.

Brannigan, John. *Orwell to the Present: Literature in England, 1945–2000*. Houndmills: Palgrave Macmillan, 2003.

Brooks, Peter. 'Changes in the Margins: Construction, Transference, and Narrative'. *Psychoanalysis and Storytelling*. Ed. Peter Brooks. Oxford: Blackwell, 1994. 46–75.

Broughton, Lynda. 'Portrait of the Subject as a Young Man: The Construction of Masculinity Ironized in "Male" Fiction'. *Subjectivity and Literature from the Romantics to the Present Day*. Eds Philip Shaw and Peter Stockwell. London: Pinter, 1991. 135–45.

Burgess, Anthony. *A Clockwork Orange*. 1962. Harmondsworth: Penguin, 1983.

Butler, Judith. *Gender Trouble: Feminism and the Subversion of Identity*. London: Routledge, 1990.

Butler, Lance St John. 'John Fowles and the Fiction of Freedom'. *The British and Irish Novel Since 1960*. Ed. James Acheson. New York: St Martin's Press, 1991. 62–77.

Camus, Albert. *The Outsider*. 1942. Trans. Joseph Laredo. Harmondsworth: Penguin, 1986.

Cannadine, David. *Class in Britain*. 1998. Harmondsworth: Penguin, 2000.

Carswell, John. Letter. *Times Literary Supplement*. 14 December 1956. 749.

Cheal, David. *The Gift Economy*. London: Routledge, 1988.

Chodorow, Nancy. *The Reproduction of Mothering: Psychoanalysis and the Sociology of Gender*. 1978. Berkeley: University of California Press, 1999.

Cohn, Dorrit. *Transparent Minds: Narrative Modes for Presenting Consciousness in Fiction*. Princeton, NJ: Princeton University Press, 1978.

Colebrook, Claire. *Gender*. Houndmills: Palgrave Macmillan, 2004.

Collins, Margery L. and Christine Pierce. 'Holes and Slime: Sexism in Sartre's Psychoanalysis'. *Philosophical Forum* 5 (1973). 112–27.

Connell, R. W. 'Psychoanalysis and Masculinity'. *Theorizing Masculinities*. Eds Harry Brod and Michael Kaufman. Thousand Oaks, CA: Sage, 1994. 11–38.

Connor, Steven. *The English Novel in History: 1950–1995*. London: Routledge, 1996.

Conradi, Peter. *Iris Murdoch: The Saint and the Artist*. Houndmills: Macmillan, 1986.

——. 'The French Lieutenant's Woman: novel, screenplay, film'. *Critical Quarterly* 24:1 (Spring 1982). 41–57.

'Contemporary Portraits'. Rev of *Lucky Jim*. *Times Literary Supplement*. 12 February 1954. 101.

Cooper, William. *Scenes from Provincial Life*. 1950. Houndmills: Macmillan, 1969.

Coward, Rosalind. *Sacred Cows: Is Feminism Relevant to the New Millenium?* London: Harper Collins, 2000.

Culler, Jonathan. 'Reading as a Woman'. 1982. *Feminisms*. Eds Robyn R. Warhol and Diane Price Herndl. New Brunswick, NJ: Rutgers University Press, 1991. 509–24.

Davies, Alistair and Peter Saunders. 'Literature, Politics and Society'. *Society and Literature 1945–1970*. Ed. Alan Sinfield. London: Methuen, 1983. 13–50.

Dennis, Nigel. *Cards of Identity*. London: Weidenfeld & Nicolson, 1955.

——. *Two Plays and a Preface*. London: Weidenfeld & Nicolson, 1958.

Doan, Laura. ' "Sexy Greedy Is the Late Eighties": Power Systems in Amis's *Money* and Churchill's *Serious Money*'. Extract in *The Fiction of Martin Amis*. Ed. Nicholas Tredell. Duxford: Icon Books, 2000. 74–8.

Dollimore, Jonathan. 'The Challenge of Sexuality'. *Society and Literature 1945–1970*. Ed. Alan Sinfield. London: Methuen, 1983. 51–85.

Dyer, Geoff. *Ways of Telling: The Work of John Berger*. London: Pluto Press, 1986.

Eco, Umberto. 'Narrative Structures in Fleming'. *Gender, Language and Myth: Essays in Popular Narrative*. Ed. Glenwood Irons. Toronto: University of Toronto Press, 1992. 157–82.

Ferrebe, Alice. 'The Gaze of the Magus: Sexual/Scopic Politics in the Novels of John Fowles'. *Journal of Narrative Theory* 34:2 (Summer 2004). 207–25.

Fetterley, Judith. *The Resisting Reader: A Feminist Approach to American Fiction*. Bloomington: Indiana University Press, 1978.

Fish, Stanley. 'Is There a Text in This Class?' *Is There a Text in This Class? The Authority of Interpretive Communities*. Cambridge, MA: Harvard University Press, 1980. 303–21.

Forster, Peter. 'How Deep Do you Dig Into a Book?' Review of *Take A Girl Like You* by Kingsley Amis. *Daily Express*. 22 September 1960. 16.

Foucault, Michel. *Discipline and Punish: The Birth of the Prison*. 1977. Trans. Alan Sheridan. New York: Vintage, 1995.

——. *The History of Sexuality Volume One: An Introduction*. 1976. Trans. Robert Hurley. Harmondsworth: Penguin, 1981.

Fowler, Edward. *The Rhetoric of Confession: Shishōsetsu in Early Twentieth-Century Japanese Fiction*. 1988. Oxford: University of California Press, 1992.

Fowles, John. *Daniel Martin*. London: Jonathan Cape, 1977.

——. 'Hardy and the Hag'. *Wormholes: Essays and Occasional Writings*. Ed. Jan Relf. London: Vintage 1999. 159–77.

——. 'Interview with John Fowles'. By James Campbell. *Contemporary Literature* 17:4 (1976). 453–69.

——. 'Notes on an Unfinished Novel'. 1969. *The Novel Today*. Ed. Malcolm Bradbury. London: Fontana, 1982. 136–50.

——. *The Aristos*. 1964. London: Triad/Granada, 1980.

——. *The Collector*. 1963. London: Triad/Panther Books, 1985.

——. *The French Lieutenant's Woman*. 1969. London: Triad/Granada, 1981.

——. *The Magus*. 1966. London: World Books, 1967.

——. *The Magus*. Rev. edn. 1977. London: Vintage, 1997.

Gardiner, Judith Kegan. *Rhys, Stead, Lessing, and the Politics of Empathy*. Bloomington: Indiana University Press, 1989.

Giddens, Anthony. *Modernity and Self-Identity: Self and Society in the Late Modern Age*. Cambridge: Polity Press, 1991.

Gindin, James. *Postwar British Fiction*. Berkeley: University of California Press, 1963.

Gray, Nigel. *The Silent Majority: A Study of the Working-Class in Post-War British Fiction*. London: Vision, 1973.

Greene, Graham. *The Heart of the Matter*. 1948. London: Vintage, 2001.

Greer, Germaine. *The Female Eunuch*. 1971. London: Paladin, 1989.

Habermas, Jürgen. *The Theory of Communicative Action*. Trans. Thomas McCarthy. Cambridge: Polity, 1987.

Haffenden, John, ed. *Novelists in Interview*. London: Methuen, 1985.

Hartman, Geoffrey H. *The Fate of Reading and Other Essays*. Chicago: University of Chicago Press, 1975.

Hartley, Anthony. *A State of England*. London: Hutchinson, 1963.

Hayman, Ronald. *The Novel Today 1967–1975*. Harlow: Longman, 1976.

Head, Dominic. *The Cambridge Introduction to Modern British Fiction, 1950–2000*. Cambridge: Cambridge University Press, 2002.

Heath, Stephen. 'Notes on Suture'. *Screen*. 18:4 (Winter 1977/8). 48–76.

Hewison, Robert. *In Anger: Culture and the Cold War 1945–60*. 1981. London: Methuen, 1988.

——. *Too Much: Art and Society in the Sixties 1960–75*. London: Methuen, 1986.

Hinde, Thomas. *Happy as Larry*. London: MacGibbon & Kee, 1957.

Hoggart, Richard. *The Uses of Literacy*. 1957. Harmondsworth: Penguin, 1958.

hooks, bell. 'writing autobiography.' *Feminisms*. Eds Robyn R. Warhol and Diane Price Herndl. New Brunswick, NJ: Rutgers University Press, 1991. 1036–9.

Hopkin, James. 'Frankie's Class Act'. Review of *White City Blue*, by Tim Lott. *The Guardian* Saturday, 8 May 1999. 4 January 2005. 10.

Hopkins, Bill. 'Author's Preface to the New Edition'. *The Leap*. London: Deverell and Birdsey, 1984. 1–4.

——. *The Divine and the Decay*. London: MacGibbon & Kee, 1957.

——. 'Ways Without a Precedent'. *Declaration*. Ed. Tom Maschler. London: MacGibbon & Kee, 1957. 131–51.

Hornby, Nick. *Fever Pitch*. 1992. London: Victor Gollancz Ltd., 1993.

——. *High Fidelity*. 1995. London: Indigo, 1996.

Intrater, Rosaline. *An Eye for an 'I': Attrition of the Self in the Existential Novel*. New York: Peter Lang, 1988.

Irigaray, Luce. 'Any Theory of the "Subject" Has Always Been Appropriated by the "Masculine" '. 1974. *Speculum of the Other Woman*. Trans. Gillian C. Gill. Ithaca, NY: Cornell University Press, 1985. 133–46.

——. 'Commodities Among Themselves'. *This Sex Which Is Not One*. 1977. Trans. Catherine Porter. Ithaca, NY: Cornell University Press, 1985. 192–7.

——. 'Women on the Market'. *This Sex Which Is Not One*. 1977. Trans. Catherine Porter. Ithaca, NY: Cornell University Press, 1985. 170–91.

Iser, Wolfgang. *The Implied Reader: Patterns of Communication in Prose Fiction from Bunyan to Beckett*. 1972. Trans. Wilhelm Fink. Baltimore, MD: Johns Hopkins University Press, 1974.

Ishiguro, Kazuo. *The Remains of the Day*. 1989. London: Faber & Faber, 1990.

Jacobus, Mary. *Reading Woman*. New York: Columbia University Press, 1986.

Jameson, Fredric. 'Periodizing the Sixties'. *Postmodernism: A Reader*. Ed. Patricia Waugh. London: Arnold, 1992. 125–52.

Johnson, B. S. *Albert Angelo*. 1964. New York: New Directions Books, 1987.

——. *All Bull: The National Servicemen*. London: Quartet Books Ltd, 1973.

——. Interview. *The Imagination on Trial: British and American Writers Discuss Their Working Methods*. Eds Alan Burns and Charles Sagnet. London: Allison & Busby, 1981. 83–94.

——. 'Perhaps it's these Hormones'. *Statement Against Corpses*. Eds B. S. Johnson and Zulfikar Ghose. London: Constable, 1964. 30–9.

——. *The Unfortunates*. 1969. London: Picador, 1999.

Jones, Ann Rosalind. 'Writing the Body: Toward an understanding of *l'écriture féminine*'. 1981. *Feminisms*. Eds Robyn R. Warhol and Diane Price Herndl. New Brunswick, NJ: Rutgers University Press, 1991. 357–70.

Joyce, James. *Ulysses*. 1922. Harmondsworth: Penguin, 1986.

Kaplan, E. Ann. 'Is the Gaze Male?' *Desire: The Politics of Sexuality*. Eds Ann Snitow, Christine Stansell and Sharon Thompson. London: Virago, 1983. 321–38.

Kimmel, Michael S. *Manhood in America: A Cultural History*. London: The Free Press, 1996.

——. 'Masculinity as Homophobia: Fear, Shame and Silence in the Construction of Gender Identity'. *Theorizing Masculinities*. Eds Harry Brod and Michael Kaufman. Thousand Oaks, CA: Sage, 1994. 119–41.

King, John. *The Football Factory*. London: Jonathan Cape, 1996.

Kinsey, Alfred C., Wardell B. Pomeroy and Clyde E. Martin. *Sexual Behaviour in the Human Male*. Philadelphia and London: W. B. Saunders Co., 1948.

Knights, Ben. *Writing Masculinities: Male Narratives in Twentieth-Century Fiction*. Houndmills: Macmillan, 1999.

Knowles, Joanne. *Nick Hornby's High Fidelity*. New York and London: Continuum, 2002.

Laing, R. D. *The Divided Self*. 1960. Harmondsworth: Penguin, 1990.

——. *The Politics of Experience and The Bird of Paradise*. 1967. Harmondsworth: Penguin, 1973.

Larkin, Philip. 'Annus Mirabilis'. *Collected Poems*. 1988. London: Faber & Faber, 1990. 167.

——. *Jill*. 1946. London: Faber & Faber, 1987.

Lawrence, D. H. *Lady Chatterley's Lover*. 1928. Harmondsworth: Penguin, 1985.

Leader, Zachary, ed. *The Letters of Kingsley Amis*. London: Harper Collins, 2000.

Le Carré, John. *The Spy Who Came in From the Cold*. 1963. London: The Reprint Society, 1964.

Lessing, Doris. *The Golden Notebook*. 1962. London: Harper Collins, 1993.

Lewis, Barry. *Kazuo Ishiguro*. Manchester: Manchester University Press, 2000.

Lodge, David. '*Lucky Jim* Revisited'. *The Practice of Writing*. Harmondsworth: Penguin, 1997. 86–7.

——. *The British Museum is Falling Down*. 1965. Harmondsworth: Penguin, 1981.

——. 'The Modern, the Contemporary, and the Importance of Being Amis'. *Critical Essays on Kingsley Amis*. Ed. Robert H. Bell. New York: G.K. Hall & Co., 1998. 40–59.

——. 'The Unreliable Narrator (Kazuo Ishiguro)'. *The Art of Fiction*. Harmondsworth: Penguin, 1992. 154–7.

Lott, Tim. *White City Blue*. London: Viking, 1999.

Lyons, John. *Language, Meaning and Context*. London: Fontana, 1981.

MacInnes, Colin. *Visions of London*. London: MacGibbon & Kee, 1969.

MacInnes, John. *The End of Masculinity: The Confusion of Sexual Genesis and Sexual Difference in Modern Society*. Buckingham: Open University Press, 1998.

MacIntyre, Alasdair. *After Virtue: A Study in Moral Theory*. London: Duckworth, 1981.

MacKinnon, Catharine. 'Feminism, Marxism, Method, and the State: An Agenda for Theory'. *Signs* 7:3 (Spring 1982). 515–44.

——. *Feminism Unmodified*. Cambridge: Harvard University Press, 1987.

MacQuarrie, John. *Existentialism*. 1972. Harmondsworth: Penguin, 1982.

McMahon, Joseph H. 'Marxist Fictions: The Novels of John Berger'. *Contemporary Literature* 23:2 (1982). 202–24.

McNab, Andy. *Bravo Two Zero*. London: Bantam, 1993.

Marwick, Arthur. *British Society Since 1945*. 1982. Harmondsworth: Penguin, 1990.

Maschler, Tom, ed. *Declaration*. London: MacGibbon & Kee, 1957.

Masters, William H. and Virginia E. Johnson. *The Human Sexual Response*. London: Churchill, 1966.

Middleton, Peter. *The Inward Gaze: Masculinity and Subjectivity in Modern Culture*. London: Routledge, 1992.

Miller, Karl. *Doubles: Studies in Literary History*. Oxford: Oxford University Press, 1987.

Millett, Kate. *Sexual Politics*. 1970. London: Virago, 1985.

Mills, Magnus. *All Quiet on the Orient Express*. 1999. London: Flamingo, 2000.

Mills, Sara. 'Reading as/like a Feminist'. *Gendering the Reader*. Ed. Sara Mills. Hemel Hempstead: Harvester Wheatsheaf, 1994. 25–46.

Mitchell, Julian. *As Far as You Can Go*. London: Constable, 1963.

Mitchell, Juliet. *Woman's Estate*. 1971. Harmondsworth: Penguin, 1977.

Moore, Suzanne. 'Slipped Discs'. Review of *High Fidelity* by Nick Hornby. *The Guardian*. 28 March 1995. 7.

Morgan, Kenneth O. *The People's Peace: British History 1945–1989*. Oxford: Oxford University Press, 1990.

Morris, Phyllis Sutton. 'Sartre on Objectification: A Feminist Perspective'. *Feminist Interpretations of Jean-Paul Sartre*. Ed. Julien S. Murphy. Pennsylvania: The Pennsylvania State University Press, 1999. 64–89.

Morrison, Blake. Introduction. *A Clockwork Orange*. Anthony Burgess. 1962. Harmondsworth: Penguin, 1996. vii–xxiv.

——. *The Movement: English Poetry and Fiction of the 1950s*. Oxford: Oxford University Press, 1980.

Mulvey, Laura. 'Visual Pleasure and Narrative Cinema'. 1975. *Visual and Other Pleasures*. Houndmills: Macmillan, 1989. 14–26.

Murdoch, Iris. 'The Existentialist Hero'. 1950. *Existentialists and Mystics*. London: Chatto & Windus, 1997. 108–15.

——. 'The Existentialist Political Myth'. 1952. Ibid. 130–45.

——. *Under the Net*. 1954. Harmondsworth: Penguin, 1963.

Murphy, Julien S. 'The Look in Sartre and Rich'. *The Thinking Muse: Feminism and Modern French Philosophy*. Eds Jeffner Allen and Iris Marion Young. Bloomington: Indiana University Press, 1989. 101–12.

Oakes, Philip. 'A New Style in Heroes.' *The Observer*. 1 January 1956. 8.

Orwell, George. *The Road to Wigan Pier*. 1937. Harmondsworth: Penguin, 2001.

Osborne, John. *Look Back in Anger*. 1957. London: Faber & Faber, 1989.

——. 'What's Gone Wrong with Women?' 1956. *Damn You, England: Collected Prose*. London: Faber & Faber, 1994. 255–8.

The Oxford English Dictionary Online. Second Edition. Oxford University Press. 13 February 2005. <http:www//dictionary.oed.com>

Parsons, Tony. Interview. 'Meet The Parent' by Lynn Barber. *The Observer,* Sunday 18th August 2002. 16.

——. *Man and Boy.* 1999. London: Harper Collins, 2000.

Parsons, Tony Victor. *The Kids.* London: New English Library, 1976.

Palmer, William J. *The Fiction of John Fowles: Tradition, Art and the Loneliness of Selfhood.* 1974. Columbia: University of Missouri Press, 1975.

Pearce, Lynne. *Feminism and the Politics of Reading.* London: Arnold, 1997.

Philips, Deborah and Ian Haywood, eds. *Brave New Causes: Women in British Postwar Fictions.* London: Leicester University Press, 1998.

Poster, Mark. *Existential Marxism in Postwar France: From Sartre to Althusser.* Princeton, NJ: Princeton University Press, 1975.

Read, Herbert. Foreword. *The Rebel.* Albert Camus. Trans. Anthony Bowen. 1953. Harmondsworth: Penguin, 1977. 7–10.

Redhead, Steve. 'Hit and Tell: a Review Essay on the Soccer Hooligan Memoir'. *Soccer and Society* 5:3 (Autumn 2004). 392–403.

Rimmon-Kenan, Shlomith. *Narrative Fiction, Contemporary Poetics.* 1983. London: Routledge, 1993.

Ritchie, Harry. *Success Stories: Literature and the Media in England, 1950–1959.* London: Faber & Faber, 1988.

Robinson, John A. T. *Honest to God.* London: S. C. M. Press Ltd., 1963.

Roof, Judith. *Come as You Are: Sexuality and Narrative.* New York: Columbia University Press, 1996.

Rosen, David. *The Changing Fictions of Masculinity.* Urbana: University of Illinois Press, 1993.

Rousseau, Jean Jacques. *The Confessions of Jean-Jacques Rousseau.* Trans. J. M. Cohen. Harmondsworth: Penguin, 1953.

Rubin, Gayle. 'The Traffic in Women: Notes on the "Political Economy" of Sex'. *Toward an Anthropology of Women.* Ed. Rayna R. Reiter. New York: Monthly Review Press, 1975. 157–210.

Rushdie, Salman. *Imaginary Homelands: Essays and Criticism 1981–1991.* Harmondsworth: Penguin, 1992.

Ryan, Kiernan. 'Sex, Violence and Complicity: Martin Amis and Ian McEwan'. *An Introduction to Contemporary Fiction: International Writing in English Since 1970.* Ed. Rod Mengham. Cambridge: Polity, 1999.

Sartre, Jean-Paul. *Existentialism.* New York: Philosophy Library, 1947.

Savran, David. *Taking It Like a Man.* Princeton NJ: Princeton University Press, 1998.

Schoene-Harwood, Berthold. *Writing Men: Literary Masculinities from Frankenstein to the New Man.* Edinburgh: Edinburgh University Press, 2000.

Schweickart, Patrocinio P. 'Reading Ourselves: Toward a Feminist Theory of Reading'. 1986. *Feminisms.* Eds Robyn R. Warhol and Diane Price Herndl. New Brunswick, NJ: Rutgers University Press, 1991. 525–50.

Schwenger, Peter. 'The Masculine Mode'. Ed. Elaine Showalter. *Speaking of Gender.* London: Routledge, 1989. 101–12.

Scott, Joan W. 'Gender: A Useful Category of Historical Analysis'. *American Historical Review* 91:5 (December 1986). 1053–75.

Sedgwick, Eve Kosofsky. *Between Men: English Literature and Male Homosocial Desire.* New York: Columbia University Press, 1985.

Sedgwick, Eve Kosofsky. *Epistemology of the Closet*. Hemel Hempstead: Harvester Wheatsheaf, 1990.

——. ' "Gosh, Boy George, You Must Be Awfully Secure in Your Masculinity" '. *Constructing Masculinity*. Eds Maurice Berger, Brian Wallis and Simon Watson. London: Routledge, 1995. 11–20.

Sennett, Richard. *The Fall of Public Man*. 1974. Cambridge: Cambridge University Press, 1977.

Showalter, Elaine. 'Ladlit'. *On Modern British Fiction*. Ed. Zachary Leader. Oxford: Oxford University Press, 2002. 60–76.

Sillitoe, Alan. *Saturday Night and Sunday Morning*. 1958. London: Pan, 1960.

Silverman, Hugh J. 'Sartre's Words on the Self'. *Jean-Paul Sartre: Contemporary Approaches to his Philosophy*. Ed. Hugh J. Silverman and Frederick A. Elliston. Brighton: Harvester, 1980. 85–104.

Silverman, Kaja. *Male Subjectivity at the Margins*. London: Routledge, 1992.

Sinfield, Alan. *Literature, Politics and Culture in Postwar Britain*. Oxford: Blackwell, 1989.

Solanas, Valerie. *SCUM Manifesto*. 1968. London: The Matriarchy Study Group, 1983.

Spencer, Neil. Interview with Robert Bly. 'Men Behaving Buddily'. *The Observer*, Review Section. 17 December 1995. 7.

Stacey, Jackie. 'Desperately Seeking Difference'. *The Female Gaze: Women as Viewers of Popular Culture*. Eds Lorraine Gamman and Margaret Marshment. London: The Women's Press, 1988. 112–29.

Stevenson, Randall. *The Oxford English Literary History Vol. 12: 1960–2000: The Last of England?* Oxford: Oxford University Press, 2004.

Stewart, Garrett. *Dear Reader: The Conscripted Audience in Nineteenth Century British Fiction*. London: The Johns Hopkins University Press, 1996.

Storey, David. *This Sporting Life*. 1960. Harmondsworth: Penguin, 1965.

——. *Radcliffe*. 1963. Harmondsworth: Penguin, 1965.

Taylor, Charles. *Sources of the Self: The Making of the Modern Identity*. Cambridge: Cambridge University Press, 1989.

Taylor, John Russell. *David Storey*. Harlow: Longman, for the British Council, 1974.

Tew, Philip. *B. S. Johnson*. Manchester: Manchester University Press, 2001.

——. 'B. S. Johnson'. *The Review of Contemporary Fiction* 22:1 (Spring 2002). 7–57.

Todd, Richard. 'The Intrusive Author in British Postmodernist Fiction: The Cases of Alasdair Gray and Martin Amis'. Extract in *The Fiction of Martin Amis*. Ed. Nicholas Tredell. Duxford: Icon Books, 2000. 70–4.

Tompkins, Jane. 'Me and My Shadow'. *Feminisms*. Eds Robyn R. Warhol and Diane Price Herndl. New Brunswick, NJ: Rutgers University Press, 1991. 1079–92.

Tredell, Nicolas. 'Telling Life, Telling Death: *The Unfortunates*'. *Review of Contemporary Fiction* 5:2 (Summer 1985). 34–41.

——. *The Fiction of Martin Amis*. Duxford: Icon Books, 2000.

Wain, John. *Hurry on Down*. 1953. Harmondsworth: Penguin, 1961.

Waugh, Evelyn. *Brideshead Revisited*. 1945. Harmondsworth: Penguin, 1982.

Waugh, Patricia. *Harvest of the Sixties*. Oxford: Oxford University Press, 1995.

——. *Metafiction: The Theory and Practice of Self-Conscious Fiction*. London: Methuen, 1984.

Wiesengrund-Adorno, Theodor. *Prisms*. Trans. Samuel and Shierry Weber. London: Spearman, 1967.

Williams, Raymond. *The English Novel From Dickens to Lawrence*. 1970. London: Hogarth Press, 1987.

Wilson, Colin. 'Beyond the Outsider'. *Declaration*. Ed. Tom Maschler. London: MacGibbon & Kee, 1957. 30–59.

——. Foreword. *The Leap*. Bill Hopkins. London: Deverell and Birdsey, 1984. v–xii.

——. *Introduction to the New Existentialism*. London: Hutchinson, 1966.

——. *Man Without a Shadow: The Diary of an Existentialist*. London: Arthur Barker Ltd., 1963.

——. *Ritual in the Dark*. London: Victor Gollancz Ltd., 1960.

——. *The Outsider*. London: Victor Gollancz Ltd., 1956.

Wilson, Elizabeth, *Only Halfway to Paradise: Women in Postwar Britain 1945–1968*. London: Tavistock, 1980.

——. *Women and the Welfare State*. London: Tavistock, 1977.

Wittig, Monique. 'The Trojan Horse'. *Feminist Issues* 4:2 (Fall 1984).

Woodcock, Bruce. *Male Mythologies: John Fowles and Masculinity*. Sussex: The Harvester Press, 1984.

Woolf, Virginia. *The Diary of Virginia Woolf*. 4 (1931–1935). Ed. Anne Olivier Bell. London: Hogarth, 1982.

Worthington, Kim L. *Self as Narrative: Subjectivity and Community in Contemporary Fiction*. Oxford: Clarendon Press, 1996.

Wyndham, Francis. Introduction. *Visions of London*. Colin MacInnes. London: MacGibbon & Kee, 1969. vii–x.

Zelizer, Viviana. *The Social Meaning of Money*. New York: Basic Books, 1994.

Index

Novels and plays are included here under both their authors and their titles; critical works are listed under author only. The letters *e.* and *n.* after page references indicate epigraphs and endnotes respectively.

Printed in the United States
70736LV00001B/151-162